知識工場
nowledge.
Knowledge is everything！

不結巴！

杜絕考試一條龍、對話一條蟲的窘境

用英語會話
［交外國朋友］

用英文交朋友，舌頭再也不打結！

張翔、薛詩怡 / 編著

Let's Make Friends Around The World.

MP3 附書附贈朗讀光碟

與老外聊開懷，絕不冷場！

看這裡！

使用說明
user's guide

1
11大日常生活聊天主題，包含美食饗宴、流行時尚、運動休閒、校園生活、寶島旅遊、異國之旅、文化交流、人際關係、職場生涯、社會議題、人生哲學。

2 流行時尚 Fashion

2
各大主題下分別發展15至18個聊天話題，全書共168個熱門話題，供讀者作為開啟話匣子的隨翻隨查、翻到就能説的得力工具書。

6. 特色小吃
Local Specialties
006

3
各話題列舉超過10條最實用的萬用好句，隨挑隨選，任選一句都能輕鬆用英文開始與外國朋友東聊西聊、就是不用擔心啞口無言！

萬用好句

1.	**Have you ever tried savory rice patties, a.k.a. pig blood cake?** 你吃過豬血糕(米血)嗎？
2.	**Crispy fried chicken is very popular among Taiwanese.** 鹽酥雞很受台灣人歡迎。
3.	**Sweet potato congee and braised pork rice are both traditional dishes in Taiwan.** 地瓜稀飯與滷肉飯都是傳統的台灣料理。
4.	**Do your parents love to eat rice tube pudding?** 你的父母親喜歡吃筒仔米糕嗎？
5.	**I will take my foreign friends to try goose with noodles.** 我要帶我的外國友人去吃鵝肉麵。

6. 特色小吃
Local Specialties
006

随書附贈外籍名師親開金口朗誦MP3正統發音光碟，一話題一音軌，老外最愛聊的168個話題，只要跟著唸，就能跟老外聊得不可開交！

各話題提供一篇虛擬實境的道地英語情境對話，供讀者宛如親臨與外國朋友用英語聊天的實況現場，無形間抓出與老外聊天聊不停的致勝關鍵！

實境對話

Paul: Do you like the food in Taiwan?
你喜歡台灣的食物嗎？

Alice: Of course. I think Taiwanese cuisine is fabulous.
當然，我覺得台式料理超棒的。

Paul: Which is your favorite?
哪一道是你最喜歡的？

Alice: I can name a whole list!
我可以列出一份最愛美食清單。

Paul: For example?
例如？

Alice: I like dumplings, beef noodles, wonton soup, hot and sour

貼心補充聊天情境時常使用到的主題式關鍵單字片語，學習會話不忘提升單字、片語力，英文能力成倍激增！

關鍵單字片語

7. **hot and sour soup** 片 酸辣湯

8. **fried rice noodles** 片 炒米粉

9. **fish ball soup** 片 魚丸湯

10. **wonton soup** 片 餛飩湯

11. **marble egg** 片 皮蛋

12. **traditional** [trə`dɪʃən] 形 傳統的

變身聊遍
天下無敵會話王

　　提升英語能力最直接、也最快速的方式，就是一逮到機會，就與以英文為母語的老外對話。然而，雖然心裡面很想這麼做，但在實際面上卻困難重重。困難點一，是我們身在台灣，老外並非俯拾即是，因此在英語學習上，環境是一大困難。困難點二，是如果真的在各個可能遇到外國朋友的場合上，得到了與外國朋友對談的機會，但卻啞口無言。之所以會發生啞口無言的情形，原因有二。第一，不知道該怎麼使用英文表達自己的意見與想法；第二，找不到該和外國朋友聊些什麼。關於環境上的困難點，張翔老師只能建議讀者出國感受母語環境；而關於第二個困難點，張翔老師則希望能透過本書來幫讀者擺脫啞口無言的窘境。

　　本書專門針對遇到老外時想要大聊特聊、但卻只能無言以對的讀者所撰寫。首先，本書精選日常生活中最有可能與外國朋友聊到的話題共168個，無論是食衣住行、吃喝玩樂等輕鬆的聊天話題，或是文化交流、社會議題以及人生哲學等較嚴肅、但卻能藉此更了解外國朋友的想法、也能訓練自己表達各種觀點的話題，本書幫讀者準備了一翻到就能說的萬用好句、以及讓讀者彷彿身歷其境的實境對話模擬參考，幫助讀者能夠在與外國朋友聊天之前先行預習、即使突然啞口無言也能一翻就能說！

張翔

用對方法，
提升英文會話力

　　英語是世界的共通語言，也因為如此成為世界上學習人數最多的語言。然而許多人在學習英語的時候，往往不得其門而入。你是不是也學了好多年英語，甚至花了大把大把的銀子，卻在真正需要使用英語做溝通的時候，只能恩恩啊啊，或是只能勉強擠出兩三個單字？好羨慕身邊可以流暢地跟外國人對談的朋友？眼紅因為英語能力而快速升遷的同事嗎？

　　不要再抱著文法書K文法規則了！也不要抱著單字片語乾啃了！

　　本書「一開口，就順口！英文生活會話怎麼聊都行」，統整時下日常生活中常有的會話主題，以單字、慣用句、示範對話等，用最有效率的方式，讓你能立即在下次遇見新朋友、新客戶時，能夠進行實用對話。不再只是「書面一條龍，會話一條蟲」。

　　現在，就跟筆者一起，以最生活化的方式，
　　讓自己的英語能力*Power Up!*

CONTENTS

PART 1
初階開口聊

PART 2
中階順口聊

CONTENTS

PART 3
進階深度聊

PART 1

Let's Chat in English!

1 初階開口聊

basic level

1.預約訂位
Making a Reservation
MP3 001

萬用好句

1.	**Have you made the reservation for our dinner on Valentine's Day?** 你訂好我們情人節晚餐的位子了嗎？
2.	**I want to make a reservation for two for Saturday at 7 pm, on May 12th.** 我想預約五月十二日星期六晚上七點的位子，兩位。
3.	**You need to make a reservation at that Japanese restaurant.** 那間日式餐廳需要訂位。
4.	**Do you know the number for that restaurant?** 你知道那間餐廳的電話號碼嗎？
5.	**Do you have a table available at 6:00 pm?** 你們晚上六點鐘還有空位嗎？
6.	**We would like a table by the window if possible.** 如果可以的話，我們想要靠窗的桌子。
7.	**That restaurant is fully booked. How about eating somewhere else?** 那間餐廳客滿了，要不要到別的地方吃呢？
8.	**Will the wait be long?** 需要等很久才有位子嗎？
9.	**There are three parties ahead of you.** 您們前面還有三組客人在候位。
10.	**We're fully booked at 7 pm. Do you want to reserve a table for 9 pm?** 晚上七點鐘的位子已經訂滿了。您要不要改訂晚上九點鐘？
11.	**This restaurant is very popular. You need to make reservations one week in advance.** 這間餐廳非常受歡迎，需要在一個星期前訂位。
12.	**How many people are there in your party?** 您們有多少人？

關鍵單字片語

1. **reservation** [ˌrɛzəˋveʃən] 名 預約

2. **lunch** [lʌntʃ] 名 午餐

3. **dinner** [ˋdɪnə] 名 晚餐

4. **restaurant** [ˋrɛstərənt] 名 餐廳

5. **Valentine's Day** 片 情人節

6. **party** [ˋpɑrtɪ] 名 團體、群

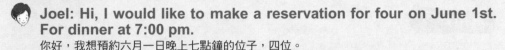

Joel: Hi, I would like to make a reservation for four on June 1st. For dinner at 7:00 pm.
你好，我想預約六月一日晚上七點鐘的位子，四位。

Ruby: Sure. One moment, please.
好的，請您稍候一下。

Joel: Thank you.
謝謝。

Ruby: Dinner for four on Friday, June 1st, right?
六月一日星期五晚上，四位，是嗎？

Joel: Yes.
是的。

Ruby: Oh, I am sorry. We are fully booked on June 1st.
噢，不好意思，我們六月一日晚上的位子都被訂滿了。

Joel: Hmm...how about June 8th?
嗯…那麼六月八日還有位子嗎？

Ruby: Let me check, please. Yes, we still have tables on June 8th. Four people at 7:00 pm, right?
我查一下。我們六月八日還有位子，一樣是四位、晚上七點鐘嗎？

Joel: Yes, thank you.
是的，謝謝。

Ruby: May I have your name, please?
請問您的大名是？

Joel: Joel Parker. P-A-R-K-E-R.
喬‧帕克。ㄆㄚ、ㄎㄜ、。

Ruby: Thank you, Mr. Parker. We look forward to seeing you on June 8th.
謝謝您，帕克先生。六月八日恭候您的光臨。

關鍵單字片語

7. **available** [əˋveləbl] 形 有空的

8. **full** [fʊl] 形 客滿的

9. **reserve** [rɪˋzɜv] 動 預約

10. **book** [bʊk] 動 預訂

11. **make a reservation** 片 預約

12. **by the window** 片 靠窗

2. 法國餐廳
In a French Restaurant
MP3 002

萬用好句

1. Have you ever been to a French restaurant?
你去過法國餐廳嗎？

2. What is your favorite French dish?
你最喜歡哪一道法國菜？

3. Have you ever eaten escargot?
你吃過蝸牛嗎？

4. I like foie gras.
我喜歡鵝肝醬。

5. Do French people eat frog legs?
法國人吃青蛙腿嗎？

6. The French have exquisite taste in food.
法國人對於食物有著極為精緻的品味。

7. The three French national culinary treasures are caviar, foie gras, and truffles.
法國有三寶，魚子醬、鵝肝醬與松露。

8. That French restaurant is always crowded.
那間法國餐廳總是客滿。

9. Many French dishes are world-renowned delicacies.
許多道法式菜餚都是世界聞名的美食。

10. I have never tried caviar before.
我從沒吃過魚子醬。

11. You should spread some cream cheese on crackers, and then add some caviar on top.
你應該先在餅乾上塗抹一些奶油乳酪，然後再把魚子醬鋪在最上面。

12. At most French restaurants, food is served as a set menu or a la carte.
大部分的法國餐廳提供套餐或單點給顧客選擇。

關鍵單字片語

1. **escargot** [ɛskɑrˋgo] 名 食用蝸牛

2. **foie gras** [fwɑˋgrɑ] 名 鵝肝醬

3. **cookery** [ˋkʊkərɪ] 名 烹飪

4. **caviar** [ˏkævɪˋɑr] 名 魚子醬

5. **truffle** [ˋtrʌfl] 名 松露

6. **culinary** [ˋkjulɪˏnɛrɪ] 形 烹飪的

實境對話

Eric: Have you ever tried French cuisine before?
你吃過法國菜嗎？

Amanda: No, never. But I heard that it's great!
從來沒有，但我聽說法國菜很棒！

Eric: It sure is! French cuisine is world-famous!
法國菜確實很棒。法國菜是世界聞名的！

Amanda: So, which dishes are your favorites?
所以，你最喜歡哪幾道菜？

Eric: I like escargot and foie gras.
我喜歡escargot與foie gras。

Amanda: What are those?
那些是什麼菜啊？

Eric: Snails and goose liver.
是蝸牛與鵝肝醬。

Amanda: Are you kidding? Are those edible?
你開玩笑吧？那些東西能吃嗎？

Eric: Of course they are, and they are very delicious.
它們當然能吃，而且還非常美味。

Amanda: That's crazy!
實在是太瘋狂了。

Eric: Maybe we can try some at a French restaurant next week, then you can find out how good they are.
或許我們下個星期可以找家法國餐廳用餐，這樣你就會知道它們有多好吃了。

Amanda: Sounds exciting! I would love to try them sometime.
聽起來很刺激！我非常願意嚐試看看。

關鍵單字片語

7. **cuisine** [kwɪˋzin] 名 菜餚

8. **exquisite** [ˋɛkskwɪzɪt] 形 精緻的

9. **renowned** [rɪˋnaʊnd] 形 有名的

10. **delicacy** [ˋdɛləkəsɪ] 名 佳餚

11. **fixed menu** 片 套餐

12. **a la carte** [ˌælɑˋkɑrt] 名 單點

3. 討論菜單
Talking about the Menu
MP3 003

萬用好句

| 1. | **Would you like to take a look at the menu?**
您要不要看一下菜單？ |

| 2. | **Can I have a menu, please?**
請給我菜單好嗎？ |

| 3. | **Are you ready to order?**
您準備好點菜了嗎？ |

| 4. | **We still need a few minutes to decide what to order.**
我們還需要幾分鐘的時間來決定點什麼菜。 |

| 5. | **What's today's special?**
今日特餐是什麼？ |

| 6. | **What do you recommend?**
你推薦哪道菜？ |

| 7. | **What is the lunch special?**
午間特餐是什麼？ |

| 8. | **What's in this dish?**
這道菜包含哪些食材？ |

| 9. | **What is Kung Pao Chicken?**
宮保雞丁是什麼？ |

| 10. | **Do you have vegetarian dishes?**
你們提供素食餐點嗎？ |

| 11. | **Do you have anything that's not spicy?**
你們是否有不辣的餐點？ |

| 12. | **We would like to have a cheeseburger, some fajitas and a salad.**
我們要點一份起司漢堡、一份法士達以及一份沙拉。 |

關鍵單字片語

1. **special** [`spɛʃəl] 名 特餐

2. **chef** [ʃɛf] 名 主廚

3. **menu** [`mɛnju] 名 菜單

4. **onion** [`ʌnjən] 名 洋蔥

5. **lamb** [læm] 名 羔羊肉

6. **recommend** [ˌrɛkə`mɛnd] 動 推薦

實境對話

Oscar: Good evening. I'm your waiter today. My name is Oscar.
您好，今晚由我來替您們服務，我的名字是奧斯卡。

Shirley: Hi, Oscar. What's your dinner special today?
嗨！奧斯卡，請問你們今晚的特餐是什麼？

Oscar: The chef's special is lamb chops and onion soup.
今天的主廚特餐是小羊排與洋蔥湯。

Shirley: Hmm...I don't feel like having lamb today. May I see the menu, please?
嗯…我今天不想吃羊肉。可以給我看看菜單嗎？

Oscar: Sure, here you are.
好的，菜單在這裡。

Shirley: Let me see...hmm...what's in the Rainbow Salad?
我看一下。嗯…「彩虹沙拉」裡面有什麼？

Oscar: There are carrots, yellow and green peppers, corn, onions and shrimp.
彩虹沙拉裡有紅蘿蔔、黃椒、青椒、玉米、洋蔥以及鮮蝦。

Shirley: Sounds delicious. I'll have a Rainbow Salad, please.
聽起來很不錯，請給我一份。

Oscar: Anything else, Ma'am?
還需要什麼嗎，女士？

Shirley: I would also like to have a hamburger.
我還要一份漢堡。

Oscar: No problem. Anything to drink, Ma'am?
沒問題。需要來點飲料嗎，女士？

Shirley: A large diet Coke, please.
請給我大杯的健怡可樂一杯。

Oscar: Sure, Ma'am. I'll be back with your order right away.
好的。您的餐點馬上為您送上。

關鍵單字片語

7. **veggie** [.vɛdʒɪ] 形 素食的

8. **spicy** [`spaɪsɪ] 形 辣的

9. **large** [lɑrdʒ] 形 大的

10. **take a look at** 片 看一看

11. **no problem** 片 沒問題

12. **right away** 片 馬上

4. 酒吧閒聊
Chatting in a Bar
MP3 004

萬用好句

1.	**Do you come to this pub often?** 你常來這家酒吧嗎？
2.	**I have never been to this pub before.** 我之前沒來過這家酒吧。
3.	**Let me buy you a drink.** 我請你喝一杯。
4.	**Do you know the bartender?** 你認識那位酒保嗎？
5.	**I am a social drinker only.** 我只在社交場合淺嚐幾口。
6.	**Would you like to have one more round?** 要不要再喝一輪？
7.	**I would like to have a glass of Whiskey.** 請給我一杯威士忌。
8.	**I first take a sip of my Budweiser and then chug down the whole thing.** 我先啜了一小口百威啤酒，然後再一飲而盡。
9.	**Don't drink too much.** 別喝太多。
10.	**I think he is drunk.** 我覺得他喝醉了。
11.	**I only drink Vodka.** 我只喝伏特加。
12.	**What do you wet your whistle with here?** 你要在這裡喝什麼酒？

 關鍵單字片語

1. **pub** [pʌb] 名 酒吧

2. **bartender** [ˋbɑrˌtɛndɚ] 名 酒保

3. **whiskey** [ˋhwɪskɪ] 名 威士忌

4. **vodka** [ˋvɑdkə] 名 伏特加

5. **Long Island iced tea** 片 長島冰茶

6. **martini** [mɑrˋtinɪ] 名 馬丁尼

實境對話

Kelly: There is a new pub on 7th Street.
第七街上開了一家新的酒吧。

John: I know. You mean "Heaven."
我知道。你說的是「天堂酒吧」。

Kelly: Yes. Have you been there?
沒錯。你去過嗎？

John: Of course. The bartender is my good friend.
當然，那裡的酒保是我的好朋友。

Kelly: Cool.
真酷。

John: What do you like to drink?
你喜歡喝什麼酒？

Kelly: I usually like to have a Long Island iced tea or a martini when I go to a pub.
我在酒吧通常會喝長島冰茶或是馬丁尼。

John: Have you ever gotten drunk at a pub?
你曾經在酒吧裡喝醉過嗎？

Kelly: No, never. I don't do that.
從來沒有。我才不幹那種事。

John: I went to "Heaven" with Adam last Friday, and he got totally drunk.
上星期五我跟亞當去「天堂酒吧」，他喝得有夠醉。

Kelly: Seriously? How bad was it?
真的嗎？他喝成什麼樣子啊？

John: He threw up on me.
他吐在我身上。

關鍵單字片語

7. **drunk** [drʌŋk] 形 喝醉的

8. **cool** [kul] 形 很酷的、很棒的

9. **chug down** 片 一飲而盡

10. **get drunk** 片 喝醉

11. **throw up** 片 嘔吐

12. **wet whistle with** 片 喝酒

5.美式速食
Fast Food

MP3 005

萬用好句

1.	**Do you like fast food?** 你喜歡速食嗎？
2.	**Teenagers and children love hamburgers and fried chicken.** 青少年與孩童喜歡吃漢堡與炸雞。
3.	**Do you want some French fries?** 你要來點薯條嗎？
4.	**Do you want your fried chicken spicy?** 你要辣味的炸雞嗎？
5.	**Can I have some ketchup?** 可以給我一些番茄醬嗎？
6.	**I want a filet-o-fish to go.** 我要外帶一份麥香魚。
7.	**I would like to have a small salad with no dressing, please.** 我要一份小的沙拉，不要沙拉醬。
8.	**Could I have a Coke, please?** 可以給我一杯可樂嗎？
9.	**I am a big fan of fast food.** 我非常喜愛速食。
10.	**I eat fast food three meals a day.** 我一天三餐都吃速食。
11.	**I hate fast food.** 我痛恨吃速食。
12.	**Fast food is really convenient.** 速食非常方便。

關鍵單字片語

1. **fast food** 片 速食
2. **teenager** [`tin.edʒɚ] 名 青少年
3. **French fries** 片 炸薯條
4. **ketchup** [`kɛtʃəp] 名 番茄醬
5. **dressing** [`drɛsɪŋ] 名 沙拉醬
6. **milk shake** 片 奶昔

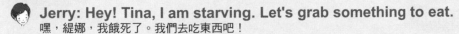

Jerry: Hey! Tina, I am starving. Let's grab something to eat.
嘿，緹娜，我餓死了。我們去吃東西吧！

Tina: Sure. What would you like to have?
好啊。你想吃什麼？

Jerry: How about fast food? Is McDonald's ok?
我們吃速食好不好？去麥當勞如何？

Tina: Oh, man! Not again! We had McDonald's yesterday and two days ago.
噢！老兄！別再吃麥當勞了！我們昨天和前天都是吃麥當勞欸。

Jerry: I like McDonald's.
我喜歡麥當勞。

Tina: Don't you ever get tired of it?
你吃不膩嗎？

Jerry: No. I am thinking about having a filet-o-fish with a strawberry milk shake today.
不會啊！我今天想吃麥香魚搭配草莓奶昔。

Tina: Ok, ok. We can have McDonald's today. But this is the last time. I don't want to eat fast food again for another three months!
好吧！我們今天可以吃麥當勞，但這是最後一次了，我接下來三個月不想再吃速食。

Jerry: If you insist.
如果你堅持的話。

Tina: I insist.
我堅持。

Jerry: Ok. Let's go now. What will you have today?
好，我們走吧。你今天想吃什麼？

Tina: A double cheese burger and a diet Coke.
我要一個雙層吉事漢堡和一杯健怡可樂。

關鍵單字片語

7. **sour** [saur] 形 酸的

8. **convenient** [kən`vinjənt] 形 方便的

9. **starving** [`stɑrvɪŋ] 形 飢餓的

10. **bored** [bord] 形 無趣的、厭倦的

11. **insist** [ɪn`sɪst] 動 堅持

12. **to go** 片 外帶

6. 特色小吃
Local Specialties

MP3 006

萬用好句

1.	**Have you ever tried savory rice patties, a.k.a. pig blood cake?** 你吃過豬血糕(米血)嗎？
2.	**Crispy fried chicken is very popular among Taiwanese.** 鹽酥雞很受台灣人歡迎。
3.	**Sweet potato congee and braised pork rice are both traditional dishes in Taiwan.** 地瓜稀飯與滷肉飯都是傳統的台灣料理。
4.	**Do your parents love to eat rice tube pudding?** 你的父母親喜歡吃筒仔米糕嗎？
5.	**I will take my foreign friends to try goose with noodles.** 我要帶我的外國友人去吃鵝肉麵。
6.	**I like to eat dumplings with hot and sour soup.** 我吃水餃喜歡搭配酸辣湯。
7.	**Would you like to have fried rice noodles and fish ball soup?** 你想不想吃炒米粉和魚丸湯？
8.	**Taiwanese beef noodles are world-famous!** 台灣的牛肉麵世界聞名！
9.	**In the summer time, people like to eat mango ice.** 夏天時，大家喜歡吃芒果冰。
10.	**Red beans with milk ice is also quite popular in summer.** 紅豆牛奶冰在夏季也很受歡迎。
11.	**My mother can make delicious wonton soup.** 我媽媽會做美味的餛飩湯。
12.	**I think marble eggs taste funny.** 我覺得皮蛋的味道很怪。

關鍵單字片語

1. **savory rice patty** 片 豬血糕

2. **crispy fried chicken** 片 鹽酥雞

3. **congee** [`kɑndʒi] 名 稀飯

4. **braised pork rice** 片 滷肉飯

5. **dumpling** [`dʌmplɪŋ] 名 水餃

6. **goose with noodles** 片 鵝肉麵

實境對話

Paul: Do you like the food in Taiwan?
你喜歡台灣的食物嗎？

Alice: Of course. I think Taiwanese cuisine is fabulous.
當然，我覺得台式料理超棒的。

Paul: Which is your favorite?
哪一道是你最喜歡的？

Alice: I can name a whole list!
我可以列出一份最愛美食清單。

Paul: For example?
例如？

Alice: I like dumplings, beef noodles, wonton soup, hot and sour soup, rice tube pudding, crispy fried chicken...
我喜歡水餃、牛肉麵、餛飩湯、酸辣湯、筒仔米糕、鹽酥雞…

Paul: Wow, you do like Taiwanese cuisine!
你真的很喜歡台灣的食物欸。

Alice: I love it!
我愛極了！

Paul: Is there anything that you have no interest in trying?
有你不想碰的台灣料理嗎？

Alice: Hmm...there are a few things that I really don't dare to try.
嗯…確實有一些我不敢嘗試的食物。

Paul: Such as?
例如？

Alice: Savory rice patties and marble eggs.
豬血糕和皮蛋。

Paul: I totally understand.
我完全理解。

關鍵單字片語

7. **hot and sour soup** 片 酸辣湯

8. **fried rice noodles** 片 炒米粉

9. **fish ball soup** 片 魚丸湯

10. **wonton soup** 片 餛飩湯

11. **marble egg** 片 皮蛋

12. **traditional** [trəˋdɪʃən!] 形 傳統的

7. 來逛夜市：路邊攤
Roadside Food Stands at Night Markets

MP3 007

萬用好句

1.	**I want to go to a night market.** 我想去逛夜市。
2.	**Shi-Lin Night Market has some of the most famous food stands in Taiwan.** 士林夜市裡有幾家台灣最知名的小吃攤。
3.	**Do you like the shaved ice at that night market?** 你喜歡那個夜市裡的刨冰嗎？
4.	**My favorite thing at this night market is tapioca milk tea.** 這個夜市裡，我最喜歡的是珍珠奶茶。
5.	**Have you tried chicken feet before?** 你吃過雞腳嗎？
6.	**I want to buy some duck tongues.** 我想買一些鴨舌。
7.	**What is double layer sausage?** 什麼是大腸包小腸？
8.	**Many Japanese tourists especially love the pearl milk tea at this drink stand.** 許多日本觀光客特別喜歡這個飲料攤賣的珍珠奶茶。
9.	**I think stinky tofu is really tasty.** 我覺得臭豆腐非常美味。
10.	**I want to order an oyster omelet.** 我想點一份蚵仔煎。
11.	**Tofu pudding is a delicious dessert.** 豆花是一道美味的甜點。
12.	**This Taiwanese meatball is extremely yummy.** 這個肉圓真的超級好吃。

關鍵單字片語

1. **night market** 片 夜市
2. **stand** [stænd] 名 攤販
3. **shaved ice** 片 刨冰
4. **tapioca milk tea / pearl milk tea** 片 珍珠奶茶
5. **double layer sausage** 片 大腸包小腸

實境對話

Angel: Where do you want to go this evening?
今晚你想去什麼地方？

Tom: I heard that Shi-Lin Night Market is quite famous. Can we go there?
我聽說士林夜市非常有名。我們可以去士林夜市嗎？

Angel: Sure. There are stands selling all kinds of different foods. We can have dinner there.
當然可以。士林夜市裡有販售各種不同食物的攤販。

Tom: Sounds great. What do you recommend I try?
聽起來真棒。你有沒有推薦什麼好吃的？

Angel: The oyster omelets, stinky tofu and Chinese meatballs are quite famous there.
那裡的蚵仔煎、臭豆腐以及肉丸都非常有名。

Tom: I would love to try them all.
我每一樣都想吃吃看。

Angel: And you could try shaved ice or tofu pudding for dessert.
甜點的部分，你可以吃刨冰或是豆花。

Tom: I also want to try pearl milk tea. I heard it's delicious!
我還想試試珍珠奶茶。聽說珍珠奶茶非常美味。

Angel: Oh, yes. You don't want to miss the tapioca milk tea.
噢！對，千萬別錯過珍珠奶茶。

Tom: It seems that there are so many kinds of yummy foods at this world-famous night market.
這個世界知名的夜市裡，似乎有許多好吃的食物。

Angel: So, are you ready to go to Shi-Lin Night Market now?
所以，你準備好往士林夜市出發了嗎？

Tom: Of course! I can't wait.
當然！我等不及了。

關鍵單字片語

6. **oyster omelet** 片 蚵仔煎

7. **stinky tofu** 片 臭豆腐

8. **eel noodles** 片 鱔魚麵

9. **tofu pudding** 片 豆花

10. **delicious** [dɪˋlɪʃəs] 形 美味的

11. **seem** [sim] 動 似乎

8. 來逛夜市：食尚玩家
Having Fun at Night Markets
008

萬用好句

1. **This is my first time visiting a night market.**
   這是我第一次逛夜市。

2. **It's amazing how many different kinds of stands there are at this night market.**
   這個夜市裡各式各樣的攤販，真令人大開眼界。

3. **You can not only eat lots of foods at night markets, but also do some shopping.**
   在夜市裡，你不僅可以大吃，還可以逛街買東西。

4. **There are all kinds of stands at night markets.**
   夜市裡有各種攤販。

5. **You can buy T-shirts or small souvenirs in night markets.**
   你可以在夜市裡買T恤或是紀念品。

6. **The best thing is, you can bargain.**
   最棒的是，你可以殺價。

7. **I bought a pair of earrings at that night market last week.**
   我上禮拜在那個夜市裡買了一副耳環。

8. **The souvenir T-shirt I bought at the night market was not only cheap, but also very special.**
   我在夜市裡買的那件紀念T恤不但便宜，而且還非常特別。

9. **This night market is crowded with tourists from all over the world.**
   這個夜市裡擠滿了來自世界各地的觀光客。

10. **I would love to come back and visit this night market again.**
    我希望有機會再回來逛逛這個夜市。

11. **I ate a lot and bought a lot of things at Feng-Chia Night Market.**
    我在逢甲夜市裡大吃，也買了很多東西。

12. **I had a lot of fun at the night market.**
    我在夜市裡玩得很開心。

關鍵單字片語

1. **souvenir** [ˋsuvəˏnɪr] 名 紀念品
2. **shopping** [ˋʃɑpɪŋ] 名 購物
3. **earring** [ˋɪrˏrɪŋ] 名 耳環
4. **tourist** [ˋturɪst] 名 觀光客
5. **foreigner** [ˋfɔrɪnɚ] 名 外國人
6. **necklace** [ˋnɛklɪs] 名 項鍊

實境對話

May: Did you take your American friend to Shi-Lin Night Market last Saturday?
你上週六帶美國朋友去逛我們的士林夜市了嗎？

Jay: Yes, I did. Benson and I went there and had a lot of fun.
有啊，班森跟我去逛士林夜市，我們玩得很開心。

May: That's wonderful. What did you guys do there?
那好極了。你們在那邊做了些什麼？

Jay: We ate a lot of delicious foods, and Benson bought some souvenirs.
我們吃了很多美食，班森還買了一些紀念品。

May: What did he eat there?
他吃了些什麼？

Jay: He tried an oyster omelet and Taiwanese meatball, but his favorite was the stinky tofu.
他吃了蚵仔煎與肉圓，但他最愛的是臭豆腐。

May: Are you kidding? I heard many foreigners don't like the smell of stinky tofu.
真的假的？我聽說很多外國人不喜歡臭豆腐的味道。

Jay: Not Benson. He loved it!
班森可不同，他愛臭豆腐！

May: Cool! And what did he buy at the night market?
真酷！那麼他在夜市裡買了些什麼呢？

Jay: He bought a necklace for his girlfriend and a cap for himself.
他買了一條項鍊要送他女朋友，還買了一頂帽子給他自己。

May: How much was the necklace?
他花多少錢買項鍊？

Jay: You won't believe it! It was only NT$100!
你一定不相信，那條項鍊只要新台幣一百元！

關鍵單字片語

7. **cap** [kæp] 名 無邊帽；棒球帽

8. **favorite** [`fevərɪt] 形 最喜愛的

9. **lovely** [`lʌvlɪ] 形 可愛的

10. **various** [`vɛrɪəs] 形 各式各樣的

11. **wonderful** [`wʌndəfəl] 形 極好的

12. **not only...but also...** 片 不僅…而且…

9.節慶辦桌
Festival Banquet
MP3
009

萬用好句

1. "Bun Dough" is a kind of Taiwanese banquet.
「辦桌」是一種台灣式的宴會。

2. "Bun Dough" means "to treat" in Taiwanese.
「辦桌」是台語，意思是「請客」。

3. People sit outdoors and enjoy a feast prepared by chefs.
人們坐在戶外，享受廚師準備的大餐。

4. Buddha's Delight is a typical Bun Dough dish.
「佛跳牆」是辦桌常見的菜餚。

5. Buddha's Delight is a very famous dish. It has scallops, sea cucumbers, ham hocks and chicken in it.
「佛跳牆」是一道很有名的菜餚，裡頭有干貝、海參、蹄膀與雞肉。

6. When there's something to celebrate, like a wedding or birthday, people hold a "Bun Dough" to treat relatives and friends.
每當有婚禮、壽誕等值得慶祝的事情時，人們就會「辦桌」來宴請親朋好友。

7. Taiwanese love to attend Bun Dough banquets.
台灣人喜歡參加辦桌宴會。

8. Bun Dough is unique to Taiwanese culture, and some scholars even write essays about it.
辦桌是一項特殊的台灣文化，有些學者甚至以它為題撰寫論文。

9. Bun Dough expresses the hospitality of the Taiwanese people.
辦桌展現台灣人的熱情。

10. Bun Dough dishes may not be fine cuisine, but they are delicious.
辦桌的菜餚或許不算精緻料理，但非常美味。

11. They also serve desserts at Bun Doughs.
辦桌也供應甜點。

12. Holding a Bun Dough is a way to bring people together.
辦桌是一種拉近人際距離的方式。

關鍵單字片語

1. **Buddha's Delight** 片 佛跳牆
2. **scallop** [`skɑləp] 名 干貝
3. **sea cucumber** 片 海參
4. **ham hock** 片 蹄膀
5. **shark fins** 片 魚翅
6. **hospitality** [ˌhɑspɪˋtælətɪ] 名 好客

實境對話

Jane: Have you ever been to a "Bun Dough"?
你有沒有吃過「辦桌」？

Benson: What is that?
那是什麼？

Jane: It's a kind of Taiwanese banquet.
「辦桌」是一種台灣式的宴席。

Benson: What's so special about it?
有什麼特別之處嗎？

Jane: Well, a "Bun Dough" is usually held outdoors.
嗯，「辦桌」通常在戶外舉行。

Benson: Outdoors? That sounds like a poolside buffet.
戶外？聽起來像是在游泳池畔舉辦的歐式自助餐。

Jane: Not exactly. At a Bun Dough, not only do the guests sit outdoors, even the chefs cook and prepare the dishes outdoors.
不太像。辦桌時，不僅客人坐在戶外，連廚師也是在戶外烹煮及準備餐點。

Benson: Then that sounds like a backyard barbeque.
那麼聽起來又像是在庭院裡舉辦的烤肉會。

Jane: Well, I don't think a "Bun Dough" is exactly the same as either of those two.
「辦桌」跟你提到的兩者都不盡相同。

Benson: Hmm..., so what is it then?
呃…，那麼「辦桌」到底是什麼？

Jane: I will attend a wedding tomorrow and they will have a "Bun Dough" after the ceremony. Do you want to come with me?
我明天要去參加一場婚禮，他們在婚禮後會「辦桌」宴客，你要不要跟我一起去？

Benson: I'd love to!
非常樂意！

關鍵單字片語

7. **ceremony** [`sɛrə,monɪ] 名 儀式

8. **typical** [`tɪpɪkl] 形 特有的

9. **delicate** [`dɛləkət] 形 精緻的

10. **express** [ɪk`sprɛs] 動 表達

11. **exactly** [ɪg`zæktlɪ] 副 精確地

12. **anyway** [`ɛnɪ,we] 副 到底、反正

10. 外送外賣
Food Delivery and Takeaway MP3 010

萬用好句

1. This Chinese restaurant has delivery service.
這間中國餐廳提供外送服務。

2. Do you deliver after 8:00 pm?
你們晚上八點後還有外送嗎？

3. I would like to order a number three and a number seven.
我想點三號餐與七號餐。

4. Can I order a number eleven and number thirteen with extra garlic?
我想點十一號跟十三號餐，可以多加一點大蒜嗎？

5. Can I have extra cheese on my pizza?
可以在我的披薩上面多加一些起司嗎？

6. May I have your address, please?
能不能告訴我您的地址？

7. My address is apartment 4, No. 168 Central Street.
我的地址是中央街168號，第四室。

8. I asked the delivery boy to keep the change as a tip.
我讓外送小弟留下零錢，當作他的小費。

9. Your order will be there in twenty minutes.
您的餐點將在二十分鐘內送達。

10. Please let me repeat your order. You ordered a fruit salad, a hamburger and a corn soup.
請讓我重複您的餐點：您點了一份水果沙拉、一個漢堡，還有一杯玉米湯。

11. The delivery person finally arrived after one hour.
外送人員終於在一個小時後抵達。

12. Can you answer the door, please? It must be our pizza!
能不能請你去應門？一定是我們的披薩到了。

關鍵單字片語

1. **delivery** [dɪˋlɪvərɪ] 名 遞送

2. **address** [əˋdrɛs] 名 地址

3. **change** [tʃendʒ] 名 零錢

4. **tip** [tɪp] 名 小費

5. **corner** [ˋkɔrnɚ] 名 轉角、角落

6. **answer the door** 片 應門

實境對話

Freya: I don't feel like going out for dinner tonight.
我今晚不想出去吃晚餐。

Larry: Ok, let's order something and have dinner at home.
好啊，那我們晚飯就點些東西在家吃。

Freya: What would you like to order?
你想點什麼來吃呢？

Larry: I feel like eating Chinese food today.
我今天想吃中國菜。

Freya: Does the Chinese restaurant on the corner have delivery service?
街角那家中國餐廳有外送服務嗎？

Larry: I am sure they do.
我確定他們有。

Freya: Good. Do you have their menu?
太好了。你有他們的菜單嗎？

Larry: Yes, it's in the drawer.
有，就在抽屜裡。

Freya: Let's see..., ok, I will have a number two and a mushroom soup.
我們來看看。好，我要一份二號餐再加一個蘑菇湯。

Larry: I will have a number six and a meatball soup.
我要一份六號餐加一個貢丸湯。

Freya: Ok. Let me make the call.
好，我來打電話。

Larry: Thanks. I am so glad that they deliver their food.
謝啦！我真高興他們可以外送餐點。

關鍵單字片語

7. **mushroom** [`mʌʃrum] 名 蘑菇

8. **meatball soup** 片 貢丸湯

9. **extra** [`ɛkstrə] 形 額外的

10. **keep** [kip] 動 保留

11. **repeat** [rɪ`pit] 動 重複

12. **arrive** [ə`raɪv] 動 抵達

11. 悠閒午茶
Enjoying Afternoon Tea
MP3 011

萬用好句

1.	**Would you like to have afternoon tea with me?** 你願意與我共享午茶時光嗎？
2.	**This coffee shop has great afternoon tea.** 這間咖啡廳有很不錯的下午茶。
3.	**They serve afternoon tea from 2:00 pm to 5:00 pm.** 他們下午兩點至五點提供下午茶。
4.	**What would you like to order?** 你想要什麼餐點？
5.	**I would like to have a piece of cheese cake and a cappuccino.** 我要一份起司蛋糕以及一杯卡布奇諾。
6.	**Would you like to have a scone and a hot Earl Grey tea?** 你要不要來一份司康以及熱的伯爵茶？
7.	**They have cinnamon scones with raisins.** 他們提供肉桂葡萄乾司康。
8.	**Please give me a piece of Boston cream pie and a cup of hot rose tea.** 請給我一份波士頓派與一杯熱的玫瑰茶。
9.	**They have very good cherry pie here.** 他們有很棒的櫻桃派。
10.	**This is the best apple pie I have ever had!** 這是我吃過最棒的蘋果派！
11.	**The cinnamon rolls here are very delicious.** 這裡的肉桂捲非常美味。
12.	**I usually like to have a cup of café latte in the afternoon.** 我通常喜歡在下午喝一杯拿鐵咖啡。

關鍵單字片語

1. **afternoon tea** 片 下午茶

2. **cheese cake** 片 起司蛋糕

3. **cappuccino** [ˌkɑpəˈtʃino] 名 卡布奇諾咖啡

4. **scone** [skon] 名 英國司康餅

5. **Earl Grey tea** 片 伯爵茶

6. **cinnamon** [ˈsɪnəmən] 名 肉桂

實境對話

Jessie: Hey! Derek, would you like to join me for a relaxing tea time?
嘿！德瑞，想不想跟我去享受一下輕鬆的午茶時光？

Derek: Sure, why not?
當然好啊。

Jessie: I know there's a new coffee shop that has great afternoon tea.
我知道一家新開的咖啡廳，他們有很棒的下午茶。

Derek: Sounds nice. What are they famous for?
聽起來不錯。他們最有名的是什麼？

Jessie: I heard that they have very tasty scones and pie.
我聽說他們的司康和派都很好吃。

Derek: I like pie.
我喜歡吃派。

Jessie: What kind of pie do you like?
你喜歡吃哪種派？

Derek: I like blueberry pie.
我喜歡藍莓派。

Jessie: I am sure they have very good blueberry pie.
我相信他們有不錯的藍莓派。

Derek: And I'd like to have Earl Grey tea.
我還想喝伯爵茶。

Jessie: I would like to have some scones and a cup of hot café latte.
我想吃司康，還想喝熱的拿鐵咖啡。

Derek: What are we waiting for? Let's go!
我們還等什麼？快走吧！

關鍵單字片語

7. **raisin** [ˋrezn̩] 名 葡萄乾

8. **Boston cream pie** 片 波士頓派

9. **cinnamon roll** 片 肉桂捲

10. **café latte** 片 拿鐵咖啡

11. **provide** [prəˋvaɪd] 動 提供

12. **be famous for** 片 以…聞名

12. 吃早午餐
Having Brunch
MP3 012

萬用好句

1. Would you like to have brunch with me?
你願意與我共進早午餐嗎？

2. Do you serve brunch here?
你們提供早午餐嗎？

3. I usually get up at 11:00 am and then have brunch before going to school.
我通常上午十一點起床，吃個早午餐再去上學。

4. I will have brunch with my friends next Sunday. Would you like to join us?
我下星期天要和朋友們共進早午餐，你要不要一起來？

5. Thank you for inviting me. But I guess I'll have to pass. I usually have breakfast at 7:00 am.
謝謝你的邀請，但我就不過去了。我通常早上七點吃早餐。

6. I didn't have lunch today, because I had brunch at around 11:00 am.
我今天沒吃午餐，因為我在上午十一點左右吃了早午餐。

7. They serve American brunch from 10:30 am to 2:00 pm.
他們提供美式早午餐的時間，是從早上十點半到下午兩點。

8. I usually have nothing but coffee in the morning.
我早上通常只喝咖啡。

9. Do you like pancakes or waffles?
你喜歡吃薄煎餅或格子鬆餅嗎？

10. I would like to have a cheese omelet with ham and onions.
我要一份火腿洋蔥起司蛋捲。

11. Would you like some fresh orange juice?
你要不要喝點新鮮的柳橙汁？

12. Can I have a sunny-side-up egg and bacon, please?
可以給我單面煎蛋加培根嗎？

關鍵單字片語

1. **brunch** [brʌntʃ] 名 早午餐

2. **breakfast** [`brɛkfəst] 名 早餐

3. **pancake** [`pæn͵kek] 名 薄煎餅

4. **waffle** [`wɑfl] 名 格子鬆餅

5. **omelet** [`ɑmlɪt] 名 煎蛋餅；煎蛋捲

6. **sunny-side-up egg** 片 單面煎蛋

實境對話

Fanny: Hey, Chase! Would you like to have brunch with me this Saturday?
嘿，卻斯！這個星期六想不想跟我一起吃頓早午餐？

Chase: Sure, why not?
當然好啊！

Fanny: I know there's a great restaurant that has a very delicious brunch buffet.
我知道有家很棒的餐廳，提供美味的自助式早午餐。

Chase: Really? I love buffets!
真的嗎？我超愛自助餐！

Fanny: They offer twenty dishes for you to choose from, and you can eat as much as you like, and the price is reasonable.
他們供應二十道菜任你吃到飽，而且價格十分合理。

Chase: How much is it for one person?
每個人多少錢？

Fanny: Only NT$300.
只要新台幣三百元。

Chase: That's not too expensive.
那不算太貴。

Fanny: I know. That's why this restaurant is so popular these days.
沒錯。所以這家餐廳最近才會這麼受歡迎。

Chase: We should really go there and give it a try.
我們一定要去親自品嘗一下。

Fanny: Should we invite Maggie and Lucy to join us?
要不要找瑪姬和露西一起去？

Chase: Definitely! The more the merrier.
那當然囉！越多人越開心！

關鍵單字片語

7. **bacon** [`bekən] 名 培根

8. **buffet** [bu`fe] 名 自助餐

9. **fresh** [frɛʃ] 形 新鮮的

10. **reasonable** [`riznəbl] 形 合理的

11. **popular** [`pɑpjələ] 形 受歡迎的

12. **The more the merrier.** 成 多多益善

13. 素食養生
Vegetarian Food
013

萬用好句

1.	**Are you a vegetarian?** 你是素食者嗎？	
2.	**Many people are vegetarians.** 許多人吃素。	
3.	**I am on a pure vegetarian diet.** 我吃全素。	
4.	**Are you a strict vegetarian?** 你吃全素嗎？	
5.	**I don't eat spring onions or garlic.** 我不吃蔥與蒜。	
6.	**Do you serve vegetarian food here?** 這裡供應素食嗎？	
7.	**I am a lacto vegetarian.** 我吃奶素。	
8.	**I am an ovo-lacto vegetarian.** 我吃蛋奶素。	
9.	**I am on a vegetarian diet that includes milk and eggs.** 我吃奶蛋素。	
10.	**I am a fruitarian.** 我吃水果素。	
11.	**He became a vegetarian for health reasons.** 他出於健康因素而改吃素。	
12.	**I haven't eaten meat for ten years.** 我已經十年不吃肉了。	

關鍵單字片語

1. **vegetarian** [ˌvɛdʒəˋtɛrɪən] 名 素食者
2. **health** [hɛlθ] 名 健康
3. **spring onion** 片 蔥
4. **garlic** [ˋgɑrlɪk] 名 蒜
5. **lacto vegetarian** 片 奶素
6. **ovo-lacto vegetarian** 片 蛋奶素

實境對話

Peter: Do you know if there's a good vegetarian restaurant near here?
你知道這附近哪裡有好的素食餐廳嗎？

Ella: No. Why do you ask? Are you a vegan now?
不知道。怎麼這麼問？你改吃素了嗎？

Peter: No, I am not. But one of my best friends is coming to visit me, and he is a vegetarian.
不，我沒吃素。但是我有個好朋友要來找我，他吃素。

Ella: I see.
原來如此。

Peter: He is a strict vegetarian, so I want to welcome him by taking him to a nice vegetarian restaurant.
他吃全素，所以我想找一家不錯的素菜餐廳，歡迎他的來訪。

Ella: A strict vegetarian?
全素是什麼意思？

Peter: He doesn't even eat spring onions or garlic, not to mention meat or eggs. And he doesn't drink milk.
他連蔥與蒜都不吃，更別說是肉類或蛋類了。他也不喝牛奶。

Ella: That does sound really strict.
聽起來相當嚴格。

Peter: And he doesn't drink alcohol, either.
他也不喝酒。

Ella: Cool! Is there a special reason why he's on such a strict vegetarian diet?
真酷！他吃素有什麼特別的理由嗎？

Peter: He believes that it's healthier.
他相信吃素比較健康。

關鍵單字片語

7. **fruitarian** [fruˋtɛrɪən] 名 水果素食者

8. **alcohol** [ˋælkə͵hɔl] 名 含酒精飲料

9. **pure** [pjʊr] 形 純粹的

10. **welcome** [ˋwɛlkəm] 動 歡迎

11. **consider** [kənˋsɪdə] 動 考慮

12. **not to mention** 片 更別說…

14. 健康蔬果
Fruits and Vegetables
MP3 014

萬用好句

1.	**Which fruit do you like the most?** 你最喜歡的水果是哪一種？
2.	**I love guavas and papayas.** 我喜歡番石榴和木瓜。
3.	**I don't like peaches.** 我不喜歡桃子。
4.	**Fruits and vegetables are good for your health.** 水果和蔬菜對你的健康有益。
5.	**I hate grapes. I don't like the skin.** 我討厭葡萄，我不喜歡葡萄的皮。
6.	**You should eat vegetables and fruits every day.** 你應該每天吃蔬菜與水果。
7.	**An apple a day keeps the doctor away.** 一天一蘋果，醫生遠離我。
8.	**I enjoy all kinds of fruit.** 我喜歡各種水果。
9.	**Carrots are good for your eyes.** 胡蘿蔔對眼睛有益。
10.	**I eat five kinds of fruit every morning.** 我每天早上吃五種水果。
11.	**Watermelon is quite popular in summer.** 西瓜在夏季很受歡迎。
12.	**Could you buy some mangos for me at the market?** 能不能請你幫我到市場買些芒果？

關鍵單字片語

1. **guava** [`gwɑvə] 名 番石榴

2. **papaya** [pə`paɪə] 名 木瓜

3. **peach** [pitʃ] 名 桃子

4. **grape** [grep] 名 葡萄

5. **carrot** [`kærət] 名 胡蘿蔔

6. **watermelon** [`wɔtə,mɛlən] 名 西瓜

Kevin: I bought a lot of fruit at the market. Do you want some?
我在市場上買了很多水果，你要不要分一些？

Linda: What do you have?
你買了哪些水果？

Kevin: I've got tangerines, strawberries, lemons and bananas.
我買了橘子、草莓、檸檬和香蕉。

Linda: Do you have pineapple? I love pineapple.
你有鳳梨嗎？我愛吃鳳梨。

Kevin: I think there's still some in the refrigerator.
我的冰箱裡應該還有一些鳳梨。

Linda: Great! Can I have it?
太好了，可以給我嗎？

Kevin: Sure.
當然可以。

Linda: I really love pineapple. It's both sweet and a little sour. I love the taste.
我真的很愛吃鳳梨。鳳梨甜中帶酸，我很愛那種口感。

Kevin: I like watermelon. It's juicy.
我喜歡吃西瓜。西瓜的水分很多。

Linda: Oh, I love watermelon, too.
噢，我也愛吃西瓜。

Kevin: I bought a big watermelon yesterday. I can share half of it with you.
我昨天買了一個大西瓜，可以分你一半。

Linda: Really? Thanks a lot!
真的嗎？太感謝了！

關鍵單字片語

7. **mango** [ˋmæŋgo] 名 芒果
8. **tangerine** [ˋtændʒəˏrin] 名 橘子
9. **pineapple** [ˋpaɪnˏæpl] 形 鳳梨
10. **refrigerator** [rɪˋfrɪdʒəˏretə] 名 冰箱
11. **half** [hæf] 形 一半的
12. **share** [ʃɛr] 動 分享

15. 付費結帳
Paying the Check
MP3 015

萬用好句

1.	**May I have the check, please?** 請給我帳單好嗎？
2.	**Do you accept credit cards?** 你們收信用卡嗎？
3.	**I am sorry, we take cash only.** 不好意思，我們只收現金。
4.	**Do you want separate checks?** 您們要分開算嗎？
5.	**Let's go Dutch.** 我們各付各的吧！
6.	**Let's split the check evenly.** 我們各付一半吧！
7.	**Let's share the bill.** 我們一起分攤帳單費用吧！
8.	**It's on me.** 我來付。
9.	**It's my treat.** 我請客。
10.	**May I have the receipt, please?** 可以給我收據嗎？
11.	**A ten-percent service charge will be added to the check.** 會多收百分之十的服務費。
12.	**I insist on paying my half.** 我堅持付我的部分。

 關鍵單字片語

1. **check** [tʃɛk] 名 帳單
2. **credit card** 片 信用卡
3. **cash** [kæʃ] 名 現金
4. **go Dutch** 片 各付各的
5. **bill** [bɪl] 名 帳單
6. **treat** [trit] 名 請客

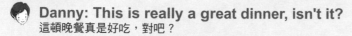

實境對話

Danny: This is really a great dinner, isn't it?
這頓晚餐真是好吃，對吧？

Carol: Yes, the steak is fantastic. I would definitely come back again.
沒錯，牛排超棒的，我以後一定還要再來吃。

Danny: Shall we go now?
我們該回去了吧？

Carol: Yes. Where is the check? How much is my steak?
嗯。帳單在哪裡？我的牛排多少錢？

Danny: Don't worry. It's my treat today.
別擔心，今天我請客。

Carol: Oh, you don't have to do that.
噢，你不需要請客啦！

Danny: You helped me a lot during the final exam. This is the least I can do to show my gratitude.
你在期末考期間幫了我很多忙，我只是想向你表達謝意。

Carol: But that's too much. Let's just go Dutch.
但是這頓飯太貴了，我們還是各付各的吧！

Danny: It's on me, really!
我來付就好，真的。

Carol: I insist on paying my half, Danny.
我堅持付我自己的這一半，丹尼。

Danny: Ok, if you insist. How about letting me buy you a coffee tomorrow?
好吧，如果你堅持的話。不如我明天請你喝咖啡？

Carol: It's a deal.
一言為定！

關鍵單字片語

7. **receipt** [rɪ`sit] 名 收據

8. **pay** [pe] 動 支付

9. **gratitude** [`ɡrætə͵tjud] 名 感謝

10. **separate** [`sɛprɪt] 形 分開的

11. **fantastic** [fæn`tæstɪk] 形 極佳的

12. **accept** [ək`sɛpt] 動 接受

1. 精緻彩妝
Cosmetics
MP3 016

萬用好句

1.	**We have lipstick in a wide range of colors. Do you want to try one?** 我們有多款顏色的唇膏，你想要試用嗎？
2.	**Do you have a base make-up in a lighter tone?** 你有顏色亮一點的遮瑕膏嗎？
3.	**BB cream is popular among teenage girls.** BB霜廣受青少女的歡迎。
4.	**The color of Angelina's lip gloss is very stunning.** 安潔莉娜的唇蜜顏色好美！
5.	**Remember, just apply a thin layer of the foundation, or you may ruin all the make-up you apply on top.** 記得，粉底只要上薄薄的一層就好，否則會毀了整個妝容。
6.	**The secret of putting on perfect make-up is to practice and be patient.** 完美彩妝的秘訣就是有耐心和反覆練習。
7.	**Gina spends more than an hour doing her make-up every morning.** 吉娜每天早上花超過一個小時的時間化妝。
8.	**You can get free samples at the counter.** 您可以在櫃檯索取免費的試用品。
9.	**It is extremely important for you to have a good powder brush.** 擁有一支好用的蜜粉刷非常重要。
10.	**This specially-designed brush can lengthen your eyelashes beyond your imagination.** 這支特製刷具可超乎想像地拉長您的睫毛。
11.	**This color palette features twelve gorgeous eye shadows, which are waterproof.** 這個眼影盤有十二款亮彩防水眼影。
12.	**Gently remove your make-up with a cotton pad.** 使用化妝棉輕柔地卸掉您的彩妝。

關鍵單字片語

1. **accessory** [æk`sɛsərɪ] 名 配件

2. **make-up** [`mek.ʌp] 名 化妝品

3. **foundation** [faʊn`deʃən] 名 粉底

4. **blend into** 片 混合

5. **mascara** [mæs`kærə] 名 睫毛膏

6. **volumize** [`vɑljəmaɪz] 動 增量

實境對話

Manny: Wow, you look fantastic today!
哇，你今天看起來真漂亮！

Pauline: Thanks! I am wearing a little bit of make-up.
謝啦！我有上一點妝。

Manny: That's why you look different. I like your eye shadow.
難怪你看起來有點不一樣。我喜歡你的眼影。

Pauline: I got it from Sogo. They're having a sale now.
我在太平洋百貨買的，目前正在特價。

Manny: Right. Mother's Day is just around the corner. Time to take advantage of the big sales going on! Do you have any recommendations?
是啊！馬上就是母親節，差不多該享受折扣了。你有沒有推薦什麼？

Pauline: Elite Cosmetics is having a Buy 1 Get 1 Free sale.
雅麗特化妝品現正買一送一。

Manny: Sounds great! I'd better run out and get my Mother's Day gift right away. See you.
聽起來真棒！我最好現在就跑去買我的母親節禮物。再會！

Pauline: Don't rush. They have an online ordering system.
別急，他們有線上訂購系統。

Manny: An online ordering system?
線上訂購系統？

Pauline: Yes. As long as you have a VIP membership, you can place orders online.
沒錯。只要你是他們的貴賓會員，你就可以在上網訂購。

Manny: It's a pity that I am not their VIP member.
很可惜我不是他們的貴賓會員。

Pauline: But I am!
可我是啊！

關鍵單字片語

7. **waterproof** [ˋwɔtəˏpruf] 形 防水的

8. **lengthen** [ˋlɛŋθən] 動 增長

9. **eyelash** [ˋaɪˏlæʃ] 名 睫毛

10. **corner of the mouth** 片 嘴角

11. **smudge** [smʌdʒ] 動 弄髒

12. **complexion** [kəmˋplɛkʃən] 名 氣色

2. 伸展台上
Runway Catwalk
MP3 017

萬用好句

1.	**Milan Fashion Week is an important event for fashion designers.** 米蘭時尚週是時裝設計師的重要盛會。
2.	**The show will present Mr. Choo's latest collection.** 這場秀將展示周先生的最新系列。
3.	**The designer came on stage at the end of the show.** 那位設計師在這場秀結束時走上舞台。
4.	**The model accidently tripped on the runway.** 那名模特兒不小心在伸展台上跌倒了。
5.	**Every model has to change five times during the show.** 在這場秀裡，每位模特兒都得換裝五次。
6.	**What should I do after I step onto the catwalk?** 站上伸展台後，我該怎麼做呢？
7.	**There are models wearing the latest collection in today's show.** 在今天的秀裡，模特兒們展示最新的設計系列。
8.	**The Victoria's Secret underwear and lingerie fashion show is one of my favorites.** 維多利亞祕密的內衣秀是我最喜歡的秀之一。
9.	**My cousin is a model. She can teach you how to walk like a catwalk beauty.** 我的堂姊是個模特兒，她可以教你如何像個時裝模特兒一樣走台步。
10.	**Millions of models would kill to be on the catwalk during Milan Fashion Week.** 數百萬名模特兒夢想能在米蘭時尚週裡走秀。
11.	**A new collection of faux fur coats will be paraded in today's show.** 今天的秀將會展示新系列的人造皮草外套。
12.	**More than fifty photographers were trying to get the best shots of the clothes and the models.** 超過五十名攝影師試著捕捉服裝和模特兒們最精彩的瞬間。

關鍵單字片語

1. **catwalk** [ˋkæt͵wɔk] 名 伸展台

2. **high fashion** 片 頂級時尚

3. **glamorous** [ˋglæmərəs] 形 富有魅力的

4. **garment** [ˋgɑrmənt] 名 服裝

5. **runway** [ˋrʌn͵we] 名 伸展台

6. **model** [ˋmɑdl] 名 模特兒

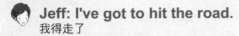

Jeff: I've got to hit the road.
我得走了

Nicole: Why? It's still early.
為何？還早耶。

Jeff: There's a fashion show on channel 11 at 8:00 tonight.
因為今晚八點在第十一台有場時尚秀。

Nicole: I had no idea that you are interested in fashion. I thought you were only into basketball.
我不知道你對時尚有興趣。我以為你只愛籃球。

Jeff: It's not an ordinary fashion show. It's the Victoria's Secret fashion show.
這可不是一般的時尚秀。這是維多利亞的祕密時尚秀。

Nicole: You mean the one with women's underwear and lingerie?
你是指那個女性內睡衣品牌嗎？

Jeff: Right. I'm taking a stage design class, and professor Lu asked us to write a report on the show.
是的。我修了一門舞台設計課，盧教授要我們做一份這場秀的報告。

Nicole: Wow! You do do your best on your homework.
哇！你真的很努力做作業。

Jeff: Of course. Besides, the show will motivate the male students like me.
當然。而且，這能提升如我這種男同學的學習動機。

Nicole: Who wants to do assignments on a Saturday night?
誰想在週六晚上做作業啊？

Jeff: Were you not listening to me? It's an underwear show!
你沒聽到我說的嗎？這可是場內衣秀耶！

Nicole: Alright, I got your point. You may leave now.
好啦，我懂你的意思，你可以離開了。

★ 關鍵單字片語

7. **in the promotion of** 片 為了促銷…

8. **couture** [ku`tʊr] 名 女性時裝

9. **trendy** [`trɛndɪ] 形 時髦的

10. **spotlight** [`spɑt‚laɪt] 名 聚光燈

11. **the latest collection** 片 最新系列

12. **camera face** 片 上相的人

3. 美容美髮
Make-up and Hairstyle

MP3 018

萬用好句

1. **I just want to get my hair trimmed a little bit.**
   我想稍微修剪一下頭髮。

2. **How long will it take to perm my hair?**
   燙我的頭髮要花多久時間？

3. **I would like to make an appointment with my stylist for this Sunday afternoon.**
   我想和我的設計師預約本週日下午。

4. **Sandy's new hairdo is very cute. She looks just like Carey Mulligan.**
   珊蒂的新髮型很可愛，她看起來就像凱芮‧穆雷根。

5. **Kenny dyed his hair green, which drives his father mad.**
   肯尼把頭髮染成綠色，讓他爸爸氣瘋了。

6. **Mandy always treats herself to a cucumber facial in the finest spa every payday.**
   蔓蒂總是在發薪日犒賞自己，到最好的護膚沙龍做臉。

7. **My mother always gets a perm every other month.**
   我媽媽總是每兩個月燙髮一次。

8. **Do you know any good hair salons? I am thinking about changing my hairstyle.**
   你推薦哪家不錯的美髮沙龍嗎？我正考慮換個髮型。

9. **Can you give me an oil massage, too?**
   可以也幫我按摩一下嗎？

10. **I want my hair cut short, please.**
    我想剪短髮，麻煩你。

11. **I'll cut your hair first, and then thin it out if necessary.**
    我會先剪短你的頭髮，如有需要的話會打薄。

12. **Jason looks much younger with his new hairdo.**
    傑森的新髮型讓他看起來更加年輕。

關鍵單字片語

1. **bang** [bæŋ] 名 瀏海

2. **salon** [sə`lɑn] 名 美髮沙龍

3. **ceramic perm** 片 陶瓷燙

4. **straight** [stret] 形 直的

5. **braid** [bred] 名 辮子

6. **trim off** 片 修剪

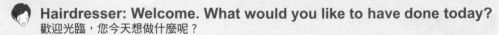

Hairdresser: Welcome. What would you like to have done today?
歡迎光臨，您今天想做什麼呢？

Customer: I want a hairstyle that makes me look more sophisticated.
我想弄個看起來較成熟的髮型。

Hairdresser: How about a short curly hairstyle?
短捲髮的造型如何？

Customer: Sounds perfect. Let's do it.
聽起來很棒，就這麼弄吧！

Hairdresser: OK. Let me wash your hair and massage your scalp first. This way, please.
好的，我先幫您洗個頭和按摩頭皮。這邊請。

Customer: The massage was so great. What's next?
按摩真是舒服。接下來呢？

Hairdresser: I'll cut your hair and thin it out a bit. Then I will give you a perm.
我會幫您剪髮，並稍微打薄，然後再燙髮。

Customer: How long will it take?
會花多久時間？

Hairdresser: About two hours. Do you want some magazines to read?
大約兩個小時。您想看點雜誌嗎？

Customer: Sure.
好呀。

Hairdresser: OK. It's done. A sophisticated short curly hairstyle!
好了，大功告成。成熟的短卷髮！

Customer: Are you kidding me? I look exactly like my mother!
你在跟我開玩笑嗎？我看起來就像我媽！

關鍵單字片語

7. **thin out** 片 打薄

8. **beauty parlor** 片 美容院

9. **hair spray** 片 髮膠

10. **split ends** 片 頭髮分岔

11. **perm** [pɜm] 動 燙髮

12. **cucumber facial** 片 做臉

4. 少一雙鞋
Not Enough Shoes
MP3 019

萬用好句

1. What is your shoe size?
您的腳多大？

2. Sorry, but we don't have size five right now.
抱歉，我們目前沒有五號尺寸。

3. Excuse me. I would like to try on these in a size six, please.
不好意思，我想要試穿這款，請給我六號。

4. We have three different colors: green, red, and black. Which one would you like?
我們有三款不同的顏色：綠色、紅色和黑色。您想要哪一款？

5. This pair of shoes is made of real leather.
這雙鞋由真皮製成。

6. Did you wear your boots in the rain?
你是不是穿著靴子淋雨？

7. You'd better try the shoes on before you buy them.
你最好在付帳購買前先試穿。

8. The new training shoes fit Jenny like a glove.
這雙新的運動鞋十分符合珍妮的尺寸。

9. Our son has outgrown his running shoes. Let's get him a new pair for Christmas.
我們兒子的慢跑鞋已經不合腳了，耶誕節送他一雙新的吧。

10. I am looking for a pair of all-weather shoes.
我正在找一雙各種天候都合穿的鞋。

11. What is this pair of shoes made of, real or synthetic leather?
這雙鞋是以真皮還是合成皮製成的？

12. How many lace holes are there in this shoe?
這隻鞋有多少個鞋帶孔？

關鍵單字片語

1. **high heels** 片 高跟鞋

2. **boot** [but] 名 靴子

3. **sandal** [`sændl] 名 (露趾)涼鞋

4. **sneaker** [`snikɚ] 名 球鞋

5. **wellie** [`wɛlɪ] 名 橡膠靴

6. **training shoes** 片 帆布膠底運動鞋

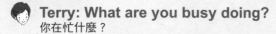

Terry: What are you busy doing?
你在忙什麼？

Jessica: I'm shopping for shoes online.
我在上網買鞋子。

Terry: Online? Don't you think you should at least try them on first?
上網買？你不覺得至少要先試穿過嗎？

Jessica: Sure. I can try on the shoes before I actually "own" them.
當然。我的確可以在「擁有」鞋子之前試穿它們。

Terry: How does that work with online shopping?
上網購物是要怎麼個試穿法？

Jessica: Well, there are plenty of online shopping Websites with a "free refund policy" now.
喔，現在有許多線上購物網站提供「免費退換服務」。

Terry: Oh? Is that so?
哦？這樣嗎？

Jessica: Yes. You can return your order within seven days if the item doesn't fit you well, or even if you don't like the color.
是啊。若尺寸不合、或是顏色你不愛，七天內都可免費退換。

Terry: Then, what about the return shipping fees?
那麼退換貨的運費怎麼算呢？

Jessica: The shipping is absolutely free.
免付運費。

Terry: Really? Are you serious?
真的嗎？你不是開玩笑的吧？

Jessica: Yes I am. Isn't it convenient? With a click on the mouse, everything is done.
當然不是。很方便吧！按下滑鼠就可搞定一切。

關鍵單字片語

7. **slipper** [`slɪpɚ] 名 拖鞋

8. **polish** [`pɑlɪʃ] 動 擦亮

9. **measure** [`mɛʒɚ] 動 測量

10. **sturdy** [`stɝdɪ] 形 經久耐用的

11. **fit like a glove** 片 合尺寸

12. **wear out** 片 磨損

5. 新鮮用語
Catchy Phrases
MP3
020

萬用好句

1.	**Allen is nothing but a geek in the eye of his classmates.** 亞倫在他同學們的眼中，不過是個怪胎。
2.	**I think Kevin and his posh car can certainly get all the attention he wants.** 我想凱文和他那台酷炫轎車一定能夠吸引到任何他想要的目光。
3.	**Jack only spent two months learning Chinese, and now he can converse in it fluently. He must have natural talent.** 傑克只學了兩個月的中文，現在就能暢談無礙。這一定是他與生俱來的能力。
4.	**I have a gut feeling that Jason can't make it.** 我有個直覺傑森不會來了。
5.	**Keep your shirt on! It takes time for the water to boil.** 耐心點！水要花點時間才會煮滾。
6.	**Sometimes it's better to bite your tongue to avoid trouble.** 有時候忍住不說，避免捲入麻煩比較好。
7.	**Do you think I'm a push-over?** 你是不是把我當成好欺負的人？
8.	**Mike was late and blew the date with his princess charming.** 麥克遲到，搞砸了他和理想情人的約會。
9.	**Do you want to try to make a slam-dunk?** 你想要試試看灌籃嗎？
10.	**Jason gets TV stoned whenever a basketball game is on.** 每次電視轉播籃球賽，傑森都目不轉睛。
11.	**Jessie was dead tired after staying up late singing karaoke.** 潔西唱了整晚的歌後，整個人累翻了。
12.	**What's wrong with you? You get wigged out every time Allen comes.** 你怎麼了？每次亞倫來，你總是一副害怕的樣子。

關鍵單字片語

1. **posh** [pɑʃ] 形 奢侈的、漂亮的

2. **poser** [`pozɚ] 名 矯揉造作的人

3. **janky** [`dʒænkɪ] 形 老舊的

4. **catchy** [`kætʃɪ] 形 引起注意的

5. **phrase** [frez] 名 詞組

6. **phat** [fæt] 形 好的、極好的

實境對話

Tom: Finally, it's time to call it a day. T.G.I.F.
終於可以下班了。T.G.I.F.。

Gina: What is T.G.I.F.?
T.G.I.F是什麼？

Tom: It's the acronym for, "Thank God it's Friday."
就是「感謝老天，終於星期五了！」的英文縮寫。

Gina: O.I.C.
噢，原來如此。

Tom: No work tomorrow, how about grabbing a drink together?
明天不用工作，一起去喝一杯吧！

Gina: I'd love to, but Mr. Hu asked me to finish this report by nine.
我很想去，但胡先生要我在九點前完成這份報告。

Tom: He always asks people to work overtime to meet an urgent deadline. It's really annoying.
他總在最後一刻要人幫他趕件，真的很討厭。

Gina: You are right, but he promised me a huge bonus once the deal is sealed.
你說的沒錯，但他答應我一旦交易成功，就要給我一份豐厚的紅利。

Tom: Don't count on it. The bonus is just an illusion.
別抱希望。這都是唬你的。

Gina: What do you mean by that?
你說這話是什麼意思？

Tom: I am saying that Mr. Hu is just a con man. He never really gives anyone the bonuses he promises.
我說胡先生是個騙子，他從來沒有真的給過他所承諾的紅利。

Gina: Oh, no! That's whacked.
噢不，那真是太糟糕了。

關鍵單字片語

7. **bling bling** 片 閃亮華麗

8. **cashed out** 片 破產的、貧窮的

9. **stoked** [stokt] 形 非常開心的

10. **kick rocks** 片 滾開、閃邊去

11. **my bad** 片 我的錯、我不好

12. **chillin'** [`tʃɪlɪn] 形 放鬆的

6. 電視節目
TV Programs
MP3 021

萬用好句

1. Teddy always fights over the remote control with his sister.
泰迪和他妹妹總是互搶電視遙控器。

2. The finale of "Friends," the popular TV series, had an amazingly high viewership rate of 22%.
受歡迎的影集《六人行》，其完結篇創下了百分之二十二的驚人收視率。

3. Who will be the guest host on the Today's Show?
《今日秀》的主持嘉賓會是誰？

4. Rumor has it that Tom Cruise is joining the cast of "True Blood."
傳言湯姆・克魯斯要加入《嗜血真愛》的演員陣容。

5. "Take Home Chef" is a popular reality show in the U.K.
《帥哥主廚到你家》是英國受歡迎的實境節目。

6. "The Big Bang Theory" is a series about four geeky scientists.
《宅男行不行》是部描述四位怪胎科學家的影集。

7. The Emmy Award are awards for TV productions in the U.S.
艾美獎是個有關美國電視製作的獎項。

8. Who do you think will be voted the Best Actor at the Emmys?
你覺得今年誰會贏得艾美獎最佳男演員？

9. Hank's wife divorced him because she couldn't stand a couch potato like him anymore.
漢克的太太因為再也無法忍受他如此愛看電視又懶散，而和他離婚。

10. "The Office" is a popular sitcom with an overall viewership of hundreds of millions worldwide.
《辦公室風雲》是部受歡迎的情境喜劇，全球有超過數億名觀眾收看。

11. "Friends" is said to be the most successful sitcom in the U.S.
《六人行》被譽為全美最成功的情境喜劇。

12. What's your favorite TV series?
你最喜歡的電視影集是什麼？

關鍵單字片語

1. **variety show** 片 綜藝節目
2. **couch potato** 片 極為懶惰的人
3. **previously on** 片 前情提要
4. **commercial** [kə`mɝʃəl] 名 廣告
5. **host** [host] 名 (男性)主持人
6. **reality show** 片 實境節目

實境對話

Kevin: The Emmys are on tomorrow night. I am so excited!
艾美獎就在明晚了，我好興奮！

Charlie: Are you? I had no idea you are that into dramas.
是噢？我不知道你這麼喜歡戲劇。

Kevin: I surely am! And you know what? Dramas today are not only entertaining but also educational.
當然囉！而且你知道嗎？現在的戲劇兼具娛樂性與教育性。

Charlie: Really? I thought dramas were just for entertainment.
是嗎？我以為戲劇只具娛樂效果。

Kevin: They can do more! Like Criminal Minds. It contains educational information about forensics and psychology.
他們可以給你更多！像是《犯罪心理》，含有關於法醫學和心理學的知識。

Charlie: Wow. I thought dramas were all about romance.
哇。我以為戲劇都在講愛情。

Kevin: Romance is indeed a common theme in dramas, but there are still other popular themes.
愛情的確是很普遍的主題，但也有其他受歡迎的主題。

Charlie: Like what?
像是什麼呢？

Kevin: For example, "The Big Bang Theory" is a hilarious sitcom that doesn't put too much emphasis on romance.
如《宅男行不行》這類詼諧的情境喜劇，不太過強調愛情。

Charlie: Sounds interesting. Seems like I need to start watching some TV shows.
聽起來不賴。也許我該開始看些電視節目了。

Kevin: Let me suggest some dramas that you'll like.
讓我推薦幾部合你味口的戲劇吧！

關鍵單字片語

7. **talk show** 片 談話節目(脫口秀)

8. **sitcom** [`sɪt͵kɑm] 名 情境喜劇

9. **remote control** 片 遙控器

10. **rating** [`retɪŋ] 名 收視率

11. **serial** [`sɪrɪəl] 名 影集

12. **season** [`sizn̩] 名 一季

7. 近期上映
Movies

MP3 022

萬用好句

1.	**What type of movies do you like the most?** 你最喜歡哪種類型的電影？
2.	**Twilight is a romance between a vampire and an ordinary girl adapted from a popular novel.** 《暮光之城》改編自著名小說，是關於吸血鬼與人類女孩的愛情故事。
3.	**The movie trailer successfully drew large audiences into the theater.** 這部電影預告成功地吸引觀眾前往戲院觀賞。
4.	**Nicole Kidman gave a stunningly great performance in Moulin Rouge, in which she not only acts well, but also sings perfectly.** 妮可·基嫚在《紅磨坊》裡演出精湛，不只演得好、也唱得好。
5.	**Who is the director of Transformers?** 《變形金剛》的導演是誰？
6.	**The making of movies has been brought up to a higher level thanks to computer graphics technology.** 多虧電腦動畫科技，電影製作已臻更高境界。
7.	**The box office sales of the new movie are not as good as expected.** 這部新電影的票房不如預期。
8.	**The Karate Kid features Jackie Chan as an Asian kungfu master.** 成龍在《功夫小子》裡主演一位亞洲功夫師父。
9.	**Do you know when the Low Cost will be on in the theaters?** 你知道《廉價航空》何時上映嗎？
10.	**Will Leonardo DiCaprio attend the premier of J. Edgar in Paris?** 李奧那多·迪卡皮歐會出席電影《強·艾德格》在巴黎的首映會嗎？
11.	**Three Idiots broke the opening box office record in India.** 《三個傻瓜》打破了印度的首映票房記錄。
12.	**The movie is rated PG, a.k.a. parental guidance.** 這部電影列為輔導級，也就是需要家長陪同觀賞。

關鍵單字片語

1. **trailer** [`trelɚ] 名 預告片

2. **box office** 片 (電影)票房

3. **thriller** [`θrɪlɚ] 名 驚悚片

4. **break the record** 片 打破記錄

5. **director** [dɚ`rɛktɚ] 名 導演

6. **screenplay** [`skrin‚ple] 名 電影劇本

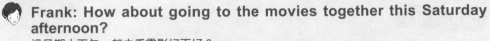

Frank: How about going to the movies together this Saturday afternoon?
這星期六下午一起去看電影好不好？

Amanda: Great idea. What do you want to see?
好主意。你想看什麼？

Frank: I am thinking about The Iron Lady. Emma said it's a must-see.
我想看《鐵娘子》，艾瑪說這部必看。

Amanda: It definitely is, but it's not showing anymore.
是沒錯，但這部片已經下檔了。

Frank: That's too bad. Do you have any other movies in mind?
真糟糕。那你有沒有想看的片？

Amanda: How about American Pie: Reunion?
那《美國派：高潮再起》怎麼樣？

Frank: Well, I'm not that interested in teeny bopper movies.
呃，我對於青少年電影興趣不太大。

Amanda: Me neither. But those kinds of movies are really relaxing.
我也還好。但這類電影的確可以紓解壓力。

Frank: You're right. Then, let's go see American Pie: Reunion together!
的確是。那就看《美國派：高潮再起》吧！

Amanda: OK. How about this Saturday afternoon at 2:30?
好的。這星期六下午兩點半怎麼樣？

Frank: Sounds perfect. How about having lunch together first?
好啊！要不要先一起吃頓午餐呢？

Amanda: Sure.
好啊。

關鍵單字片語

7. **chase scene** 片 追逐戲

8. **character** [`kærɪktə] 名 角色

9. **leading role** 片 主角

10. **cast** [kæst] 名 卡司(演員名單)

11. **perform** [pə`fɔrm] 動 表演

12. **Sci-Fi** [`saɪ`faɪ] 名 科幻電影

8.**熱門音樂**
Pop Music
MP3 023

萬用好句

1.	**The Black Eyed Peas is one of my favorite bands.** 黑眼豆豆是我最喜歡的樂團之一。
2.	**You can get the latest pop music updates on Billboard.com.** 你可在告示牌排行榜的網頁上得到最新流行音樂資訊。
3.	**Adele is still at No. 1 on the Billboard this week.** 艾戴爾本週仍居告示牌排行榜第一名。
4.	**50 cent is a very popular rapper with teenagers.** 五角是位廣受年輕人歡迎的饒舌歌手。
5.	**Who is the composer of this song?** 這首歌的作曲者是誰？
6.	**Mandy enjoys indulging herself in jazz music after work.** 蔓蒂喜歡在下班後聽爵士樂放鬆。
7.	**Cats has been one of the most popular musicals for decades.** 《貓》劇數十年來為最受歡迎的音樂劇之一。
8.	**Gina is a huge fan of Justin Timberlake. She has a complete collection of his albums.** 吉娜很喜歡賈斯汀。她有他的全套專輯。
9.	**The release of Katy Perry's latest album is scheduled for July 1st.** 凱蒂・佩瑞的最新專輯預計於七月一日發售。
10.	**If you order Lady Gaga's album now, you can get a free limited edition poster.** 如果您現在預購女神卡卡的專輯，就可獲得一張免費的限量版海報。
11.	**iTunes is an Internet platform where you can download the latest music at bargain prices.** iTunes是個可讓你以優惠價格下載最新音樂的網路平台。
12.	**Mayday is going to give a live concert on New Year's Eve.** 五月天將在跨年夜舉辦現場演唱會。

關鍵單字片語

1. **Billboard** [`bɪl͵bord] 名 告示牌排行榜

2. **soundtrack** [`saund͵træk] 名 原聲帶

3. **R&B** [`ar͵ænd`bi] 名 節奏藍調

4. **hot** [hɑt] 形 受歡迎的、暢銷的

5. **album** [`ælbəm] 名 專輯

6. **release** [rɪ`lis] 動 發行

實境對話

Host: It's FM 100. You are listening to "Love Request." Everybody express your love! Hello, this is Jenny. Who's calling?
這裡是調頻一百，您正在收聽「愛的點唱機」。愛要說出來！嗨，我是珍妮。怎麼稱呼你？

Jason: This is Jason. I want to request a song for my wife.
我是傑森，我想點歌給我太太。

Host: Which song would you like to request for her?
你想點什麼歌給她？

Jason: "P.S. I Love You" by the Beatles.
披頭四的「備註：我愛你」。

Host: It's a classical love song. Why did you choose that song?
這是一首經典情歌。為什麼你選了這首歌呢？

Jason: I want to tell her that although life is not as easy as we had imagined it would be, I will always love her and cherish her with all my heart.
我想跟她說，雖然生活不如我們想像般容易，我永遠愛她，也會全心全意珍惜她。

Host: That's so sweet of you!
你真貼心！

Jason: It's really nothing. She has been very good to me.
這沒什麼。她一直都對我很好。

Host: May I ask how long you have been married?
我可以請問你們結婚多久了嗎？

Jason: Seven years. It is our anniversary today.
七年了。今天是我們的結婚紀念日。

Host: Happy Anniversary! How are you going to celebrate?
週年快樂！你們要怎麼慶祝？

Jason: We will have a nice dinner together at W hotel.
我們今晚要在W飯店共進晚餐。

關鍵單字片語

7. **artist of the year** 片 年度最佳歌手

8. **debut** [dɪˋbju] 名 初次登台、首次露面

9. **reportedly** [rɪˋportɪdlɪ] 副 據報導

10. **pop** [pɑp] 形 流行的

11. **single** [ˋsɪŋgl] 形 單一的

12. **lyric** [ˋlɪrɪk] 名 歌詞

萬用好句

1. Let's enjoy the Swedish rock festival at the Wall live house tonight.
今晚，一同享受在這牆音樂展演空間舉辦的瑞典搖滾音樂祭吧！

2. Music by Enigma always makes my skin crawl.
謎樂團的音樂總讓我起雞皮疙瘩。

3. Soul music is the combination of gospel music and R&B.
靈魂樂融合聖歌音樂和節奏藍調。

4. Which genre of music do you like the most?
你最喜歡的音樂類型是？

5. Mr. Kennedy wants to introduce aboriginal music on his record.
甘迺迪先生想在他的專輯裡採用原住民音樂的概念。

6. The music of Mozart is an archetype of the Classical style.
莫札特的音樂是古典樂的代表。

7. I can hardly understand the concept behind Bjork's music.
碧玉歌曲的概念對我來說很難理解。

8. Larry Huang is a famous aboriginal composer, whose music conveys the nature-loving spirit of aboriginal culture.
黃賴瑞是位著名的原住民編曲家，他的音樂傳達了原住民文化裡喜愛大自然的精神。

9. Because she has record-breaking album sales even though she's not well-known, Yozoh is the best singer I can think of.
雖然不太有名、卻能創造專輯銷售佳績，窈窕小姐是我心中最棒的歌手。

10. I have a full collection of Radiohead's CDs.
我有電台司令專輯的完整收藏。

11. Mandy finally made her debut at the NSO as the violinist.
蔓蒂終於以小提琴手的身分加入國家交響樂團。

12. Can you tell me who the composer of the song is?
可以告訴我這首歌的作曲者是誰嗎？

關鍵單字片語

1. **genre** [`ʒɑnrə] 名 種類

2. **dynamic** [daɪ`næmɪk] 形 有活力的

3. **classical** [`klæsɪk]] 形 古典的

4. **aboriginal** [ˌæbə`rɪdʒən]] 形 原住民的

5. **rhythm** [`rɪðəm] 名 韻律、節奏

6. **creep** [krip] 名 毛骨悚然的感覺

實境對話

Will: What is the name of this song? It's very nice.
這首歌叫什麼名字？很好聽。

Jessica: It's Canon. My favorite song.
這是我最喜歡的歌，卡農。

Will: Every time I ride in your car, you always listen to this song.
我每次坐你的車，你都在聽這首歌。

Jessica: This song helps me escape from the chaos of the city.
這首歌可以帶我逃離城市的喧囂。

Will: I see. Isn't it the theme song of "My Sassy Girl"?
這樣啊。這首不就是《我的野蠻女友》的主題曲嗎？

Jessica: Yes, that's right. The full name of the song is "Variations on the Canon by Pachelbel" by George Winston.
沒錯，就是那首歌，它是喬治·溫斯頓的歌，全名是《帕海貝爾卡農變奏曲》。

Will: Really? I thought the name of that song was only "Canon."
是嗎？我以為那首歌就叫做《卡農》。

Jessica: Actually, Canon is the name for a specific kind of melody, rather than a particular song.
事實上，卡農是一種旋律的名稱，並不是某首曲名。

Will: Is that so? I didn't know that.
真的啊？我都不知道。

Jessica: Yeh. One of the most famous songs in this style is George Winston's Canon, which is how it got that name.
真的啊！這種旋律最有名的就是喬治·溫斯頓的卡農，所以這首歌就成為卡農的招牌。

Will: I never knew that. I have really learned something.
我從來沒聽說過。我真的學到東西了。

Jessica: How about you? Tell me about your favorite music.
那你呢？有沒有什麼喜歡的音樂？

關鍵單字片語

7. **make skin crawl** 片 起雞皮疙瘩

8. **unique** [ju`nik] 形 獨特的

9. **Baroque** [bə`rok] 形 巴洛克風格的

10. **pioneer** [ˌpaɪə`nɪr] 動 作為…的先驅

11. **remixed version** 片 混音版本

12. **a symphony of** 片 與…和諧

10. **時尚派對**
Fashion Party

M P 3
025

萬用好句

1. **I would kill for your shoes! Where did you get them?**
   我好想要你這雙鞋！你在哪買的？

2. **What's the theme of this fashion party?**
   這個時尚派對的主題是什麼？

3. **Wherever Kevin is, there is always fun.**
   有凱文的地方總是充滿歡樂。

4. **At a fashion party, you can get updates on the latest fashion news.**
   在時尚派對裡，你可以得到最新的時尚訊息。

5. **The party is being held in cooperation with Louis Vuitton and Hermes.**
   這個派對和路易威登及愛馬仕合作舉辦。

6. **The 100th guest to arrive will win a free Hermes handbag.**
   第一百名蒞臨者可免費獲得一個愛馬仕手提包。

7. **Every member will get an invitation to Breeze Night.**
   每位會員將收到微風之夜的邀請函。

8. **The brand is scheduled to reveal its new collection of handbags at the party next week.**
   這個品牌預計於下週派對上發表最新的手提包系列。

9. **Gina decided to throw a private house party to celebrate the 10th anniversary of her brand.**
   為慶祝個人品牌十週年，吉娜決定舉辦一場私人派對。

10. **Do you think it's the model or the dress that's so stunning?**
    你覺得是模特兒的關係，還是那件洋裝實在是太美了？

11. **For the convenience of our guests, only finger food will be served at the party.**
    為了賓客的便利，這場派對只供應手抓小食物。

關鍵單字片語

1. **fabulous** [`fæbjələs] 形 極好的

2. **costume** [`kɑstjum] 名 服裝、裝束

3. **enjoy oneself** 片 享受、喜愛

4. **life of the party** 片 派對中的靈魂人物

5. **theme** [θim] 名 主題

6. **charmer** [`tʃɑrmɚ] 名 有魅力的人

實境對話

Reporter: Can you tell us about the upcoming fashion show?
可以跟我們說一下即將到來的這場時裝秀嗎？

Chen: Sure. It is to celebrate our 50th anniversary, and our designers are going to show their new fashion collections.
好的。這場秀是為了慶祝我們的五十週年紀念，我們的設計師會展示新系列的設計。

Reporter: Is it true that your top model, Lil Q, will be in the show?
你們的首席模特兒琳兒·Q也會參加這次的秀，是真的嗎？

Chen: It's true. Lil Q will come back from France and step onto the stage for the first time since she got married.
是真的。琳兒·Q會從法國回來，在她婚後首次登台。

Reporter: Her fans must be very excited.
她的粉絲一定會很興奮。

Chen: Yes, they are.
他們的確非常興奮。

Reporter: Is there anything else special about the show?
這場秀還有什麼特別的嗎？

Chen: Yes. The 100th attendee to arrive at the party will win a 20% discount off for a whole year.
有的。第一百位入場者可享全年八折優惠。

Reporter: That's definitely great news for all the fashion lovers.
這真是所有時尚愛好者的好消息。

Chen: It sure is. Please check our website at beautyup.com for information about how to attend.
當然。請至我們的網站beautyup.com查詢入場資訊。

Reporter: Fashion lovers, don't miss it! Thank you, Miss Chen.
時尚愛好者，別錯過囉！陳小姐，謝謝您。

Chen: Thank you.
謝謝你。

關鍵單字片語

7. **finger food** 片 可用手拿取的小點心

8. **component** [kəm`ponənt] 名 構成要素

9. **all the rage** 片 正在流行的

10. **cocktail** [`kɑk,tel] 名 雞尾酒

11. **ruin** [`rʊɪn] 動 破壞、毀壞

12. **celebrate** [`sɛlə,bret] 動 慶祝

11. **街頭藝術**
Street Arts
MP3
026

萬用好句

1.	There is some huge graffiti of Obama on the back of the building. 這棟大樓後方有一幅歐巴馬的大型塗鴉。
2.	There are many street performers on High Street in Edinburgh. 愛丁堡的高街上有許多街頭表演者。
3.	She plays Guzheng on the street and makes some money. 她在街上演奏古箏賺錢。
4.	Street performance, the practice of performing in public places by street musicians and mime performers, is entertaining. 街頭表演是由街頭音樂家或是默劇表演者在公眾場所進行的表演，具有娛樂性。
5.	The performer pretends to be a statue, which makes many passersby gasp at each of his movements. 那個表演者扮成一座雕像，使許多路過的民眾在他移動時尖叫。
6.	Jason used to be a street violinist in the park on weekends. 傑森以前曾經於週末時，在公園表演小提琴。
7.	The British singer Sting was once a street performer. 英國歌手史汀當過街頭藝人。
8.	The city hall welcomes the buskers and provides them with budget dorms. 市政府歡迎街頭藝人，並提供他們費用低廉的宿舍。
9.	How can I apply for a busking permit? 我該如何申請街頭表演許可證？
10.	The street performers along the River Thames are unforgettable. 泰晤士河沿岸的街頭表演者令人難忘。
11.	You can get a glimpse of teenage subculture by watching street performers. 從街頭表演中，你可以窺見青少年的次文化。
12.	The city is always bristling with buskers and tourists on holidays. 這座城市假日總是充斥著街頭藝人和觀光客。

關鍵單字片語

1. **spray** [spre] 動 噴漆、噴霧
2. **graffiti** [græˋfitɪ] 名 牆上塗鴉
3. **public art** 片 公眾藝術
4. **put up** 片 設立、設置
5. **ink** [ɪŋk] 名 墨水
6. **prolific** [prəˋlɪfɪk] 形 富創造力的

實境對話

Amanda: What are you doing, Jack?
傑克，你在做什麼？

Jack: I am practicing the guitar.
我在練吉他。

Amanda: Are you going to give a performance?
你將要有表演嗎？

Jack: Not yet, but soon. I'm going to apply for a busker permit.
還沒，但快了。我要去申請街頭藝人許可證。

Amanda: What is a busker permit?
街頭藝人許可證是什麼？

Jack: City Hall is going to have a qualifying test for buskers. Whoever passes the test can get a busker permit.
市政廳為街頭藝人舉辦資格考試。通過考試者，就能獲得街頭藝人許可證。

Amanda: What is so special about a busker permit?
這張街頭藝人許可證有什麼特別之處？

Jack: If you have a permit, you can perform in an area especially-designated for buskers, and you don't have to worry so much about safety.
有了街頭藝人許可證，你就可以在特別規劃的區域內表演，不用過於擔心安全問題。

Amanda: I kind of heard about this on TV. But I'm really surprised that you can play guitar.
我好像在電視上聽過，不過我很驚訝你會彈吉他。

Jack: I can't. But how hard can it be?
我不會啊。不過會有多難？

Amanda: You are right. Practice makes perfect. When is the test?
你說的沒錯，練習造就完美。資格考是什麼時候？

Jack: It's in two days. This Saturday.
就在兩天後，這星期六。

關鍵單字片語

7. **accordionist** [ə`kɔrdɪənɪst] 名 手風琴手

8. **be inspired by** 片 被⋯激發靈感

9. **subculture** [`sʌb͵kʌltʃ] 名 次文化

10. **mime** [maɪm] 名 默劇

11. **busker** [`bʌska] 名 街頭藝人

12. **flash mob** 片 快閃族

萬用好句

1.	**Who is the blonde beauty over by the counter?** 吧台那邊那位金髮美女是誰？
2.	**Are you alone, or did you come here with your friends?** 你自己一個人，還是跟朋友一起來？
3.	**The bartender is my close friend, therefore I can get free drinks.** 我跟這裡的酒保很熟，所以我可以免費拿酒。
4.	**There are two bouncers over seven feet tall in front of the club.** 夜店前面有兩個超過七呎高的保鑣。
5.	**Whoever joins the pole dance competition can have a cocktail on the house.** 凡是參加鋼管舞競賽的人，都可以得到一杯本店招待的雞尾酒。
6.	**How about grabbing something to eat after we finish this drink?** 喝完這杯後，要不要一起去找些東西吃？
7.	**The girl Tom hit on at the bar last night happened to be my wife.** 湯姆昨天晚上在酒吧搭訕的女孩碰巧是我老婆。
8.	**It is very enjoyable to have drinks with a couple of friends in a cocktail lounge.** 和三五好友一起在酒吧喝點酒，真是一大享受。
9.	**If you are looking for a place to relax, Carter's Club is your best choice.** 如果你想找個地方放鬆一下，卡特酒吧是你的首選。
10.	**I am going to get a drink. Can I get you one?** 我要去點飲料。要幫你點一杯嗎？
11.	**I think Jessica has a crush on the guy drinking at the bar.** 我覺得潔西卡看上在吧台喝酒的那個男人。
12.	**How often do you go clubbing?** 你多常去夜店？

關鍵單字片語

1. **clubbing** [`klʌbɪŋ] 名 去夜店
2. **lounge bar** 片 雅座酒吧
3. **bar** [bɑr] 名 吧台

4. **hit on** 片 搭訕
5. **dude** [djud] 名 傢伙
6. **on the rocks** 片 加冰塊

實境對話

Kevin: Hey, check out the blonde lady over there.
喂，看那邊那個金髮美女。

Jane: Which one?
哪一個？

Kevin: The one wearing a pink ribbon by the counter.
櫃檯旁，綁粉紅色蝴蝶結的那個。

Jane: Do you mean the one in the red dress?
你是說穿紅色洋裝的那個嗎？

Kevin: That's right. I think I'm in love! I am going to buy her a drink.
沒錯。我想我戀愛了。我要去請她喝杯飲料。

Jane: As your best friend, I suggest you not do that.
身為你的好朋友，我建議你不要。

Kevin: Why not? Does she have a date?
為什麼不？她有攜伴前來嗎？

Jane: No, I don't think she's got a date.
沒有，我覺得她沒人陪。

Kevin: Then why not?
那為什麼？

Jane: I think she is way out of your league.
我覺得你配不上她。

Kevin: That's nonsense. Why don't you support me a little bit?
說那什麼話！你為什麼不挺我呢？

Jane: I really want to, but I can't. I am her older sister. I can't see you together with her.
我很想，但是我沒辦法。我是她姊，我不覺得你們相配。

Kevin: Oh.
噢。

關鍵單字片語

7. **on the house** 片 本店招待

8. **bouncer** [`baʊnsɚ] 名 保鏢

9. **wingman** [`wɪŋmæn] 名 同行夥伴

10. **wasted** [`westɪd] 形 喝醉的

11. **pole dance** 片 鋼管舞

12. **chick** [tʃɪk] 名 小妞(輕挑語)

13. 奢華精品
Luxuries

MP3
028

萬用好句

1. Not everyone can afford a cashmere scarf.
不是每個人都能負擔得起一條喀什米爾羊毛圍巾。

2. The handbag was made by an experienced Italian craftsman.
這個手提包是由一名老經驗的義大利工匠製作。

3. Hermes is one of the most luxurious brands in the world.
愛馬仕是世界上最奢華的品牌之一。

4. Amanda really knows her signature style.
亞曼達很瞭解她自己的穿衣風格。

5. The diamond is so fabulous that Helena cannot resist taking out her credit card.
那顆鑽石是如此美麗，以致於海蓮娜忍不住拿出她的信用卡。

6. Designer brands tend to incorporate new elements into their designs.
設計師品牌喜歡在設計中加入新的元素。

7. Jessica's latest jewelry collection is well-received in the market.
潔西卡最新一季的珠寶設計在市場上反應很好。

8. Luxury goods are usually associated with affluence, rather than necessity.
奢侈品通常與富裕聯想在一起，而非與必需品。

9. This handbag cost me a fortune.
這個手提包花了我好大一把銀子。

10. Tourists are limited to the purchase of only two handbags at Louis Vuitton in Paris.
在巴黎的路易威登，每位觀光客限額購買兩個手提包。

11. The car made of fiber glass and titanium costs 2 million dollars.
這輛車以玻璃纖維和鈦打造而成，要價兩百萬元。

12. The word is that Mercedes Benz will reveal its newest model in summer.
賓士車廠據傳將在夏季公布最新車款。

關鍵單字片語

1. **luxury** [`lʌkʃərɪ] 名 奢侈品

2. **cashmere** [`kæʃmɪr] 名 喀什米爾羊毛

3. **edgy** [`ɛdʒɪ] 形 前衛的

4. **elite** [e`lit] 名 精英

5. **silk** [sɪlk] 名 絲綢

6. **jewelry** [`dʒuəlrɪ] 名 珠寶

實境對話

Elvis: I really like your handbag! Where did you get it?
我喜歡你的手提包！你在哪裡買的？

Jennifer: You have an excellent taste. This is Hermes, and it took a big effort for me to get it.
你真有品味。這是愛馬仕包，花了我好大一番心血才得到。

Elvis: A big effort? How's so?
好大一番心血？怎麼說？

Jennifer: It's a limited bag. There are only two hundred around the globe. And I am one of the lucky owners.
這是限量包，全球只有兩百個。我是其中一名幸運持有者。

Elvis: Wow! So, did you pay extra money for it?
哇，所以你有額外多付錢嗎？

Jennifer: Money alone won't ensure that you can get a limited edition bag.
錢不能保證你一定買得到限量包。

Elvis: Then how did you get it?
那麼是怎麼得到的？

Jennifer: I'd waited in line in front of the Hermes store for a whole week before the new bag was released.
新包發售前，我在愛馬仕門口排隊等了一整個禮拜。

Elvis: A whole week! Don't tell me that you even slept in front of the store!
一整個禮拜？別跟我說你還在店門口睡覺！

Jennifer: Of course, I did! If you left, you gave up the chance! It was worth it!
當然啦！一走掉，就是放棄機會了！非常值得！

Elvis: So people do get crazy when it comes to luxuries.
所以一提到奢侈品，人類的確會發癲。

關鍵單字片語

7. **boutique** [bu`tik] 名 精品店

8. **fancy** [`fænsɪ] 形 別緻的

9. **brand** [brænd] 名 品牌

10. **idle rich** 片 非常富有

11. **in the lap of luxury** 片 非常富有

12. **life style** 片 生活方式

14. 逛街血拼
Shopping Spree
029

萬用好句

1. **Gina always goes shopping after big exams.**
吉娜總在大考過後逛街購物。

2. **You can get free coupons once you log onto our website.**
一登入我們的網站，就能得到免費的折價券。

3. **Amanda never just buys what she needs, so her mother is very concerned about the way she squanders money.**
亞曼達從不依需求購物，她媽媽對於她揮霍金錢的行徑十分掛慮。

4. **Keep the receipt in case you want a refund.**
把收據留著，以免你想要退貨。

5. **We offer free delivery on all purchases over 3,000 dollars.**
購物超過三千元可享免運費。

6. **The cash register is out of order.**
收銀機故障了。

7. **Everything with a blue tag is 50% off.**
藍色標籤的商品都打五折。

8. **Whenever Jason sees something he likes, he always pays through the nose for it.**
每當傑森看到喜歡的東西，他總是不經考慮就買了。

9. **Where can I get a free catalogue?**
我可以在哪裡取得免費型錄？

10. **Where is the Men's Department?**
男裝部在哪裡？

11. **How would you like to pay? By credit card or cash?**
您要使用信用卡還是現金付款？

12. **Keep an eye on your handbag and belongings, and beware of pickpockets.**
留意您的手提包及隨身財物，小心防範扒手。

關鍵單字片語

1. **window shopping** 片 逛街

2. **log onto** 片 登入

3. **coupon** [`kupɑn] 名 優惠券

4. **size** [saɪz] 名 尺寸

5. **pay for** 片 為⋯付款

6. **on sale** 片 拍賣中

實境對話

Clerk: How can I help you, Sir?
先生，需要什麼服務嗎？

Warren: I'm looking for a birthday gift for my daughter.
我想買份生日禮物送我女兒。

Clerk: Oh, I see. Do you have anything special in mind?
這樣啊。您有想買什麼嗎？

Warren: I'm thinking about getting something fancy.
我想買些別緻的東西。

Clerk: We have dresses, handbags, and shoes with lots of bling.
我們有洋裝、手提包以及閃亮的鞋子。

Warren: A dress would be nice. Can you help me choose one?
洋裝應該不錯！你可以幫我挑選嗎？

Clerk: My pleasure. What's her favorite color?
這是我的榮幸。她最喜歡什麼顏色？

Warren: I think pink is.
我想是粉紅色。

Clerk: Let's see. How about one of these two? This one has rosettes on the skirt, and that one has tiny bows on the shoulder. Either would be an excellent choice.
我看看…這兩件如何？這件裙擺上有玫瑰花，那件肩膀上有小蝴蝶結。兩件都很值得買。

Warren: I will take the one with the rosettes.
我買有玫瑰花的那件。

Clerk: Great! What size is she?
好的！她是什麼尺寸？

Warren: Medium.
中號尺寸。

Clerk: OK. One moment, please.
好的。請稍等一下。

關鍵單字片語

7. **customer** [`kʌstəmɚ] 名 顧客

8. **spend** [spɛnd] 動 花費

9. **squander** [`skwɑndɚ] 動 浪費

10. **buy a lemon** 片 花錢買到爛東西

11. **the in-thing** 片 正流行的事物

12. **pay through the nose** 片 盲目購買

15. **消費電子**
Electronic Devices

MP.3 030

萬用好句

1.	**Rumor has it that the iPad 3 will be available in early July.** 謠傳iPad 3將在七月上旬上市。
2.	**How many USB ports does this laptop have?** 這台筆電有幾個USB插槽？
3.	**The latest ultrabook is a hit on the market.** 最新的超薄筆電在市場上造成轟動。
4.	**Teens are crazy about Smartphones and related APPs.** 青少年對智慧型手機以及相關的應用程式十分著迷。
5.	**The teenager thumb culture has made them so adept at typing that some of them have even stopped hand-writing anything.** 青少年的拇指文化讓他們習慣於打字，有些人甚至不寫字了。
6.	**The notebook is equipped with the latest fingerprint recognition technology.** 這台筆記型電腦配備最新的指紋辨識系統。
7.	**You can buy an additional lens for only 500 dollars with the purchase of any camera.** 購買新相機，只要花五百元就能多擁有一個鏡頭。
8.	**The new processor makes doing everything faster than it used to be.** 新的處理器加快了處理事情的速度。
9.	**This digital camcorder is said to be the lightest in the market.** 這台數位錄影機據說是市面上最輕的。
10.	**iRobot makes our life more efficient and easier.** 居家打掃機器人讓我們的生活更有效率、更輕鬆。
11.	**You should really throw away your old cell phone.** 你真該把你的舊手機給丟了。
12.	**I need some advice on choosing a camera for my daughter.** 我需要一些建議，以挑選一台相機給我女兒。

關鍵單字片語

1. **Smartphone** [`smɑrt.fon] 名 智慧型手機

2. **earplug** [`ɪr.plʌg] 名 耳塞式耳機

3. **intuitive** [ɪn`tjuɪtɪv] 形 直覺的

4. **wireless** [`waɪrlɪs] 形 無線的

5. **take advantage of** 片 利用

6. **necessity** [nə`sɛsətɪ] 名 需求

實境對話

Daughter: Dad, can I talk to you for a second?
爸，我可以跟你說一下話嗎？

Father: Sure, sweetheart. What is it?
好啊，小寶貝。什麼事？

Daughter: You know I have a midterm next week, right?
你知道我下週要期中考，對吧？

Father: Yes, you have been studying really hard these days.
沒錯，你這些天一直都很用功。

Daughter: Yes I have. Dad, I was wondering if I could get a reward after the test.
我是的。爸，我在想，考完試後，是不是可以給我一點獎賞？

Father: What do you have in mind, sweetie?
親愛的，你想要什麼？

Daughter: I want a new cell phone.
我想要一支新的手機。

Father: What for? Is there anything wrong with yours?
為何？你現在這支壞掉了嗎？

Daughter: No, it works fine. It's just that I want a Smartphone. That way, I can surf the Internet anytime, and you can make video calls to me wherever I am.
還正常。我想要一隻智慧型手機。如此無論何時我都可以上網，你也可隨時和我視訊通話。

Father: Sounds like a good way to make sure you are safe and secure when you're out. Well, O.K., I'll buy you a Smartphone.
聽來是個確認你出外時安全的好工具。好啊，我會買一支智慧型手機給你。

Daughter: Thanks, Dad!
謝了，爸！

Father: You're welcome.
不客氣。

關鍵單字片語

7. **efficient** [ɪˋfɪʃənt] 形 有效率的

8. **touch pad** 片 觸控板

9. **APP** 縮 應用軟體程式

10. **purchase** [ˋpɝtʃəs] 動 購買

11. **thumb culture** 片 拇指族

12. **kit** [kɪt] 名 配套元件

1. 上健身房
In the Gym
MP3 031

萬用好句

1.	**I always warm-up before working out.** 我總在健身前先暖身。
2.	**How long have you been working out?** 你健身多長時間了？
3.	**The gym equipment should be shared by everyone working out in the gym.** 健身房使用者應共同使用館內設備。
4.	**Every gym member should follow the gym regulations.** 每位健身房會員都應遵守館內規定。
5.	**Mary does aerobics three times a week.** 瑪麗每週做三次有氧運動。
6.	**Daniel has been hogging the treadmill for one and a half hours.** 丹尼爾已霸佔跑步機一個半小時了。
7.	**Excuse me. Is anyone using this machine?** 不好意思，請問這台機器有人使用嗎？
8.	**Who is your personal trainer?** 誰是你的私人教練？
9.	**Going to the gym is a good way to stay in shape.** 上健身房是保持身材的好方法。
10.	**How can I get a membership for this gym?** 我要如何成為健身房的會員？
11.	**We have yoga classes from 7 p.m. to 9 p.m. every Wednesday and Friday.** 我們每週三、五晚間七點到九點有瑜伽課程。
12.	**We have weights ranging from 2.5 lbs to 100 lbs. You'd better start with the 2.5 lb weights.** 我們有從二點五磅到一百磅的舉重鐵餅，你最好從二點五磅開始。

關鍵單字片語

1. **fitness** [`fɪtnɪs] 名 健康

2. **dumbbell** [`dʌm͵bɛl] 名 啞鈴

3. **abdominal bench** 片 腹部訓練椅

4. **bicep** [`baɪsɛp] 名 二頭肌

5. **feel the burn** 片 感覺正在燃燒脂肪

6. **treadmill** [`trɛd͵mɪl] 名 踏步機

實境對話

Rick: Welcome to Fitness Gym. How can I help you?
歡迎來到窈窕健身房。有什麼我可以幫您的嗎？

Amanda: Hi! I would like some information about getting a membership.
嗨，我想了解你們的入會資訊。

Rick: We have 3 different plans: the bronze, silver, and golden pass.
我們有三種不同方案：銅牌會員、銀牌會員以及金牌會員。

Amanda: What is the difference between them?
有什麼不一樣的地方？

Rick: It depends on what facilities and lessons you want.
這與您所想要使用的器材以及想上的課程有關。

Amanda: Well, I always enjoy relaxing in a steam room after working out, and I'm thinking about starting yoga lessons.
我很喜歡在運動後進蒸汽室放鬆一下；最近也想開始學瑜伽。

Rick: Then our golden pass is the perfect choice for you. You can enjoy all the facilities and attend all the lessons for free for a whole year.
那麼您很適合加入我們的金牌會員，可全年免費享用所有健身設備、並參加所有課程。

Amanda: What lessons do you offer?
你們有哪些課程？

Rick: We have yoga lessons every morning and cycling lessons every evening.
我們每天早上有瑜伽課，晚上則有飛輪有氧課。

Amanda: How much is the golden pass?
金牌會員要多少錢？

Rick: It's $12,000 for a year. We're offering a 20% discount now.
一年一萬兩千元，目前正在打八折。

關鍵單字片語

7. **towel** [`tauəl] 名 毛巾

8. **membership** [`mɛmbɚˌʃɪp] 名 會員資格

9. **military press** 片 肩部推舉機

10. **increase** [ɪn`kris] 動 增加

11. **pace** [pes] 名 步速、速度

12. **regularly** [`rɛgjələlɪ] 副 規律地

2. 美國職籃 NBA
MP3 032

萬用好句

1.	**Lebron James swept the floor last night.** 雷霸龍昨天晚上橫掃全場。
2.	**Who was the MVP of the game last night?** 誰是昨天晚上的最有價值球員？
3.	**The Hornets are definitely going to win the championship this year.** 黃蜂隊今年一定會贏得總冠軍。
4.	**It was such a pity that the Heat didn't win the championship.** 熱火隊沒能贏得總冠軍真的很可惜。
5.	**Who will be the new coach after Phil Jackson retires?** 誰會在菲爾傑克森退休後接任教練？
6.	**It was reported that Derrick Rose agreed to extend his contract with the Bulls.** 據報導，德瑞克羅斯同意和公牛隊續約。
7.	**Kobe Bryant shot a triple-double once again tonight.** 寇比今晚再度達成大三元。
8.	**Though he sprained his toe in the previous game, Derrick Rose still sidelined the Bulls and won the game.** 雖然腳趾在前一場比賽中扭傷，羅斯還是幫助公牛隊贏得比賽。
9.	**The Mavericks have remained undefeated for a week, a sure sign to many of their fans that they will win the championship this year.** 小牛隊已經維持一週不敗，這對許多小牛隊的球迷而言，是贏得總冠軍的徵兆。
10.	**Steve Novak just had his best game of the season.** 史提夫諾瓦克剛打了一場他本季最棒的比賽。
11.	**Jeff Green might miss the whole season due to his heart surgery.** 由於心臟手術，傑夫格林或許得錯過整個球季。
12.	**The coach said regretfully that the guard will be out for two games because of his lower back problem.** 教練遺憾地表示，由於下背傷的問題，那名後衛必須缺席兩場比賽。

★ 關鍵單字片語

1. **triangle offense** 片 三角進攻
2. **franchise player** 片 王牌球員
3. **dribble** [`drɪbl] 動 運球

4. **rebound** [`ri͵baʊnd] 名 籃板球
5. **foul** [faʊl] 名 犯規
6. **shooting** [`ʃutɪŋ] 名 投籃

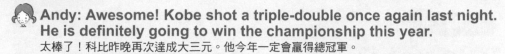

Andy: Awesome! Kobe shot a triple-double once again last night. He is definitely going to win the championship this year.
太棒了！科比昨晚再次達成大三元。他今年一定會贏得總冠軍。

Peter: Not with Lebron James and Derrick Rose in the league. They both have a lot of potential and are much younger than Kobe.
但別忘了聯盟裡有雷霸龍和德瑞克羅斯。他們都很有潛力，而且比科比年輕多了。

Andy: Experience is what matters most. I believe the Lakers will become the champions under Kobe's excellent leadership.
球賽裡重要的是經驗。我相信湖人隊在科比優異的帶領下，會是一支冠軍隊伍。

Peter: I hope you are right. Let's wait and see.
希望你是對的。我們就靜觀其變吧。

Andy: Then which team do you think will win this season?
那你覺得這一季哪一隊會獲勝？

Peter: Actually, I think the Bulls will.
事實上我覺得會是公牛隊。

Andy: The Bulls? Because of Derrick Rose?
公牛隊？因為德瑞克羅斯嗎？

Peter: Exactly.
沒錯。

Andy: But I don't think he can beat either Kobe or Lebron.
但我想他是沒辦法打敗科比或雷霸龍的。

Peter: Maybe he's not the toughest player in the league, but he's definitely the best player to take the team to the top.
他或許不是聯盟裡最強的球員，但他一定是能帶領球隊走向巔峰的最佳球員。

Andy: You've got a good point.
你說的有道理。

關鍵單字片語

7. **quarter** [`kwɔrtə] 名 一節

8. **defense** [dɪ`fɛns] 名 防守

9. **slam dunk** 片 灌籃

10. **off-season games** 片 季後賽

11. **three-point line** 片 三分線

12. **turnover** [`tɜn͵ovə] 名 失誤

3. 美國職棒 · MLB

MP3 033

萬用好句

1.	**The Mets and the Yankees are both in New York.** 大都會隊和洋基隊都在紐約。
2.	**The Yankees and the Red Sox have been rivals for decades.** 洋基隊和紅襪隊是數十年來的世仇。
3.	**Which team do you think might win the World Series?** 你覺得哪一隊會贏得世界大賽？
4.	**The American League and the National League are in the MLB.** 大聯盟裡分美國聯盟和國家聯盟。
5.	**Clayton Kershaw beat out many other great pitchers to win the Cy Young Award this year.** 克雷頓科夏擊敗許多優秀的投手，贏得今年的賽揚獎。
6.	**The MLB All-Star Game this year will be held in Kansas City.** 今天大聯盟明星賽將在堪薩斯城舉辦。
7.	**Ichiro Suzuki made a nice homerun and ended the game.** 鈴木一朗擊出全壘打結束比賽。
8.	**Wang decided to join the Nationals after his contract with the Yankees expired.** 與洋基隊的合約終止後，王建民決定加入華盛頓國民隊。
9.	**Kuo is warming up in the bullpen under the coach's instructions.** 在教練的指導下，郭泓志正在牛棚進行熱身。
10.	**The coach asked the pitcher to do his very best in the 9th inning.** 教練要求投手在九局上半用盡全力。
11.	**J. Shields is the top performer on the Rays' pitching staff.** 詹姆斯薛爾斯是光芒隊最優秀的投手。
12.	**Derek Holland, the Rangers' top pitcher, had a 2.5 ERA in 22 starts until last Friday.** 直到上週五為止，遊騎兵隊頂尖投手德瑞克荷蘭主投二十二場，自責分率僅二點五。

關鍵單字片語

1. **Hall of Fame** 片 名人堂

2. **pitcher** [`pɪtʃɚ] 名 投手

3. **catcher** [`kætʃɚ] 名 捕手

4. **curve ball** 片 曲球

5. **double play** 片 雙殺打

6. **bullpen** [`bʊl͵pɛn] 名 牛棚

實境對話

Kenny: Turn to Channel 7. Hurry up!
轉到第七台。快！

Gwen: Why are you in such a hurry? You just got home a minute ago!
你為何這麼著急？不是才剛回到家？

Kenny: The Nationals baseball game is on now.
現在有場國民隊的比賽。

Gwen: I thought the New York Yankees was your favorite team.
我以為紐約洋基隊才是你的最愛。

Kenny: It used to be, but ever since they gave up Wang, I'm not a loyal fan anymore.
以前是，但自從他們放棄王建民後，我就不再是他們的忠實球迷了。

Gwen: Really? I didn't know about that. When did that happen?
真的嗎？我不知道這件事。這是什麼時候的事？

Kenny: Are you kidding me? It's not news anymore. They gave him up last season because of his injury.
你在開玩笑嗎？這不是新聞了喔。因為他的傷勢，上一季他們就已將他釋出了。

Gwen: That's too bad. So which team is he playing for now?
真是糟糕。所以他現在效力於哪一隊？

Kenny: He is on the Washington Nationals now. Today is his first game since he signed on.
他現在效力於華盛頓國民隊，今天是他簽約後的第一場比賽。

Gwen: Then it's definitely a must-see game this season.
那這可是本季必看的一場比賽。

Kenny: Absolutely! That's why I raced all the way home. Now, do you want to join me?
真的！這就是我一路衝回家的原因。你想要和我一起看比賽嗎？

關鍵單字片語

7. **home plate** 片 本壘板

8. **steal a base** 片 盜壘

9. **league** [lig] 名 聯盟

10. **one-base hit** 片 一壘安打

11. **bases loaded** 片 滿壘

12. **changeup** [`tʃɛndʒ،ʌp] 名 變速球

4.中華職棒 CPBL

MP3 034

萬用好句

1.	I always enjoy watching live games at Xinzhuang Baseball Stadium. 我總在新莊棒球場享受現場比賽。
2.	The Lamigo Monkeys are expected to win the championship this year. 那米哥桃猿隊今年預期能拿下冠軍。
3.	Many CPBL teams are devoted to charity. 許多中華職棒球隊致力於慈善事業。
4.	Many baseball teams in the CPBL have baseball camps for young students during the winter vacation. 許多中華職棒隊伍都在寒假期間為年輕學子舉辦棒球營。
5.	The Sinon Bulls have recruited Lin Chen-Hua with a huge signing bonus. 興農牛隊以高價簽約金網羅林晨樺。
6.	Chen Wei-Yin decided to sign a contract with the Baltimore Orioles. 陳偉殷決定與巴爾的摩金鶯隊簽約。
7.	Lin Hong-Yu earned the title of 2011 Homerun King with 22 homeruns. 林泓育以二十二支全壘打贏得二○一一年全壘打王。
8.	Who's your favorite coach in the CPBL? 誰是你中華職棒聯盟裡最喜歡的教練？
9.	Hsu Sheng-Ming is one of the top coaches in the CPBL. 徐生明是中華職棒最優秀的教練之一。
10.	Which team is going to play against the Lamigo Monkeys tonight? 今天晚上哪一隊會和桃猿隊對決？
11.	Ever since the gambling scandal, many famous players have been rejected from the CPBL, such as Chen Chih-Yuan. 自從簽賭醜聞後，許多著名的球員如陳致遠，被拒於中華職棒門外。
12.	The championship game between the Elephants and the Bulls is scheduled on June 22nd, next Sunday. 象牛冠軍決戰訂於下週日，六月二十二號。

關鍵單字片語

1. **homerun** [`hom,rʌn] 名 全壘打

2. **inning** [`ɪnɪŋ] 名 局

3. **hit-and-run** [`hɪtṇ`rʌn] 形 打帶跑的

4. **infielder** [`ɪn,fildɚ] 名 內野手

5. **pitch** [pɪtʃ] 動 投球

6. **triple play** 片 三殺守備

Jason: The CPBL is in its 23rd season.
中華職棒目前正在第二十三季。

Rain: 23rd season? Wow, that's really a long time.
第二十三季？哇，那真的很久了。

Jason: That is long. I have watched the CPBL games for 18 years.
是很久了，我已經看中華職棒十八年了。

Rain: How did you start watching the CPBL games?
你怎麼會開始看中華職棒的？

Jason: My dad always hogged the TV at dinner time, so I had no choice but to watch baseball games with him, and thus became a little fan myself.
我爸總在晚餐時間霸佔電視，所以我只能和他一起看球賽，然後也變成小球迷了。

Rain: Ah....that's so sweet. Then, who is your favorite team?
啊…好溫馨喔。那你最喜歡哪一隊？

Jason: It used to be the Elephants, but the Lamigos are my favorite now.
以前是兄弟象，但我現在最愛桃猿隊。

Rain: What made you change teams?
是什麼讓你改變了？

Jason: As you know, there was a gambling scandal in CPBL years ago, and many players in the Brother Elephants were involved.
你知道的，幾年前中華職棒有簽賭醜聞，有很多兄弟象的球員涉案。

Rain: You must have felt very depressed then.
你當時一定很沮喪。

Jason: You are right.
沒錯。

關鍵單字片語

7. **take base** 片 安全上壘

8. **hit** [hɪt] 動 打擊

9. **foul ball** 片 界外球

10. **sinker** [ˋsɪŋkɚ] 名 下墜球

11. **slider** [ˋslaɪdɚ] 名 滑球

12. **perfect game** 片 完全比賽

5. 滿貫網球
Tennis
MP3 035

萬用好句

1.	**Roger Federer quit the game because of his arm injury.** 費德勒因為手臂受傷而退出比賽。
2.	**Nadal is expected to win the next ATP tournament, the US Open.** 外界預期納達爾將會贏得美國網球公開賽。
3.	**The Australian Open and the US Open are played on hard courts.** 澳洲公開賽和美國公開賽都在硬地球場上進行。
4.	**"The Grand Slam" refers to the four major tournaments: the Australian Open, the US Open, the French Open, and Wimbledon.** 「大滿貫」是指澳洲公開賽、美國公開賽、法國公開賽以及溫布頓網球賽等四大公開賽事。
5.	**When is Maria Sharapova's next match?** 莎拉波娃的下一場比賽是什麼時候？
6.	**Obviously, 2011 was the best year for Novak Djokovic in his career.** 很明顯，二〇一一年是喬柯維奇職業生涯中最棒的一年。
7.	**Andy Murray is currently ranked No. 4 in the world.** 安迪墨瑞是目前世界排名第四的選手。
8.	**Are you planning to stay up to watch the Wimbledon finals tonight?** 你打算熬夜觀看溫布頓冠軍賽嗎？
9.	**Jessica is interested in tennis, and she is also a semi-professional player in Taiwan.** 潔西卡一直對網球很有興趣，她同時也是台灣半職業的選手。
10.	**Caroline Wozniacki has impressed the public with not only her good looks but also her strong two-handed backhand.** 沃茲妮亞琪讓大家不只對她的美貌、也對她強勁的雙手反拍印象深刻。
11.	**It's a pity that Lu received a bye in the 4th round at Wimbledon.** 盧彥勳在溫布頓第四輪被淘汰，很可惜。
12.	**Serena Williams is the best tennis player I can think of.** 在我心中，小威廉斯是最棒的網球員。

關鍵單字片語

1. **court** [kort] 名 球場

2. **baseline** [`beslaɪn] 名 底線

3. **deuce** [`djus] 名 平手

4. **match** [mætʃ] 名 比賽

5. **ace** [es] 名 發球得分

6. **cross court** 片 對角擊球

實境對話

Gina: The guy in the Rolex commercial is so handsome.
那個勞力士廣告裡的男生簡直帥呆了！

Ken: You mean Roger Federer? He is indeed a Prince Charming.
你是說費德勒嗎？他的確能夠迷倒眾生。

Gina: Do you know who he is?
你知道他是何方神聖哦？

Ken: Sure. He's a famous tennis player, maybe the best in the world.
當然。他是非常有名的，或許是世界第一的網球選手。

Gina: Really? Can you tell me more about him?
真的嗎？你可以多跟我說一些他的事嗎？

Ken: No problem. He is a Swiss professional tennis player who held the ATP No.1 position for 237 consecutive weeks.
好啊。他是瑞士的職業網球選手，也是連續兩百三十七週的ATP冠軍。

Gina: ATP? What is that?
ATP？那是什麼？

Ken: ATP stands for the Association of Tennis Professionals. It organizes world tennis tours for men.
ATP代表「職業網球協會」，主辦世界男子網球巡迴賽。

Gina: Sounds like he is an excellent tennis player.
他聽起來是個很棒的網球選手。

Ken: He really is. But it's a pity that he isn't the No. 1 currently.
他的確是。但很可惜目前他不是世界第一。

Gina: So who sits on the throne now?
那現在誰是世界第一呢？

Ken: Novak Djokovic, but I believe Roger Federer can certainly take the championship back this season.
是喬柯維奇，但我相信費德勒這一季會把冠軍奪回來的。

關鍵單字片語

7. **Grand Slam** 片 大滿貫

8. **volley** [ˋvɑlɪ] 動 截擊

9. **server** [ˋsɜvɚ] 名 發球方

10. **advantage set** 片 長盤制

11. **best of three** 片 三盤兩勝制

12. **backhand** [ˋbækˋhænd] 名 反手拍

6. 倒掛金鉤
Soccer
MP3 036

萬用好句

1. **Iker Casillas is considered to be one of the best goalkeepers in Europe.**
卡西拉斯被認為是歐洲最棒的守門員之一。

2. **Jason was overjoyed when Spain won the 2010 World Cup.**
西班牙贏得二○一○年世界盃的時候，傑森狂喜不已。

3. **Messi has been the FIFA World Player of the Year 2 years in a row.**
梅西已經連續兩年贏得世界足球先生的稱號。

4. **Messi scored a goal at the last minute and took the championship home.**
梅西在最後一分鐘射門進球，把冠軍打包回家。

5. **Which team do you root for?**
你支持哪一支球隊？

6. **The announcement that Ronaldo will be traded to Barcelona will definitely make headlines.**
將羅納度交易到巴塞隆納的消息將會成為新聞頭條。

7. **Dan was shown a red card and had to leave the field immediately.**
丹被發紅牌，必須要立刻離場。

8. **The game was tied until Henry scored a goal in the PK.**
這場比賽一直到亨利在PK戰得分之前，一直是平手狀態。

9. **Tripping or attempting to trip an opponent is a serious violation.**
絆倒或是企圖絆倒對手是很嚴重的犯規。

10. **How about a soccer game at the riverbank park this afternoon?**
今天下午要不要到河堤公園踢一場足球比賽？

11. **Didi used to say, "If we don't treat the ball with love, she won't do what we want her to do."**
迪迪曾經說：「如果我們不以愛對待球，她就不會聽話。」

12. **Real Madrid is referred to as the Undefeated Vessel.**
皇家馬德里被稱作無敵艦隊。

關鍵單字片語

1. **score** [skor] 動 得分 名 分數

2. **goalkeeper** [`gol‚kipɚ] 名 守門員

3. **backfield** [`bæk‚fild] 名 守衛區

4. **break loose** 片 擺脫(防守)

5. **penalty area** 片 罰球區

6. **referee** [‚rɛfə`ri] 名 裁判

實境對話

Kelly: What are you checking air ticket information for?
你看機票資訊做什麼？

Tom: I am going to the FIFA World Cup!
我要去看世界盃！

Kelly: I didn't know you were such a devoted soccer fan.
我不知道你是個狂熱的足球迷。

Tom: I'm not exactly. I am not supporting any particular team.
倒也不是，我沒有特別支持哪一隊。

Kelly: Then why do you want to fly all the way there?
那你為何想要飛越重洋呢？

Tom: I just enjoy the heat and passion of being part of the crowd during a game. Once you've experienced it, it's hard to forget.
我只是很享受比賽中球迷們的熱情和狂熱。你一旦體驗過，就很難忘記。

Kelly: I've never been to any game. Maybe I should give it a try.
我從來沒去看過球賽，或許我該試試看。

Tom: That's a great idea. You can come with me.
好主意。你可以跟我一起去。

Kelly: Excellent! I'm a big fan of Real Madrid, so let's go cheer for Spain!
太好了！我是皇家馬德里的球迷，所以就讓我們去為西班牙歡呼吧！

Tom: I can book tickets. How about Spain against Brazil?
我來訂票。西班牙對巴西的比賽如何？

Kelly: Nice. Both teams won the championship before.
好耶！這兩隊都曾把冠軍帶回家過。

Tom: Then it will surely be a great game. Let's keep our fingers crossed it is.
那麼這一定會是場很精采的比賽。就讓我們祈禱吧！

關鍵單字片語

7. **free kick** 片 任意球

8. **injury time** 片 傷停補時

9. **match ban** 片 禁賽規定

10. **defend** [dɪˋfɛnd] 動 防守

11. **dribbling** [ˋdrɪblŋ] 名 盤球、帶球

12. **hacking** [ˋhækɪŋ] 名 攻擊對手的腳

7. 高爾夫球
Golf

MP3
037

萬用好句

1. **Yani Tzeng is undoubtedly one of the top golf players in the world.**
曾雅妮無疑是全球最頂尖的高爾夫球選手之一。

2. **Golf is one of the most popular sports in Korea.**
高爾夫球是南韓最受歡迎的運動之一。

3. **Because golf is hot these days, ESPN is going to broadcast a program every Saturday morning to teach people how to master golf.**
因應最近的高球熱潮，ESPN體育台將於每週六早上播出教觀眾精通高爾夫球的節目。

4. **All the tournament participants are shown on LPGA.com.**
所有參賽選手都列名在LPGA的網站上。

5. **Jack believes playing golf with clients can help him bond with them.**
傑克認為和客戶打高爾夫球有助於和他們建立感情。

6. **How long does it take to get to the nearest golf course?**
從這裡到最近的高爾夫球場要多久時間？

7. **Amanda didn't roll in a birdie putt until the No. 15.**
一直到第十五洞，亞曼達才打出博蒂。

8. **Jay insisted that he lost the game because of a bunker at No. 17.**
傑伊堅持他輸了比賽是因為球在第十七洞被打入沙坑。

9. **You can get up-to-date wrap-ups of golf games online.**
你可以在網路上得到最新的高球賽事完整報導。

10. **I used to play golf with my dad every Sunday morning.**
我以前每個週日早晨都和父親打高爾夫球。

11. **It is extremely important to have a good grip to add both power and height to your golf swing.**
打高爾夫球時，完美的握杆對於增加揮杆的強度和高度非常重要。

12. **To make a good putt, never forget to take into account the wind and the grain of the grass.**
要打出好的推杆，別忘了考慮風向和草種。

關鍵單字片語

1. **O.B.** 縮 出界

2. **hole in one** 片 一杆進洞

3. **caddie** [`kædɪ] 名 杆弟或球僮

4. **birdie** [`bɜdɪ] 名 低於標準杆一杆

5. **course** [kors] 名 高爾夫球場

6. **just middle** 片 正中球心

實境對話

Derek: Do you have any plans for the coming weekend?
你這個週末有什麼計畫嗎？

Gina: Not yet. Do you have any good ideas?
還沒。你有什麼好主意嗎？

Derek: How about going for a golf game?
來場高爾夫球賽如何？

Gina: A golf game? Since when do you play golf?
高爾夫球賽？你什麼時候開始打高爾夫的？

Derek: I don't. I just want to watch the LPGA tournament in Taiwan.
我沒打過，我只是想去看在台灣舉辦的LPGA高爾夫球錦標賽。

Gina: LPGA? What is that?
LPGA？那是什麼？

Derek: LPGA stands for the Ladies Professional Golf Association, which is an American organization for female golfers.
LPGA的全名是「女子職業高爾夫球協會」，這是個美國的組織，專為女性高球手設立。

Gina: I thought they only held games in the U.S.
我以為比賽只在美國進行。

Derek: Actually, they have tournaments around the world. This is their first time in Taiwan.
事實上，全世界都有巡迴賽。這是第一次在台灣舉行。

Gina: No wonder you want to go to the game.
難怪你想去看比賽。

Derek: Exactly, and Yani Tzeng will be in the game, too.
沒錯，而且曾雅妮也會參賽。

Gina: Well, then let's go cheer her on!
那麼，我們去幫她加油吧！

關鍵單字片語

7. **swing** [swɪŋ] 動 揮杆

8. **bunker** [`bʌŋkə] 名 沙坑

9. **circuit** [`sɜkɪt] 名 巡迴賽

10. **fluke** [fluk] 動 僥倖打中

11. **howe** [hau] 名 第十八洞

12. **double eagle** 片 低於標準杆三杆

8. 賽車競技
Car Racing

MP.3
038

萬用好句

1. **Ferrari driver Alonso has won the World Championship twice.**
法拉利車手阿隆索已經贏得兩次世界冠軍了。

2. **Jack's father is the biggest fan of his racing career.**
在傑克的賽車生涯中，他的父親是他最忠實的粉絲。

3. **Motorsports are very popular among teenagers.**
汽車運動很受青少年的歡迎。

4. **Mr. Sicard will make the DAMS shine in their GP2 program because of his in-depth knowledge of endurance racing.**
西卡德先生將會以他所擁有的耐力賽車知識，讓DAMS車隊在GP2賽事裡發光發熱。

5. **Ferrari is one of the best teams in F1, and also the only one to have continuously competed in the F1 World Championship.**
法拉利是一級方程式賽車裡最棒的車隊之一，同時也是唯一一連續角逐冠軍獎盃的隊伍。

6. **Race queens always attract the attention of most male spectators.**
賽車女郎總是吸引多數男性觀眾的目光。

7. **Do you know the difference between rallying and formula 1 races?**
你知道越野賽與一級方程式賽車的差別在哪嗎？

8. **Red Bull Racing is hoping to take home the championship again with its superstar Sebastian Vettel.**
紅牛車隊希望維多能再度將冠軍獎盃帶回家。

9. **Lotus is going to unveil its new motorsport line-up this afternoon.**
今天下午，蓮花車廠將公布新的賽車系列。

10. **The Dakar Rally is one of the most famous off-road rallies.**
達卡越野賽是最有名的非公路競賽之一。

11. **The speed of car races always gets me super excited.**
賽車的速度總是讓我非常興奮。

12. **Which is your favorite team, Ferrari or Red Bull?**
你喜歡哪一個車隊，法拉利還是紅牛？

關鍵單字片語

1. **bounce back** 片 恢復之前的水準
2. **Grand Prix** 片 國際汽車大賽
3. **a set of** 片 一組、一套
4. **mechanic** [məˋkænɪk] 名 汽車技師
5. **pit lane** 片 維修站
6. **rallycross** [ˋrælɪˏkrɔs] 名 汽車越野大賽

Hannah: This is a cool poster--a red race car with a hot race queen. You do like pretty girls, don't you?
這張海報好酷──紅色賽車和性感的賽車女郎。你真的很喜歡美女，對吧？

Paul: I do, but they're not the best part of the poster.
我是啊，但是美女並不是這張海報最棒的地方。

Hannah: What are you talking about? I can't see anything else but the car and the girl.
你在說什麼？除了車跟美女，我什麼都沒看到。

Paul: The car is the reason why it's on my bedroom wall.
這輛賽車就是這張海報會被貼在我房間牆上的原因。

Hannah: But I can't see anything special about that race car.
但我看不出這輛賽車有什麼特別之處。

Paul: Are you kidding me? Can't you see how beautiful the blood red color is?
你在開我玩笑嗎？你認不出這亮麗的血紅色？

Hannah: Sorry, but I know very little about car racing.
對不起，但是我對賽車不太懂。

Paul: I understand, but you must have heard of Ferrari, right?
沒關係，但你一定聽過法拉利，對吧？

Hannah: Of course, it's a world-famous car brand.
當然，那是世界知名的車廠。

Paul: Yes, and the red is their signature color in Formula One.
沒錯，而紅色就是它們在一級方程式比賽中的標誌色。

Hannah: And the color for their brand as well!
也是他們廠牌的顏色！

Paul: You're right, and that's why they are called "the Red Flash."
你說的對，這就是它們被稱作「紅色閃電」的原因。

關鍵單字片語

7. **accelerate** [æk`sɛlə,ret] 動 加速

8. **transmission** [træns`mɪʃən] 名 變速器

9. **automatic** [,ɔtə`mætɪk] 形 自動的

10. **manual** [`mænjuəl] 形 手動的

11. **racer** [`resə] 名 賽車手

12. **trophy** [`trofɪ] 名 獎盃

9. 倫敦奧運
The Olympic Games
MP3 039

萬用好句

1. Do you know what year the first modern Olympics were held?
你知道第一屆現代奧運是在哪一年舉辦的嗎？

2. I heard that the London Olympics will feature twenty-six sports.
我聽說倫敦奧運將舉辦二十六項賽事。

3. I think the Olympics is the most important sports event on Earth.
我覺得奧運是世界上最重要的運動賽事。

4. I'm going back to London this July to see the Olympics.
我將於今年七月回到倫敦，參與奧運盛會。

5. Olympic shooting events fall broadly into three types, which are Pistol, Rifle and Shortgun.
奧運射擊項目廣泛地包含三類：手槍、來福槍和短槍。

6. Do you know who has been nominated to be the torchbearers?
你知道誰被提名為聖火傳遞者嗎？

7. The Olympic torchbearers have always been one of the highlights of the Games.
傳遞奧運聖火者一直是競賽的關注焦點之一。

8. When do the tickets to the Olympic Football Tournament go on sale?
什麼時候開始販售奧運足球賽的門票？

9. Rumor has it that Pink Floyd will reunite at the 2012 London Olympics.
謠傳平克佛洛伊德樂團將於二〇一二年倫敦奧運重組。

10. The mascots of the 2012 Olympics are Wenlock and Mandeville.
溫勒克和曼德維爾是倫敦奧運的吉祥物。

11. Where can I get ticket information for the 2012 Olympics?
我在哪裡可以獲得二〇一二年奧運的門票販售資訊？

12. Sandra told me she would take the flight next Saturday morning to London to experience the passion of the Olympic Games.
珊卓跟我說，她下週六早上要搭機去倫敦體驗奧運的熱情。

關鍵單字片語

1. **event** [ˋɪvɛnt] 名 競賽項目

2. **opening ceremony** 片 開幕儀式

3. **Triathlon** [traɪˋæθlɑn] 名 鐵人三項

4. **doping** [ˋdopɪŋ] 名 使用禁藥

5. **medal** [ˋmɛdl] 名 獎牌

6. **gymnastics** [dʒɪmˋnæstɪks] 名 體操

Fiona: Have you seen the commercial for the 2012 Olympic Games?
你有看過二〇一二年奧運的廣告嗎？

Paul: Of course. It has been on TV almost every five minutes.
當然有，電視上幾乎每五分鐘就播出一次。

Fiona: You're over exaggerating. Then, you should know where they are being held, right?
你太誇張了。那你知道這次在哪裡舉行嗎？

Paul: They're in London, aren't they? Why are you asking?
不是在倫敦嗎？你問這幹嘛？

Fiona: I'm thinking about going there. Do you want to go with me?
我想去看比賽。你想和我一起去嗎？

Paul: That's a good idea, but I heard that the tickets are hard to get.
好主意，但是我聽說門票很難買耶。

Fiona: Don't worry. I can get tickets on the website. What games do you want to go to?
別擔心，我可以在網站上買到門票。你想看什麼比賽？

Paul: How about tennis or football?
網球或足球怎麼樣？

Fiona: Football is a good idea. I am a big fan of David Beckham.
足球是個好主意。我是大衛貝克漢的超級球迷。

Paul: He is such a great football player. I think England will be a dark horse with him on the team.
他是個很棒的足球員。我想英國隊有他，將會是一匹黑馬。

Fiona: Absolutely! Then we have to make room reservations and book air tickets.
當然了！那我們得來預訂飯店和機票。

關鍵單字片語

7. **judo** [`dʒudo] 名 柔道

8. **beach volleyball** 片 沙灘排球

9. **athletic** [æθ`lɛtɪk] 形 運動員的

10. **bodybuilding** [`bɑdɪˌbɪldɪŋ] 名 健身法

11. **injury** [`ɪndʒərɪ] 名 受傷、傷勢

12. **controversy** [`kɑntrəˌvɝsɪ] 名 爭議

10. 游泳池畔
Swimming
MP3 040

萬用好句

1. Swimming is one of my favorite exercises. How about you?
游泳是我最愛的運動之一。你呢？

2. Remember to warm up before you get into the pool.
記得在下水前先暖身。

3. Many teenage boys get a tan to attract girls.
許多青少年想要晒黑吸引女孩注意。

4. The lifeguard was absent when the accident happened.
那名救生員意外發生時不在現場。

5. Young kids love the water slide most.
滑水道一向是小孩子的最愛。

6. Don't forget to dry yourself off when you get out of the pool, so you don't catch a cold.
離開游泳池的時候別忘了擦乾，以免你感冒了。

7. Jenny is good at swimming. She can do the freestyle and backstroke.
珍妮擅長游泳，她會游自由式和仰式。

8. Excuse me. Where can I get extra starting blocks?
不好意思，我可以在哪取得多的浮板？

9. You can rent a locker for five dollars at the counter.
你可以向櫃檯租用五元的置物櫃。

10. My father swims at least twenty laps each morning, which is the secret to his excellent health.
我爸爸每天早上至少游二十圈，這就是他十分健康的秘訣。

11. Just relax your body, and you can float in the water.
只要放鬆身體，你就可以漂浮在水中。

12. What are the advantages of swimming?
游泳的好處有哪些？

關鍵單字片語

1. **lifeguard** [`laɪf.ɡɑrd] 名 救生員

2. **tan** [tæn] 動 晒成棕褐色

3. **sunscreen** [`sʌn.skrin] 名 防曬乳

4. **butterfly stroke** 片 蝶式

5. **freestyle** [`fri.staɪl] 名 自由式

6. **dive** [daɪv] 動 跳水

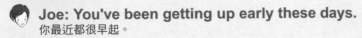

Joe: You've been getting up early these days.
你最近都很早起。

Amanda: Yes. I have a swimming class at the community center.
是啊，我去社區活動中心上游泳課。

Joe: A swimming class? I didn't know they have classes there.
游泳課？我不知道他們有開課。

Amanda: They didn't until last month. They have hired a coach who gives swimming lessons every Wednesday.
一直到上個月才有的。他們雇了位教練，每週三上游泳課。

Joe: What do you do in the class?
你們課堂上都做些什麼？

Amanda: Our coach has been a swim coach for 5 years, and he used to be a lifeguard, so safety always comes first with him.
我們的教練已經當游泳教練五年了，他以前是救生員，所以他很重視安全。

Joe: What do you mean?
這是什麼意思？

Amanda: He always asks us to warm up before getting into the pool, even if someone is late for class.
他總是要我們在下水前暖身，即使你已經遲到了。

Joe: Sounds like he's a great coach.
他聽起來像是個好教練。

Amanda: And he always reminds us to put on sunscreen. He said too much sun exposure might cause skin cancer.
而且他總是提醒我們要擦防曬。他說過度曝曬可能會導致皮膚癌。

Joe: Maybe I can go to his class, too. What time is the class?
或許我也可以去上他的課，這堂課是幾點啊？

Amanda: It starts at five thirty in the morning.
早上五點半開始。

關鍵單字片語

7. **breaststroke** [ˋbrɛst͵strok] 名 蛙式

8. **swim between flags** 片 保持在泳道內

9. **swimsuit** [ˋswɪmsut] 名 (女)泳衣

10. **put on** 片 穿上

11. **swimming cap** 片 泳帽

12. **floaty** [ˋflotɪ] 名 臂上浮圈

11. 海灘衝浪
Surfing
MP3
041

萬用好句

1. Penghu Island is ideal for surfing because of its sandy beach breaks.
澎湖島因為沙質海灘而成為理想的衝浪地點。

2. Surfing can be for recreational fun or for professional sport.
衝浪可以是休閒娛樂，也可以是職業運動。

3. Surf safety and awareness are of great importance to every surfer.
對衝浪者來說，衝浪安全和衝浪注意事項是十分重要的。

4. Never let go of your surfboard and be aware of other surfers.
絕對不要放開你的衝浪板，並且留意其他衝浪者。

5. Jenny and Jamie have been into surfing ever since they were 14.
珍妮和潔米從她們十四歲起就愛上了衝浪。

6. Do you know any good surf spots around here?
你知道這附近哪裡有好的衝浪點嗎？

7. You can rent a surfboard from any surf school by the beach, and take lessons to experience the excitement of surfing.
你可以在海灘邊任何一家衝浪學校租借衝浪板或是參加課程，體驗衝浪的刺激。

8. Wearing a leash can keep your board close to you and keep it from becoming a hazard to other surfers.
戴著鏈繩可以讓衝浪板保持在你的周圍，避免造成其他衝浪者的危險。

9. Everyone who surfs should be certified in CPR and basic first aid.
每個衝浪者都應該要通過心肺復甦術和基本急救法的認證。

10. A good surfer always keeps an eye on changing weather conditions and is aware of the danger of too much sun exposure.
一名好的衝浪者會隨時留心天候的變化以及太陽曝曬的危險。

11. What are the requirements for a good surfboard?
好的衝浪板應具備哪些條件？

12. Queensland, Australia is called a paradise for surfers.
澳洲的昆士蘭享有衝浪天堂的美名。

關鍵單字片語

1. **seize the timing** 片 把握時機

2. **surfer** [`sɜfə] 名 衝浪者

3. **wave** [wev] 名 海浪

4. **surfboard** [`sɜf͵bord] 名 衝浪板

5. **paddle out** 片 向外滑行

6. **stand up** 片 站立在衝浪板上

實境對話

Jeff: Did you see Jason?
你有看到傑森嗎？

Amy: Yes, 20 minutes ago. Why?
有啊，二十分鐘之前。怎麼了？

Jeff: He's supposed to meet me here before getting into the water.
他應該要在下水前先和我在這裡碰面的。

Amy: Look! He's right over there on the beach.
你看！他就在海灘那裏。

Jeff: What is he doing there? According to the weather report, we will have the best waves before noon.
他在那裡做什麼？根據氣象報告，我們在中午前會有比較好的浪。

Amy: According to what I know, he's been waxing his surfboard for 20 minutes.
我只知道他已經替他的衝浪板上了二十分鐘的蠟。

Jeff: 20 minutes? Does he have 3 surfboards to wax?
二十分鐘？他是有三個衝浪板要上蠟嗎？

Amy: I'm sure he only has 1. But I think I know what he's doing.
我確定他只有一個。不過我想我知道他在做什麼了。

Jeff: What is he doing?
他在幹嘛？

Amy: Don't you see those blondes right next to him? I think he is trying to get some attention from those girls.
你沒看到他旁邊的金髮妞嗎？我想他正試著要吸引那些女孩的注意。

Jeff: That's enough! He did exactly the same thing last week. I really wonder whether he's here to surf or just to show off and pick up girls.
真是夠了！他上星期也做了一樣的事。我真懷疑他是來衝浪、還是來炫耀把馬子。

關鍵單字片語

7. **current** [`kɜənt] 名 洋流

8. **leash** [liʃ] 名 綁腳繩

9. **rashguard** [`ræʃ‚gɑrd] 名 防磨衣

10. **sluggish** [`slʌgɪʃ] 形 遲鈍的

11. **as deep as possible** 片 儘可能深潛

12. **cutback** [`kʌt‚bæk] 名 切迴轉彎

12. 強身打 Wii
Let's Play Wii
MP3 042

萬用好句

1.	**There are five different games for your enjoyment in Wii Sports.** Wii運動聖地裡有五種不同的運動可供您遊樂。
2.	**Jeremy just bought Wii Sports Resort last weekend.** 傑瑞米上週末剛買了Wii運動度假聖地。
3.	**While bowling on Wii, just imagine the remote is an extremely light bowling ball and throw it as usual.** 在玩Wii保齡球時，只要想像遙控器是顆非常輕的保齡球，就像平常一樣丟出去就好。
4.	**Wii is a lot of fun and the boxing really gets the heart pumping.** Wii非常有趣，拳擊遊戲也能讓心跳加速。
5.	**How about playing a baseball game on Wii, just you and me?** 要不要來場Wii的棒球賽，就我們兩個？
6.	**Wii is a good exercise choice for those who don't like going out to the gym or exercising with other people.** 對於那些不想上健身房、或不想和別人一起運動的人來說，Wii是個很好的運動選擇。
7.	**What is your favorite Wii game?** 你最喜歡的Wii遊戲是什麼？
8.	**Jeremy invited us to have a Wii fight with him at his place.** 傑瑞米邀請我們去他家參與Wii大戰。
9.	**With Wii, you can canoe anytime at home just with a simple click on the mouse.** 有了Wii，你只需按按滑鼠，就可隨時在家裡划獨木舟。
10.	**Wii and Kinnect are both ideal choices for family reunion fun during the Chinese New Year.** Wii和Kinnect都是農曆新年期間全家團聚歡樂的好選擇。
11.	**Both of my parents enjoy competing with each other on Wii.** 我的父母很喜歡和對方玩Wii比輸贏。
12.	**You can put your personal record in Wii and take it anywhere.** 你可以把個人紀錄儲存在Wii裡面，並帶著它四處征戰。

 關鍵單字片語

1. **remote controller** 片 遙控器
2. **direction** [dəˋrɛkʃən] 名 方向
3. **balance board** 片 平衡板

4. **console bundle** 片 操縱組
5. **motion sensor** 片 動作感測器
6. **pick up** 片 學習

實境對話

Lauren: No way! That's the third time I have been struck out. You can't be that good!
不會吧！這已經是我第三次被三振了，你不可能那樣厲害的！

Frank: Face the music! I am really good at Wii.
面對現實吧！我玩Wii真的很厲害。

Lauren: How can you be so confident?
你怎麼能這麼有自信？

Frank: My family always plays Wii together on weekends.
我們家人總是在週末一起玩Wii。

Lauren: No wonder you are so good at this.
難怪你這麼厲害。

Frank: I am not just good. I'm the best!
我不只是厲害而已，我超強的！

Lauren: Don't be so cocky. Let's play another game. Maybe I will beat you.
別太自傲。我們再比一場，或許我能擊敗你。

Frank: Are you sure that you want to challenge me? My cousins call me the Wii God.
妳確定要向我挑戰？我的表弟們都說我是「Wii之神」。

Lauren: Stop bragging.
別再吹牛了。

Frank: O.K. Tell me which game you want to play, bowling or Frisbee?
好。那跟我說你想玩哪個遊戲，保齡球還是飛盤？

Lauren: Let's go bowling.
就玩保齡球吧。

Frank: No problem. Don't weep when you lose.
沒問題。輸的時候可別哭啊。

關鍵單字片語

7. **Nunchuck** [`nʌntʃʌk] 名 Wii左手操縱桿

8. **respond** [rɪˋspɑnd] 動 反應、回應

9. **multiplayer** [ˋmʌltɪˏpleɚ] 形 多位玩家的

10. **jab** [dʒæb] 動 以拳猛擊

11. **against** [əˋgɛnst] 介 對抗

12. **position** [pəˋzɪʃən] 名 位置

13. 中國功夫
Chinese Kung Fu
MP3 043

萬用好句

1.	**Ip Man is a popular movie about the life of a Kung Fu legend.** 《葉問》是一部關於一位功夫傳奇人物一生的著名電影。
2.	**Shaolin and Wudang are different schools of Kung Fu.** 少林和武當是不同門派的功夫。
3.	**Chinese martial arts have been a hot topic in Hollywood movies.** 中國武術一直是好萊塢電影的熱門題材。
4.	**Bruce Lee and Jackie Chan are my favorite action movie stars.** 李小龍和成龍是我最喜歡的動作明星。
5.	**Who is your favorite Kung Fu star, Jet Li or Jackie Chan?** 誰是你最喜歡的功夫明星，李連杰還是成龍？
6.	**Kung Fu is not only used for self-defense, self-development, and physical exercise, but also for spiritual enlightenment.** 功夫不只用來自衛、自我鍛鍊和運動，同時也能涵養心性。
7.	**Before you decide on a particular school for further involvement, it's always better to read, visit, ask, compare and experience.** 在決定進一步練習特定的功夫門派前，最好能夠先多讀、多看、多問、多比較和多體驗。
8.	**"Chi" refers to the inner life force that is the essence of Kung Fu.** 「氣」指的是內在的生命能量，也是功夫的精髓所在。
9.	**The Shaolin Temple has been an important fountainhead of Kung Fu.** 少林寺一直是中國功夫的重要發源地。
10.	**Thai Chi is a widely practiced form of Chinese Kung Fu done as a healthy exercise nowadays.** 太極功夫現在是廣為流行的健康運動。
11.	**It takes years of practice to master Chinese Kung Fu.** 要花好幾年的時間才能精通中國功夫。
12.	**Where can I take Kung Fu lessons in the neighborhood?** 這附近哪裡可以學中國功夫？

關鍵單字片語

1. **martial arts** 片 武術
2. **beginner** [bɪˋgɪnɚ] 名 初學者
3. **Tai Chi** 片 太極拳
4. **Kung Fu** 片 中國功夫
5. **strength** [strɛŋθ] 名 力量
6. **flexibility** [ˌflɛksəˋbɪlətɪ] 名 靈活度

實境對話

Hank: What are you watching?
你在看什麼？

Jessica: I'm watching Shaolin Soccer.
我在看《少林足球》。

Hank: Again? You have watched it at least 20 times.
又看？你已經看了至少二十遍。

Jessica: I know. It's one of the best movies made by Stephen Chow.
我知道啊。這是周星馳最棒的電影之一。

Hank: I really can't see what's so special about the movie.
我真不懂這部電影有什麼特別的。

Jessica: It's amazing that it combines the principles of Chinese Kung Fu and Western soccer which makes it such a great movie.
他結合中國武術和西方足球，做出一部這麼棒的電影。

Hank: You do have a point.
你的確言之有理。

Jessica: In fact, many of my friends started learning Kung Fu after watching this movie.
事實上，我有很多朋友在看了這部電影以後，就開始學功夫了。

Hank: Really?
是嗎？

Jessica: Absolutely! And I'm planning to join them.
沒錯！而且我也打算去學。

Hank: Oh, please. You don't even walk to the nearby grocery store. How could you handle being kicked and jabbed?
得了吧！你連走路去附近的雜貨店都懶，是要怎麼應付那些拳腳功夫？

Jessica: Don't underestimate me! Take this!
別小看我！看招！

關鍵單字片語

7. **physical condition** 片 體能狀況

8. **joint** [dʒɔɪnt] 名 關節

9. **damage** [`dæmɪdʒ] 動 傷害

10. **fist** [fɪst] 名 拳

11. **vigorous** [`vɪgərəs] 形 精力充沛的

12. **training** [`trenɪŋ] 名 訓練

14. 自由搏擊
Kickboxing
MP3 044

萬用好句

1. **Kickboxing is derived from karate, Muay Thai, and Western boxing.**
自由搏擊是從空手道、泰拳和西方拳擊演變而來。

2. **Kickboxing refers to a group of martial arts and stand-up combat sports based on kicking and punching.**
自由搏擊是指各種武術和以腳踢和拳擊為主的站立格鬥技術結合。

3. **How about joining a martial arts club with me?**
要不要跟我一起加入自由搏擊俱樂部？

4. **Melvin Guillard impressed the audience with his martial arts skills.**
梅爾文吉拉德以他的武打技術讓觀眾印象深刻。

5. **Mark Coleman is my favorite fighter in the UFC Hall of Fame.**
馬克柯曼是我在終極格鬥賽名人堂裡最喜歡的選手。

6. **Where can I get information about the upcoming UFC events?**
我可以在哪裡獲得終極格鬥賽的最新消息？

7. **Henry is a huge UFC fan, and he never misses any local games.**
亨利是終極格鬥賽的大粉絲，他從不錯過任何一場當地的比賽。

8. **Because of its intense kicking and punching, kickboxing is definitely the biggest calorie-burning sport.**
自由搏擊含有大量的腳踢和拳擊，絕對是最消耗卡路里的運動。

9. **My idol, Bruce Lee, has had a great impact on modern kickboxing.**
我的偶像李小龍對於現代自由搏擊有很大的影響。

10. **Many kickboxing fighters train themselves to build stronger and more defined arms and legs to increase their chances of winning every fight.**
許多自由搏擊選手為了贏得每一場打鬥，都會鍛鍊自己有更強壯、結實的手臂和雙腿。

11. **More and more people are now joining kickboxing classes to improve their fitness.**
現在，越來越多的人參加自由搏擊學校健身。

關鍵單字片語

1. **protection** [prə`tɛkʃən] 名 保護

2. **facility** [fə`sɪlətɪ] 名 設備

3. **slow down** 片 減慢速度

4. **cross** [krɔs] 名 直拳

5. **uppercut** [`ʌpə͵kʌt] 名 上勾拳

6. **side kick** 片 側踢

實境對話

Yvonne: Do you remember my cousin, Jeff?
你記得我的表弟傑夫嗎？

Kevin: Of course. He plays computer games all day in his room.
當然記得，他整天在房裡打電動。

Yvonne: Yes, he used to indulge himself in computer games.
沒錯，他曾經沉迷於電動。

Kevin: What do you mean by "used to"?
你說「曾經」是什麼意思？

Yvonne: He quit when he joined the Kickboxing Club.
自從他參加自由搏擊社之後，他就不打電動了。

Kevin: Do you mean the one doing lots of kicking and punching?
你是說有很多腳踢跟拳擊的那個社團？

Yvonne: That's it. He is very fit and strong now.
沒錯。他現在很健壯。

Kevin: Wow. I'm surprised. I would not have imagined that such a pale boy like him would participate in kickboxing.
哇，這可嚇到我了。我不能想像，像他那樣的蒼白小伙子居然會打自由搏擊。

Yvonne: What's more, he's not doing this just for fun. He is signing up for the Ultimate Fighting competition this year.
還有，他可不是玩玩而已。他要報名參加今年的終極格鬥賽。

Kevin: Really? I heard it's a very tough match. Many fighters get seriously hurt during the match.
真的假的？我聽說那是個很粗暴的比賽。很多參賽者都在比賽中嚴重受傷。

Yvonne: That's why my aunt wants to ask you a favor; talk Jeff out of it. He really admires you.
這就是為什麼我姑姑想請你幫忙說服傑夫不要參加比賽，他一直很崇拜你。

Kevin: O.K. I'll try, but I can't promise anything.
好吧。我會試試看，可是我不能保證些什麼喔。

關鍵單字片語

7. **palm strike** 片 掌擊

8. **form** [fɔrm] 名 套路

9. **Muay Thai** 片 泰拳

10. **body combat** 片 拳擊有氧

11. **kickboxing** [`kɪk‚bɑksɪŋ] 名 自由搏擊

12. **punch** [pʌntʃ] 動 用拳猛擊

15. 體育新聞
Sports News
045

萬用好句

1. **ESPN is one of the leading world sports news agencies.**
ESPN是體育新聞的世界領導媒體之一。

2. **My husband tunes into the sports news at nine every evening.**
我丈夫每晚九點準時收看體育新聞。

3. **The sportscaster has received a lot of complaints because of his inappropriate judgment calls during the Real Madrid match.**
由於在比賽中對皇家馬德里的不當批評，那名體育播報員收到很多抱怨。

4. **That famous sportscaster is also a well-known sports blogger.**
那位有名的體育新聞播報員也是位知名體育部落客。

5. **Sports Today shows clips of all the best plays of the day.**
《今日體育新聞》會有本日最精采的賽事剪輯。

6. **What are today's sports headlines?**
今天的體育新聞頭條是什麼？

7. **What channel is ESPN sports news on?**
ESPN體育新聞在哪個頻道？

8. **Mr. Watson used to be a famous sportscaster on Channel 8.**
華生先生曾經是第八頻道的知名體育播報員。

9. **Just call our hotline after the news and answer our question correctly, and you can win free tickets to the game between the Lakers and the Heat.**
只要在新聞後撥打我們的熱線答對問題，你就可以贏得免費的湖人對熱火隊的球賽門票。

10. **Each week, the Sports News has exclusive reports on sporting events.**
體育新聞每週提供最詳盡的體育動態報導。

11. **There will be an inside story on Jeremy Lin at 3 this afternoon.**
今天下午三點會有關於林書豪的詳細報導。

12. **Do you prefer ESPN or VL sports news?**
你比較喜歡ESPN、還是緯來體育新聞？

關鍵單字片語

1. **sportscaster** [`sports,kæstɚ] 名 體育主播

2. **news clip** 片 新聞片段

3. **headline** [`hɛd,laɪn] 名 頭條

4. **NCAA** 縮 美國大學運動協會

5. **hockey** [`hɑkɪ] 名 曲棍球

6. **TV schedule** 片 電視節目表

實境對話

Jay: Did you see the sports report? Kobe Bryant is going to retire!
你有看體育新聞嗎？科比布萊恩要退休了！

May: No! It can't be true! That report must be wrong.
不！不可能是真的！報導一定是錯的。

Jay: I don't believe it, either. Although Kobe is not young anymore, the Lakers still count on him to help win the championship.
我也不相信。雖然科比已經不年輕了，湖人隊還是仰賴他贏得冠軍。

May: Did the news say the reason why Kobe wants to retire?
新聞有說為什麼科比想退休嗎？

Jay: Not exactly. I just caught the headline only.
不算有，我只是瞄到頭條新聞。

May: The anchor must be lying. I bet he supports the Heat!
那個記者一定在亂說。我打賭他一定是熱火隊的球迷！

Jay: He might be! By the way, did you watch last night's game?
他可能是喔！對了，你有看昨晚的比賽嗎？

May: No, but I watched the replay this morning.
沒有，但是我看了今天早上的重播。

Jay: Me, too. Don't you think the commentator was ridiculous? He said Kobe can't get his glory back.
我也是。你不覺得那個播報員很誇張嗎？他說科比不能再享昔日光輝了。

May: Nonsense. Kobe is the best player in the league not only because of his skills, but also his experience.
一派胡言！科比之所以是聯盟裡最棒的球員，不只是因為他的技巧，還有他的經驗。

Jay: I couldn't agree with you more.
我非常同意你。

關鍵單字片語

7. **live** [laɪv] 形 現場轉播的

8. **delay-live** [dɪˋle͵laɪv] 形 延遲轉播的

9. **report** [rɪˋport] 名 報導

10. **comment** [ˋkɑmənt] 動 名 評論

11. **turning to** 片 將焦點轉到某一則新聞

12. **reporter** [rɪˋportɚ] 名 記者

1.歡樂迎新
Welcome Party
MP3
046

萬用好句

1.	Don't forget about the welcome party next Friday. 別忘了下個星期五的迎新派對。
2.	The welcome party will be held next Saturday, not Friday. 迎新派對是在星期六舉行、不是星期五。
3.	There will be cocktails and refreshments at the welcome party. 迎新派對上提供雞尾酒與茶點。
4.	What time will the welcome party begin? 迎新派對幾點鐘開始？
5.	I can't believe that the welcome party lasted for five hours! 我不敢相信迎新派對竟長達五個小時！
6.	I am so excited about meeting all the newcomers. 即將與新生相見，讓我感到相當興奮。
7.	He got totally drunk at the welcome party. 他在迎新派對上喝個爛醉。
8.	What's the dress code for the welcome party? 迎新派對的服裝規定是什麼？
9.	We have to wear suits and ties. 我們必須穿西裝打領帶。
10.	Can I wear jeans to the welcome party? 我可以穿牛仔褲去參加迎新派對嗎？
11.	I met an old friend at the welcome party. I didn't know that we go to the same school. 我在迎新派對上遇見一位老朋友，我不知道我們竟然上了同一所學校。
12.	There were at least two hundred people at the welcome party yesterday. 昨天的迎新派對上至少有兩百個人。

關鍵單字片語

1. **orientation party** 片 迎新茶會

2. **suit** [sut] 名 西裝

3. **refreshment** [rɪˋfrɛʃmənt] 名 茶點

4. **welcome party** 片 迎新派對

5. **jeans** [dʒinz] 名 牛仔褲

6. **department** [dɪˋpɑrtmənt] 名 系所

實境對話

Cindy: Hi, Danny. I heard that you went to the welcome party yesterday. Was it fun?
嗨，丹尼。我聽說你昨天去參加了迎新派對，好玩嗎？

Danny: Yes, it was nice. I made many new friends at the party.
對啊，挺好玩的。我在派對上認識了許多新朋友。

Cindy: That's great.
那還真不錯。

Danny: And there will be a welcome party held by our department next Saturday.
下個星期六，我們系上還會辦一場迎新派對。

Cindy: Wow! That one will be exciting, too.
哇！這場派對應該也會相當刺激吧？

Danny: I think so, too. There will be beer and a barbeque at the welcome party.
我也這樣想。迎新派對上會供應啤酒與烤肉。

Cindy: Really? Can I go, too?
真的嗎？我也可以參加嗎？

Danny: I guess so. The invitation says that we can invite friends to go with us.
我想應該可以吧！邀請函上說我們可以帶朋友一起去。

Cindy: Cool!
太酷了！

Danny: And it will be held by the poolside!
而且，這場迎新派對還是在游泳池畔舉行的喔！

Cindy: Really? I can't wait!
真的嗎？我真等不及想參加了！

Danny: I can't wait, either!
我也等不及了！

關鍵單字片語

7. **barbeque** [`bɑrbɪ͵kju] 名 烤肉

8. **invitation** [͵ɪnvəˋteʃən] 名 邀請函

9. **poolside** [`pulsaɪd] 名 游泳池畔

10. **hold** [hold] 動 舉辦

11. **last** [læst] 動 持續

12. **dress code** 片 服裝規定

2.校園巡禮
Orientation
047

萬用好句

1.	**Your campus is really beautiful.** 你們的校園真美麗。
2.	**How do you like our campus?** 你覺得我們的校園如何？
3.	**Where is the administration office?** 教務處在哪裡？
4.	**The library is right next to the swimming pool.** 圖書館就在游泳池的旁邊。
5.	**I have to return these books to the library before tomorrow.** 我必須在明天之前把這些書還回圖書館。
6.	**You have to show your student I.D. to get into the library.** 你必須出示學生證才能進入圖書館。
7.	**The cafeteria is always crowded during lunch time.** 學校的自助餐廳在午餐時間總是非常擁擠。
8.	**Can you meet me at the student lounge at four-thirty?** 你四點半的時候可以在學生交誼廳跟我碰面嗎？
9.	**That building over there is the gymnasium.** 那棟建築物是體育館。
10.	**Some students are having physical training in the gymnasium.** 有些學生正在體育館裡進行體能訓練。
11.	**If you need anything, you can go to the student center and ask for help.** 如果你有需要，你可以到學生中心去請求協助。
12.	**I need to buy something from the student store.** 我需要去學生商店買些東西。

關鍵單字片語

1. **campus** [`kæmpəs] 名 校園

2. **administration office** 片 教務處

3. **library** [`laɪˌbrɛrɪ] 名 圖書館

4. **student I.D.** 片 學生證

5. **gymnasium** [dʒɪm`nezɪəm] 名 體育館

6. **student center** 片 學生中心

實境對話

Joel: Do you like your campus?
你喜歡你的校園嗎？

Lisa: Sure, I love it. It's very convenient.
當然，我愛極了。我們校園超方便的。

Joel: Oh, really?
喔，真的嗎？

Lisa: The student store is open 24-7. The gymnasium and the swimming pool are big and clean.
學生商店全年無休，而且體育館與游泳池又大又乾淨。

Joel: Sounds really good!
聽起來真棒！

Lisa: I especially love our library. Our library has just been renovated, and everything in it is new and modern.
我特別喜歡我們學校的圖書館。我們的圖書館剛剛翻修過，所以裡面的一切設備都是新的，而且很現代化。

Joel: Do you spend a lot of time in the library?
你常常待在圖書館嗎？

Lisa: Yes, I do.
是啊。

Joel: I think your campus is very beautiful.
我覺得你們校園好漂亮。

Lisa: It is truly a nice one! When I have no class, I enjoy riding my bike and looking around the campus.
真的很漂亮！我沒有課的時候，我會騎著腳踏車在校園裡到處看看。

Joel: How relaxing!
真是悠閒！

Lisa: I know. That's why I love my school so much!
是啊，所以我非常喜愛我的學校！

關鍵單字片語

7. **beautiful** [`bjutəfəl] 形 美麗的

8. **physical** [`fɪzɪkl] 形 體能的

9. **modern** [`mɑdən] 形 現代化的

10. **relaxing** [rɪ`læksɪŋ] 形 令人放鬆的

11. **return** [rɪ`tɜn] 動 歸還

12. **renovate** [`rɛnə‚vet] 動 維修

3. 討論選課
Course Selections
MP3 048

萬用好句

1. **Which courses are you taking this semester?**
你這學期要修哪些課？

2. **I don't want to take Professor Winston's history class.**
我不想修溫斯頓教授的歷史課。

3. **What time does your first class begin?**
你的第一堂課幾點開始？

4. **How many credits are you taking?**
你要修幾個學分？

5. **I plan to take 20 credits.**
我打算修二十個學分。

6. **I still need 16 credits to graduate.**
我還需要十六個學分才能畢業。

7. **I think I am going to drop that course.**
我想我大概會退掉那門課。

8. **When is the deadline to add or drop courses?**
加退選課程的截止日期是什麼時候？

9. **I heard that Professor Richardson's class is very interesting.**
我聽說理查森教授的課很有趣。

10. **I have enrolled in the English writing course on Tuesdays.**
我已經選了每週二的英文寫作課。

11. **Don't forget to register for this course before Thursday.**
別忘了在星期四之前選好這門課。

12. **I am so tired of this course-selection thing!**
我真厭倦選課這玩意兒！

關鍵單字片語

1. **course** [kors] 名 課程

2. **semester** [səˋmɛstə] 名 學期

3. **history** [ˋhɪstərɪ] 名 歷史

4. **credit** [ˋkrɛdɪt] 名 學分

5. **graduate** [ˋgrædʒʊˏet] 動 畢業

6. **selection** [səˋlɛkʃən] 名 選擇

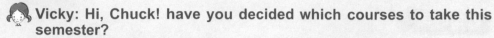

Vicky: Hi, Chuck! have you decided which courses to take this semester?
嗨，查克！你決定這學期要修哪些課了嗎？

Chuck: Hi, Vicky. No, not yet. I am still thinking about it.
嗨，維琪。不，還沒，我還在考慮中。

Vicky: Do you want to take Professor Lee's class?
你想修李教授的課嗎？

Chuck: Hmm..., I don't know. I heard that he is a very strict teacher.
嗯…，我不知道。我聽說他是個非常嚴格的老師。

Vicky: He is very strict, and he is a very good teacher, too.
他很嚴格，而且他也是個非常好的老師。

Chuck: I'll have to think about it.
我得考慮考慮。

Vicky: Ok. How many courses do you plan to take this semester?
好吧。你這學期要選幾門課？

Chuck: I plan to take two courses.
我打算修兩門課。

Vicky: Only two courses?
只修兩門課？

Chuck: I only need twelve credits to graduate.
我只需要再修十二個學分就可以畢業了。

Vicky: That's nice. So what's your plan for the semester?
真好，所以你這學期的計畫是什麼？

Chuck: I plan to take urban planning on Monday and graphic design on Tuesday.
我打算修週一的都市計劃和週二的平面設計。

關鍵單字片語

7. **urban planning** 片 都市計劃

8. **graphic design** 片 平面設計

9. **drop** [drɑp] 動 退選

10. **add** [æd] 動 加選

11. **register** [`rɛdʒɪstə] 動 登記

12. **enroll** [ɪn`rol] 動 登記

4.夜衝夜遊
Night Out
MP3 049

萬用好句

1.	**Young people love to ride scooters in groups all night and have fun together.** 年輕人喜歡在晚上成群騎著摩托車一起去玩。
2.	**Do you want to join us for a night ride?** 你想跟我們去夜遊嗎？
3.	**How many people will join us?** 多少人要跟我們一起去？
4.	**I guess I'll pass. I am afraid of ghosts.** 我想我還是不去好了，我怕鬼。
5.	**I want to join you guys, but my scooter is broken.** 我想跟你們去，但是我的摩托車拋錨了。
6.	**Let's go for a night ride after the midterm exam!** 我們期中考過後去夜遊吧！
7.	**They plan to depart from the Shi-lin Night Market at 11:00 pm and then ride all the way to Tam-shui, so they are taking a nap now.** 他們計畫晚上十一點從士林夜市出發，接著再一路騎車到淡水，所以他們現在正在補眠。
8.	**Don't forget to fill up the tank before we depart.** 別忘了在出發前先加滿油。
9.	**We can enjoy the sunrise on Yang-ming Mountain.** 我們可以在陽明山上看日出。
10.	**I went on a night ride last night, and I am exhausted now.** 我昨晚去夜衝，現在整個人累得要命。
11.	**You have to be very careful when you ride at night.** 晚上騎車要非常小心。
12.	**I don't want to stay up all night just to ride my scooter.** 我不想要整晚熬夜騎摩托車。

關鍵單字片語

1. **scooter** [`skutɚ] 名 輕型摩托車
2. **night ride** 片 夜遊、夜衝
3. **ghost** [ɡost] 名 鬼
4. **tank** [tæŋk] 名 油箱
5. **sunrise** [`sʌn͵raɪz] 名 日出
6. **exhausted** [ɪɡ`zɔstɪd] 形 精疲力竭的

Judy: I am so tired today.
我今天好疲倦。

Frank: What's wrong? Didn't you sleep well last night?
怎麼了？你昨晚沒睡好嗎？

Judy: I didn't even sleep last night.
我昨晚根本沒睡。

Frank: Really? Why not?
真的嗎？為什麼不睡？

Judy: I was out last night.
我昨晚出去了。

Frank: Out? Where?
出去？去哪裡？

Judy: I went for a night ride with my classmates.
我跟同學們去夜衝了。

Frank: You guys are crazy!
你們真瘋狂！

Judy: This was my first time, and I think it was really fun.
這是我第一次參加夜衝，但是我覺得很好玩。

Frank: I don't understand. What's so fun about riding a scooter all night long?
我不懂。一整晚都在騎摩托車有什麼好玩的？

Judy: We went to many places in one night, and we saw the sunrise from Yang-ming Mountain!
我們一個晚上去了好多地方，而且還從陽明山上看到日出耶！

Frank: It doesn't sound fun to me at all, ha, ha!
對我而言，聽起來一點都不有趣。哈哈！

關鍵單字片語

7. **careful** [`kɛrfəl] 形 小心的

8. **crazy** [`krezɪ] 形 瘋狂的

9. **join** [dʒɔɪn] 動 參加

10. **depart** [dɪ`pɑrt] 動 出發

11. **be afraid of** 片 害怕

12. **out of order** 片 拋錨、故障

5. 自我介紹
Self Introduction
MP3 050

萬用好句

1.	**Please allow me to introduce myself first.** 請先讓我自我介紹。
2.	**I am Lucas, and I am from Taipei, Taiwan.** 我是盧卡斯，我來自台灣的台北市。
3.	**May I have your last name, please?** 能不能請告訴我您貴姓？
4.	**Would you please tell me your name again?** 能不能請您再告訴我一次您的大名？
5.	**It's nice to meet you.** 很高興認識你。
6.	**You look familiar to me. Have we met before?** 你看起來很面熟，我們之前見過嗎？
7.	**Do you remember me? We met last summer at David's party.** 你還記得我嗎？我們去年夏天在大衛的派對上見過。
8.	**There are five people in my family--my parents, my two younger brothers and I.** 我家有五個人，我的雙親、兩個弟弟，還有我。
9.	**I live near the Taipei City Hall MRT station.** 我住在台北市政府捷運站附近。
10.	**I am 23 years old, and I am still a student. I'm working on an MBA degree at NTU.** 我今年二十三歲，還是個學生。我現在在台灣大學攻讀企業管理碩士學位。
11.	**Is he from Germany?** 他是不是德國人？
12.	**I used to live in Kyoto, Japan when I was little.** 我小時候住在日本京都。

關鍵單字片語

1. **last name** 片 姓氏

2. **MBA** 縮 企業管理碩士

3. **NTU** 縮 台灣大學

4. **accent** [`æksɛnt] 名 口音

5. **assistant** [ə`sɪstənt] 名 助理

6. **familiar** [fə`mɪljə] 形 熟悉的

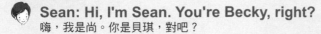

實境對話

Sean: Hi, I'm Sean. You're Becky, right?
嗨，我是尚。你是貝琪，對吧？

Becky: Hi. Yes, I'm Becky. Have we met?
嗨。是的，我是貝琪，我們見過嗎？

Sean: We were both at Professor Hoffman's party last night.
我們昨晚都參加了霍夫曼教授的派對。

Becky: Oh, yes! Now, I remember. How are you doing?
喔，對！我現在想起來了。你好嗎？

Sean: I'm fine, thank you.
我很好，謝謝。

Becky: The party last night was really fun, wasn't it?
昨晚的派對真的很有趣，不是嗎？

Sean: It sure was. Hey, Becky, I noticed that you have a British accent. Are you from the U.K.?
是啊。嘿，貝琪，我發現你說話有點英國腔，你是英國人嗎？

Becky: Yes, I am. I'm from London.
對，我是從倫敦來的。

Sean: Cool. How long have you been here in Taipei?
酷耶，你在台北多久了？

Becky: I have been living in Taipei for almost two years now.
我住在台北已經快要兩年了。

Sean: Did you come here to study?
你來這裡唸書嗎？

Becky: No, I came here for work. I am Professor Hoffman's assistant.
不，我是來這裡工作的。我是霍夫曼教授的助理。

關鍵單字片語

7. **both** [boθ] 形 兩者都

8. **British** [`brɪtɪʃ] 形 英國的

9. **allow** [ə`lau] 動 允許

10. **introduce** [ˌɪntrə`djus] 動 介紹

11. **notice** [`notɪs] 動 注意

12. **almost** [`ɔlˏmost] 副 幾乎

6.課堂私語
Chit Chat in Class
MP3 051

萬用好句

1.	**What is your favorite subject?** 你最喜歡哪一門課？
2.	**Did you like Professor Coleman's speech?** 你喜歡寇曼博士的演講嗎？
3.	**I totally forgot to do my homework!** 我完全忘記做功課了！
4.	**What is the assignment for today?** 今天的作業是什麼？
5.	**What chapter are we on?** 我們上到哪一章？
6.	**What class do you have next?** 你下一堂是什麼課？
7.	**I don't understand Professor Dickson's lecture.** 我聽不懂狄克森教授的課。
8.	**Who is the girl sitting next to Linda?** 那個坐在琳達旁邊的女孩是誰？
9.	**Why didn't you come to class this morning?** 你為什麼今天早上沒來上課？
10.	**May I borrow your notes?** 我能向你借筆記嗎？
11.	**Raise your hand if you have questions or comments.** 如果你有問題或是意見，可以舉手提出。
12.	**I am taking five courses this semester.** 我這學期修了五門課。

關鍵單字片語

1. **subject** [ˋsʌbdʒɪkt] 名 科目

2. **professor** [prəˋfɛsɚ] 名 教授

3. **speech** [spitʃ] 名 演講

4. **assignment** [əˋsaɪnmənt] 名 作業

5. **lecture** [ˋlɛktʃɚ] 名 授課

6. **comment** [ˋkɑmɛnt] 名 意見

實境對話

Guy: Did you go to the marketing class this morning?
你今天早上有沒有去上行銷課？

Nina: Yes, I did, and you weren't there.
有，我去上了。可是你翹課了。

Guy: I overslept.
我睡過頭了。

Nina: That's a pity. Professor Jackson's lecture today was really inspiring.
真可惜，傑克森教授今天的授課內容非常有啟發性。

Guy: Did you take notes?
你有沒有作課堂筆記？

Nina: I did. You can borrow my notes if you want.
我作了筆記。如果你想借，我可以借給你。

Guy: Thanks a lot. You are really a good friend.
謝啦，你真是個好朋友。

Nina: You're welcome. Why did you oversleep?
別客氣。你為什麼會睡過頭啊？

Guy: I was doing my accounting class assignment until 4:00 am this morning.
我的會計學作業寫到凌晨四點鐘。

Nina: I didn't know you were taking accounting. How is Professor King?
我不知道你修了會計學，金恩教授教得如何？

Guy: I never understand his lectures. I have to study by myself or ask my classmates for help.
我根本聽不懂他的課，我都靠自己唸書或是請同學幫忙。

Nina: Poor you!
你真可憐！

關鍵單字片語

7. **marketing** [`mɑrkɪtɪŋ] 名 行銷學

8. **accounting** [ə`kaʊntɪŋ] 名 會計學

9. **poor** [pʊr] 形 可憐的

10. **forget** [fə`gɛt] 動 忘記

11. **borrow** [`bɑro] 動 借入

12. **oversleep** [`ovə`slip] 動 睡過頭

7. 切磋課業
Discussing Homework

MP3 052

萬用好句

1. I don't understand this chapter. Can you explain it to me, please?
我不了解這一章的內容，能請你教我嗎？

2. Do you have time? Can we discuss today's assignment for five minutes?
你有時間嗎？我們可不可以花五分鐘討論一下今天的作業？

3. Have you finished reading chapter ten?
你已經讀完第十章了嗎？

4. He is the most outstanding student in the class.
他是班上最傑出的學生。

5. I usually listen to music while doing my homework.
我做功課時通常會聽著音樂。

6. You can't watch TV and study at the same time.
你不可能邊看著電視、又邊讀書。

7. The teacher asked us to preview lessons eight and nine.
老師要求我們預習第八課與第九課。

8. It's important to review what you learned after class.
下課後複習所學的內容相當重要。

9. Can you show me how to solve this math question?
能不能請你教我解這道數學題目？

10. I am so tired of studying all night long.
我已經厭倦了整晚唸書。

11. What did the teacher say about this chapter? I don't remember!
關於這一章，老師說了什麼？我不記得了！

12. Study harder and you will get better grades.
再用功一點，你就會得到更好的成績。

關鍵單字片語

1. **plain English** 片 白話英文

2. **outstanding** [`aʊt`stændɪŋ] 形 傑出的

3. **absent** [`æbsn̩t] 形 缺席的

4. **understand** [ˌʌndə`stænd] 動 瞭解

5. **preview** [`priˌvju] 動 預習

6. **review** [rɪ`vju] 動 複習

實境對話

Gary: Have you finished today's assignment?
今天的作業你已經寫完了嗎？

Nina: Yes, I have. Why do you ask?
我寫完了啊！你為什麼要這麼問？

Gary: I have some questions about the assignment. Can you help me?
我有一些問題，你能幫幫我嗎？

Nina: Sure. Which questions are you having a problem with?
那當然，你不會哪幾題？

Gary: Number fourteen and number nineteen.
第十四題與第十九題。

Nina: Let me see.
我來看一下。

Gary: I don't even understand the language in the questions. Were they written in plain English?
我連題目都看不懂，這些題目是用白話英文寫成的嗎？

Nina: Of course. Wait a minute! I see what your problem is.
當然是啊，等一下！我知道你的問題出在什麼地方了。

Gary: What?
我的問題出在什麼地方？

Nina: You were absent last Tuesday, and questions fourteen and nineteen are related to the lecture given that day.
你上個星期二缺席，但是第十四題與第十九題與當天的課程內容有關。

Gary: No wonder I don't understand a thing!
難怪我完全不懂！

Nina: Don't worry. I'll teach you how to answer those questions.
別擔心，我來教你解題。

關鍵單字片語

7. **solve** [sɑlv] 動 解答

8. **worry** [`wɜɪ] 動 擔心

9. **while** [hwaɪl] 連 當…的時候

10. **at the same time** 片 同時

11. **of course** 片 當然

12. **no wonder** 片 難怪

8. 小組討論
Group Discussion

MP3
053

萬用好句

1. **This week's assignment is a team project.**
這個星期的作業是要撰寫分組報告。

2. **The teacher divided the class into twelve groups.**
老師把全班分成十二個小組。

3. **There are four people on a team.**
四個人一組。

4. **Tommy, Adam, Nelson and I are on the same team.**
湯米、亞當、尼爾森與我在同一組。

5. **It is important to cooperate with your team members.**
與小組成員合作是很重要的。

6. **I like to work in teams.**
我喜歡團隊合作。

7. **Our team will meet up this afternoon to discuss our project.**
我們小組今天下午會聚在一起，討論我們的報告。

8. **During our discussion, there were some disagreements.**
我們討論的過程中，有一些意見不合的情況。

9. **Disagreements are unavoidable.**
意見不合總是難以避免。

10. **When there is a disagreement, the majority rules.**
有意見不合的情況時，少數服從多數。

11. **Helen makes no contributions to her team.**
海倫對她的小組沒有貢獻。

12. **She never shows up for discussions.**
她從不在小組討論時現身。

關鍵單字片語

1. **team project** 片 小組報告

2. **meet up** 片 遇見、聚集

3. **divide** [dəˋvaɪd] 動 劃分

4. **discuss** [dɪˋskʌs] 動 討論

5. **responsible** [rɪˋspɑnsəbḷ] 形 負責的

6. **contribution** [ˏkɑntrəˋbjuʃən] 名 貢獻

實境對話

Max: How is your team project going?
你的小組報告進展如何？

Peggy: It's ok.
還可以。

Max: You don't sound too excited about it. What's wrong?
你聽起來好像不太愉快，小組發生了什麼事嗎？

Peggy: Well, you know, one of my team members is Robert.
呃，你知道的，羅伯在我們這一組。

Max: What's wrong with Robert?
羅伯有什麼不好的地方嗎？

Peggy: If you ask me, he is not a very responsible person.
如果你問我的意見，我認為他不是個負責的人。

Max: Really? What does he do?
真的嗎？他做了什麼事？

Peggy: The problem is not what he does do, but what he doesn't do.
問題不在於他做了什麼事，而是他沒做什麼事。

Max: I guess I understand what you mean.
我想我大概瞭解你的意思了。

Peggy: He never shows up for our discussions, and he didn't even try to participate in our team project.
他從不來參加討論，他甚至不試圖參與我們的小組報告。

Max: Can you do anything about it?
你們能不能想辦法解決這個問題呢？

Peggy: Other team members are thinking about kicking him off of our team!
其他的組員想把他踢出我們小組！

關鍵單字片語

7. **cooperate** [koˋɑpə‚ret] 動 合作

8. **participate** [pɑrˋtɪsə‚pet] 動 參與

9. **The majority rules.** 成 少數服從多數

10. **show up** 片 現身

11. **the same** 片 相同的

12. **kick out** 片 剔除、除名

9. 上台報告
Presentations

MP3 054

萬用好句

1. **Did you like my presentation?**
你喜歡我的報告嗎？

2. **The opening of your presentation is very interesting.**
你報告的開頭部份很有趣。

3. **I think your presentation was well-organized.**
我覺得你的報告內容很有組織。

4. **It is important to make eye-contact with the audience.**
與觀眾眼神交會是很重要的。

5. **You shouldn't use too many gestures.**
你不該使用太多手勢。

6. **Can you speak louder? We can't hear you in the back.**
可以請你大聲一點嗎？我們坐在後面聽不到你的聲音。

7. **I think your presentation needs to be improved.**
我認為你的報告內容需要改善。

8. **Don't be nervous.**
不要緊張。

9. **Be sure to make your point of view clear and strong.**
你的立場一定要堅定且清晰。

10. **Your presentation didn't seem to match the topic.**
你的報告內容似乎與主題不相關。

11. **What is your conclusion?**
你的結論是什麼？

12. **If you emphasized that issue more, your presentation would be much better.**
如果你能夠多強調那個議題，你的報告會出色許多。

關鍵單字片語

1. **presentation** [ˌprizɛnˋteʃən] 名 報告

2. **audience** [ˋɔdɪəns] 名 聽眾

3. **gesture** [ˋdʒɛstʃə] 名 手勢

4. **viewpoint** [ˋvjuˌpɔɪnt] 名 觀點

5. **conclusion** [kənˋkluʒən] 名 結論

6. **attractive** [əˋtræktɪv] 形 吸引人的

實境對話

Mona: I will give a presentation in class tomorrow.
我在明天的課堂上要上台報告。

Jack: Wow, cool! What is your topic?
哇，酷斃了！你的題目是什麼？

Mona: The Development of the Movie Industry.
《電影產業的發展》。

Jack: Are you nervous?
你很緊張嗎？

Mona: To be honest, yes.
坦白說，我很緊張。

Jack: Don't be nervous. I'm sure you will do well tomorrow.
別緊張，我相信你會表現得很好。

Mona: Thank you. I hope so.
謝謝你，我也希望如此。

Jack: Remember to make eye contact with your audience.
記得要與你的聽眾們進行眼神交流。

Mona: That's right. My teacher always reminds me of that, too.
沒錯，我的老師也總是提醒我這一點。

Jack: Did your teacher remind you of other things?
你的老師還有提醒你其他事情嗎？

Mona: He said that I use too many gestures.
他說我的手勢太多了。

Jack: Ok. If you keep those pointers in mind, your presentation should be no problem.
好，如果你都記得這些事，你的報告應該就不會有問題了。

關鍵單字片語

7. **organized** [`ɔrgən‚aɪzd] 形 有組織的

8. **loud** [laʊd] 形 大聲的

9. **nervous** [`nɜvəs] 形 緊張的

10. **firm** [fɜm] 形 堅定的

11. **sharp** [ʃɑrp] 形 清晰的

12. **improve** [ɪm`pruv] 動 改善

10. 準備考試
Exam Preparation

MP3 055

萬用好句

1.	**The midterm exam will be next week.** 下個星期是期中考。
2.	**I reviewed my notes three times last night.** 我昨晚將我的筆記複習了三次。
3.	**I didn't study at all for the final exam.** 期末考我完全沒有準備。
4.	**This is an open-book exam.** 這是一場可以參考書本的考試。
5.	**I have two more chapters to study.** 我還有兩個章節要唸。
6.	**Let's form a study group and prepare for the exam together.** 我們來組個讀書小組，一起準備考試。
7.	**Cheating on the exam is not allowed.** 考試中不可以作弊。
8.	**Did you stay up all night studying for the exam?** 你為了準備考試而整晚熬夜嗎？
9.	**I got a perfect score on the test today.** 今天的小考我得到滿分。
10.	**Do you need a tutor?** 你需要家教嗎？
11.	**I forgot everything after the exam.** 我一考完試就什麼都忘光了。
12.	**The exam covered chapters one to three.** 考試範圍為第一章到第三章。

關鍵單字片語

1. **midterm exam** 片 期中考
2. **final exam** 片 期末考
3. **open-book exam** 片 翻書考
4. **chapter** [`tʃæptɚ] 名 章節
5. **study group** 名 讀書小組
6. **cheating** [`tʃitɪŋ] 名 作弊

Sophia: Oh, my God! The midterm exam will be next Monday!
喔，我的老天啊！下週一就要期中考了！

David: Scary. I haven't studied at all!
真可怕，我一點書都沒唸！

Sophia: Me, neither. What should we do?
我也沒唸，我們應該怎麼辦才好？

David: Don't panic. We still have Saturday and Sunday.
別慌張，我們還有星期六與星期天可以準備。

Sophia: What do you suggest?
你建議我們怎麼做？

David: We can study together. You read the first two chapters and I will take care of chapters three and four.
我們可以一起準備。你唸前兩章，我來負責第三章與第四章。

Sophia: Sounds like a plan.
計畫聽起來不錯。

David: But I think we have to start right away.
但我想我們還是必須馬上開始準備。

Sophia: Sure. Let's grab something to eat first and then go to my place.
當然。我們先去吃點東西，然後就到我家去唸書。

David: Ok..., but wait a minute.
沒問題…，不過等一下。

Sophia: What's wrong?
怎麼了？

David: I don't have my textbook with me!
我沒帶課本！

關鍵單字片語

7. **a perfect score** 名 滿分

8. **panic** [`pænɪk] 動 恐慌

9. **stay up** 片 熬夜

10. **take care of** 片 處理

11. **at all** 片 絲毫、根本

12. **prepare for** 片 為…作準備

11. 社團活動
Club Activities

MP3 056

萬用好句

1. **I am thinking about joining a club.**
   我想要加入社團。

2. **Which club do you want to join?**
   你想參加什麼社團？

3. **Are you interested in joining the astrology club?**
   你想參加占星社嗎？

4. **The hiking club meets every Saturday at 8:00 am.**
   健行社每週六早上八點鐘聚會。

5. **It's a good way to meet people.**
   這是認識朋友的好方法。

6. **He is a member of this fraternity.**
   他是這個兄弟會的會員。

7. **Do you want to go to that sorority party?**
   你想去參加那個姊妹會的派對嗎？

8. **I signed up for the movie club yesterday.**
   我昨天加入了電影社。

9. **Do you know anyone in the art club?**
   你認識美術社的人嗎？

10. **I have no idea what that club is.**
    我完全不知道那個社團是做什麼的。

11. **Don't forget to attend the club meeting at 3:00 pm.**
    別忘了下午三點鐘去參加社團會議。

12. **I am the president of the singing club.**
    我是合唱社的社長。

關鍵單字片語

1. **club** [klʌb] 名 社團

2. **astrology** [əˋstrɑlədʒɪ] 名 占星學

3. **hiking** [ˋhaɪkɪŋ] 名 健行

4. **fraternity** [frəˋtɜnətɪ] 名 兄弟會

5. **sorority** [səˋrɔrətɪ] 名 姊妹會

6. **president** [ˋprɛzədənt] 名 會長、主席

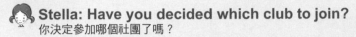

Stella: Have you decided which club to join?
你決定參加哪個社團了嗎？

Chuck: Not really. I am interested in a few clubs, but I haven't decided which one I should join.
還沒有。我對幾個社團都有興趣，但是我還沒決定要參加哪一個。

Stella: Is Omega on your list?
「歐米茄」有在你的候選社團名單上嗎？

Chuck: Omega? What is that?
「歐米茄」？那是什麼東西？

Stella: It's the best fraternity on campus.
「歐米茄」是學校裡最好的兄弟會。

Chuck: What is a "fraternity"?
什麼是「兄弟會」？

Stella: It's a club for male students only. You have to be one of the top students to become their pledge.
兄弟會只有男學生可以參加，而且你必須要名列前茅，才能夠成為兄弟會的新進會員。

Chuck: The criterion sounds very strict.
門檻聽起來相當嚴格。

Stella: That's quite true.
確實是如此。

Chuck: I don't think I am interested in joining a fraternity.
我想我應該沒什麼興趣參加兄弟會。

Stella: So, what do you have in mind?
那麼你想參加什麼社團？

Chuck: I might join either the chess club or the swimming club.
要不就參加西洋棋社，要不就參加游泳社。

關鍵單字片語

7. **chorus** [`korəs] 名 合唱團

8. **pledge** [plɛdʒ] 名 新進會員

9. **criterion** [kraɪ`tɪrɪən] 名 標準

10. **strict** [strɪkt] 形 嚴格的

11. **be interested in** 片 對…感興趣

12. **either...or...** 片 要不…，要不…

12. **住校生活**
Living on Campus
MP3 **057**

萬用好句

1.	**I live in the school dormitory.** 我住在學校宿舍。
2.	**I have two roommates.** 我有兩位室友。
3.	**The policy is that four students share one dorm room. But there are only three of us in our room.** 規定是一個房間住四個人，但是我們房間只住了三個人。
4.	**There is a laundromat in the basement of our dorm.** 我們宿舍的地下室有一間洗衣房。
5.	**I usually do my laundry on Thursday evenings.** 我通常在星期四晚上洗衣服。
6.	**I can't put up with my roommate anymore.** 我再也無法忍受我的室友了。
7.	**My roommate is a really messy person.** 我室友真的是個很髒亂的人。
8.	**My roommates and I get along very well.** 我的室友們與我相處愉快。
9.	**The cafeteria is right next to our dorm.** 學校的自助餐廳就在我們宿舍隔壁。
10.	**It's hard to have privacy in the dorms.** 住宿舍很難擁有隱私權。
11.	**Do you live in a co-ed dorm?** 你住在男女混宿的宿舍嗎？
12.	**There is a student lounge in the dorm.** 宿舍裡面有個學生交誼廳。

關鍵單字片語

1. **dormitory** [`dɔrmə,tɔrɪ] 名 宿舍

2. **roommate** [`rum,met] 名 室友

3. **policy** [`pɑləsɪ] 名 政策

4. **laundromat** [`lɑndrəmæt] 名 洗衣間

5. **basement** [`besmənt] 名 地下室

6. **cafeteria** [,kæfə`tɪrɪə] 名 自助餐廳

Clair: Hey, Charles. What are you doing?
嘿，查爾斯，你在做什麼？

Charles: I am reading the ads in the Student Paper. I'm looking for an apartment.
我在看《學生報》上的廣告，我要找房子。

Clair: What's wrong? Don't you want to live in the dorm anymore?
怎麼了？你不想繼續住在宿舍裡了嗎？

Charles: To be honest, I want to move out of the dorm immediately.
坦白說，我想要立刻搬出去。

Clair: What happened? Did you have a fight with your roommate?
發生了什麼事？你和你的室友吵架了嗎？

Charles: Correct. He is really nasty. I just can't stand him any longer!
沒錯。他真的很不衛生，我再也沒有辦法忍受他了！

Clair: Why don't you just talk to him?
你為什麼不跟他談一談？

Charles: We've talked about this many times, but he never changes!
我們針對這個問題談了好多遍，他卻一點也不願改變！

Clair: I see.
我明白了。

Charles: Even though I don't really want to move out of this comfortable dorm, I will.
雖然我真的不想搬出這間舒服的宿舍，但我一定會搬走的。

Clair: I know. If you really can't get along with your roommate, maybe it's better for you to find a new place.
我懂。如果你真的跟室友處不來，或許找個新地方住會比較好。

⭐關鍵單字片語

7. **privacy** [ˋpraɪvəsɪ] 名 隱私

8. **lounge** [laʊndʒ] 名 休息室、交誼廳

9. **messy** [ˋmɛsɪ] 形 凌亂的

10. **co-ed** [ˋkoˋɛd] 形 男女學生一起的

11. **nasty** [ˋnæstɪ] 形 髒亂的

12. **look for** 片 尋找

125

13. **外宿生活**
Living off Campus
058

萬用好句

1.	**How much is the rent?** 房租多少錢？
2.	**How much is the security deposit?** 押金多少錢？
3.	**Are utilities included?** 水電費包含在內嗎？
4.	**How long is the lease?** 租期多長？
5.	**A six-month lease is the minimum.** 至少要租六個月。
6.	**I will rent for at least one year.** 我至少會租一年。
7.	**The lease will expire on December 31, 2013.** 租約在二〇一三年十二月三十一日到期。
8.	**What's the penalty for breaking the lease?** 違反租約的話，罰金怎麼算？
9.	**Is the room furnished?** 這個房間附家具嗎？
10.	**When can I move in?** 我什麼時候可以搬進來？
11.	**I'd like to move in as soon as possible.** 我想趕快搬進去。
12.	**Would you like to renew the lease?** 你要續約嗎？

 關鍵單字片語

1. **rent** [rɛnt] 名 房租

2. **security deposit** 片 押金

3. **utilities** [ju`tɪlətɪz] 名 水電費

4. **lease** [lis] 名 租約

5. **minimum** [`mɪnəməm] 名 最低限度

6. **penalty** [`pɛn]tɪ] 名 罰金

實境對話

Clair: Have you found a studio apartment yet?
你找到套房了嗎？

Charles: Yes, I just found a nice one yesterday.
嗯，我昨天才剛找到一間很不錯的套房。

Clair: Great! Where is it?
那真好！在什麼地方？

Charles: It's about a ten-minute walk from our school.
走路到我們學校大約十分鐘的距離。

Clair: That's very convenient.
這樣很方便欸。

Charles: I know. And the rent is affordable.
沒錯，而且房租也在我負擔得起的範圍內。

Clair: How much is it?
多少錢？

Charles: It's NT$10,000 per semester. Utilities included.
每個學期新台幣壹萬元，包含水電。

Clair: Is it furnished?
有沒有附家具呢？

Charles: Yes. There's a single bed, a desk, a chair, and a wardrobe.
有啊！裡面有一張單人床、一張書桌、一張椅子，還有一個衣櫥。

Clair: What about a television and air conditioner?
那麼，電視機和冷氣機呢？

Charles: Oh, yes. It has those, too. And there is also a tiny refrigerator!
喔，對，那些也有。而且還有一台小冰箱！

關鍵單字片語

7. **studio apartment** 片 套房

8. **single bed** 片 單人床

9. **wardrobe** [`wɔr͵rob] 名 衣櫥

10. **furnished** [`fɜnɪʃt] 形 附家具的

11. **expire** [ɪk`spaɪr] 動 到期

12. **affordable** [ə`fɔrdəbl] 形 負擔得起的

14. **離別依依**
Saying Goodbye
MP3 059

萬用好句

1.	**I will never forget you.** 我不會忘記你的。
2.	**Thank you for all your help.** 謝謝你的全力協助。
3.	**I am deeply grateful for your support.** 我真的很感激你的支持。
4.	**Please do stay in touch.** 請務必保持聯絡。
5.	**Thank you for being there for me.** 謝謝你一直挺我。
6.	**I really hate to say goodbye.** 我討厭說再見。
7.	**Don't forget to give me a call sometime.** 有空別忘了打電話給我。
8.	**I have to go now.** 我必須要走了。
9.	**I wish you could stay longer.** 我真希望你可以待久一點。
10.	**Remember to send my regards to your family.** 請記得代我向你的家人問安。
11.	**When will I see you again?** 我何時可以再見到你？
12.	**Take good care of yourself.** 好好照顧你自己。

關鍵單字片語

1. **support** [sə`port] 名 支持

2. **goodbye** [ˌɡud`baɪ] 名 再見

3. **regard** [rɪ`ɡɑrd] 名 問候

4. **leave** [liv] 動 離開

5. **kiss goodbye** 片 吻別

6. **visit** [`vɪzɪt] 動 拜訪

實境對話

Madeline: Why the long face?
幹嘛拉長了臉？

Jeremy: My American friend, Benson, is leaving tomorrow.
我的美國朋友班森明天就要走了。

Madeline: So soon? I thought he just arrived here a couple of days ago.
這麼快啊？我還以為他才來這裡沒幾天。

Jeremy: He has been visiting Taipei for a week.
他已經在台北待一個星期了。

Madeline: Why is he leaving so soon? Can't he stay a little bit longer?
他為什麼要這麼早回去？他不能多留幾天嗎？

Jeremy: He has to return because his classes will begin soon.
因為快開學了，所以他必須回去。

Madeline: I see.
我懂了。

Jeremy: I really hate to say goodbye. Benson and I had so much fun together.
我真不願意跟他道別，班森和我一起玩得相當開心。

Madeline: Cheer up. You two can still keep in touch by e-mail!
打起精神來，你們兩個人還是可以靠著互通電子郵件來保持聯絡啊！

Jeremy: That's true. And he promised to come back again next summer.
這倒是真的，而且他承諾明年夏天會再來玩。

Madeline: Or you can visit him in New York.
你或許也可以去紐約拜訪他啊。

Jeremy: I will. I plan to visit him during Christmas.
我會去啊，我打算聖誕節的時候去找他。

關鍵單字片語

7. **promise** [ˋprɑmɪs] 動 承諾

8. **sometime** [ˋsʌmˌtaɪm] 副 改天

9. **stay in touch** 片 保持聯絡

10. **take care** 片 珍重

11. **a couple of** 片 數個、兩三個

12. **a little bit** 片 一點點、少許

15. 申請學校
Applying for Schools
MP3 060

萬用好句

1.	**I am thinking about studying in the US.** 我打算到美國唸書。
2.	**Which school are you thinking of applying to?** 你考慮申請哪一所學校？
3.	**Which are better? Public schools or private ones?** 公立學校與私立學校，哪種學校比較好？
4.	**Is there some place in particular that you are thinking of going?** 你有沒有特別想去的地區？
5.	**I've heard that there are several good schools in Boston.** 我聽說波士頓地區有幾所不錯的學校。
6.	**I am applying to Harvard University.** 我要申請哈佛大學。
7.	**You can apply online or download the application forms.** 你可以在線上申請，或者從線上下載申請表。
8.	**When is the application deadline?** 申請的截止日期是什麼時候？
9.	**You need to take the TOEFL and GRE tests.** 你必須要考「托福」與「美國研究生入學考試」。
10.	**I am applying for business school.** 我要申請商學院。
11.	**You need to submit your application forms, two recommendations and three essays before the deadline.** 你需要在截止日期前寄出你的申請表、兩封推薦信以及三份論文。
12.	**I've got the admission letter yesterday.** 我昨天收到入學許可了。

關鍵單字片語

1. **application** [ˌæpləˈkeʃən] 名 申請書

2. **recommendation** [ˌrɛkəmɛnˈdeʃən] 名 推薦信

3. **deadline** [ˈdɛdˌlaɪn] 名 截止日期

4. **TOEFL** 縮 托福考試

5. **form** [fɔrm] 名 表格

6. **essay** [ˈɛse] 名 論文

實境對話

Betty: I am thinking about getting a Master's degree abroad.
我想到國外去唸個碩士學位。

Vincent: That's cool! Where do you want to go?
那很好啊！你想去哪個國家？

Betty: The United States.
美國。

Vincent: Any specific school?
有特別想要申請的學校嗎？

Betty: I hope I can go to UCLA or UC Berkeley.
如果可以的話，我希望去唸加州大學洛杉磯分校、或是柏克萊分校。

Vincent: What will you major in?
你要主修什麼？

Betty: I am not sure yet. Business administration or finance, I think.
我還不確定。我想應該是企業管理或是財務金融吧。

Vincent: Nice. Then you'll have to take the GMATs.
真好。那麼你需要有「管理學研究生入學資格考試」的成績。

Betty: I know. I heard they are really difficult.
我知道，我聽說那種考試很難考。

Vincent: It won't be easy, but I think you can do well on the exam.
那種考試確實不容易，但是我想你一定可以考出好成績。

Betty: Thank you for the encouragement.
謝謝你的鼓勵。

Vincent: That's what friends are for!
這是朋友該做的！

關鍵單字片語

7. **Master's degree** 片 碩士學位

8. **statistics** [stə`tɪstɪks] 名 統計學

9. **finance** [faɪ`næns] 名 財金

10. **particular** [pə`tɪkjələ] 形 特定的

11. **specific** [spɪ`sɪfɪk] 形 特定的

12. **major** [`medʒə] 動 主修

PART 2

Let's Chat in English!

2 中階順口聊

intermediate level

1.首都走透透：台北、陽明山
The Capital: Taipei

MP3
061

萬用好句

1.	**The Raohe and Shihlin night markets are both famous in Taipei.** 台北的饒河夜市和士林夜市都很有名。
2.	**You must try the local Taiwanese snacks like tofu pudding and fried chicken at the Shihlin Night Market.** 到士林夜市，你一定要嚐嚐台灣當地小吃，如豆花和炸雞排。
3.	**Having exotic meals in restaurants in Taipei is like travelling around the world.** 在台北的異國餐廳用餐，就像是環遊了世界一周。
4.	**Jinguashi tells the history of gold-mining in Taiwan.** 金瓜石述說著台灣的淘金歷史。
5.	**The display in the Yingge Ceramics Museum is comprehensive.** 鶯歌陶瓷博物館的展覽非常多樣化。
6.	**Taipei is a sleepless city with many bars and clubs to go to.** 台北是個不夜城，有許多酒吧和夜店可去。
7.	**If you want to find clothes at bargain prices, go to Wufenpu.** 如果你想以便宜的價格買到衣服，就去五分埔逛逛。
8.	**Yanmingshan is the best spot for viewing the night scenery of Taipei city.** 陽明山是觀賞台北市夜景的最佳地點。
9.	**The lantern display at Sun Yat-sen Memorial Hall is amazing.** 國父紀念館的燈會很壯觀。
10.	**To reminisce about your childhood, you should take the Ferris' Wheel in Miramar Entertainment Park.** 若想回味童年，一定得去搭乘美麗華摩天輪。
11.	**Yingge is well-known for its colorful pottery.** 鶯歌之所以出名，是因為它多彩多姿的陶藝品。
12.	**You can get information about the city at any MRT station.** 你可在任一捷運站獲得本市資訊。

關鍵單字片語

1. **pleasure** [`plɛʒɚ] 名 樂趣

2. **hot spring resort** 片 溫泉旅館

3. **sulphur spring** 片 硫磺泉

4. **reminisce** [ˌrɛməˋnɪs] 動 追憶

5. **beneficial** [ˌbɛnəˋfɪʃəl] 形 有益的

6. **transparent** [trænsˋpɛrənt] 形 透明的

實境對話

Eva: Good morning, Sir. How can I assist you today?
先生，早安。我可以幫您什麼嗎？

Josh: Good morning. I want to take the MRT to Sun Yat-sen Memorial Hall. Which line should I take?
早安，我想搭捷運到國父紀念館，我應該搭哪一線呢？

Eva: You can take the blue line to Sun Yat-sen Memorial Hall.
您可以搭乘藍線到國父紀念館站。

Josh: Great. What if I want to go to Yamingshan later today?
太棒了。如果我今天晚一點想去陽明山呢？

Eva: Then you need to take Bus 260 or Bus 126 at Taipei Main Station.
那麼您就必須到台北車站搭乘260號公車、或是126號公車。

Josh: O.K. What places do you recommend I go to?
我知道了。還有哪些推薦的景點嗎？

Eva: Of course, the National Palace Museum is excellent.
當然有。故宮博物院是個很棒的選擇。

Josh: What is so special about it?
那裡有什麼特別的？

Eva: You can see a lot of Chinese art there.
您可以在那裡看到許多中國的藝術品。

Josh: It sounds cool. How can I get there?
聽起來很不錯。我要怎麼到那裡呢？

Eva: Take the red line to Shilin, and then take red bus 30.
搭乘捷運紅線到士林站，然後轉搭紅30號公車。

Josh: Thank you for your help. That's really nice of you.
謝謝你的協助。你人真好。

★ 關鍵單字片語

7. **MRT station** 片 捷運車站

8. **cab** [kæb] 名 計程車

9. **capital** [`kæpətl] 名 首都

10. **shopping mall** 片 購物中心

11. **five-star** [`faɪv, stɑr] 形 五星級的

12. **characteristic** [ˌkærəktə`rɪstɪk] 形 獨特的

2.造訪港都：高雄、愛河
Kaohsiung

MP3 062

萬用好句

1.	**Many tourists come to Kaohsiung for the seascape.** 許多觀光客為了海景而來高雄。
2.	**You can enjoy either the attractive harbor or the rich urban life in Kaohsiung.** 在高雄，你可以享受迷人的港灣或是市區的繁華。
3.	**The TV series "Black and White" was shot in Kaohsiung.** 電視影集《痞子英雄》就是在高雄拍攝的。
4.	**Kaohsiung has glistening colorful nights.** 夜晚的高雄多姿多采。
5.	**The sunset at Sizih Bay is so stunning.** 西子灣的夕陽美翻了。
6.	**I love the vendors behind the Hanshin Department Store.** 我喜愛那些在漢神百貨後方的小攤子。
7.	**The Pier-2 Art Center holds art exhibitions from time to time.** 駁二藝術特區不時舉辦藝術展覽。
8.	**Can you suggest any local cultural tour in Kaohsiung?** 你能否推薦高雄當地的文化之旅？
9.	**You can enjoy fresh seafood in Chi-Gin Harbor.** 你可在旗津港享用新鮮海產。
10.	**You can try DIY paper-umbrella making in Meinung.** 你可在美濃體驗自製紙傘。
11.	**Couples love to take the ferry along the Love River.** 情侶們喜愛乘船遊愛河。
12.	**What do you like the most about Kaohsiung?** 你最喜歡高雄的什麼？

關鍵單字片語

1. **night scenery** 片 夜景

2. **harbor** [`hɑrbɚ] 名 港灣

3. **exhibition** [ˌɛksəˋbɪʃən] 名 展覽

4. **wharf** [hwɔrf] 名 碼頭

5. **ferry** [`fɛrɪ] 名 渡輪

6. **Sizih Bay** 片 西子灣

實境對話

Adam: Have you seen the movie "Black and White"?
你有看過電影《痞子英雄》嗎？

Peggy: Of course! Mark Chao is so handsome and cool!
當然有！趙又廷真是帥又酷！

Adam: Then how about joining me on my trip to Kaohsiung next week?
那下週跟我一起去高雄如何？

Peggy: Is there a connection between these two topics?
這兩件事有關嗎？

Adam: What? Don't you know that most of the scenes in "Black and White" are shot in Kaohsiung? And they even have a "Black and White Festival" in Kaohsiung right now!
什麼？你不知道痞子英雄大部分場景都在高雄拍攝嗎？高雄現在還有痞子英雄特展耶！

Peggy: Cool! Can I go to the South District Police Department?
酷！我可以去南區分局嗎？

Adam: Sure. It's right next to the True Love Pier.
當然。那就在真愛碼頭旁。

Peggy: Is there anything special you want to do besides that?
除了特展外，你還有什麼特別想做的事嗎？

Adam: Yes. We can go to the Pier-2 Art Center afterwards. We can't miss the creative art exhibitions there.
有。之後我們可以去駁二特區。我們決不能錯過那裡舉辦的創意藝文展。

Peggy: How could I?
我怎麼能呢？

Adam: Right. It is a great chance to get closer to your hero.
是啊。這是你和你的英雄更加接近的機會。

Peggy: You got it! Count me in!
說得有理！我也要去！

關鍵單字片語

7. **Love River** 片 愛河

8. **take** [tek] 動 搭乘

9. **cycling** [`saɪklɪŋ] 名 騎乘單車

10. **nearby** [`nɪr͵baɪ] 副 鄰近地

11. **windmill** [`wɪnd͵mɪl] 名 風車

12. **prosperity** [prɑs`pɛrətɪ] 名 繁華

3. 山海小城：九份、淡水
Jioufen and Tamshui

MP3 063

萬用好句

1. **Jioufen was a traditional gold mining town.**
九份是座傳統金礦小鎮。

2. **Jioufen Old Street reminds people of the good ol' days.**
九份老街令人憶起過往的美好時光。

3. **The taro and sweet potato balls in Jioufen are delicious.**
九份的芋圓和番薯圓很美味。

4. **Jay Chou graduated from Tam-Kang Senior High School.**
周杰倫畢業於淡江高中。

5. **The peddlers along the Tamshui Old Street are my favorite.**
淡水老街沿路的攤販是我的最愛。

6. **The Tamshui Historical Museum in New Taipei City is an historical building from the Dutch Colonial times.**
新北市淡水博物館(紅毛城)是荷蘭殖民時期的歷史建築。

7. **Fisherman's Wharf in Tamshui is a hot place to go on a date.**
淡水漁人碼頭是情侶約會的熱門景點。

8. **Have you ever taken the boat in Tamshui?**
你有在淡水搭過船嗎？

9. **The famous movie "A City of Sadness" was shot in Jioufen.**
著名電影《悲情城市》在九份拍攝。

10. **The Love Bridge in Tamshui got its romantic name because it was opened on February 14th.**
淡水的情人橋因於二月十四日啟用，而擁有這個浪漫的名字。

11. **The souvenir shops on Jishan Street are always crowded.**
基山街上的紀念品商店總是擠滿了人。

12. **What is the most efficient way to travel around Jioufen?**
旅遊九份最有效率的方式是？

關鍵單字片語

1. **town** [taun] 名 小鎮

2. **humanistic story** 片 人文故事

3. **rich** [rɪtʃ] 形 富有…的

4. **geographic** [ˌdʒɪə`græfɪk] 形 地理的

5. **certainly** [`sɜtn̩lɪ] 副 確實地、確定地

6. **good ol' days** 片 過往美好歲月

實境對話

Gina: Look! That's the taro ball stall! You must try one.
你看！是芋圓攤耶！你一定得嚐嚐看。

Larry: Taro balls? What are those?
芋圓？那是什麼？

Gina: It's a famous dessert made of taro in Jioufen. You can also order one mixed with sweet potatoes as well.
是九份有名的小吃，用芋頭製成。你也可以點一碗混有番薯圓的綜合口味。

Larry: Sounds great. I'll have one!
聽起來很棒。我來一份吧！

Gina: And there are the ice cream spring rolls. They're my favorite!
還有冰淇淋春捲，是我的最愛！

Larry: I've heard of spring rolls, but ice cream spring rolls?
我聽過春捲，但是冰淇淋春捲是？

Gina: It's a creative snack here in Jioufen. Unlike traditional spring rolls, they put ice cream and sweet peanut powder in them.
是九份的創意小吃。與傳統春捲不同的是，裡面包有冰淇淋和花生粉。

Larry: Wow, you are an expert on snacks!
哇，你真是個小吃專家！

Gina: No big deal. You will find even more stalls on Jishan Street.
這不算什麼。基山街上還有更多小吃攤呢！

Larry: I am starving. Do you have any recommendations?
我好餓噢。你有任何推薦品嗎？

Gina: The best part of the local markets in Taiwan is that you can try everything along the street, as long as you still have room for more food.
這就是台灣傳統市集最棒的地方了。只要你還能吃，你可以吃遍整條街。

Larry: Perfect! Let's go!
太棒了！我們走吧！

關鍵單字片語

7. **taro ball** 片 芋圓

8. **fish ball** 片 魚丸

9. **be home to** 片 為…的故鄉

10. **mine** [maɪn] 名 礦井、礦山

11. **overlook** [ˌovɚˋluk] 動 俯視

12. **peddler** [ˋpɛdlɚ] 名 小販

4. 海濱暢遊：北海岸、基隆、東北角
Keelung and the Coastline
MP3
064

萬用好句

1.	You can go to the Keelung City Tourist Information Center to get information on accommodations. 你可前往基隆市遊客中心詢問住宿資訊。
2.	The Miaokou Gourmet Street is another popular place for gourmets. 基隆廟口是另一個適合老饕前往的知名景點。
3.	My favorite local snack, Ding-Bian-Cuo, is shredded rice paste from the rim of a heated pot. 我最愛的小吃——鼎邊銼，是沿著滾燙鍋邊煮熟的碎米糊。
4.	Pig's blood soup might be scary to some foreigners. 豬血湯對某些外國人來說很可怕。
5.	Fulong Beach is popular for its golden sand. 福隆海水浴場因為它的金色沙粒而受歡迎。
6.	I love going to the Yehliu Geopark with my family. 我喜歡和家人一同前往野柳地質公園。
7.	He suggests we cycle along the northeast coastline. 他建議我們騎單車遊覽東北角。
8.	Seafood lovers can't miss the Fugi Wharf. 海鮮愛好者絕不能錯過富基漁港。
9.	The Eighteen Lords Temple is renowned for granting worshipers wishes. 十八王公廟以靈驗著稱。
10.	The northeast coastline attracts many photography lovers. 東北角吸引許多攝影愛好者。
11.	The Shihsanhang Museum of Archaeology is worth visiting. 十三行博物館值得一訪。
12.	Sitting in an exotic café along Repulse Bay is relaxing. 閒坐淺水灣具異國風情的咖啡館，感覺好放鬆。

關鍵單字片語

1. **fish market** 片 魚市場

2. **shut down** 片 關閉

3. **azure** [`æʒɚ] 形 蔚藍的

4. **gourmet** [`ɡʊrme] 名 老饕

5. **Repulse Bay** 片 淺水灣

6. **photography** [fə`tɑɡrəfɪ] 名 攝影

Frank: Have you seen the news? They said Yehliu Geopark is going to be shut down for four months.
你有看到新聞嗎？野柳地質公園將關閉四個月。

Mona: Is that true? Why?
真的嗎？為什麼？

Frank: They said there are very few tourists these days.
說是因為最近遊客量變少。

Mona: That's such a pity. The landscape in Yehliu is so special.
真可惜。野柳的景色很特別。

Frank: I couldn't agree more. I still remember how amazed I was the first time I saw the sea cave and the famous Queen's Head rock formation.
真的。猶記初見海洞穴和著名的女王頭時，我有多驚訝。

Mona: Me, too. And the Fairy Shoe, which I used to believe might be a real fairy stopping by.
我也是。還有仙女鞋，我以前真的以為有仙女駐足。

Frank: You were such an adorable kid.
你以前真可愛。

Mona: Luckily, they will only shut it down for four months, right?
還好只會關閉四個月，對吧？

Frank: Yes. They are going to reopen in the summer.
沒錯，夏天時就會重新開放了。

Mona: Great! I think it's time to take my little girl there.
太棒了！我想是該帶我小女兒去那兒走走了。

Frank: Good idea! Can Lisa and I join you?
好主意！我和莉莎可以加入你們嗎？

Mona: Of course! We couldn't be happier to have you two join us.
當然可以！有你們加入，我們再開心不過了。

關鍵單字片語

7. **cape** [kep] 名 海角

8. **stop at** 片 停留於…

9. **seascape** [`si,skep] 名 海景

10. **wave attack** 片 波浪侵蝕

11. **imaginative** [ɪ`mædʒə,netɪv] 形 有想像力的

12. **the Queen's Head** 片 女王頭

5.桃竹苗之旅
Taoyuan, Hsinchu and Miaoli
MP3 065

萬用好句

1.	**The Nanzhuang Trout Festival in Miaoli is in November.** 苗栗南庄的鱒魚節十一月舉辦。
2.	**Dahu is known as the hometown of strawberries.** 大湖被稱作草莓的故鄉。
3.	**You can taste various wines in the Dahu Winery.** 在大湖酒莊，你可以品嚐各式美酒。
4.	**You'll be delighted with the Hakka culture and arts in Miaoli.** 在苗栗，你可以徜徉於客家文化與藝術。
5.	**I recommend the linguini noodles and spring rolls in the food court in front of the City Guardian Temple in Hsinchu.** 我推薦新竹城隍廟前美食街的細麵跟春卷。
6.	**You can see many scenic spots while cycling along the 17-kilometer coastline of Hsinchu.** 沿新竹十七公里的海岸線騎乘自行車，你能欣賞到許多景點。
7.	**The Mei-Chu Games between the Tsing-Hua and Chiao-Tung Universities always excite the students.** 清華大學和交通大學的梅竹賽總讓學生們感到興奮。
8.	**You must attend the Hakka Tung Blossom Festival at least once.** 你至少得去參加一次客家桐花季。
9.	**Tung blossoms look just like snow from a distance.** 從遠方望來，桐花看起來就像雪。
10.	**I want to walk on the Skywalk at the Little Wu-Lai Scenic Resort.** 我想漫步在小烏來風景區的天空步道上。
11.	**You can feel the history of Daxi by walking around the streets.** 漫步在大溪街上，你能感受到它的歷史。
12.	**Smangus is a well-preserved forest area in Hsinchu.** 司馬庫斯是新竹保存良好的林區。

關鍵單字片語

1. **food stand** 片 小吃攤

2. **Hakka** [`hɑk`kɑ] 形 客家的

3. **odorous** [`odərəs] 形 富有香氣的

4. **in advance** 片 事先

5. **flat noodles** 片 粄條

6. **food court** 片 美食街

Jessica: Larry, what is your plan for the coming spring break?
賴瑞，接下來的春假你有什麼計劃？

Larry: I am going to Smangus with my high school friends.
我要和高中朋友去司馬庫斯。

Jessica: Smangus? Where is that?
司馬庫斯？在哪裡？

Larry: It's an aboriginal tribe in Hsinchu County.
那是在新竹的一個原住民部落。

Jessica: An aboriginal tribe?
原住民部落？

Larry: Yes, it is located in an isolated area in Jianshi county in Hsinchu. The area is so beautiful that the tribe who lives there has been nicknamed "God's tribe."
是的。它位於新竹縣尖石鄉，因為很漂亮而贏得「神之部落」的美名。

Jessica: Have you booked the hotel yet? Maybe I can join you.
你訂好旅館了嗎？也許我可以和你們一起去。

Larry: I am sorry, but there is no hotel in Smangus.
抱歉，司馬庫斯沒有旅館。

Jessica: No hotel? Then where are you going to stay?
沒有旅館？那你們要住哪裡？

Larry: There is one B&B with only six rooms. So you must make a reservation far in advance.
那裡有一間民宿，但只有六個房間，所以一定要事先預約。

Jessica: Six rooms?
六個房間？

Larry: I think that is the only way to keep the place from being overrun by tourists.
我想那是讓這個地方不會有過量觀光客的唯一方法。

關鍵單字片語

7. **worship** [ˋwɝʃɪp] 動 祭拜

8. **rice noodles** 片 米粉

9. **coastline** [ˋkost͵laɪn] 名 海岸線

10. **straw raincoat** 片 蓑衣

11. **wood sculpture** 片 木製雕塑品

12. **trout** [traʊt] 名 鱒魚

6.好山好水：集集、埔里、日月潭

Nantou

MP3
066

萬用好句

1. **Nantou is famous for its scenery and spring-like weather.**
南投以美景和四季如春的氣候聞名。

2. **Sun Moon Lake is the largest lake in Taiwan.**
日月潭是台灣最大的湖。

3. **The reflections of the hills and the mountains on Sun Moon Lake are crystal clear.**
日月潭湖面映出的山丘倒影看起來很清晰。

4. **Jiji Train Station still looks the same as it did in the old days.**
集集火車站保有古早的風味。

5. **I learned about the paper industry at Puli Paper Factory.**
我在埔里紙廠學到了有關造紙業的知識。

6. **Where can I sign up for the DIY paper-making course?**
我要去哪裡報名造紙課程？

7. **Do you know any must-see places in Puli?**
你知道埔里有哪些必去的景點嗎？

8. **Puli is known for its pure water and juicy pears.**
埔里以清澈的水質和多汁的水梨聞名。

9. **Because of the clear water and fair weather, Nantou is the most important tea plantation area in Taiwan.**
由於擁有清澈的水質和良好的天氣，南投是台灣最重要的產茶區。

10. **I'm taking part in the Sun Moon Lake Swimming Carnival.**
我要參加萬人泳渡日月潭活動。

11. **There is not only a paper culture museum but a café and a DIY activity center included in the Puli Paper Factory Tour.**
埔里造紙工廠之旅不只有參觀紙類文化博物館，還有咖啡廳跟DIY中心的行程。

12. **If you enjoy nature, don't forget to visit the Verdant Tunnel in Jiji.**
如果你喜愛大自然，別忘了到集集的綠色隧道走走。

關鍵單字片語

1. **fruit-picking** [ˋfrut͵pɪkɪŋ] 名 採水果

2. **orchard** [ˋɔrtʃəd] 名 果園

3. **sake vinasse** 片 清酒粕

4. **earthquake** [ˋɝθ͵kwek] 名 地震

5. **brewery** [ˋbruərɪ] 名 釀酒廠

6. **pleasing** [ˋplizɪŋ] 形 令人欣喜的

實境對話

Jerry: Are you available this Saturday?
你這週六有空嗎？

Maggie: Yes. Is there anything special going on?
有啊。有什麼特別的事嗎？

Jerry: I'm taking you to Sun Moon Lake for our anniversary.
我想帶你去日月潭慶祝我們的結婚紀念日。

Maggie: Do you mean it? Sun Moon Lake? We are not touring, but celebrating our anniversary.
你說真的嗎？日月潭？我們不是去觀光，而是要慶祝紀念日噢。

Jerry: I know, and that's why I am taking you there. The Sun Moon Lake Music Festival will start this Friday.
我知道，所以我要帶你去那裡。日月潭音樂節這週五開始。

Maggie: A music festival? Sounds great.
音樂節？聽起來不錯。

Jerry: It's more than great. There will be all kinds of entertainment, including your favorite--Tang Meiyun Taiwanese Opera.
比不錯更棒！那裡會有很多節慶表演，包括你最愛的唐美雲歌仔戲。

Maggie: Really? I love their live performances very much.
真的嗎？我很喜歡他們的現場表演。

Jerry: There are also fireworks after all the festivities.
所有的節慶表演結束之後，還會有煙火。

Maggie: Fireworks by Sun Moon Lake? That's so romantic.
日月潭邊的煙火？太浪漫了。

Jerry: I am glad you like the plan.
我很高興你喜歡這樣的安排。

Maggie: It will be the best anniversary ever!
這會是最棒的結婚紀念日！

關鍵單字片語

7. **serene** [sə`rin] 形 寧靜的

8. **pineapple cake** 片 鳳梨酥

9. **pick flowers** 片 採花

10. **black stinky tofu** 片 黑皮臭豆腐

11. **situated** [`sɪtʃu.etɪd] 形 位於…的

12. **Lushan** [`luʃɑn] 名 廬山

7. 彰化：鹿港小鎮、肉圓
Changhua

MP3
067

萬用好句

1. **Changhua is the best at preserving its culture.**
彰化保存絕佳的文化資產。

2. **Changhua's historical areas attract lots of tourists.**
彰化的歷史景點吸引了大量的觀光客。

3. **I can't resist eating beauty's eyes and green bean cakes in Lukang.**
我無法抗拒鹿港的鳳眼糕和綠豆糕的美味。

4. **The Changhua County Government will hold a Chinese New Year Celebration on January 1st on the lunar calendar.**
彰化縣政府將於農曆一月一號舉辦春節慶祝大會。

5. **Paguashan is always packed with worshipers all year round.**
八卦山一年到頭總是擠滿了信徒。

6. **Did you know that Changhua is the granary of Taiwan?**
你知道彰化是台灣的穀倉嗎？

7. **Lukang is popular for its cultural areas and local snacks.**
鹿港之所以受歡迎，是因為它的文化景點和當地小吃。

8. **You can book a guided tour of the Confucius Temple.**
你可以先預約孔廟導覽。

9. **Excuse me. How can I get to the Longshan Temple in Lukang?**
不好意思，我要怎麼去鹿港龍山寺？

10. **Walk straight for two blocks, and the Changhua Art Museum will be on your left.**
直走過兩個街區後，你會在左手邊看到彰化藝術博物館。

11. **How much is the admission fee?**
入場費是多少錢？

12. **Moru Lane is only about 70 cm wide, so it's difficult for women to squeeze through it.**
摸乳巷大約只有七十公分寬，因此女性必須擠身通過。

關鍵單字片語

1. **ancient** [`enʃənt] 形 古代的

2. **architecture** [`ɑrkə,tɛktʃə] 名 建築物

3. **meatball** [`mit,bɔl] 名 肉圓

4. **granary** [`grænərɪ] 名 穀倉

5. **local snack** 片 當地小吃

6. **guided tour** 片 導覽

實境對話

Amanda: Let's go to Changhua for the Lantern Festival!
我們去彰化賞燈吧！

Andy: Why Changhua?
為何是彰化？

Amanda: Didn't you hear the news? The Changhua city government is holding the Taiwan Lantern Festival this year.
你沒聽說嗎？彰化市政府主辦今年的台灣燈會。

Andy: Thanks, but I'm really not interested in the Lantern Festival.
謝了，但我對燈會沒什麼興趣。

Amanda: Why not? There will be lots of different beautiful lanterns and many stalls along the way.
為什麼？那裡有許多不同的漂亮花燈，且沿路會有很多攤位。

Andy: I know, but the crowd almost suffocated me last year.
我知道。但去年的人潮差點讓我窒息而死。

Amanda: You are exaggerating.
你太誇張了。

Andy: I'm serious! And it took me five hours to drive to Miaoli.
我是說真的！而且去年我開了五個小時的車才到苗栗。

Amanda: Five hours? Are you kidding me?
五個小時？你在開玩笑嗎？

Andy: Not one bit. So if you really want to go to the Lantern Festival, be prepared for the crowds and traffic jam.
才沒有。所以如果你真的很想去燈會，可要對人潮和塞車有點心理準備。

Amanda: I might need to take a train or go there two days early.
我或許得搭火車，或提前兩天出發。

Andy: At least you won't spend hours in the traffic jam.
至少你可省下塞車的時間。

關鍵單字片語

7. **folk** [fok] 形 民俗的

8. **creative arts** 片 創意藝術

9. **one-bite cookie** 片 一口酥

10. **green bean cakes** 片 綠豆糕

11. **beauty's eyes** 片 鳳眼糕

12. **traffic jam** 片 塞車

8. 古城之旅：台南古蹟、鹽水蜂炮
Tainan

MP3
068

萬用好句

1. Tainan is a city of history and culture.
台南是歷史文化之城。

2. The Beehive Fireworks in Yanshui Town are held to celebrate the Lantern Festival.
鹽水蜂炮是慶祝元宵節的活動。

3. Anping Tree House has unique architecture.
安平樹屋是一棟很有特色的建築。

4. I used to believe that the Anping Tree House was haunted.
我曾以為安平樹屋鬧鬼。

5. Tainan City always reminds you of the golden years of the past.
台南市讓你回想起過往的黃金歲月。

6. I strongly recommend the shrimp rolls in Tainan City.
我強烈推薦台南蝦捲。

7. The milkfish congee is a traditional food in Tainan.
虱目魚粥是台南的傳統食物。

8. Which do you prefer, the rice pudding or the steamed rice cake?
你較喜歡米糕還是碗粿？

9. The Chihkan Tower was built in the Dutch Colonial Period.
赤崁樓建於荷蘭殖民時期。

10. Excuse me. Where is the Eternal Fortress?
不好意思，億載金城在哪裡？

11. It is necessary to wear a helmet and a thick raincoat when you attend the Beehive Firework Festival.
參加蜂炮節時，安全帽與厚雨衣是必要裝備。

12. Buying a Tainan pass will save you a lot on admission fees to different historical scenic spots.
購買台南觀光通行證可省下許多古蹟景點的入場費。

關鍵單字片語

1. **shrine** [ʃraɪn] 名 聖祠

2. **antiquity** [æn`tɪkwətɪ] 名 古蹟

3. **stroll** [strol] 動 漫步

4. **in the distance** 片 在遠方

5. **preserve** [prɪ`zɜv] 動 保存

6. **historical** [hɪs`tɔrɪkl] 形 歷史的

實境對話

Karen: Aren't you going on vacation this weekend?
你這週末不是要去渡假嗎？

Frank: Yes, I am so excited about it.
對啊，我好興奮哦。

Karen: Then why are you packing a helmet and a raincoat in your luggage? Those don't look like holiday essentials to me.
那你為何打包放安全帽和雨衣？在我看來不像是度假用品。

Frank: They are if you are going to Yanshui in Tainan.
如果是去台南的鹽水，它們就是必要的了。

Karen: What do you mean?
什麼意思啊？

Frank: We plan to watch the Beehive Firework Show. Multiple launches of bottle rockets will shoot out in all directions.
我們要去看鹽水蜂炮，許多沖天炮會朝四面八方炸。

Karen: So that's why you need those. To protect yourself?
所以你才需要那些東西來保護自己？

Frank: That's right. Some people even wear a mask.
沒錯。有些人甚至會戴面具。

Karen: How did this dangerous festival get so popular?
這種危險的節慶怎麼會受歡迎？

Frank: It used to be a religious ceremony. And then it became popular beause of the great fireworks display and all the excitement surrounding it.
這以前是一項宗教儀式，後來因為煙火秀和刺激感而大受歡迎。

Karen: You really need to be careful.
你得要小心點。

Frank: Don't worry. See! I'm even carrying a medical kit with me.
別擔心。你看！我還帶了醫藥箱呢。

關鍵單字片語

7. **helmet** [`hɛlmɪt] 名 安全帽

8. **protection** [prə`tɛkʃən] 名 保護措施

9. **cautious** [`kɔʃəs] 形 謹慎的

10. **the Eternal Fortress** 片 億載金城

11. **Tantz Noodles** 片 擔仔麵

12. **Coffin Board** 片 棺材板

🏁 9. 春天吶喊：墾丁、南灣
Kenting

MP3 069

萬用好句

1.	Kenting is a paradise for for young people with all its sunny beaches. 墾丁因為有陽光沙灘而成為年輕人的天堂。
2.	Have you seen the colorful underwater world in Nanwan? 你見過南灣美麗的海底世界嗎？
3.	Band applications for the Spring Scream should be received by October 11. 想參加春天吶喊的樂團，必須在十月十一日前提出申請。
4.	Spring Scream is an outdoor music festival held in April. 春天吶喊是在四月舉辦的戶外音樂節。
5.	Spring Scream was organized by two Americans in 1995. 春天吶喊在一九九五年由兩位美國人所創辦。
6.	You will see lots of bands at Spring Scream every year. 每年在春天吶喊，你會看到非常多的樂團。
7.	The National Museum of Marine Biology & Aquarium is a well-liked scenic spot for both children and adults. 國立海洋生物博物館是大人和小孩都喜愛的景點。
8.	I am looking forward to the sleepover in the National Museum of Marine Biology & Aquarium. 我很期待夜宿海生館的行程。
9.	My friend loves going surfing in Nanwan. 我朋友喜愛到南灣衝浪。
10.	Let's try a typical restaurant on Kenting's main street. 我們就在墾丁大街上選一家特色小吃店試試吧！
11.	Have you ever been to Spring Scream? 你有去過春天吶喊嗎？
12.	How can I sign up for surfing lessons? 我該如何報名衝浪課程？

⭐ 關鍵單字片語

1. **paradise** [`pærə͵daɪs] 名 天堂

2. **beach** [bitʃ] 名 海灘

3. **Spring Scream** 片 春吶音樂會

4. **live band** 片 現場演奏樂團

5. **bikini** [bɪˋkinɪ] 名 比基尼泳裝

6. **water sports** 片 水上運動

實境對話

Ann: What are you doing, David?
大衛，你在做什麼？

David: I am booking a ticket to Kenting.
我在訂到墾丁的票。

Ann: Kenting? It's still a little bit cold for water sports, isn't it?
墾丁？現在去玩水上運動不會有點冷嗎？

David: You're right, but I am not going to do water sports.
你說的沒錯，但我不是要去玩水上運動。

Ann: Then where will you go? The National Museum of Marine Biology & Aquarium? You don't even like sea animals!
那你要去哪裡？海生館？你根本就不喜歡海洋生物啊！

David: No, I am going to Spring Scream.
不是，我是要去春天吶喊。

Ann: Oh! I've heard that it's an international music event.
喔！聽說那是個國際性的音樂盛會。

David: Yes. Bands from all over the world participate in this event.
是啊，將會有來自全球各地的樂團參加。

Ann: Sounds interesting. Tell me more.
聽起來很有趣，多跟我說一點。

David: OK. There will be several stages in multiple places. You can lie on the beach while listening to great music.
好啊。在不同地方會有好幾個舞台，你可以躺在沙灘上享受好音樂。

Ann: Wow! It sounds like a dream.
哇！聽起來真夢幻。

David: Yes, a heavenly dream. Do you want to join me?
沒錯，如天堂般的夢境。你要一起來嗎？

Ann: Absolutely!
當然要！

關鍵單字片語

7. **attend** [əˋtɛnd] 動 參加

8. **stage** [stedʒ] 名 舞台

9. **festive** [ˋfɛstɪv] 形 喜慶的、歡宴的

10. **including** [ɪnˋkludɪŋ] 介 包含、包括

11. **tropical** [ˋtrɑpɪkl] 形 熱帶的

12. **touching** [ˋtʌtʃɪŋ] 形 感人的

10. **居高臨下：玉山、阿里山**
Yushan and Alishan

MP3
070

萬用好句

1.	**Alishan Forest Railway was originally built to transport timber.** 阿里山森林鐵路原先是為了運送木材而鋪設。
2.	**Watching the sunrise from Alishan is beyond description.** 阿里山的日出美不勝收。
3.	**Walking among the Sacred Trees can relax your body and soul.** 漫步神木群中可放鬆你的身心靈。
4.	**Yushan is one of the best places for hiking in Taiwan.** 玉山是台灣最棒的健行地點之一。
5.	**Yushan is the toughest mountain to hike because it has lots of snow.** 大雪令玉山成為最具挑戰性的健行地點。
6.	**We can take the small train to the peak to watch the sunrise.** 我們可以搭乘小火車到山頂看日出。
7.	**The Yushan area contains five peaks.** 玉山地區包含五峰。
8.	**How can I get a mountain permit to enter the Yushan National Park?** 我該如何取得玉山國家公園的登山證？
9.	**You need to check the weather conditions before you start your Yushan hiking trip.** 前往玉山健行前，務必先查詢天候狀況。
10.	**Yushan's main peak is popular because it has the best view.** 玉山主峰因為景色絕美而受歡迎。
11.	**The Alishan Railway is one of the only three remaining mountain railways in the world.** 阿里山鐵路是世上現存唯三條高山鐵路之一。
12.	**You can check the daily sunrise time at the Alishan Information Center.** 你可以在阿里山遊客中心查詢當日日出時間。

關鍵單字片語

1. **pavilion** [pə`vɪljən] 名 涼亭

2. **aroma** [ə`romə] 名 香氣

3. **railway** [`rel,we] 名 鐵路、鐵道

4. **rice in a bamboo tube** 片 竹筒飯

5. **beyond description** 片 難以形容

6. **maple** [`mepl] 名 楓樹

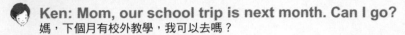

Ken: Mom, our school trip is next month. Can I go?
媽，下個月有校外教學，我可以去嗎？

Mom: Of course, sweetheart. Where are you going?
親愛的，當然可以。你們要去哪裡？

Ken: Alishan, and we are going to stay in Fenchihu.
阿里山，我們會住在奮起湖。

Mom: That's great! Will you go watch the sunrise?
太棒了！你們會去看日出嗎？

Ken: Yes, and the teacher told us that we have to get up by four am in order to catch the sunrise.
沒錯，而且老師說我們要在四點起床，才看得到日出。

Mom: That's the price of seeing the stunningly beautiful sunrise.
想看美得驚人的日出，就得有所付出。

Ken: Have you ever been to Alishan before, Mom?
媽，你有上過阿里山嗎？

Mom: Actually, my first date with your father was in Alishan.
事實上，我第一次和你爸約會就是在阿里山。

Ken: Really? Where did you go?
真的嗎？你們去了哪裡？

Mom: We watched the sunrise on the top of Alishan, and then hiked all the way to Fenchihu for the rice in bamboo.
我們在阿里山山頂看了日出，然後一路健行到奮起湖吃竹筒飯。

Ken: Wow! It sounds so romantic.
哇！聽起來真浪漫。

Mom: It was, especially because there were sakura flowers blooming everywhere.
是很浪漫，特別是那裡到處都是盛開的櫻花。

關鍵單字片語

7. **permit** [`pɜmɪt] 名 許可證

8. **the sea of clouds** 片 雲海

9. **hilltop** [`hɪlˌtɑp] 名 山頂

10. **Fenchihu** [`fəntʃɪhu] 名 奮起湖

11. **landscape** [`lændˌskep] 名 風景

12. **tea plantation** 片 茶園

11. 居高臨下：合歡山、雪山
Hehuanshan and Hsuehshan

MP3 071

萬用好句

1.	**Hehuanshan is an ideal place to escape from the summer heat.** 合歡山是避暑勝地。
2.	**Hehuanshan is one of the few subtropical areas where it snows.** 合歡山是亞熱帶地區少數會降雪的地點之一。
3.	**Can you recommend a place for me to stay in Hehuanshan?** 你能推薦我合歡山上的住宿地點嗎？
4.	**Hehuanshan always attracts many tourists who come to see the snow.** 合歡山總是吸引大量遊客前來賞雪。
5.	**Where can I get a road map of Hehuanshan?** 我可以在哪裡取得合歡山的交通指南呢？
6.	**Did you go to the Hsuehshan National Forest Recreation Area?** 你去了雪山國家森林遊樂區嗎？
7.	**Bird watching is also very popular in Hsuehshan.** 雪山的賞鳥活動也很受歡迎。
8.	**An Ma Mansion is the best place to find a visitor center, accommodations, and restaurants in one spot.** 鞍馬山莊有遊客中心、住宿地點和餐廳。
9.	**Only vehicles under nine passengers are allowed into Hsuehshan National Forest Recreation Area.** 乘坐九人以下的車輛才准進入雪山國家森林遊樂區。
10.	**You can stay in Cingjing if you are going to Hehuanshan.** 如果你要去合歡山，可以住宿清境。
11.	**Hehuanshan is a popular scenic spot for hiking enthusiasts.** 合歡山是受健行愛好者歡迎的景點之一。
12.	**The Central Cross-Island Highway makes it much easier to travel to Hehuanshan.** 中部橫貫公路使得前往合歡山的路途變得容易許多。

關鍵單字片語

1. **traffic guide** 片 交通指南

2. **spend** [spɛnd] 動 花費(時間、金錢)

3. **safety** [`seftɪ] 名 安全

4. **worth the effort** 片 值得一切努力

5. **route** [rut] 名 路徑

6. **ensure** [ɪn`ʃʊr] 動 確保

實境對話

Tina: Isn't this a nice picture!
這真是張美照！

Frank: I took it on the top of Hehuanshan with my friends.
這是我和朋友在合歡山山頂上拍的。

Tina: Hehuanshan? I didn't know you like hiking in the mountains.
合歡山？我不知道你喜歡高山健行。

Frank: That was my first time, and I learned a lot from it.
那是我第一次高山健行，而且我學到了很多。

Tina: What do you mean?
你的意思是？

Frank: I used to think hiking in mountains must be hard and boring, but it turned out to be extremely fun and exciting.
我以前覺得高山健行是件辛苦又無聊的事，但其實非常有趣又令人興奮。

Tina: Me, too. I thought hiking in mountains was for old men.
我也是，我覺得高山健行是老人家做的事。

Frank: Actually it took a lot of effort. It took us seven hours to get to the top, not to mention the fifteen kilogram backpacks we carried.
其實非常費力。光是抵達山頂就花了我們七個小時，更別說我們還背著十五公斤的行李。

Tina: Fifteen kilograms? What did you do there? Build a house?
十五公斤？你們是去那裡蓋房子嗎？

Frank: Kind of. We took a tent with us for the night, and some other equipment for cooking and safety.
差不多囉，我們帶了一個過夜用帳棚，和一些烹飪用具及安全裝備。

Tina: You must have been exhausted when you got to the top.
你到達山頂時鐵定是筋疲力盡。

Frank: I was, but the great scenery was totally worth it.
是啊，但一看到山頂的景色就覺得一切的辛苦都值得。

關鍵單字片語

7. **climbing gear** 片 登山設備

8. **stay alert on** 片 保持警戒

9. **peak** [pik] 名 尖端、頂峰

10. **challenging** [`tʃælɪndʒɪŋ] 形 有挑戰性的

11. **jeopardy** [`dʒɛpədɪ] 名 危險

12. **the backbone of Taiwan** 片 台灣之脊

12. 宜蘭：傳藝中心、太平山
Ilan

MP3
072

萬用好句

1.	**Ilan is a city with beautiful natural scenery and amicable people.** 宜蘭是個擁有美麗的自然景色與友善居民的城市。
2.	**Caoling Historic Trail is excellent for people who love hiking.** 草嶺古道對健行愛好者來說是極佳的選擇。
3.	**Gueishan Island is shaped like a sleeping turtle.** 龜山島的外形像隻沈睡的烏龜。
4.	**You can book a room in Taipingshan online.** 你可線上預約太平山住宿。
5.	**I don't want to put off my holiday to Taipingshan.** 我不想延後我的太平山假期。
6.	**I bought snow chains for our trip to Taipingshan.** 為了去太平山的旅行，我買了雪鏈。
7.	**Jiuzhize is an outdoor hot spring in Taipingshan.** 鳩之澤是位於太平山的戶外溫泉。
8.	**Camping is not allowed in the Taipingshan National Forest Recreation Area.** 太平山國家森林遊樂區裡不准露營。
9.	**The National Center for Traditional Arts in Ilan preserves traditional Taiwanese culture and arts, such as Taiwanese opera.** 宜蘭傳藝中心保存台灣傳統藝術，如歌仔戲。
10.	**Many artistic groups put on shows at regular intervals in the National Center for Traditional Arts.** 許多藝術團體定期在傳藝中心表演。
11.	**The tour to Taipingshan allowed me to escape from the chaos of the city.** 太平山之旅讓我遠離城市喧囂。
12.	**Can you recommend some must-see places in Ilan?** 你可以推薦一些宜蘭的必去景點嗎？

關鍵單字片語

1. **spread over** 片 遍佈…

2. **cultural estates** 片 文化資產

3. **Lanyang Plain** 片 蘭陽平原

4. **rejuvenate** [rɪˋdʒuvənet] 動 恢復精神

5. **meadowfoam** [ˋmɛdo͵fom] 名 菅芒花

6. **handicraft** [ˋhændɪ͵kræft] 名 手工藝

實境對話

Josh: Wendy, aren't you from Ilan?
溫蒂，你不是宜蘭人嗎？

Wendy: Yes. Why?
是啊，怎麼啦？

Josh: I am taking my girlfriend to Ilan. Where should we go?
我要帶女朋友去宜蘭，我們該去哪些地方呢？

Wendy: You could take her to Jiaoxi to enjoy the nice hot springs. You'll love it if you are tired of the city chaos.
你可以帶她去礁溪泡溫泉。若你對於城市喧囂感到厭倦，就會愛上那裡。

Josh: What about during the day? Where can we go?
那白天呢？我們可以去哪裡？

Wendy: I recommend Taipingshan if she likes nature.
如果她喜歡大自然，我推薦太平山。

Josh: But she hates any outdoor activities.
但她討厭戶外活動。

Wendy: Then you can go to the National Center for Traditional Arts. You can learn a lot about the history of the local arts there.
那你們可以去傳藝中心。在那裡，你可以學到許多關於當地藝術的歷史。

Josh: Good idea. Where else?
好主意。還有嗎？

Wendy: There are many souvenir shops and bakeries with local snacks in Jiaoxi. It's a good place for shopping.
礁溪有很多紀念品商店和當地糕餅店，是個逛街的好地方。

Josh: Sounds perfect! Thank you so much.
聽起來太棒了！非常謝謝你。

Wendy: You're welcome.
不客氣。

關鍵單字片語

7. **put on** 片 上演

8. **smoked duckling** 片 鴨賞

9. **souvenir shop** 片 紀念品店

10. **accessible** [æk`sɛsəbl] 形 可接近的

11. **Luodong night market** 片 羅東夜市

12. **leisurely** [`liʒəlɪ] 副 悠閒地

13. 花蓮：太魯閣國家公園
Hualien

MP3 073

萬用好句

1.	**Hualien is beautiful with its vast fields, rugged cliffs, and endless sky that melts into the sea.** 花蓮很美，有廣闊的平原、崎嶇的峭壁和無限延伸、與海平面融為一體的天空。
2.	**You need a permit to get into the Taroko Gorge National Park.** 你需要登山證才能進入太魯閣國家公園。
3.	**I participated in the Taroko International Marathon last year.** 我去年參加了太魯閣國際馬拉松。
4.	**Taroko National Park was established during the Japanese Colonial Period.** 太魯閣國家公園建立於日據時代。
5.	**I found the landscape in Taroko National Park stunning.** 我覺得太魯閣國家公園的風景美得驚人。
6.	**You have a variety of accommodation choices around Taroko National Park, including Buluowan and Tianxiang.** 太魯閣國家公園附近有許多住宿地點可選擇，如布洛灣和天祥。
7.	**What are some suggested tours of Taroko National Park? Are there any tips when touring Taroko National Park?** 太魯閣國家公園的旅遊建議景點及旅遊小秘訣有哪些？
8.	**Where can I take the free Taroko shuttle?** 我可以去哪裡搭乘太魯閣免費接駁車？
9.	**You can stay in the Tianxiang Youth Activity Center.** 你可以住宿天祥青年活動中心。
10.	**We learned about the local culture at the Buluowan Service Station.** 我們在布洛灣服務站學到了當地的文化。
11.	**You can take the Taroko Gorge Trail to the Eternal Spring Shrine, and then have your lunch at Buluowan.** 你可以沿太魯閣峽谷步道信步至長春祠，然後在布洛灣用午餐。

關鍵單字片語

1. **facial tattoo** 片 紋面(臉部刺青)

2. **aboriginal settlement** 片 原住民聚落

3. **vast** [væst] 形 廣闊的

4. **breeze** [briz] 名 微風

5. **rugged** [`rʌgɪd] 形 高低不平的

6. **Taroko Gorge** 片 太魯閣峽谷

實境對話

Fran: What sports do you do in your free time?
你空閒時做些什麼運動？

Larry: I usually jog. Sometimes I join a marathon for fun.
通常是慢跑，有時會因為好玩而參加馬拉松。

Fran: I have been thinking about starting jogging.
我正考慮開始慢跑。

Larry: Really? Then maybe you can take part in the Taroko International Marathon with me next month.
真的嗎？或許你可以和我一同參加下個月的太魯閣國際馬拉松。

Fran: It doesn't sound like something for a layman like me.
聽起來不像是我這種門外漢可以參加的。

Larry: Not at all. The Taroko International Marathon has different groups for professionals and novices. Besides, it will be wonderful to jog between the Taroko Gorges.
一點也不。太魯閣國際馬拉松分職業組和業餘組，且在峽谷間慢跑感覺一定很好。

Fran: Right. Jogging in such a beautiful place must be great.
也對，在這麼漂亮的地方慢跑鐵定很棒。

Larry: Just join me, and we can start training tomorrow.
和我一起去吧，我們明天就可以開始訓練。

Fran: How many kilometers do I have to run?
我要跑幾公里？

Larry: As a novice, you would be in the five-kilometer group.
身為新手，你可以參加五公里組。

Fran: Five kilometers? That sounds OK for me.
五公里？聽起來還可以。

Larry: Of course it will be! And don't forget you've got me as your coach!
當然！別忘了你有我這個教練！

關鍵單字片語

7. **trail** [trel] 名 小徑

8. **crafted** [`kræftɪd] 形 製作精美的

9. **Swallow Grotto** 片 燕子口

10. **cliff** [klɪf] 名 懸崖

11. **trail condition** 片 小徑路況

12. **tour suggestion** 片 旅遊建議

14. 出海去：澎湖
Penghu

MP3 074

萬用好句

1.	**The Kite Festival at Guanyin Pavilion is a popular international event for kite flyers from all over the world.** 小鳥兜風節是受全球風箏愛好者歡迎的國際盛會。
2.	**Penghu is a paradise for water sports lovers.** 澎湖是水上運動愛好者的天堂。
3.	**The Double-Heart of Stacked Stones in Shihu fishing village is a world-famous scenic spot.** 石滬漁村的「雙心石滬」是世界著名景點。
4.	**You can try the local cuisine in Magong city.** 你可在馬公享用當地美食。
5.	**Brown sugar cakes are a typical local snack.** 黑糖糕是當地特色小吃。
6.	**The local fresh seafood in Penghu is popular with tourists.** 澎湖在地的新鮮漁產很受遊客歡迎。
7.	**There is a Fireworks Festival in Penghu every summer.** 每年夏季澎湖會有花火節。
8.	**Why is Penghu also called "the Chrysanthemum Island"?** 為何澎湖又被稱作「菊島」？
9.	**Where can I take a boat to go night fishing?** 我可以在哪裡搭船夜釣？
10.	**During the Fireworks Festival, there will be a fireworks show every Monday and Thursday.** 花火節期間，每週一和四會有煙火秀。
11.	**You can't miss the Four-Eyed Well if you visit Penghu.** 造訪澎湖時，不能錯過「四眼井」。
12.	**Cactus pears are the local specialty of Penghu.** 仙人掌果是澎湖當地的特色食物。

關鍵單字片語

1. **refresh** [rɪ`frɛʃ] 動 消除…疲勞
2. **get tired of** 片 對…感到厭煩
3. **in season** 片 產季中
4. **brown sugar cake** 片 黑糖糕
5. **fly a kite** 片 放風箏
6. **windsurfing** [`wɪndˌsɜfɪŋ] 名 風帆衝浪

實境對話

Mr. Huang: Good morning. Welcome to Paradise Motorcycle Rental. How can I help you?
早安，歡迎光臨樂園機車出租店。需要什麼服務呢？

Jessica: Good morning. I want to rent a motorcycle for two days.
早安，我想租兩天機車。

Mr. Huang: OK. It's eight hundred dollars total. Please fill in this form, and here is the key.
好的，總共八百元。請填寫這張表格，這是車鑰匙。

Jessica: Thank you. Are there any must-see places on the island?
謝謝。這裡有什麼必去景點嗎？

Mr. Huang: You must visit the Double-Heart of Stacked Stones.
你一定要去參觀「雙心石滬」。

Jessica: I've heard about that. What about the Four-Eyed Well?
我有聽過。那「四眼井」如何？

Mr. Huang: Oh, it's worth visiting because of its 400 years of history.
喔，四眼井有超過四百年的悠久歷史，很值得一看。

Jessica: Is it far from here?
它離這裡很遠嗎？

Mr. Huang: Not at all. It will only take you five to ten minutes to drive there. And, be sure to try the brown sugar cakes.
一點也不，騎車只要五至十分鐘。另外，記得嚐嚐黑糖糕。

Jessica: No problem. I really love sweets.
沒問題，我非常喜愛甜點。

Mr. Huang: Enjoy your trip in Penghu. See you in two days.
好好享受你的澎湖之旅吧！兩天後見。

Jessica: I'm sure I will. Thank you.
我會的，謝謝你。

關鍵單字片語

7. **sea urchin** 片 海膽

8. **attraction** [ə`trækʃəl] 名 觀光景點

9. **marine** [mə`rin] 形 海生的、海產的

10. **animal** [`ænəml] 名 動物

11. **vessel** [`vɛsl] 名 船、艦

12. **be able to** 片 能夠⋯

15. 出海去：蘭嶼、綠島
Orchid Island and Green Island

MP3
075

萬用好句

1. Lanyu is like a natural park isolated on the ocean.
蘭嶼像是獨立於海上的天然公園。

2. You can feed the cute sika deer in the Formosa Sika Deer Biology Park.
你可在梅花鹿生態公園餵食可愛的梅花鹿。

3. Spending a night in the Green Island Prison must be interesting.
在綠島監獄過夜一定很有趣。

4. We rented a motorcycle to tour around Lanyu.
我們租了一輛摩托車以觀光蘭嶼。

5. How much is the rent for a 100 c.c. motorcycle for a day?
租一輛100cc的摩托車一天要多少錢？

6. We need to respect the Yami tribe's lifestyle on Lanyu Island.
我們要尊重蘭嶼雅美族的生活方式。

7. A traditional underground lodge is a good example of the wisdom of the Yami tribe for surviving in the hot humid weather.
傳統地下屋展示雅美族人如何因應溼熱的天氣。

8. It's amazing to see hundreds of flying fish jumping out of the ocean.
數百隻飛魚躍出海面，看起來很壯觀。

9. How can I sign up for the tour to catch flying fish at night?
我該如何參加夜間捕飛魚之旅？

10. What is the best season for traveling to Green Island?
前往綠島的最佳季節是何時？

11. Sunrise Hot Spring is an ocean-bed hot spring.
朝日溫泉是一座海床溫泉。

12. Seaweed meatballs are a local speciality of Green Island.
海藻肉圓是綠島當地的名產。

關鍵單字片語

1. **leisure** [`liʒɚ] 名 空閒時間

2. **speciality** [ˌspɛʃɪˈælətɪ] 名 名產

3. **tribal culture** 片 部落文化

4. **flying fish** 片 飛魚

5. **seaweed** [`siˌwid] 名 海藻

6. **motorcycle rental** 片 摩托車租賃

實境對話

Gary: Did you watch the Plungons' show this Tuesday?
你有看這週二的「撲蠬共」嗎？

Amanda: Do you mean "Super Taste"? Of course I did. The hosts are so funny, and they always go to the most interesting places.
你是說「食尚玩家」嗎？我當然有。他們超好笑的，而且總是帶你到最有趣的地方。

Gary: Too bad that I had to work overtime. Where did they go?
可惜我那晚加班。他們去了哪裡？

Amanda: They were on Green Island.
他們去了綠島。

Gary: Green Island? Isn't it an island prison?
綠島？不就是監獄之島嗎？

Amanda: That's not true at all. The Green Island even has one of the only three ocean-bed hot springs in the world.
完全不正確。世界上三座海床溫泉之一就在綠島。

Gary: So did they introduce any interesting scenic spots?
那他們介紹了什麼好玩的地方嗎？

Amanda: They went to the hot spring and the prison.
他們泡了溫泉，也去了監獄。

Gary: What? What did they do in the prison?
什麼？他們去監獄做什麼？

Amanda: Actually, the prison is partly open to the public now. And you can even stay in the prison B&B if you make a reservation.
事實上，目前監獄部分開放給遊客。而且如果你事先預約，還可以入住監獄民宿。

Gary: It sounds interesting and a bit weird.
聽起來既有趣又有點詭異。

Amanda: It is, but it could be the most unique tour of your life.
的確，但這會是你一生中最特別的旅程。

關鍵單字片語

7. **snorkel** [`snɔrkl] 動 浮潛

8. **hot spring** 片 溫泉

9. **coral bleaching** 片 珊瑚白化

10. **cruise** [krus] 動 漫遊

11. **Kuroshio** [kuˋloʃɪo] 名 黑潮

12. **commune** [kəˋmjun] 動 融為一體

1. 計畫出遊
Travel Plans
MP3 076

萬用好句

1. **Do you have any plans for the coming holiday?**
接下來的假期你有什麼計劃？

2. **If you book your tickets online, you can get low early-bird prices!**
若你線上訂票，可享有早鳥優惠價！

3. **It is essential for you to make sure that you have all your travel documents, including your passport and travel visa.**
確認是否備齊所有旅行文件是有必要的，包括你的護照及旅行簽證。

4. **Have you made hotel reservations yet?**
你訂好旅館了嗎？

5. **Perhaps it is a good idea to buy a guidebook or even a phrase book before your tour.**
或許在出發旅行前買本旅遊書、甚至是外語手冊會是個好主意。

6. **It is also a good idea to buy local currency in advance.**
預先購買當地貨幣也是個好主意。

7. **You can also buy some traveler's checks at a local bank, so you won't have to carry too much cash with you during your trip.**
你也可以在本地銀行購買旅行支票，這樣旅途中就不需攜帶太多現金。

8. **Do you have any places of interest in mind?**
你有沒有想去什麼地方玩？

9. **Joan always makes a list of must-see sights before her trip, just to make sure she has no regrets later.**
瓊安總在旅行前開一張想去景點的清單，以確保不會有任何遺憾。

10. **Are you planning to go anywhere this winter?**
你今年冬天要去什麼地方嗎？

11. **I usually travel light because I don't like carrying heavy bags.**
我通常輕便旅行，因為我不喜歡攜帶很重的袋子。

12. **What package tours do you have?**
你們提供哪些套裝行程？

關鍵單字片語

1. **itinerary** [,aɪˋtɪnə,rɛrɪ] 名 旅行計劃

2. **tour operator** 片 旅行社

3. **currency exchange** 片 匯兌

4. **guide book** 片 旅遊書

5. **phrase book** 片 外語手冊

6. **packing list** 片 打包清單

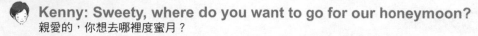

實境對話

Kenny: Sweety, where do you want to go for our honeymoon?
親愛的，你想去哪裡度蜜月？

Gina: Can we go to Paris? It's my dream to visit Paris with you.
我們可以去巴黎嗎？我夢想和你一起去巴黎。

Kenny: Good choice. Paris is considered a romantic city.
選得好。巴黎是個浪漫的城市。

Gina: Thank you, sweetheart. Which travel agency should we go to? Do you know any travel agents?
親愛的，謝謝你。我們要找哪一間旅行社？你有認識的嗎？

Kenny: Actually, I'm thinking about doing things myself.
事實上，我在考慮自己處理。

Gina: Are you sure? Isn't there too much to do?
你確定嗎？不會很繁瑣嗎？

Kenny: Not at all. I've checked some websites, and it looks like that's a more feasible solution to getting a better-quality tour.
一點也不會。我已研究過一些網站，這看來可行，而且會給我們品質更好的旅程。

Gina: Sounds great. Does that mean I can shop as much as I want?
聽起來很不錯。我是不是可以盡情的購物呢？

Kenny: Absolutely. I can book tickets for the on-sale season and the closest hotel to the shopping mall.
絕對可以。我可以預訂購物季的機票，和最靠近購物中心的旅館。

Gina: Really?
真的嗎？

Kenny: For you, I will do anything.
為了你，我什麼都願意做。

Gina: Oh, sweetheart. I love you so much.
噢，親愛的，我好愛你喔。

關鍵單字片語

7. **early-bird** [`ɝlɪ`bɝd] 形 早起者的

8. **travel insurance** 片 旅遊保險

9. **travel agency** 片 旅行社

10. **plan** [plæn] 動 名 計畫

11. **scenic spot** 片 景點

12. **map** [mæp] 名 地圖

2. 自助vs.跟團
Private or Packaging Tour
MP3 077

萬用好句

1.	**We should pay the tour guide 5 US dollars per day during the trip.** 旅途中，我們應每天支付導遊五元美金。
2.	**This is my first time traveling alone.** 這是我第一次獨自旅行。
3.	**Please keep an eye on your belongings during the trip.** 旅程中，請留意您的隨身行李。
4.	**The tour guide was so funny that everyone on the bus burst into laughter after hearing his joke.** 導遊很風趣，遊覽車上的每個人聽了他的笑話都開懷大笑。
5.	**Please meet up in the hotel lobby at five tomorrow morning.** 請於明天早上五點在旅館大廳集合。
6.	**Let's share travel information with other travelers in the lobby!** 我們和其他在大廳的旅客分享旅遊情報吧！
7.	**Maria and her newlywed husband are joining a five-day package tour to Italy for their honeymoon.** 瑪麗亞和新婚丈夫的蜜月旅行，是義大利五日套裝行程。
8.	**Kevin is such an experienced tour guide that he can always take his group to the best scenic spot.** 凱文是個很有經驗的導遊，他總是可以帶團前往最棒的景點。
9.	**Remember to keep your passport with you at all times.** 記得隨身攜帶護照。
10.	**Jenna is going to set off on a solo trip to France, Switzerland, and Germany next month.** 珍娜下個月即將前往法國、瑞士和德國自助旅行。
11.	**We have several tour packages. Which one do you prefer?** 我們有數款套裝行程，你較喜歡哪一個？
12.	**Do you know any great places to go around here?** 你知道這附近有什麼好玩的地方嗎？

關鍵單字片語

1. **solo traveler** 片 單獨旅行客

2. **car rental** 片 租車

3. **photo ID** 片 有照片的證件

4. **cautious** [ˋkɔʃəs] 形 謹慎的

5. **pickpocket** [ˋpɪk.pɑkɪt] 名 扒手

6. **keep an eye on** 片 小心、留意

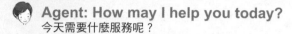

Agent: How may I help you today?
今天需要什麼服務呢？

Peggy: I'm looking for a tour for Easter. What do you have?
我在看復活節假期的行程。你們有些什麼團？

Agent: We have several tours during the Easter holiday. Where do you want to go, Korea or Bali Island?
我們有數個復活節假期團。你想去韓國還是峇里島？

Peggy: I don't know. Can you introduce the tours to me?
我不知道耶，你可以介紹一下嗎？

Agent: Of course. We have two tours to Korea featuring shopping or film locations for K-pop dramas. Both of them are very popular with young girls. I believe you could make many friends on the tour.
當然。我們有兩個到韓國購物和參觀韓劇景點的團，都很受年輕女性歡迎。相信你可以在旅程中交到很多朋友。

Peggy: What about Bali Island?
那峇里島呢？

Agent: Bali Island is for those who would like to escape from the city chaos. You can have a lulur spa treatment, which is a massage and rosebud bath.
峇里島是為那些想逃離都市喧囂者準備的。你可以享受露露三溫暖——按摩加玫瑰浴。

Peggy: It sounds very attractive.
聽起來很吸引人。

Agent: Indeed it is. And now we offer a special discount for anyone who pays in cash.
的確，而且我們現在提供付現客人特別折扣。

Peggy: Great! I can pay in cash. When is the departure date?
太棒了！我可以付現。出發日是何時？

關鍵單字片語

7. **go sightseeing** 片 觀光

8. **K-pop drama** 片 熱門韓劇

9. **day trip** 片 一日遊

10. **money belt** 片 貼身錢袋

11. **tip** [tɪp] 名 小費 動 給小費

12. **tour guide** 片 導遊

3.機上閒談
Plane Chat
MP3
078

萬用好句

1. **Can I see your boarding pass, please?**
可以看一下您的登機証嗎？

2. **I need a hand putting my luggage into the overhead compartment.**
我需要人幫忙把行李放入座位上方的行李櫃。

3. **Excuse me. Can I have some more bread?**
不好意思，可以再給我一些麵包嗎？

4. **Would you like something to drink?**
您想喝點什麼？

5. **When does the in-flight duty-free sale start?**
機上免稅品何時開始銷售？

6. **Do you need a Customs and Immigration Form?**
您需要一張入境報關表嗎？

7. **Since it's a short flight, the flight attendants will be serving light refreshments, instead of a meal.**
由於本航班為短程飛行，機組員將提供小點心，而不提供正餐。

8. **You are in row eleven, seat C.**
您的座位在第十一排的 C 座。

9. **You can always ask the flight attendant for a pillow if you're tired.**
如果累了，您可隨時向空服員索取枕頭。

10. **It is a little bit cold in the cabin. Can I have an extra blanket?**
機艙內有點冷。可以再給我一條毯子嗎？

11. **The lavatory is occupied.**
洗手間有人。

12. **Please remain in your seat until we taxi to the gate.**
在飛機滑行至機艙口前，請您留在座位上。

關鍵單字片語

1. **reading light** 片 閱讀燈

2. **flight attendant** 片 空服員

3. **seat number** 片 座位號碼

4. **tray table** 片 用餐盤

5. **upright** [`ʌp͵raɪt] 形 直立的

6. **seat belt** 片 安全帶

實境對話

Flight Attendant: Madam, what can I get for you?
女士，有什麼需要幫忙的嗎？

Karen: It's a bit cold in the cabin. Can I have another blanket?
機艙裡有點冷，我可以再要一條毯子嗎？

Flight Attendant: No problem. Is that all?
沒問題。這樣就可以了嗎？

Karen: It would be great if I could have some hot tea, too.
如果可以再給我杯熱茶就太好了。

Flight Attendant: Sure. I'll bring your hot tea in a few minutes.
好的，熱茶馬上來。

Flight Attendant: We have beef, chicken and fish today. Which one do you prefer?
我們今天有牛肉、雞肉和魚肉。您想要哪一種？

Karen: Fish, please.
請給我魚肉。

Flight Attendant: Can I get you anything to drink?
您要喝點什麼？

Karen: Do you have juice?
你們有果汁嗎？

Flight Attendant: Yes, we have apple juice and pineapple juice. Which one do you prefer?
有的，我們有蘋果汁和鳳梨汁。您要哪一種？

Karen: Pineapple juice. Thank you.
鳳梨汁，謝謝。

Flight Attendant: You're welcome.
不客氣。

關鍵單字片語

7. **aisle** [aɪl] 名 走道

8. **emergency exit** 片 緊急逃生口

9. **assist** [əˋsɪst] 動 協助

10. **fasten** [ˋfæsn̩] 動 繫緊

11. **luggage** [ˋlʌgɪdʒ] 名 行李

12. **service** [ˋsɝvɪs] 名 服務

4. 出境入境
Departure and Arrival

MP3 079

萬用好句

1. **Please have your passport out when you go through the security.**
通過安檢處時,請出示您的護照。

2. **Do you have anything to declare?**
你需要申報任何物品嗎?

3. **What is the purpose of your visit?**
你這次旅行的目的是?

4. **How long will you stay in this country?**
你會在這個國家待多久?

5. **Have you ever been to this country before?**
你曾來過這個國家嗎?

6. **Tourists are not allowed to stay beyond three months.**
旅客不得停留超過三個月。

7. **May I take a look at your passport and Customs declaration form?**
我可以看一下您的護照與申報表嗎?

8. **Which carrousel will our luggage be at?**
我們的行李會在幾號轉盤?

9. **Please make sure you have your luggage claim ticket with you.**
請確認您持有行李收據。

10. **I am sorry, but no liquids over 100ml can be taken on board.**
很抱歉,但超過一百毫升的液體不得帶上飛機。

11. **Please take off your boots before passing through the X-ray checkpoint.**
通過 X 光掃瞄機前,請脫掉您的靴子。

12. **Do you know where I can get a wheelchair?**
你知道我可以到哪裡取得輪椅嗎?

 關鍵單字片語

1. **liquid** [`lɪkwɪd] 名 液體

2. **terminal** [`tɜmən!] 名 航空站

3. **counter** [`kauntə] 名 櫃檯

4. **passport** [`pæs,port] 名 護照

5. **visa** [`vizə] 名 簽證

6. **destination** [,dɛstə`neʃən] 名 目的地

實境對話

Customs Officer: Can I see your passport, please?
可以看一下你的護照嗎？

Mandy: Yes. Here you are.
好的，在這裡。

Customs Officer: What is the purpose of your trip?
你這次旅行的目的是？

Mandy: I am visiting my college friend in New Jersey.
我到紐澤西拜訪我的大學朋友。

Customs Officer: How long will you stay?
你會待多久？

Mandy: About a month. Here is my return ticket.
大約一個月。這是我的回程票。

Customs Officer: OK. Are you staying with your friend while you are here, or are you staying in a hotel?
好的。你會和朋友一起住，還是住旅館？

Mandy: I am going to stay with my friend and her family.
我會和朋友還有她的家人一起住。

Customs Officer: Do you have anything to declare?
你有物品要申報嗎？

Mandy: No.
沒有。

Customs Officer: OK. You may proceed. Enjoy your trip.
好的。你可以離開了。祝你旅途愉快。

Mandy: Thank you.
謝謝。

Customs Officer: Next!
下一位！

關鍵單字片語

7. **X-ray machine** 片 X 光掃描機

8. **declare** [dɪˋklɛr] 動 申報

9. **Customs** [ˋkʌstəmz] 名 海關

10. **flight number** 片 班機號碼

11. **baggage claim** 片 行李提領

12. **contraband** [ˋkɑntrə͵bænd] 名 違禁品

萬用好句

1.	**I would like to book two adjoining rooms for my parents and myself.** 我要替爸媽和自己訂兩間相鄰的房間。
2.	**When is check-out time?** 退房時間是什麼時候？
3.	**The bellboy will take your bags to your room for you now.** 現在門僮會替您把行李拿進房裡。
4.	**Your room number is 406. Please take the lift on the right to the fourth floor.** 您的房號是406，請搭乘右手邊的電梯至四樓。
5.	**Do you still have any lakeview rooms?** 你們還有湖景房嗎？
6.	**I am afraid that the hotel is fully booked tonight.** 今晚飯店恐怕是客滿了。
7.	**You can check in anytime after two in the afternoon.** 下午兩點後可隨時入住。
8.	**We only have one vacancy left, and it is a double room.** 我們只剩一間雙人房。
9.	**What time would you like your wake-up call?** 您希望明天早上幾點叫您起床？
10.	**The towels in the room are hotel property and should not be taken when you leave.** 房間內的毛巾屬飯店財產，離開時不得帶走。
11.	**How much is a twin room?** 兩張單人床的房間多少錢？
12.	**I would like a room with a king-size bed.** 我要一間加大床的房間。

 關鍵單字片語

1. **check in** 片 入住

2. **check out** 片 退房

3. **king-size bed** 片 加大床

4. **amenities** [ə`minətɪz] 名 便利設施

5. **double room** 片 雙人房

6. **brochure** [bro`ʃur] 名 小手冊

Receptionist: Welcome to Grand Plaza Hotel. May I help you?
歡迎光臨格蘭登大飯店。有什麼可以為您服務的？

Larry: How much is a double room for one night?
雙人房一晚多少錢？

Receptionist: We have 2 types of double rooms. A lakeview room is 2,500 dollars, and a mountain view room is 2,200 dollars.
我們有兩種雙人房。湖景房是兩千五百元，山景房則是兩千兩百元。

Larry: Can I see Sun Moon Lake from the lakeview room?
我可從湖景房看到日月潭嗎？

Receptionist: Of course. A complimentary breakfast is also included.
當然；另附免費早餐。

Larry: Then, I will take the lakeview room. Can I check in now?
那給我湖景房。我現在可以入住嗎？

Receptionist: I am sorry, but the room won't be ready until three in the afternoon.
很抱歉，房間下午三點才會準備好。

Larry: Really? But I would like to take the two o'clock cable car.
真的嗎？但我想搭乘兩點鐘的纜車。

Receptionist: You can put your luggage in our storage room, and pick it up later when you check in.
您可將行李寄放於儲藏室，稍晚入住時再取回。

Larry: Do I have to pay to store my luggage?
寄放行李需要付費嗎？

Receptionist: No, it's a free service for our guests.
不用，這是提供給每位住客的免費服務。

Larry: That's awesome!
太棒了！

關鍵單字片語

7. **adjoining** [ə`dʒɔɪnɪŋ] 形 鄰接的

8. **wake-up call** 片 電話叫醒服務

9. **cable car** 片 纜車

10. **include** [ɪn`klud] 動 包含

11. **storage room** 片 儲藏室

12. **charge** [`tʃɑrdʒ] 動 收費

6.城市之旅
City Tour
MP3 081

萬用好句

1.	**Never leave your bag unattended in a train station.** 車站內，請隨時留意您的行李。
2.	**How much is a round-trip ticket to Paddington?** 到派丁頓站的來回票多少錢？
3.	**There are many buildings from the Renaissance era in the city.** 這座城市裡有許多文藝復興時期的建築。
4.	**While we were on our way to the subway station, a strange building caught our eye.** 在我們前往地鐵站的途中，一棟奇特的建築物吸引我們的注意。
5.	**Excuse me. Where is the nearest subway station?** 不好意思，離這裡最近的地鐵站在哪裡？
6.	**How long will it take if we travel by tube to King's Cross?** 若我們搭乘地鐵到國王十字站，要花多久時間？
7.	**If you want to visit the Louvre, take the metro to the Louvre Rivoli stop.** 若你想參觀羅浮宮，可搭乘地鐵至羅浮宮西摩里站。
8.	**Do you know the closest tube station to the British Museum?** 你知道離大英博物館最近的地鐵站嗎？
9.	**The train comes every five minutes.** 火車每五分鐘來一班。
10.	**The train was late due to an accident in Times Square Station.** 火車因時代廣場站的事故而誤點。
11.	**The subway is definitely the cheapest and the most convenient way to tour around a big city.** 地鐵絕對是在大城市裡最便宜也最便利的旅遊方式。
12.	**A day pass is available to tourists for $5, which allows you to take the train an unlimited number of times within a 24-hour period.** 遊客可購買五美元的單日通行票，可於二十四小時內不限次數乘坐。

關鍵單字片語

1. **subway** [`sʌb‚we] 名 地鐵
2. **metropolis** [mə`trɑplɪs] 名 都會區
3. **suburban** [sə`bɜbən] 形 郊區的
4. **on schedule** 片 準點
5. **platform** [`plæt‚fɔrm] 名 月台
6. **kiosk** [kɪ`ɑsk] 名 (月台上的)小店

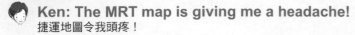

Ken: The MRT map is giving me a headache!
捷運地圖令我頭疼！

Gina: Calm down. What's wrong?
冷靜點，怎麼了？

Ken: My friend from France is visiting me next month. I am planning a Taipei tour for us. I'm thinking about taking the MRT.
我的法國朋友下個月要來訪，我正在規劃台北之旅，我想搭捷運。

Gina: That's a great choice. You can tour around Taipei in a not only cheap but also efficient way.
那是個好選擇。你可以用既便宜又有效率的方式觀光台北。

Ken: I know, but the MRT map is so complicated that I don't know what to do. I don't want to waste a lot of time or money on our trip.
我知道，但捷運地圖太複雜了，我不知該怎麼辦。這趟旅行我不想浪費太多時間和金錢。

Gina: What about getting an MRT pass?
買張捷運通行證如何？

Ken: What is that?
那是什麼？

Gina: It's a day pass, which allows you to take the MRT as many times as you want in a single day.
那是張單日通行證，你可在一天內不限次數搭乘捷運。

Ken: Is that true? Even if I have to take it more than 10 times a day?
真的嗎？即使我一天內要搭乘超過十次？

Gina: Yes, and no extra fees will be charged. In addition, if you have to take a bus, you get a discount if you have an MRT pass.
沒錯，且不收取額外費用。而且如果你得搭巴士，也會有折扣。

Ken: That's awesome! Thank you for sharing this.
太棒了！謝謝你告訴我。

關鍵單字片語

7. **second class** 片 二等艙

8. **conductor** [kənˋdʌktə] 名 車掌

9. **return ticket** 片 來回票

10. **fare** [fɛr] 名 票價

11. **locker** [ˋlɑkə] 名 置物櫃

12. **one-way ticket** 片 單程票

7.漫步鄉間
Trip to the Country
MP3
082

萬用好句

1.	**The Napa Winery offers tours to get an inside look at wine-making.** 納帕酒莊提供深度釀酒之旅。
2.	**How many kinds of wine can I taste during my visit to the winery?** 造訪酒莊期間,我可以品嚐多少種酒類?
3.	**You can rent a car and explore the countryside.** 你可以租輛車探索鄉間。
4.	**You can also enjoy a multi-course lunch at a scenic winery with other guests from all over the world.** 你也可以和來自世界各地的其他客人,在風景優美的釀酒區享受多道餐點的午餐。
5.	**Strolling through the grape vineyards and smelling the fragrance of mellow wine is one of the biggest delights in life.** 漫步在葡萄園區,聞著醇厚的酒香,是人生一大樂事。
6.	**We have a winery boutique where you can buy all kinds of wine and champagne.** 在我們的釀酒廠禮品店,您可買到各種酒和香檳。
7.	**What is so special about this winery tour?** 這個酒廠之旅有何特別之處?
8.	**Traveling in the countryside is always relaxing.** 到鄉間旅行總是好放鬆。
9.	**It is the perfect time for family bonding while enjoying a country tour.** 享受鄉村之旅,是聯繫家庭感情的絕佳時機。
10.	**How about a trip to the country to get closer to Mother Nature?** 何不來段鄉村之旅,與大自然更親近?
11.	**I'm looking for a quick getaway to a beautiful countryside this fall.** 我正在尋找這個秋天可以前往旅遊的美麗鄉間。
12.	**Mr. Watson's winery has a cheese and wine-tasting for all the guests.** 華生先生的酒莊提供客人起司和品酒。

關鍵單字片語

1. **winery** [`waɪnərɪ] 名 酒莊

2. **brew** [bru] 動 釀造、釀製

3. **cottage** [`katɪdʒ] 名 農舍

4. **farm** [farm] 名 農場

5. **vineyard** [`vɪnjəd] 名 葡萄園

6. **getaway** [`gɛtə,we] 名 逍遙遊

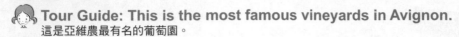
實境對話

Tour Guide: This is the most famous vineyards in Avignon.
這是亞維農最有名的葡萄園。

Mr. Watson: Wow, it's so beautiful.
哇，太漂亮了。

Tour Guide: Yes, it is. These vineyards are not only famous for having the best-quality wine, but are also the most beautiful.
沒錯。這座葡萄園因品質良好的酒和絕佳的風景聞名。

Mr. Watson: Can we take pictures?
我們可以拍照嗎？

Tour Guide: Of course. You will have one hour to tour the vineyards, and there is wine-tasting at the entrance.
當然可以。您有一小時的時間遊覽葡萄園，並可在入口處品酒。

Mr. Watson: Wine-tasting? Is that for free?
品酒？是免費的嗎？

Tour Guide: Wine-tasting is totally free, and if you find something great to bring back home, you can purchase it at the boutique on the right.
品酒是完全免費的。另外，若您發現不錯的伴手禮，可在右手邊的紀念品商店購買。

Mr. Watson: And the brochure says there is a guided wine-making tour available as well?
手冊上說有個釀酒導覽，是嗎？

Tour Guide: Yes, you can register at the front desk. They will take you to the wine cellar and vineyards, and you can learn about different kinds of grapes.
沒錯，您可在前方櫃枱登記，他們會帶您前往酒窖和葡萄園，認識各種不同的葡萄。

Mr. Watson: It sounds great.
聽起來很棒。

關鍵單字片語

7. **countryside** [`kʌntrɪ‚saɪd] 名 鄉間

8. **course** [kors] 名 一道菜

9. **meadow** [`mɛdo] 名 草地

10. **produce** [prə`djus] 動 製造

11. **pack a picnic** 片 打包野餐

12. **wine tasting** 片 品酒

8. **浪漫歐洲**
Europe

MP3
083

萬用好句

1.	**Edinburgh, the capital of Scotland, has been a tourist hot spot for a long time.** 蘇格蘭的首都愛丁堡，一直是熱門的觀光景點。
2.	**Let's enjoy traditional English afternoon tea at the Ritz Hotel.** 我們到麗池飯店享用傳統英式下午茶吧！
3.	**Have you heard of Loch Ness and Nessie?** 你聽說過尼斯湖和水怪嗎？
4.	**The changing of the Guard at Buckingham Palace takes place at 11:30 every other day from May till the end of July.** 白金漢宮的守衛交接，從五月至七月底，每兩天於十一點半舉行。
5.	**The Castle of Versailles used to be a royal castle and is one of the most popular scenic spots now.** 凡爾賽宮曾是皇家城堡，是現在最熱門的觀光景點之一。
6.	**There are more than thirty museums in Paris.** 巴黎擁有超過三十座博物館。
7.	**Excuse me. Can you tell me where the Eiffel Tower is?** 不好意思，可以告訴我艾菲爾鐵塔在哪裡嗎？
8.	**It takes only two hours by Eurostar from Paris to London.** 搭乘歐洲之星列車，從巴黎到倫敦僅需兩小時。
9.	**In the countryside villages in England, such as Cotswolds, you can enjoy a tranquil atmosphere and an old-fashioned spirit.** 在英國的鄉村小鎮如柯茲窩，你可以享受寧靜氣氛和古典情懷。
10.	**Do you know where the Sherlock Holmes Museum is located?** 你知道福爾摩斯博物館在哪嗎？
11.	**David and I are going to the museum to appreciate the Mona Lisa.** 大衛和我要去博物館欣賞《蒙娜麗莎的微笑》。
12.	**If you love Peter Rabbit, you shouldn't miss the Lake District.** 若你喜愛彼得兔，你絕不能錯過湖區。

關鍵單字片語

1. **Windsor Castle** 片 溫莎堡
2. **afternoon tea** 片 下午茶
3. **cultural heritage** 片 文化遺產
4. **Buckingham Palace** 片 白金漢宮
5. **double-decker** [`dʌbl`dɛkɚ] 名 雙層巴士
6. **fascinating** [`fæsn͵etɪŋ] 形 迷人的

實境對話

Frank: Welcome to London, the greatest city in the world!
歡迎到世界上最棒的城市——倫敦！

Penny: I'm so excited! Where are you taking me today?
我好興奮！你今天要帶我去哪裡？

Frank: I am going to show you the best of London. Do you have your Oyster card with you?
我要讓你看見最棒的倫敦。你有帶蚵仔卡(地鐵預付卡)嗎？

Penny: Check!
有！

Frank: OK. Let's go to King's Cross Station first!
好。那我們先出發到國王十字站吧！

Penny: Is that where the British Museum is?
是不是大英博物館那站？

Frank: No, but it's even cooler! We are going to Hogwarts!
不是，但比那更酷！我們要去霍格華茲。

Penny: What? Are you kidding me?
什麼？你在跟我開玩笑嗎？

Frank: Not at all. Do you remember Platform 9 ¾ where Harry Potter and his friends got onto the Hogwarts Express?
才不是。你記得哈利波特和他的朋友搭乘霍格華茲列車的「九又四分之三月台」嗎？

Penny: Of course! That scene really impressed me.
當然！那場景讓我印象深刻。

Frank: It's right at King's Cross Station, and there is even a trolley in the wall that looks like it's taking you to Hogwarts.
那場景就在國王十字站。那裡的牆上還有個推車，看起來就像要帶你前往霍格華茲。

Peter: Wow! What are we waiting for? Let's go now!
哇！那我們還在等什麼？現在就出發吧！

關鍵單字片語

7. **express** [ɪk`sprɛs] 名 快車

8. **Stonehenge** [`ston`hɛndʒ] 名 史前巨石柱群

9. **Eurostar** [`juro`star] 名 歐洲之星列車

10. **discover** [dɪs`kʌvɚ] 動 發現

11. **village** [`vɪlɪdʒ] 名 村莊

12. **park** [park] 名 公園

9. 悠遊美國
The U.S.A.
MP3
084

萬用好句

1. **Times Square is always crowded on New Year's Eve.**
除夕夜，時代廣場總是擠滿民眾。

2. **New York, the Big Apple, is home to the New York Knicks.**
紐約又稱作「大蘋果」，是紐約尼克隊的家鄉。

3. **The Statue of Liberty is a famous New York City landmark.**
自由女神像是紐約市著名的地標。

4. **What is the best way to get to the Statue of Liberty?**
到自由女神像的最佳方式是？

5. **If you're lucky, you might run into Tom Cruise in Beverly Hills.**
如果你運氣好，或許可在比佛利山莊遇見湯姆克魯斯。

6. **Taking the hop-on hop-off bus is the fastest way to tour the city.**
搭乘觀光巴士是遊覽市區最快的方式。

7. **Los Angeles is a dynamic city featuring a wide variety of tours and attractions.**
活力之都洛杉磯，有著各種觀光行程和景點。

8. **Strolling down the sandy beach and simply sitting back and relaxing is one of the best things you can do in the Los Angeles area.**
沿著沙灘散步、任意坐下放鬆，是你可以在洛杉磯享受的樂事之一。

9. **Do you know any interesting restaurants in Los Angeles?**
你知道洛杉磯有哪家有意思的餐廳嗎？

10. **Maybe we can schedule a trip to Yellowstone this summer.**
今年夏天，我們或許可以安排一趟黃石公園之旅。

11. **Universal Studios is a popular theme park featuring scenes from movies where you can get a sense of filmmaking.**
環球影城是個受歡迎的電影主題樂園。在那裡，你可以體驗電影製作。

12. **What's your favorite place in New York?**
你最喜歡紐約的哪個地方？

關鍵單字片語

1. **Broadway** [`brɔdˌwe] 名 百老匯

2. **stadium** [`stedɪəm] 名 體育館

3. **save** [sev] 動 節省

4. **theme park** 片 主題樂園

5. **city pass** 片 城市通行證

6. **skyscraper** [`skaɪˌskrepɚ] 名 摩天大樓

實境對話

Sandy: What are your plans for summer vacation?
你的暑假有什麼計劃？

Josh: I am taking part in an exchange program.
我要參加交換學生計劃。

Sandy: Cool! Where are you going?
酷！你要去哪裡？

Josh: New York.
紐約。

Sandy: Really? I love New York!
真的嗎？我愛紐約！

Josh: Have you ever been there before? Can you recommend some must-see attractions?
你曾去過那裡嗎？可以推薦我一些必去景點嗎？

Sandy: I went to New York two years ago. You can visit the Metropolitan Museum of Art. It's a great museum.
我兩年前去過紐約。你可以去參觀大都會博物館，那是個很棒的博物館。

Josh: Can you recommend any great musicals?
可以推薦我好看的音樂劇嗎？

Sandy: Rent is my favorite, and you must go to Time Square and Central Park. Both are very popular scenic spots.
《吉屋出租》是我的最愛。你一定要去時代廣場和中央公園，這兩處都是很受歡迎的景點。

Josh: OK. Let me write that down. Is there anything else?
好的，讓我寫下來。還有別的嗎？

Sandy: It's also a great opportunity to catch Linsanity! Go see the Knicks and Jeremy Lin!
這也是個趕上林來瘋熱潮的佳機！去看看尼克隊和林書豪吧！

Josh: Of course! It's at the top of my must-do list!
當然！那是我第一件必辦之事！

關鍵單字片語

7. **plenty of** 片 許多

8. **crowded** [`kraʊdɪd] 形 擁擠的

9. **on your visit** 片 在你造訪時

10. **entrance fee** 片 入場費

11. **hop-on hop-off bus** 片 觀光巴士

12. **Statue of Liberty** 片 自由女神像

181

10. 非洲風情
Africa
MP3
085

萬用好句

1.	**Seeing the great migration on an African safari is the chance of a lifetime.** 到非洲草原觀賞動物大遷徙是一生一次的機會。
2.	**Would you like to stay at a hotel, or in a tent while on safari?** 你的非洲之旅想住旅館，還是草原上的帳篷？
3.	**Cape Town is the second-most populous city in South Africa, where you can find many luxury hotels.** 開普頓是南非第二大城，你可以在那找到許多奢華旅館。
4.	**We were just two feet away from the lion, which made my heart pump hard relentlessly.** 我們離獅子只有兩英呎遠，這讓我的心臟跳個不停。
5.	**You can hear the calls of wild animals on an African safari.** 你可以在旅程中於非洲大草原上聽見野生動物的呼喚。
6.	**Mary longs to take her honeymoon in the African wilderness.** 瑪麗想去野性非洲度蜜月。
7.	**How much is a guided safari tour?** 導遊陪同的大草原旅行團要多少錢？
8.	**This agency specializes in tailor-made African tours for the rich.** 這家旅行社專為富有客戶量身打造非洲之旅。
9.	**Do you have any recommendations regarding a trip to Africa?** 你對非洲之旅有什麼建議嗎？
10.	**African safaris are best when the animals are easy to find and in dense numbers.** 非洲狩獵之旅最棒的一點，是可以輕易觀察到數量龐大的動物。
11.	**Is going on an African safari dangerous?** 參加非洲狩獵之旅危險嗎？
12.	**There are many wildlife parks and reserves in South Africa.** 南非有許多野生動物公園和保護區。

關鍵單字片語

1. **safari** [səˋfɑrɪ] 名 非洲(狩獵)旅行

2. **hunting** [ˋhʌntɪŋ] 名 狩獵

3. **zebra** [ˋzibrə] 名 斑馬

4. **relentless** [rɪˋlɛntlɪs] 形 不間斷的

5. **nocturnal** [nɑkˋtɝnḷ] 形 夜行性的

6. **wilderness** [ˋwɪldənɪs] 名 荒野

實境對話

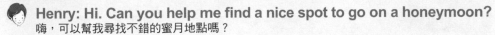

Henry: Hi. Can you help me find a nice spot to go on a honeymoon?
嗨，可以幫我尋找不錯的蜜月地點嗎？

Agent: Sure. How many days are you taking for your honeymoon?
當然好，你們蜜月想去幾天？

Henry: About two weeks, and I'm thinking about going abroad.
大約兩週，我考慮要出國。

Agent: OK. How about Africa? It's become very popular recently.
好。非洲如何？最近那裡很受歡迎。

Henry: Africa? But I don't want to go hunting.
非洲？但我不想打獵。

Agent: Africa is more than that. It's a natural paradise. Imagine having lunch while monkeys swing by your side and then falling to sleep with the owls and giraffes, far away from the chaos of the city. Just you, your lovely new wife, and Mother Nature.
非洲不只能打獵。那裡是自然界天堂。想像猴子晃到你身旁陪你吃午餐，貓頭鷹和長頸鹿伴你入眠，遠離城市喧囂。只有你、你親愛的新婚妻子，和大自然。

Henry: Sounds perfect.
聽起來很棒。

Agent: Doesn't it? We also provide a honeymoon suite and a professional local guide who can take you deep into the jungle.
可不是嗎？我們也提供蜜月套房和專業當地導遊，可帶你深入叢林。

Henry: Will I have any chance to see lions and leopards?
我有機會看到獅子和豹嗎？

Agent: Of course, and many other animals. It will be the closest that you've ever been to wild animals.
當然有，以及許多其他的動物。這會是你和野生動物靠最近的機會。

Henry: I hope my fiancée doesn't faint at the sight of a real lion.
希望我未婚妻在看到真的獅子時不會昏倒。

關鍵單字片語

7. **national park** 片 國家公園

8. **gorilla** [gəˋrɪlə] 名 大猩猩

9. **survive** [səˋvaɪv] 動 存活

10. **game** [gem] 名 獵物

11. **jeep** [dʒip] 名 吉普車

12. **leopard** [ˋlɛpəd] 名 豹

11. 中東探索
The Middle East
MP3 086

萬用好句

1.	**Do you want to join us for a trip to Dubai next month?** 下個月想和我們一起去杜拜嗎？
2.	**Dubai is a city full of contrasts, where you can find traditional Arabian culture and modern skyscrapers.** 杜拜是座充滿對比的城市，可見傳統阿拉伯文化和現代摩天大樓。
3.	**You can hire a local guide and rent a jeep to cross the desert.** 你可僱用當地導遊和租用吉普車橫越沙漠。
4.	**Though it is very hot in Dubai, you can go skiing and have a snowball fight in the indoor ski dome.** 雖然杜拜非常熱，你卻可以在室內滑雪場滑雪和打雪仗。
5.	**It is improper for women to expose any part of their body in Arabian countries.** 在阿拉伯國家，女性裸露身體的任何部分是不恰當的。
6.	**It is illegal to take photos of passersby in most Arabian countries.** 在多數阿拉伯國家，拍攝路人的照片是違法的。
7.	**Females should wear a headscarf before entering a mosque.** 進入清真寺前，女性應穿戴頭紗。
8.	**Sand-surfing is a popular sport because it is very exciting.** 滑沙因為很刺激而成為熱門運動。
9.	**Pork is not served in most Middle Eastern restaurants.** 大部分中東餐廳不供應豬肉。
10.	**Don't forget to bring the sunblock and your sunglasses with you.** 別忘了帶防曬乳和太陽眼鏡。
11.	**Women cannot wear miniskirts in Arabian countries.** 在阿拉伯國家，女人不能穿著迷你裙。
12.	**What customs should I be aware of if I am going to Dubai for a trip?** 若我去杜拜旅遊，我應知道哪些習俗？

關鍵單字片語

1. **Abu Dhabi** 片 阿布達比

2. **helicopter** [`hɛlɪ͵kɑptɚ] 名 直升機

3. **luxurious** [lʌg`ʒʊrɪəs] 形 奢華的

4. **conflict** [`kɑnflɪkt] 名 衝突

5. **experience** [ɪk`spɪrɪəns] 動 體驗

6. **mosque** [mɑsk] 名 清真寺

實境對話

Dan: Sandy, why are you wearing a miniskirt?
珊蒂，你為什麼穿著迷你裙？

Sandy: Isn't it cute on me? It's my favorite holiday clothing.
我穿起來很可愛吧？這是我度假時最愛穿的。

Dan: Don't you know that we are now in Dubai?
你不知道我們在杜拜嗎？

Sandy: So what? What's that got to do with my skirt?
那又如何？這跟我的裙子有什麼關係嗎？

Dan: In most Arabian countries, it's improper for women to expose any part of their body, let alone wear a miniskirt.
在多數阿拉伯國家，女性裸露身體是很不恰當的，更別提穿著迷你裙了。

Sandy: I don't care how they see me. It's just who I am: a visitor from a non-Arabian country.
我不在乎人們怎麼看我。這就是我，一個來自非阿拉伯國家的觀光客。

Dan: OK. But you just can't wear that today.
好吧，但你今天就是不能這樣穿。

Sandy: Why not?
為什麼不能？

Dan: We are going to a mosque today, and no woman without a robe can enter.
我們今天要去清真寺，女性得穿長袍才能進去。

Sandy: Really? What should I do now?
真的嗎？那我現在該怎麼辦？

Dan: I think you'd better go back to your room and change.
我想你最好回房間換個衣服。

Sandy: OK. I'll be right back.
好的，我馬上回來。

★ 關鍵單字片語

7. **ride a hot balloon** 片 搭乘熱氣球

8. **sightseeing tour** 片 觀光之旅

9. **Arabian** [əˋrebɪən] 形 阿拉伯的

10. **extremely** [ɪkˋstrimlɪ] 副 極端地

11. **camel** [ˋkæml] 名 駱駝

12. **duration** [djʊˋreʃən] 名 期間

12. 行腳中國
China

MP3 087

萬用好句

1.	The Yangtze River is the longest in China and the third longest in the world, and it offers a perfect escape for nature lovers. 長江是中國最長、世界第三長河，也是自然愛好者的絕佳去處。
2.	The Great Wall of China was built thousands of years ago. 中國的萬里長城建造於數千年前。
3.	The Great Wall of China was built for border control and defense. 萬里長城出於邊境控管和防禦目的而建造。
4.	The Great Wall of China is listed as a World Heritage site. 萬里長城被列為世界遺產。
5.	Rumor has it that the Great Wall can be seen from space. 謠傳可從外太空看見萬里長城。
6.	Being an important military gateway, Shanhaiguan Pass in Hebei is nicknamed "the First Pass of the World." 河北山海關因為防禦敵人入侵的重要性，而獲「天下第一關」名號。
7.	Zhangjiajie is the inspiration for the fictional landscape of Avatar. 張家界是阿凡達電影場景的原型。
8.	What do you think about taking a trip to Jiuzhaigou Valley? 去九寨溝旅行如何？
9.	You can visit Yunnan to experience ethnic variety. 你可造訪雲南，體驗民族多樣性。
10.	What documents do I need to submit to apply for a visa to visit China? 申請中國觀光簽證，我需繳交哪些文件？
11.	If you are traveling solo, you can hire a local tour guide downtown. 若你獨自旅行，可在市中心僱請當地導遊。
12.	Can you tell me about the guided tours to China that your tour agency offers? 可以介紹我一些貴旅行社的中國團嗎？

關鍵單字片語

1. **karst** [kɑrst] 名 石灰岩地形
2. **UNESCO** 縮 聯合國教科文組織
3. **ruins** [`ruɪnz] 名 遺跡
4. **plateau** [plæ`to] 名 高原
5. **lakebed** [`lek.bɛd] 名 湖床
6. **trek** [trɛk] 動 長途旅行

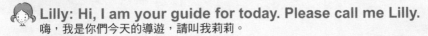

Lilly: Hi, I am your guide for today. Please call me Lilly.
嗨，我是你們今天的導遊，請叫我莉莉。

Will: Nice to meet you, Lilly. Where are we going today?
莉莉，很高興認識你。我們今天要去哪裡？

Lilly: I'm taking you to the Great Wall of China.
我要帶各位前往萬里長城。

Will: I've heard of that. How long is the wall exactly?
我聽說過。這座牆到底有多長？

Lilly: It is a series of fortifications, measuring 8851.8 km.
萬里長城是由許多防禦工事組成的，總長8851.8公里。

Will: I saw a documentary that said an emperor killed millions of people to build this wall. But I still can't understand why he built it at such a high cost.
我在記錄片裡看過，曾有皇帝殺了數百萬人來建築這座城牆。但是我一直不懂，為何要付出這麼大的代價來築這道牆。

Lilly: In ancient China, there were barbarians from the north who invaded, robbed villages, and were thus a great threat to national security. The Great Wall was built to protect the empire against intrusions.
在中國古代，北方有許多野蠻人會入侵邊境，掠奪城鎮，因此對國家安全造成很大的威脅。萬里長城是為了保護帝國不受侵略而建成的。

Will: Now I see.
現在我就懂了。

Lilly: And there is even a Great Wall marathon.
而且，現在甚至還有萬里長城馬拉松。

Will: Wow, I wonder who would dare take part in such a demanding competition.
哇，我懷疑有誰敢參加這場吃力的比賽。

關鍵單字片語

7. **be located in** 片 位於…

8. **gigantic** [dʒaɪˋgæntɪk] 形 巨大的

9. **the Great Wall** 片 萬里長城

10. **safety concern** 片 安全考量

11. **discover the charm** 片 發現魅力

12. **embankment** [ɪmˋbæŋkmənt] 名 堤岸

13. 遊東南亞 Southeast Asia
MP3 088

萬用好句

1. Thao Maha Brahma in Thailand is a must-see for many tourists.
泰國的四面佛是許多觀光客的必訪景點。

2. Many visitors go to the Floating Market for an exotic experience.
許多觀光客前往水上市場體驗異國風情。

3. There are many peddlers along the way to the Great Palace.
前往大皇宮的路上，沿途有許多小販。

4. The tuk-tuk is an iconic form of transportation in Bangkok.
庫庫車是泰國曼谷的特色交通工具。

5. There are many bars in Bangkok, the city that never sleeps.
曼谷是座不夜城，有許多酒吧。

6. The magnificent Angkor Wat is one of the wonders of the world.
吳哥窟是世界奇景之一。

7. Thailand and Cambodia are both Buddhist countries.
泰國和柬埔寨皆屬佛教國家。

8. Do you know the difference between the temples and shrines in Thailand and in Cambodia?
你知道泰國和柬埔寨的佛寺有何差別嗎？

9. Taking a cruise on Tonle Sap Lake is a popular daytrip in Cambodia.
東龍灣一日遊在柬埔寨很受歡迎。

10. How much is the day trip to the elephant farm in Chiang Mai?
清邁大象牧場一日遊的費用是多少？

11. Thailand is a paradise for massage and spa lovers, with various beauty shops and massage parlors along the way.
泰國是喜愛按摩和三溫暖人士的天堂，你可在路上找到各式美容院和按摩店。

12. Thai massage is a massage style that involves stretching and deep massage.
泰式按摩包含拉筋以及深層按摩。

關鍵單字片語

1. palace [ˋpælɪs] 名 宮殿
2. floating market 片 水上市場
3. Thao Maha Brahma 片 四面佛
4. Buddha [ˋbudə] 名 佛陀
5. coconut milk 片 椰奶
6. tuk-tuk [ˋtuktuk] 名 庫庫車(一種載客機車)

實境對話

Frank: How about going abroad this summer vacation?
這個暑假出國玩如何？

Tina: That's a great idea. Where do you want to go?
好主意。你想去哪裡？

Frank: How about Thailand?
泰國怎麼樣？

Tina: What is fun to do in Thailand?
泰國有什麼好玩的呢？

Frank: Thailand is not only famous for its unique cultural attractions, such as the Great Palace, but it's also a shopping paradise.
泰國不但以像大皇宮等獨特的文化景點著名，也同時是個購物天堂。

Tina: Sounds tempting. Is there anything else to do there?
聽來很吸引人。還有什麼好玩的嗎？

Frank: You can have fun in the various bars in Bangkok, and the Thao Maha Brahma downtown is famous for granting wishes.
你可在曼谷的各種酒吧玩得盡興，而市中心的四面佛則以靈驗著稱。

Tina: It sounds like a city of many faces.
聽來是個多樣化的城市。

Frank: In addition, if you're interested in riding an elephant, you can go to Chiang Mai, where there is an elephant school.
此外，若你對騎大象有興趣，你可以前往清邁的大象學校。

Tina: Cool! I've never ridden an elephant before!
酷！我從沒騎過大象！

Frank: So, can I book the tickets to Thailand for both of us?
那我可以來訂我們去泰國的機票了嗎？

Tina: Sure!
當然可以！

關鍵單字片語

7. **monk** [mʌŋk] 名 僧侶

8. **temple** [`tɛmpl] 名 寺廟

9. **nightlife** [`naɪtlaɪf] 名 夜生活

10. **magnificent** [mæg`nɪfəsənt] 形 壯麗的

11. **bargain** [`bɑrgɪn] 動 討價還價

12. **vicinity** [və`sɪnətɪ] 名 鄰近地區

14. **東亞之旅**
East Asia
MP3 089

萬用好句

1.	**Do you know where I can buy a kimono as a souvenir?** 你知道在哪可買到和服當紀念品嗎？
2.	**On a tour to a traditional Korean palace, you will have an opportunity to dress up as an ancient emperor or empress.** 參觀傳統韓國皇宮時，你將有機會打扮成古代帝王或王后。
3.	**Which do you prefer, the kimchi hot pot or the miso hot pot?** 你喜歡泡菜鍋還是味噌鍋？
4.	**I really don't understand why North and South Korea have remained hostile towards each other for such a long time.** 我真的不了解為何南北韓可以長期維持敵對狀態。
5.	**You can take the shuttle bus or the airport express to the city.** 你可以搭乘接駁巴士或是機場快捷專車到市區。
6.	**Kyoto, the ancient capital of Japan, has an abundance of historic buildings.** 京都是日本古都，歷史古蹟豐富。
7.	**The garden art of Japan is characteristic of its Zen philosophy.** 日本的庭院藝術以禪學為特色。
8.	**Johnny is going to South Korea for the Girls' Generation's concert.** 強尼要去南韓看少女時代的演唱會。
9.	**Ski resorts in South Korea always attract many ski lovers.** 南韓的滑雪場總是吸引許多滑雪愛好者。
10.	**Do you know there's a specially designed Hello Kitty airplane?** 你知道世上有凱蒂專機嗎？
11.	**Mary told me that you went on a tour to Jeju Island last month.** 瑪麗跟我說，你上個月去濟州島玩了一趟。
12.	**Hikers should carry a bear bell with them at all times in case of a bear attack.** 健行者應隨時隨身攜帶熊鈴以防熊襲。

★ 關鍵單字片語

1. **shuttle bus** 片 接駁車

2. **Hokkaido** [hɔˋkaɪdo] 名 北海道

3. **kaiseki** [ˋkaɪˌsɛkɪ] 名 懷石料理

4. **kimono** [kɪˋmono] 名 和服

5. **cherry blossom** 片 櫻花

6. **inspire** [ɪnˋspaɪr] 動 給⋯靈感

實境對話

Laura: How many times have you been to Japan?
你去過日本幾次？

Frank: Maybe five or six. I am not sure. Why are you asking?
也許是五、六次吧，我不確定。為何問這個？

Laura: I am thinking about traveling to Japan during the summer vacation. Can you give me any suggestions?
我暑假想去日本旅行。你能給我一些建議嗎？

Frank: Of course. Where do you want to go?
當然。你要去哪裡？

Laura: I am thinking about Hokkaido or Tokyo. What do you think?
我在考慮北海道或是東京，你覺得呢？

Frank: If you want to embrace nature, go to Hokkaido; if you're into modern cities and crazy about shopping, go to Tokyo.
若你想擁抱大自然，就去北海道；若你對現代都市及瘋狂購物有興趣，就去東京。

Laura: Well, I'm kind of interested in both.
嗯，我對大自然和都市都有興趣耶。

Frank: Then you should visit Kyoto, where you can enjoy beautiful scenery and go on a shopping spree.
那你應該去京都，一個你可享受美景、也可大肆逛街的地方。

Laura: Wow. Sounds like the perfect spot for me.
哇，聽起來是最適合我的景點。

Frank: I can give you some information of Kyoto via E-mail.
我可以透過電子郵件提供你一些京都相關資訊。

Laura: That would be fantastic. Thank you. How about your summer plans?
那太好了，感謝你。你的暑假想怎麼過？

Frank: I'm still thinking about it. What do you think of Australia?
還在計畫中。你覺得澳洲怎麼樣？

關鍵單字片語

7. **highlight** [`haɪ͵laɪt] 名 最精彩的部分

8. **ski resort** 片 滑雪場

9. **shabu-shabu** [ʃɑ`buʃɑbu] 名 涮涮鍋

10. **tour around** 片 四處遊覽

11. **perfectly** [`pɝfɪktlɪ] 副 完美地

12. **festival** [`fɛstəv] 名 節慶、祭典

15. 打工度假
Working Holidays

MP3
090

萬用好句

1.	**Taking a working holiday is now fashionable among young people.** 打工度假現在很受年輕人歡迎。
2.	**In the cherry season, Mr. Watson hires some more part-time workers in his orchard.** 在櫻桃產季，華生先生的果園會多僱一些臨時工。
3.	**Jason used to milk the cows on Mr. George's farm.** 傑森曾在喬治先生的農場擠牛奶。
4.	**Taking a working holiday is an economical way to travel.** 打工度假是較經濟的旅遊方式。
5.	**People under 31 are eligible to apply for a working holiday visa.** 未滿三十一歲者皆可申請澳洲打工度假簽證。
6.	**Do you provide food and accommodation for part-time workers?** 您有提供臨時工食宿嗎？
7.	**How much is the hourly pay?** 每小時時薪多少？
8.	**Anyone who is interested in finding a part-time job in Australia can upload his or her résumé to this website.** 想在澳洲找份兼職工作的人，可將履歷上傳至本網站。
9.	**How many days are you going to stay in Melbourne?** 你要在墨爾本待幾天？
10.	**Kakadu National Park is a must-see for people on a working holiday to Australia.** 卡卡杜國家公園是澳洲打工度假者的必去景點。
11.	**How often will I get paid, biweekly or weekly?** 我會領雙週薪還是週薪？

關鍵單字片語

1. **backpacker** [`bæk͵pækɚ] 名 背包客
2. **part-time job** 片 臨時工作
3. **kangaroo** [͵kæŋɡə`ru] 名 袋鼠
4. **kiwifruit** [`kiwɪ͵frut] 名 奇異果
5. **upload** [ʌp`lod] 動 上傳
6. **in particular** 片 尤其是、特別是

實境對話

Peter: How long have you been working and traveling here in Australia?
你在澳洲這裡打工度假多久了？

Ada: Just one month. How about you?
一個月而已，你呢？

Peter: I have been here for almost one year.
我已經在這裡幾乎一年了。

Ada: Wow, quite long. Can you give me some job-finding tips?
哇，很久了耶。你可以給我些找工作的建議嗎？

Peter: Sure. It would be my pleasure. What kind of job do you prefer?
當然。這是我的榮幸。你想找什麼樣的工作？

Ada: I love animals, so it would be great if I could get a job on a farm.
我喜歡動物，所以如果可以找到牧場的工作就太棒了。

Peter: You can find some interesting jobs in the local classified ads, or you may register on the local job-search websites.
你可在當地的分類廣告找到些有趣的工作，或者你也可以註冊當地的工作搜尋網站。

Ada: OK. Then what is your favorite city?
了解。那你最喜歡哪一個城市？

Peter: I have been to Sydney, Melbourne, Canberra and Brisbane, but Darwin is my favorite.
我去過雪梨、墨爾本、坎培拉和布里斯本，但達爾文是我的最愛。

Ada: What do you like about it the most?
你最喜歡它的什麼地方？

Peter: Maybe it's the lifestyle there that I am into.
或許是那裡的生活方式吧。

關鍵單字片語

7. **classified ad** 片 分類廣告

8. **a maximum of** 片 最大值…、最多

9. **job search** 名 找工作

10. **eligible** [`ɛlɪdʒəbl]] 形 有資格的

11. **hostel** [`hɑstl]] 名 青年旅社

12. **working holiday** 片 打工度假

1. 溫馨節慶：耶誕、感恩、復活節

Western Holidays

MP3
091

萬用好句

1.	**Merry Christmas and a Happy New Year!** 聖誕快樂、新年快樂！
2.	**In Western culture, Christmas time is for family reunions.** 在西方文化裡，聖誕節是全家團聚的日子。
3.	**Many families gather together on Christmas Eve.** 許多家庭在平安夜齊聚一堂。
4.	**Having a turkey dinner is a tradition on Thanksgiving.** 享用火雞大餐是感恩節的傳統。
5.	**Children always look forward to an Easter egg hunt.** 小朋友們總是期待著復活節的尋蛋遊戲。
6.	**On Thanksgiving, you give thanks and blessings to your family and friends.** 在感恩節，你可以感謝並祝福你的親朋好友。
7.	**An Easter egg hunt is a game in which decorated eggs are hidden for children to find.** 復活節的尋蛋遊戲裡，你先藏起彩蛋，再讓小朋友們去尋找。
8.	**People put on their finery and join the Easter parade.** 人們會穿上最華麗的衣服參加復活節遊行。
9.	**My cousins tugged the wishbone at both ends, wondering who could win the opportunity to have their wish come true.** 表弟們拉著許願骨的兩端，想著誰能有機會實現願望。
10.	**Jenna has invited me over to have Thanksgiving dinner with her.** 珍娜已經邀我和她一起過感恩節了。
11.	**You will see many colorful light bulbs during the Christmas season.** 在耶誕季節，你會看到許多七彩的燈泡。
12.	**Little Jessie hung a big red sock over the fireplace for Santa.** 小潔西把大紅襪掛在壁爐上，等待聖誕老人。

關鍵單字片語

1. **Last Supper** 片 最後的晚餐

2. **angel** [ˋendʒl] 名 天使

3. **Christmas carol** 片 耶誕頌歌

4. **Christmas Eve** 片 平安夜

5. **decorate** [ˋdɛkə‚ret] 動 裝飾

6. **ornament** [ˋɔrnəmənt] 名 裝飾品

實境對話

Jason: Merry Christmas!
耶誕快樂！

Amy: Is that you, Jason? I haven't seen you for months.
你不是傑森嗎？好幾個月沒見到你了。

Jason: I just got back from Shanghai yesterday.
我昨天才剛從上海回來。

Amy: No wonder. This is a nice party, isn't it?
難怪。這個派對很棒吧？

Jason: It is. Linda totally deserves her nickname "Party Queen." Did you see all those flashing Christmas lights?
沒錯，琳達果然不負她派對女王的美名。你有看到那些閃爍的聖誕燈嗎？

Amy: Of course I did. They are almost everywhere.
當然有，幾乎到處都是。

Jason: And she even bought a pine Christmas tree! And look at the mistletoe! It's the greenest I've ever seen.
她甚至買了一棵聖誕松樹！而且你看看槲寄生！那是我看過最翠綠的。

Amy: You are right. It's really green.
沒錯，真的很綠。

Jason: Do you know the tradition regarding mistletoe?
你知道有個關於槲寄生的聖誕傳說嗎？

Amy: No. What is it?
不知道，是什麼啊？

Jason: According to an ancient custom, a man and a woman who meet under a hanging mistletoe are obliged to kiss.
根據一項古老的習俗，在槲寄生下相遇的男女要接吻。

Amy: Really? Then, it looks like we should be kissing now.
真的嗎？看來我們現在得給彼此一個吻了。

關鍵單字片語

7. **turkey** [ˋtɝkɪ] 名 火雞

8. **mistletoe** [ˋmɪsḷ͵to] 名 槲寄生

9. **harvest** [ˋhɑrvɪst] 動 名 收穫

10. **egg hunt** 片 復活節尋蛋遊戲

11. **chocolate** [ˋtʃɑkəlɪt] 名 巧克力

12. **dye** [daɪ] 動 把…染上顏色

2.歡欣節慶：年節、端午、中秋節
Chinese Holidays

092

萬用好句

1.	The Dragon Boat Festival is in memory of Qu-Yuan, who drowned himself because of his deep concern for his country. 端午節是為了紀念屈原，因為憂國而投江身亡。
2.	The Mid-Autumn Festival is a time for family gatherings. 中秋節是全家團聚的時刻。
3.	Kids always get excited about getting red envelopes. 領壓歲錢的時候，小孩們總是很興奮。
4.	Do you want to join the Dragon Boat race? 你想要參加龍舟競賽嗎？
5.	I love moon cakes, even though they are high-calorie snacks. 即使月餅是高熱量的點心，我還是愛吃。
6.	On Chinese New Year's Eve, there will be a celebration and fireworks in the City Hall Plaza. 除夕夜在市府廣場會有慶祝晚會和煙火秀。
7.	On January 2nd on the lunar calendar, married daughters will come home and have dinner with their parents. 農曆正月初二，出嫁的女兒要回家和父母吃飯。
8.	Both rice dumplings and moon cakes are our traditional food. 粽子和月餅都是我們的傳統食物。
9.	Ice cream moon cakes are very delicious. Where did you get them? 冰淇淋月餅非常好吃，你在哪裡買的？
10.	My grandmother used to make rice dumplings by herself. 我奶奶以前都會親手包粽子。
11.	Do you know the legend behind the Moon Festival and the moon cakes? 你知道中秋節和月餅的傳說嗎？
12.	Red is the color of celebration and happiness in Chinese culture. 紅色在中國文化裡是喜慶的顏色。

關鍵單字片語

1. **dragon boat** 片 龍舟

2. **paddle** [`pæd!] 動 用槳划船

3. **drum** [drʌm] 名 鼓

4. **rice dumpling** 片 粽子

5. **moon cake** 片 月餅

6. **pomelo** [`pɑməlo] 名 柚子

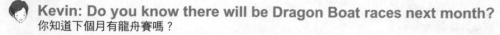

Kevin: Do you know there will be Dragon Boat races next month?
你知道下個月有龍舟賽嗎？

Laura: Dragon Boat races? What are they?
龍舟賽？那是什麼？

Kevin: They are a traditional event during the Chinese Dragon Boat Festival. People race in dragon-shaped boats.
那是端午節的傳統活動，人們會划龍型船參賽。

Laura: Sounds cool! How many tickets do you have?
聽起來很酷！你有幾張票？

Kevin: Tickets? No, I am inviting you to participate in the race with me.
票？沒有，我在邀你和我一起參加比賽。

Laura: Are you serious?
你是認真的嗎？

Kevin: Of course. The Foreign Student Union will enter one team in the race, and we need 20 rowers, a drummer, and a helmsman.
當然，外籍學生會要出一隊參加比賽，我們需要二十名划槳手、一名鼓手跟一名舵手。

Laura: I thought you have to be very strong to compete in a boat race.
我以為要很強壯才能參加賽舟。

Kevin: Not at all. Boat racing is a team sport. It's teamwork that will make you a winner.
一點也不。賽舟是團隊運動，只有團隊合作才能讓你獲勝。

Laura: OK. Count me in! I will start working out.
好吧。算我一份！我要開始健身了。

Kevin: No, you don't have to. What we need is a good drummer. You used to be a drummer in a band, didn't you?
不，你不用。我們需要的是一名好的鼓手，你以前在樂團裡擔任鼓手，對吧？

關鍵單字片語

7. **firecracker** [`faɪr,krækə] 名 鞭炮

8. **red envelope** 片 壓歲錢(紅包)

9. **reunion dinner** 片 團圓飯

10. **red couplet** 片 春聯

11. **race** [res] 名 競賽、競速

12. **Moon Festival** 片 中秋節

MP3 093

3. 開放保守
The Attitude towards Sex

萬用好句

1. Asian people are usually shy about talking about sex.
亞洲人通常羞於討論性議題。

2. Sex is a taboo subject in Chinese culture, and thus sex education wasn't part of the education system until very recently.
性在中華文化裡是個禁忌，因此一直到最近才成為學校教育的議題。

3. Sex education is considered important in Western school systems.
性是西方學校教育裡的一個重要議題。

4. Many Western parents talk about sex to their teenage kids.
許多西方父母會和他們的青少年孩子討論性議題。

5. Would you talk about sex with your children?
你會和你的孩子討論性嗎？

6. Ah-Yu's father forbids her to date any boy before she turns twenty.
阿玉的父親禁止她在二十歲以前和任何男生約會。

7. In contrast, Charlotte's father has encouraged her to have healthy relationships with boys ever since her sixteenth birthday.
相反的，夏綠蒂的父親在她十六歲生日後就鼓勵她和男孩有健康的交往關係。

8. David and his father have talked about the topic of contraception.
大衛已與他的父親談論避孕的話題。

9. Have you ever had a one night stand?
你有過一夜情嗎？

10. Traditional Chinese culture tends to repress people's desires.
傳統中國文化傾向壓抑人們的慾望。

11. Most Western teenagers are encouraged to speak out.
在西方，大部分的青少年會被鼓勵說出他們的想法。

12. What do you think of trial marriages?
你對試婚有什麼看法？

關鍵單字片語

1. **conservative** [kənˋsɜvətɪv] 形 保守的

2. **reaction** [rɪˋækʃən] 名 反應

3. **tolerable** [ˋtɑlərəbl] 形 可容忍的

4. **versus** [ˋvɜsəs] 介 與⋯相對

5. **sex partner** 片 性伴侶

6. **sex attitude** 片 性態度

實境對話

Hank: Did you read the article in the newspaper about trial marriages?
你有看報上那篇關於試婚的文章嗎？

Helen: No. What is that?
沒有，那在講什麼？

Hank: It's a temporary arrangement: a couple live together for a period of time to see if they are compatible enough to get married.
試婚是一種暫時性的安排。兩個人一起住一段時間，來看彼此是否適合結婚。

Helen: If I ever did that, my parents would definitely kill me.
如果我這樣做，我爸媽一定會殺了我。

Hank: Really? But it's very common among people of our generation.
真的嗎？但這在我們這一輩很普遍呢。

Helen: My parents are both traditional Chinese parents. They believe that a decent girl cannot have sex unless she's married.
我爸媽都是傳統的中國人，他們覺得一個好人家的女孩要到婚後才能發生性關係。

Hank: Even if the guy you move in with is your fiancé?
即使和你一起住的人是你未婚夫嗎？

Helen: Sadly, that is the case.
很遺憾，是這樣沒錯。

Hank: Wow! Did people in the old days ever live together before getting married?
哇，以前的人婚前會同住嗎？

Helen: No, and some of them didn't even see each other until the night they got married.
不會，他們有些人甚至到結婚那晚才見到面。

關鍵單字片語

7. **protective** [prə`tɛktɪv] 形 保護的

8. **decent** [`disn̩t] 形 正派的

9. **brave** [brev] 形 勇敢的

10. **one night stand** 片 一夜情

11. **preventive** [prɪ`vɛntɪv] 形 預防的

12. **repress desires** 片 壓抑慾望

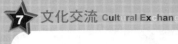

4.氣候差異
The Climate
MP3 094

萬用好句

1.	It is usually very hot and humid in summer in Taiwan. 台灣夏天通常又熱又潮濕。
2.	Do you know the difference between a typhoon and a hurricane? 你知道颱風和颶風的差別嗎？
3.	What is the weather like in June in California? 加州六月的天氣怎麼樣？
4.	Weatherfirst.com is updated four times a day with the latest information for travelers to the United States. 氣象先機網站，一天會更新四次最新天氣訊息給前往美國的遊客。
5.	Most foreigners can't stand the humid weather in Taiwan. 大多數的外國人無法忍受台灣潮濕的氣候。
6.	The temperate climate in Taiwan attracts many tourists. 台灣溫和的氣候吸引許多遊客。
7.	Taipei has high humidity all year round. 台北一年四季都非常潮溼。
8.	Maria always checks the local weather forecast for her destination before she leaves for vacation. 瑪利亞總在出發度假前先確認當地的天氣狀況。
9.	One of the biggest challenges of living abroad is to adapt oneself to the local weather. 住在國外最大的挑戰之一就是適應當地的天氣。
10.	Remember to bring skin lotion with you. It is very dry in London. 記得要帶乳液，倫敦很乾燥。
11.	It seldom snows in Taiwan in the winter, except on the high mountains. 台灣很少在冬天下雪，除非在高山上才會降雪。
12.	When is the rainy season on Bali? 峇里島的雨季在什麼時候？

關鍵單字片語

1. **dry** [draɪ] 形 乾燥的
2. **humid** [`hjumɪd] 形 潮溼的
3. **temperature** [`tɛmprətʃə] 名 氣溫
4. **weather condition** 片 天氣狀況
5. **forecast** [`for͵kæst] 名 動 預報
6. **desert** [`dɛzɚt] 名 沙漠

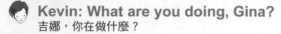

實境對話

Kevin: What are you doing, Gina?
吉娜，你在做什麼？

Gina: I am making a packing list. I am going to study in the U.K.
我在擬打包清單，我準備要去英國念書。

Kevin: Congratulations! I believe you will certainly learn a lot.
恭喜你！我相信你一定能學到很多。

Gina: Thank you. Can you give me some advice? I remember you have been there, too.
謝謝你。你可以給我些建議嗎？我記得你也去過那裡。

Kevin: Hmm...First, don't take those heavy sweaters with you.
嗯…首先，不要帶厚重的毛衣。

Gina: Really? But I've heard that it is freezing cold in the winter there.
真的嗎？但我聽說那裡冬天天寒地凍耶。

Kevin: It is, but they have heating inside. Just take a warm parka or a coat with you.
沒錯，但那裡室內都有暖氣。你只要帶溫暖的附帽毛夾克和大衣就好。

Gina: OK. What else?
好，還有嗎？

Kevin: You'll need sunglasses when it snows.
下雪的時候你會用到太陽眼鏡的。

Gina: Sunglasses. Let me write that down.
太陽眼鏡，讓我寫下來。

Kevin: And remember to take a rainproof jacket and a hat with you and an umbrella. It rains a lot in England.
記得帶防雨外套和帽子。還有雨傘，英國很常下雨。

Gina: Sure, thanks!
好的，謝了！

關鍵單字片語

7. **typhoon** [taɪˋfun] 名 颱風

8. **rainy season** 片 雨季

9. **frost** [frɔst] 動 結霜 名 霜

10. **heat wave** 片 熱浪

11. **thunder shower** 片 雷陣雨

12. **snow** [sno] 動 下雪 名 雪

5. 溝通表達方式
Ways of Communication

MP3
095

萬用好句

1. **Certain gestures may be offensive in some countries.**
在一些國家，有些手勢可能是很不禮貌的。

2. **Cross-cultural differences may cause misunderstanding.**
跨文化間的差異可能會引起誤會。

3. **In Taiwan, Sunday is the last day of the week.**
在台灣，星期天是一週的最後一天。

4. **Communicating across cultures begins with the basic understanding that one size does not fit all.**
跨文化間的溝通，始於了解到一套溝通方式並非適用全世界。

5. **In England, "cheers" means "thank you" and "you are welcome."**
在英格蘭，「cheers」的意思是「謝謝你」和「不客氣」。

6. **I am sorry, but I don't really get Kenny's joke.**
抱歉，但是我真的不懂肯尼的笑點。

7. **Our foreign clients asked us to make our presentation first.**
我們的外國客戶要求我們先進行簡報。

8. **Sometimes it is hard to understand people from other cultures because of differences in communication styles.**
有時候因為不同的溝通習慣，很難理解不同文化背景的人。

9. **What do you mean by that?**
你那樣說是什麼意思？

10. **Mr. Watson's heavily accented English is hard to understand.**
華生先生帶有濃厚腔調的英文很難聽懂。

11. **Chinese people tend to be as circumlocutory as possible to show their politeness while making requests.**
中國人在做出請求時，會儘量婉轉以示禮貌。

12. **A smile is always the best way to express your friendliness.**
微笑最能表達你的友善。

關鍵單字片語

1. **talkative** [ˋtɔkətɪv] 形 健談的

2. **taciturn** [ˋtæsɚ͵tɝn] 形 寡言的

3. **express oneself** 片 表達觀點

4. **convince** [kənˋvɪns] 動 說服

5. **refer to** 片 提到、談及

6. **converse** [kənˋvɝs] 動 談話

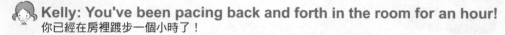

Kelly: You've been pacing back and forth in the room for an hour!
你已經在房裡踱步一個小時了！

Josh: I'm sorry, but I just can't help it.
對不起，但我就是忍不住一直走來走去。

Kelly: What's wrong with you? You look really nervous.
你怎麼了？你看起來真的很緊張耶。

Josh: I have a conference with our Australian clients tomorrow. I have to talk them into signing a contract with us.
我明天要和澳洲客戶開會，我得說服他們和我們簽約。

Kelly: You'll be fine. Calm down!
你會做得很好的，冷靜點！

Josh: I doubt it.
我很懷疑。

Kelly: Why is that?
為什麼這麼說呢？

Josh: A few months ago, I was sent to meet a potential Indian client. I got so nervous that I shook hands with her.
幾個月前，我被派去見一位印度的潛在客戶。我真的很緊張，所以我與她握手。

Kelly: What's the big deal? Everybody does that.
那又怎麼樣？每個人都會和人握手的。

Josh: My client was female. In India, females don't shake hands with males. Besides, I kept looking at the ground.
我的客戶是名女性。在印度，女性不和異性握手。而且，我還一直盯著地上。

Kelly: I understand. She thought you were being rude.
我懂了，她覺得你很粗魯無禮。

Josh: Exactly! She got furious, and I lost the contract as well.
沒錯！她氣瘋了，我也沒簽成合約。

關鍵單字片語

7. **directly** [də`rɛktlɪ] 副 直接地

8. **big deal** 片 重要大事

9. **shake hands** 片 握手

10. **nonverbal** [ˌnɑn`vɝbl] 形 非言語的

11. **get the point cross** 片 讓對方理解

12. **negotiate** [nɪ`goʃɪˌet] 動 協商

6. 酒國文化
Alcohol

MP3 096

萬用好句

1.	**Can we run a tab?** 我們可以等晚上結束後再付款嗎？
2.	**I'll have a whisky on the rocks.** 我要一杯威士忌加冰塊。
3.	**A margarita, and make it a double, please.** 請給我雙份瑪格麗塔。
4.	**Our Happy Hour is from 6 p.m. to 8 p.m.** 晚上六點到八點是我們的優惠時間。
5.	**What kind of beer do you have on tap?** 櫃檯有哪種啤酒？
6.	**When is last call?** 最後叫酒的時間是什麼時候？
7.	**Do you have any appetizers or snacks?** 你們有開胃菜或零食嗎？
8.	**I'll have another one.** 我要再來一杯。
9.	**Smoking is not allowed in our bar.** 我們酒吧裡禁菸。
10.	**Can I get another round?** 我可以再來一杯嗎？
11.	**Sir, I have to cut you off since you are already inebriated.** 先生，我不能拿酒給您了，您已經喝醉了。
12.	**The bouncer refused Jason and his friends' admittance since they were under 18.** 保鑣不讓傑森和他的朋友進場，因為他們未滿十八歲。

關鍵單字片語

1. **mix** [mɪks] 動 混和

2. **beverage** [`bɛvərɪdʒ] 名 飲料

3. **Bloody Mary** 片 血腥瑪麗

4. **swizzle stick** 片 調酒棒

5. **run a tab** 片 記在帳上

6. **pitcher** [`pɪtʃɚ] 名 壺

實境對話

Bartender: Good evening, Ma'am. What can I do for you?
晚安女士，有什麼我可以幫您的？

Woman: A whisky on the rocks, please.
請給我威士忌加冰塊。

Bartender: Excuse me. Can I see your identification, please? I need to make sure you are over eighteen.
對不起，我可以先看你的身分證嗎？我要確定你超過十八歲了。

Woman: That's so sweet of you. Do I look underage? Here you are. I am almost twenty-five.
你嘴真甜，我看起來像未成年的女孩嗎？你看吧，我都快二十五歲了。

Bartender: I just need to make sure. You do look young.
只是確認一下，您看起來真年輕。

Woman: Thank you. Do you have peanuts or popcorn?
謝謝你。你們有花生或爆米花嗎？

Bartender: Sure, and they are free as long as you order a drink.
當然有，只要有點酒就免費。

Woman: When is last call? I am expecting a friend.
最後叫酒是幾點？我在等一個朋友。

Bartender: It's eleven thirty. We close at twelve.
十一點半，我們十二點打烊。

Woman: Cool! We still have three hours to party!
酷！我們還有三小時可以狂歡！

Bartender: Enjoy your night.
好好享受今晚吧。

Woman: Thank you.
謝謝你。

關鍵單字片語

7. **ice bucket** 片 冰桶

8. **last call** 片 最後叫酒的時間

9. **coaster** [ˋkostɚ] 名 杯墊

10. **shaker** [ˋʃekɚ] 名 調酒器

11. **license** [ˋlaɪsn̩s] 名 執照

12. **another round** 片 再來一杯

7. 工作與休閒的均衡性
Work And Leisure

MP3 097

萬用好句

1.	**Working hard is necessary, but a workaholic can destroy his productivity and health.** 認真工作是必要的，但是工作狂只會毀了他的生產力和健康。
2.	**Workaholism is a type of mental disorder.** 工作狂是一種心理上的失調症。
3.	**All work and no play makes Jack a dull boy.** 只工作不消遣，使人遲鈍。
4.	**Working too much may negatively affect your health.** 過度工作可能會對健康造成負面影響。
5.	**Don't sacrifice your relationships for work.** 不要為了工作而犧牲你的人際關係。
6.	**Taking regular breaks can make you more efficient.** 定期休息可以讓你更有效率。
7.	**Most Asian employees spend most of their lives working too hard at the expense of their quality of life.** 大多數的亞洲勞工花大半輩子的時間過於認真工作，而犧牲掉和家人相聚的時間。
8.	**Many Asian workers aren't able to find a work-life balance.** 許多亞洲勞工無法達到工作與生活的平衡。
9.	**It is important to strike a balance between work and leisure.** 在工作和休閒間找到平衡點是很重要的。
10.	**How often do you go on a vacation?** 你多常度假？
11.	**Leisure and pleasure are not a waste of time. They can boost your energy for future work and challenges.** 休閒和娛樂不是浪費時間，而是替你未來的工作和挑戰做準備。
12.	**Does your life have a balance between work and fun?** 你的工作和娛樂有達到平衡嗎？

關鍵單字片語

1. **weekend activity** 片 週末活動
2. **boost** [bust] 動 幫助
3. **on vacation** 片 度假
4. **quality time** 片 能和家人相聚的時間
5. **workaholic** [ˏwɝkəˋhɔlɪk] 名 工作狂
6. **relax** [rɪˋlæks] 動 放輕鬆

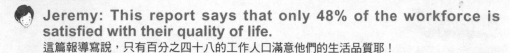

Jeremy: This report says that only 48% of the workforce is satisfied with their quality of life.
這篇報導寫說，只有百分之四十八的工作人口滿意他們的生活品質耶！

Joan: That's right on the mark. I am certainly not part of that 48%.
報導說得沒錯。我絕對不是那百分之四十八。

Jeremy: Really? Aren't you satisfied with your life now?
真的嗎？你不滿意現在的生活嗎？

Joan: Haven't you noticed my working hours? 12 hours a day!
你沒注意到我的工作時數嗎？一天十二個小時耶！

Jeremy: I thought you enjoyed the sense of accomplishment you get from work.
我以為你很享受工作帶來的成就感。

Joan: I used to, but I have been thinking about my quality of life lately.
以前是，但我最近開始思考我的生活品質。

Jeremy: I guess you're right to think about that, but you'll get promoted soon, won't you?
我想你的確是該思考一下，但你快要升職了，不是嗎？

Joan: That means I'll be even busier than now, and I'd rather spend time playing soccer with my son.
那表示我會比現在更忙，我寧願花時間陪我兒子踢足球。

Jeremy: How about weekends? You can be with your son then.
那週末呢？你週末的時候就可以陪你兒子了。

Joan: That's not possible. My boss believes that it's my responsibility to get the job done no matter how much time it takes--even on weekends.
不可能的。我老闆覺得把工作做好是我的責任，他才不管我花了多少時間、甚至是週末。

關鍵單字片語

7. **reinvigorate** [ˌriɪnˋvɪgəˌret] 動 重振

8. **loosen up** 片 使鬆弛

9. **passion for work** 片 工作熱忱

10. **produce** [prəˋdjus] 動 生產

11. **beneficial** [ˌbɛnəˋfɪʃəl] 形 有益的

12. **stressed out** 片 承受過多壓力的

8. 生活作息
Daily Routine
MP3 098

萬用好句

1. **Some Western people prefer taking a shower in the morning.**
有些西方人喜歡在早上淋浴。

2. **Parents always ask their children to maintan a certain routine.**
父母總會要求小孩維持規律的生活。

3. **I'm not used to the busy pace of life in Taipei.**
我不習慣台北忙碌的生活步調。

4. **The Chinese think punctuality is a virtue.**
中國人認為準時是一種美德。

5. **Chinese people tend to arrive a bit earlier than the scheduled time to show their earnestness.**
中國人會提早一些赴約，以表示他們的誠意。

6. **Let's take a short break and have a cup of tea together.**
我們休息一下，一起喝杯茶吧。

7. **I have been longing for the laid-back lifestyle in Spain.**
我一直很嚮往西班牙的悠閒生活。

8. **When do you usually go to bed?**
你通常都幾點睡覺？

9. **Do you usually have a snack before going to bed?**
你通常睡前會吃宵夜嗎？

10. **Most Taiwanese enjoy going to night markets for snacks.**
大部分台灣人喜歡去夜市買小吃。

11. **In some European countries, people don't have dinner until eight in the evening.**
在一些歐洲國家，不到晚上八點不會吃晚餐。

12. **Many people sleep in and have brunch on weekends.**
許多人週末睡得晚，就吃一餐早午餐。

關鍵單字片語

1. **laid-back** [`led͵bæk] 形 悠閒的

2. **punctuality** [͵pʌŋktʃʊˋælətɪ] 名 準時

3. **regular** [ˋrɛgjələ] 形 規律的

4. **alarm clock** 片 鬧鐘

5. **shower time** 片 淋浴時間

6. **stick to schedule** 片 遵守表定時間

實境對話

Karen: How was your trip to Greece?
你的希臘之旅如何？

Frank: Not as much fun as I had expected.
不如我想像中的有趣。

Karen: Why not? I thought you'd been longing to visit Greece!
怎麼會？我以為你一直想去希臘呢！

Frank: It used to be my dream holiday--before my visit.
那曾經是我的夢想假期——在我去以前。

Karen: You are confusing me. Isn't it beautiful?
你讓我搞混了，那裡不美嗎？

Frank: It surely is. The scenery is too beautiful to be true.
的確很美。風景美得不像真的。

Karen: Then what was the problem?
那是怎麼了？

Frank: It's their lifestyle. It's too laid-back. People there have a long rest in the afternoon, and the stores don't open again until three, but then they close again at five.
是他們的生活方式，太悠閒了。下午會休息很久，商店到三點才再開，但五點就關了。

Karen: Sounds like heaven for everyone! Beautiful scenery and a stress-free life!
聽起來像是天堂！美麗的風景和沒壓力的生活！

Frank: Not for me. I enjoy the bustle of the cities.
對我可不是，我喜歡城市裡的繁華。

Karen: I never knew that you preferred a busy lifestyle.
我從來不知道你喜歡忙碌的生活方式。

Frank: I just can't stand doing nothing for the whole afternoon.
我只是無法一整個下午都閒著，什麼事都不做。

關鍵單字片語

7. **luncheon** [`lʌntʃən] 名 正式午餐會

8. **brunch** [brʌntʃ] 名 早午餐

9. **teatime** [`ti͵taɪm] 名 下午茶時間

10. **take a break** 片 休息片刻

11. **lunch break** 片 午休時間

12. **take a rest** 片 休息一下

9. 文化衝擊
Culture Shock

MP3
099

萬用好句

1.	**My friends are interested in the traditions performed at temples.** 我的朋友對於廟宇的傳統儀式很感興趣。
2.	**Kathy doesn't dare try pig intestines.** 凱西不敢嘗試豬腸。
3.	**Some foreigners think pig-blood cakes are disgusting.** 一些外國人認為豬血糕很噁心。
4.	**Culture shock is common among immigrants and foreign tourists.** 文化衝擊在移民者和外國遊客身上很常見。
5.	**In Paris, people greet each other with a cheery "bonjour" even if they don't know each other.** 在巴黎，儘管不認識彼此，人們還是以歡欣的口氣用「早安」向彼此打招呼。
6.	**Greeting by kissing on the cheeks terrified me at first.** 開始的時候，我被見面時親臉頰的行為嚇了一大跳。
7.	**Asians consider it rude to meet a person's gaze for too long; however, it's just the opposite in some western cultures.** 亞洲人認為直視對方太久不禮貌，然而在一些西方文化是完全相反的。
8.	**Words might refer to different objects in different countries; for example a rubber is an eraser in India, but it is a slang for a condom in the U.S.** 一個字在不同國家代表不同物品，像「rubber」在印度是指橡皮擦，在美國則指保險套。
9.	**It took Jack five months to adjust to the Taiwanese culture.** 傑克花了五個月的時間適應台灣文化。
10.	**Do you like Chinese cuisine and the traditions surrounding it?** 你喜歡中華飲食文化嗎？
11.	**Convenience stores provide all kinds of services.** 便利商店提供各式各樣的服務。

關鍵單字片語

1. **cultural difference** 片 文化差異

2. **adjust to** 片 適應

3. **tradition** [trə`dɪʃən] 名 傳統

4. **way of thinking** 片 思考方式

5. **culture shock** 片 文化衝擊

6. **image** [`ɪmɪdʒ] 名 形象、印象

實境對話

Lynn: Do you want to try this?
你想要試試看這個嗎？

Hank: What is that? Another delicious local Taiwanese snack?
那是什麼？另一種美味的台灣當地小吃嗎？

Lynn: Yes, it's a pig-blood cake. It's my favorite.
沒錯，這是豬血糕，我的最愛。

Hank: What? Pig blood? Gross!
什麼？豬血？噁心！

Lynn: Come on! Just give it a try. Trust me, you won't regret it!
拜託！試試看嘛，相信我，你不會後悔的！

Hank: Err...What is that? Maybe I can have some of that.
呃…，那是什麼？或許我可以吃那個。

Lynn: Oh, it's a fried chicken butt. They are also very delicious.
喔，那是炸雞屁股，那也很好吃。

Hank: Chicken butts?
雞屁股？

Lynn: Yes. It has the beautiful nickname of "Seven-kilometer Scent," suggesting that it is so good you can smell it even from seven kilometers away.
沒錯。它有個很美的綽號「七里香」，意思是它太香了，你在七里外就可以聞到它的香味。

Hank: Of course you can! They are butts!
你當然聞得到！那是屁股耶！

Lynn: Please! Just one bite and you'll love it!
拜託！一口就好，你會愛上它的！

Hank: OK., just one small bite.
好，就一小口哦。

關鍵單字片語

7. **cultural values** 片 文化價值

8. **believe** [bɪ`liv] 動 相信

9. **affirm** [ə`fɜm] 動 確認、證實

10. **philosophy** [fə`lɑsəfɪ] 名 哲學

11. **behavior** [bɪ`hevjə] 名 行為

12. **be aware of** 片 意識到…

10. 入境隨俗
Customs

MP3 100

萬用好句

1.	**When in Rome, do as the Romans do.** 入境隨俗。
2.	**What do local people usually have for breakfast?** 當地人早餐通常都吃什麼？
3.	**In most homes in Taiwan, you have to take off your shoes before entering.** 在台灣大多數的家庭，你進門前要先脫鞋。
4.	**Christians pray before they enjoy a meal.** 基督教徒在享受大餐前，要先禱告。
5.	**The lottery is very hot in Taiwan, so some tourists will try their luck as well.** 樂透在台灣很夯，有些觀光客也想試試手氣。
6.	**Jeremy saw many truck drivers chewing betel nut along the way.** 傑若米看到很多卡車司機沿路嚼著檳榔。
7.	**I don't like fast food like hamburgers, so I had noodles instead.** 我不喜歡吃像漢堡那種速食，所以我選擇吃麵。
8.	**I have started teaching foreigners Taiwanese.** 我開始教外國人台語。
9.	**What do you think of the temple traditions and the parade?** 你對廟會和迎神賽會有什麼看法？
10.	**Remember not to touch the fruit while doing grocery shopping in Europe.** 記得在歐洲採買雜貨時，不要觸摸水果。
11.	**Many foreign workers can't get used to the high-pressure work environment here in Taiwan.** 許多外籍員工不能習慣台灣這裡的高壓工作環境。
12.	**As a Christian, Kevin avoids visiting temples in Taiwan.** 身為一名基督徒，凱文避免去參觀台灣的廟宇。

關鍵單字片語

1. **social practices** 片 社會習俗
2. **experience** [ɪk`spɪrɪəns] 名 經驗
3. **worship** [`wɝʃɪp] 動 崇拜
4. **feast** [fist] 名 盛宴
5. **taboo** [tə`bu] 名 禁忌
6. **custom** [`kʌstəm] 名 風俗習慣

實境對話

Frank: What are they burning along the streets?
他們在路邊燒什麼啊？

A-Yu: That's ghost money. It's a custom during Ghost Month.
在燒紙錢，這是鬼月的習俗。

Frank: Ghost Month? What is that?
鬼月？那是什麼？

A-Yu: The seventh month of the lunar calendar is called Ghost Month. That's when the ghosts come and visit our world.
農曆七月又叫「鬼月」。鬼月期間，鬼魂會回到陽間。

Frank: Oh, it's like Halloween, isn't it?
喔，就像是萬聖節，對吧？

A-Yu: Kind of. But we have many customs related to ghosts.
有點像，但我們有很多與鬼魂有關的習俗。

Frank: What do you mean?
什麼意思？

A-Yu: We will have a hand puppet show or Taiwanese folk opera in most cases. And we burn the ghost money to give blessings.
大部分的時候，我們會有布袋戲或是歌仔戲，而且會藉由燒紙錢來給予祝福。

Frank: Cool! Do you also do that at home?
法蘭克：酷耶！你們家也這樣做嗎？

A-Yu: Of course. Do you want to join us?
當然，你想要一起來參與嗎？

Frank: Sure! I am going to burn ghost money and the latest ghost iPad for them. I believe I'll be very much blessed next year!
好呀！我要燒紙錢和最新的紙iPad給祂們。我相信明年一定會被好好保佑。

A-Yu: Haha, I believe you will.
哈哈，我相信你會的。

關鍵單字片語

7. **get accustomed to** 片 習慣…

8. **guideline** [`gaɪd‚laɪn] 名 指導方針

9. **cultural habits** 片 文化習慣

10. **make sense** 片 有意義

11. **violated** [vaɪə`letɪd] 形 違反的

12. **vendor** [`vɛndɚ] 名 攤販

11. **傳統習俗：婚喪**
Marriage and Funerals

MP3
101

萬用好句

1. Jake stepped forward and took the bride's hand.
傑克走上前，牽起新娘的手。

2. In China, matchmakers arrange blind dates.
在中國，由媒人安排相親。

3. The betrothed were not allowed to see each other until the wedding night in ancient China.
在古代中國，未婚夫妻一直到新婚當晚才能見到彼此。

4. The bride's sister made a toast during the rehearsal dinner.
新娘的姊姊在婚禮預演晚宴上致詞。

5. In Chinese tradition, white is the color for funerals.
在中國傳統裡，白色是葬禮的顏色。

6. We decided to write our own wedding vows.
我們決定自己撰寫婚禮誓詞。

7. In Western culture, blue is a common wedding color.
在西方文化裡，藍色是婚禮常見的顏色。

8. Where did the wedding custom of "something old, something new, something borrowed, and something blue" come from?
婚禮習俗「舊的、新的、借來的、藍色的東西」，是從哪來的呢？

9. Jason asked the best man to hold the wedding ring.
傑森要求伴郎替他保管戒指。

10. In funerals, "white envelopes" contain condolence money.
在葬禮上，「白包」裡裝的就是慰問金。

11. The traditional color for attending a funeral service in Western culture is solid black, without any stripes or patterns.
在西方文化裡，參加喪禮的傳統顏色是純黑色，不帶任何條紋或花樣。

12. The bereaved son held a memorial service for his father.
那個喪父的兒子替他父親舉辦了追思儀式。

關鍵單字片語

1. **the auspicious time** 片 良辰吉時
2. **matchmaker** [`mætʃˌmekə] 名 媒人
3. **funeral** [`fjunərəl] 名 葬禮
4. **condolence** [kən`doləns] 名 弔唁
5. **console with** 片 以…加以安慰
6. **bachelor party** 片 單身漢派對

實境對話

Hank: Your wedding day is two weeks away. Are you nervous?
兩週後就要舉辦你的婚禮了，你會緊張嗎？

Diana: Of course! There are so many things that have to be done!
當然緊張啊！有好多事情要做呢！

Hank: Calm down. Take a deep breath. I can help you!
冷靜，深呼吸。我可以幫你！

Diana: Thank you. That's very nice of you.
謝謝你，你人真好。

Hank: Come on! I am your best friend. It's my duty to help.
拜託！我是你最好的朋友，這是我應該做的。

Diana: What about "something old, something new, something borrowed, something blue, and a silver sixpence in your shoe"?
「舊的東西、新的東西、借來的東西、藍色的東西，和鞋子裡的六便士銀幣」該怎麼辦？

Hank: What are those?
那是什麼？

Diana: It's an old English custom. They're like good luck charms.
這是古老的英國習俗，就像是幸運符一樣。

Hank: I've never heard of them. What do they mean?
我從來沒聽過，它們有什麼意義嗎？

Diana: Well, they symbolize continuity, optimism for the future, happiness and fidelity respectively. A sixpence in the shoe is a wish for good fortune.
它們各代表家族延續、對未來的期待、快樂、和忠誠。鞋子裡的六分錢則是希望未來富有。

Hank: OK. No worries. I will take care of that.
好，別擔心，包在我身上。

Diana: Thank you so much!
真的很謝謝你！

關鍵單字片語

7. **ceremony** [ˈsɛrəˌmonɪ] 名 典禮

8. **bridesmaid** [ˈbraɪdzˌmed] 名 伴娘

9. **newlywed** [ˈnjulɪˌwɛd] 名 新人

10. **bouquet** [buˈke] 名 捧花

11. **betrothed** [bɪˈtrɔθt] 名 未婚夫(妻)

12. **wedding gown** 片 婚紗

12. 傳統習俗：儒道文化
Confucianism

MP3 102

萬用好句

1. **Confucianism is very important in Chinese culture.**
儒家思想在中華文化裡，是很重要的一環。

2. **Teacher's Day is also Confucius's birthday.**
教師節同時也是孔子的誕辰。

3. **Confucianism provided ancient Chinese society with an education system and strict conventions of social etiquette.**
儒家思想提供古代中國社會一套教育體制和嚴謹的社會禮教習俗。

4. **Lao-Tzu is the founder of philosophical Taoism.**
老子是哲學理論道家的創立者。

5. **Can anyone explain more about Confucius's philosophy?**
有人可以解釋孔子的哲學思想嗎？

6. **The Analects describe the spirit of Confucianism.**
論語講述了儒家思想的精隨。

7. **The Analects is based on Confucius's discussions with his students.**
論語是孔子與學生間的討論文選。

8. **Many students will go to the Confucius Temple and ask for blessings and good luck on their exams.**
許多學生會去孔廟祈求考試能順利好運。

9. **Taoism has had great influence on the philosophy of feng shui.**
道家對風水哲學有很大的影響。

10. **Chuang-Tzu was another important Taoist philosopher.**
莊子也是道家重要的哲學家。

11. **Confucianism philosophizes about how society should be organized.**
儒家思想解釋了社會組織的哲學。

12. **On the other hand, Taoism is more about the observation of nature and the discovery of the Tao.**
另一方面，道家學說則與觀察自然和悟道有關。

關鍵單字片語

1. **Confucius** [kənˋfjuʃəs] 名 孔子

2. **philosopher** [fəˋlɑsəfə] 名 哲學家

3. **idea** [aɪˋdiə] 名 想法

4. **moral values** 片 道德價值

5. **disciple** [dɪˋsaɪpl] 名 門徒、弟子

6. **Analects** [͵ænəˋlɛkts] 名 論語

實境對話

Kenny: Why are so many people over there?
那裡怎麼聚集了那麼多人？

Xio-Hua: Oh! It's a Confucius Temple.
喔！那是孔廟。

Kenny: I've never seen a temple with so many people.
我從來沒看過一間廟有這麼多人。

Xio-Hua: It's because they are watching the eight-row dance.
那是因為他們在看八佾舞。

Kenny: A dancing show? I thought you said it's a temple!
舞蹈表演嗎？我以為你說那是間廟！

Xio-Hua: It is, but they're celebrating Confucius's birthday.
那是廟沒錯，但是他們在慶祝孔夫子誕辰。

Kenny: He must be very important to you.
他對你們一定很重要。

Xio-Hua: You can tell his great importance from his nickname, "the First and Greatest Teacher."
你從他的別稱「至聖先師」，就可以知道他的重要性了。

Kenny: Is that why today is known as Teacher's Day?
那是之所以設今天為教師節的原因嗎？

Xio-Hua: That's right. Besides, many students who are about to take exams will worship him for good luck.
沒錯。而且很多考生會拜他求好運。

Kenny: Have you ever worshipped him before a big exam?
你有在大考前拜過他嗎？

Xio-Hua: I used to. But since I am majoring in English, I don't find it useful anymore.
以前有。但自從我主修英文，我覺得這可能沒有用了。

關鍵單字片語

7. **Lao-Tzu** [ˋlauˋtz] 名 老子

8. **Taoism** [ˋtau͵ɪzəm] 名 道家學說

9. **Tao Te Ching** 片 道德經

10. **solitary** [ˋsɑlə͵tɛrɪ] 名 隱士

11. **etiquette** [ˋɛtɪkɛt] 名 禮節

12. **Confucian** [kənˋfjuʃən] 名 儒家

13. 傳統習俗：家族
The Clan

MP3
103

萬用好句

1.	A family in harmony will prosper in everything. 家和萬事興。
2.	A family with an old person has a living golden treasure. 家有一老，如有一寶。
3.	Dinner is bonding time in our family. 晚餐是我家聯繫感情的時間。
4.	Family bonding results from different activities that keep parents and children living in harmony. 家庭聯繫感情來自於讓父母和孩子保持良好和諧關係的各種活動。
5.	Most traditional Chinese families value boys more than girls. 大部分傳統的中國家庭偏愛男孩勝於女孩。
6.	Some Western teenagers refer to their parents by their first names. 一些西方的青少年會直接以父母的名字稱呼他們。
7.	Jason is named after his great-grandfather. 傑森是以他的曾祖父命名的。
8.	The whole family used to live in the same village. 這個家族以前全住在同一個村子裡。
9.	In the past, in traditional Chinese families, the marriage partners for female members were decided by their fathers or brothers. 過去，在傳統的中國家庭裡，女性的婚姻是由她們的父兄決定。
10.	In Chinese culture, a married woman is no longer considered a member of her original family. 在中國文化裡，已婚女性不再被認為是原生家庭的一員。
11.	Traditionally, the oldest male is in charge of all the family affairs. 傳統上，長男掌管所有家內事宜。
12.	How do you celebrate a family member's birthday? 你們都怎麼為家族成員慶生？

關鍵單字片語

1. **sibling** [`sɪblɪŋ] 名 兄弟姊妹

2. **attach to** 片 與…有親情聯繫

3. **bond** [bɑnd] 動 情感聯繫

4. **keep in harmony** 片 維持和諧

5. **grow up** 片 成長

6. **family value** 片 家庭價值

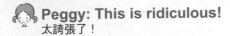

實境對話

Peggy: This is ridiculous!
太誇張了！

Andy: What's wrong? Why are you so angry?
怎麼了？你怎麼這麼生氣？

Peggy: I just read a novel. It's about a Chinese woman forced to marry a guy she has never met.
我剛剛在看小說。是有關一個中國女性，她被逼要嫁給一個她從沒見過的男人。

Andy: Actually, that was life in ancient China.
事實上，這就是古代中國的生活。

Peggy: Are you kidding me? She hadn't even seen the guy before!
你開玩笑嗎？她見都沒見過那男的耶！

Andy: In the past, parents arranged their children's marriages.
過去，父母可以決定孩子的婚姻。

Peggy: I am angry at the character's mother for saying nothing.
我很氣主角的媽媽，竟然一句話都沒說。

Andy: Chinese women were obedient to their husbands.
昔日的中國女性要順從丈夫的決定。

Peggy: Really? How about the sons? Could women discipline their sons?
真的嗎？那兒子呢？女人們可以管教兒子嗎？

Andy: They could until their sons became adults.
可以，但當兒子成年之後，就不能管教了。

Peggy: It sounds really unfair to the women. I'm so happy that I was not born in ancient China.
聽起來對女性很不公平。真慶幸我不是生在古代的中國。

Andy: So am I.
我也這樣想。

關鍵單字片語

7. **support system** 片 支持系統

8. **emotional** [ɪˋmoʃən] 形 情感上的

9. **lasting** [ˋlæstɪŋ] 形 持續的

10. **unfair** [ʌnˋfɛr] 形 不公平的

11. **link** [lɪŋk] 名 動 連結、聯繫

12. **reliable** [rɪˋlaɪəbl] 形 可依靠的

14. 西風東漸
Westernization
MP3
104

萬用好句

1.	**Westernization in Taiwan is obvious in many respects.** 台灣的西方化顯見於許多方面。
2.	**Western culture and values are seeping into our society.** 西方文化和價值觀正悄悄地滲入我們的社會。
3.	**What do you think of the Westernization of Chinese culture?** 你對中華文化的西方化有什麼看法？
4.	**My friend believes that having a Western boyfriend or girlfriend means climbing the social ladder.** 我的朋友相信有個外籍男友或女友，身分就高級了。
5.	**People enjoy the merry holiday atmosphere of Christmas.** 人們很享受聖誕節帶來的歡欣氣氛。
6.	**Many people enjoy having a light salad for health reasons.** 許多人出於健康因素而喜歡吃清爽的沙拉。
7.	**My grandfather thinks it's weird to eat steak.** 我的祖父認為吃牛排很奇怪。
8.	**Which do you prefer, Western coffee or Eastern tea?** 你喜歡哪一個，西方的咖啡還是東方的茶？
9.	**I brought my foreign friend to an exotic restaurant for dinner.** 我帶外國朋友到異國餐廳享用晚餐。
10.	**Many Asian girls are making an effort to look exotic.** 許多亞洲女孩努力讓自己看起來像外國人。
11.	**Studying abroad is a good chance to experience life in a foreign country.** 出國留學是去國外體驗生活的一個好機會。
12.	**Western cooking, with less smoke in the kitchen, is healthier than traditional Chinese deep-frying.** 比起傳統中國火炒的方式，西方的無煙烹調較為健康。

關鍵單字片語

1. **westernize** [`wɛstə‚naɪz] 動 西方化

2. **industry** [`ɪndəstrɪ] 名 工業、企業

3. **trendy** [`trɛndɪ] 形 時髦的、流行的

4. **version** [`vɜʒən] 名 版本

5. **old school** 片 守舊的人

6. **change** [tʃendʒ] 動 改變

實境對話

A-min: Mom, do you remember what day next Friday is?
媽，你記得下週五是什麼日子嗎？

Mom: Of course I do. It's your birthday, my sweet pea.
我當然記得，是你的生日啊，親愛的。

A-min: Thank you, Mom. How will we celebrate my birthday?
媽，謝謝你。我們要怎麼慶祝我的生日？

Mom: I am thinking about making it big since it's your fifteenth birthday.
既然是你的十五歲生日，我想要擴大慶祝。

A-min: Cool! Will I have a big birthday cake and a great party?
酷！我會有大的生日蛋糕和派對嗎？

Mom: No, sweetheart. We are doing it in the Chinese way.
親愛的，不用。我們要用中國方式來慶祝。

A-min: The Chinese way? What's that?
中國方式？那是什麼？

Mom: We will have thin noodles on your birthday to represent longevity.
我們會在生日吃麵線，代表長壽。

A-min: That's so old-fashioned! My friends all celebrate in the Western way--a big birthday cake and a great party with friends.
好老套！我的朋友都用西方的方式慶祝了──大的生日蛋糕，還有能與朋友同樂的派對！

Mom: We are Chinese and should do it in the Chinese way!
我們中國人應該用中國的方式慶祝！

A-min: Mom, please! I really want to have a birthday cake like everyone else does!
媽，拜託！我真的很想跟其他人一樣有生日蛋糕！

Mom: OK. I'll make you a birthday cake made of rice instead.
好，我會另外幫你做個生日年糕。

關鍵單字片語

7. **thin noodles** 片 麵線

8. **be related to** 片 與…有關

9. **in contact with** 片 與…有聯繫

10. **colony** [`kɑlənɪ] 名 殖民地

11. **longevity** [lɑn`dʒɛvətɪ] 名 長壽

12. **two-sided** [`tu`saɪdɪd] 形 兩邊的

15. **東風西漸**
Orientalization

MP3
105

萬用好句

1.	**Drinking Chinese tea is the latest fashion now.** 中國茶是最近的新流行。
2.	**My French professor loves sushi and shabu-shabu very much.** 我的法籍教授非常喜歡壽司和涮涮鍋。
3.	**The Qipao has made its way into the international world of high fashion.** 中國旗袍打入了國際高級時裝界。
4.	**How about getting a dressmaker to make a Chinese Cheongsam, or Mandarin gown, for you as a souvenir?** 找位裁縫師，幫你訂做一件中國旗袍當做紀念品如何？
5.	**Chinese characters convey the beauty of Chinese culture.** 中國文字展現中華文化之美。
6.	**There will be a Taiwanese Local Snack Fair in June in London.** 倫敦六月會有一場台灣當地小吃展。
7.	**We went to Jason Wu's fashion show. His designs were amazing.** 我們去看吳季剛的時尚展，他的設計實在令人吃驚。
8.	**Chinese calligraphy is definitely one of the most treasured traditional arts in the world.** 中國書法絕對是世界上最有價值的傳統藝術之一。
9.	**Did you know soccer originated in ancient China?** 你知道足球源於古代中國嗎？
10.	**It's certainly an exotic experience to visit London's Chinatown during the Chinese New Year.** 在中國新年期間去倫敦的唐人街玩，一定會是個很特別的異國經驗。
11.	**Yoga originated in India and has become popular in the West.** 瑜伽源自於印度，後來在西方大受歡迎。
12.	**Ginseng is known for its nourishing and healthful effects.** 人參以滋養進補的功效著稱。

關鍵單字片語

1. **oriental** [ˌorɪˈɛntl̩] 形 東方的
2. **alter** [ˈɔltɚ] 動 改變
3. **transform** [trænsˈfɔrm] 動 轉變
4. **to the point of** 片 到達…的程度
5. **culturally** [ˈkʌltʃərəlɪ] 副 文化上
6. **acculturate** [əˈkʌltʃəˌret] 動 文化適應

實境對話

Kenny: Are you available this Saturday?
你這星期六有空嗎？

Xio-Hua: Yes. Why?
有啊，怎麼啦？

Kenny: Would you please go shopping with me?
你可以陪我去購物嗎？

Xio-Hua: Of course. What are you going to buy?
當然可以，你要買什麼？

Kenny: I need to buy a gift for my boss. He is a fan of Eastern culture. Do you have any suggestions?
我要買禮物給我老闆，他很迷東方文化，你有建議嗎？

Xio-Hua: Sure. More and more westerners are starting to appreciate Eastern culture. Does he collect anything?
當然，有越來越多西方人開始欣賞東方文化。他有蒐集些什麼嗎？

Kenny: He is totally into Chinese characters. He even has a tattoo of a Chinese character.
他很迷中國字。他甚至還有個中文字的刺青。

Xio-Hua: Then we can get him "The Four Treasures of the Study."
那我們可以買「文房四寶」給他。

Kenny: That's a good idea! Where should we go?
好主意！我們要去哪裡買？

Xio-Hua: We can go to the Central Market in Chinatown.
我們可以去唐人街的中央市場。

Kenny: Wonderful! He will be thrilled to get this present.
太棒了！他看到禮物一定會開心死了。

Xio-Hua: Haha, I hope he likes it.
哈哈，我希望他會喜歡。

關鍵單字片語

7. **religion** [rɪˋlɪdʒən] 名 宗教

8. **adopt** [əˋdɑpt] 動 採用、吸收

9. **either...or...** 片 不是…就是…

10. **have effects on** 片 對…有影響

11. **depend on** 片 取決於

12. **voluntary** [ˋvɑlənˏtɛrɪ] 形 自願的

PART 3

Let's Chat in English!

3 進階深度聊

advanced level

1. 第一印象
First Impressions
MP3
106

萬用好句

1.	**Making a great first impression is the key to a successful job interview.** 良好的第一印象是成功工作面試的重要關鍵。
2.	**When you first meet someone, it only takes a quick glance to evaluate him or her.** 當你首次遇見某人,有時只需稍瞥一眼,就能對其下評斷。
3.	**A friendly smile can help create a good first impression.** 一抹友善的微笑有助建立良好的第一印象。
4.	**Never judge a book by its cover.** 人不可貌相。
5.	**Jeff put on his best suit, trying to impress his future father-in-law.** 傑夫穿上他最棒的西裝,要讓他未來的岳父印象深刻。
6.	**A good handshake is vital to making a great first impression.** 好的握手方式對於建立良好的第一印象很重要。
7.	**People form their first impression of you based on your hygiene, your clothing and your personality.** 人們根據你的衛生、穿著與個性建立對你的第一印象。
8.	**First impressions are formed on the basis of a person's appearance, including communication skills and personal conduct.** 第一印象建立在個人的外在表現上,包括溝通技巧及個人行為。
9.	**First impressions may sometimes be misleading.** 第一印象有時會誤導人。
10.	**As a famous matchmaker, Mrs. Watson is good at assisting her clients in making great first impressions on each other.** 身為有名的媒人,華生太太很擅長協助客戶在彼此身上留下好印象。
11.	**Never underestimate the impact of first impressions.** 絕對不要低估第一印象的影響力。

關鍵單字片語

1. **first impression** 片 第一印象
2. **expect** [ɪk`spɛkt] 動 期待
3. **smile** [smaɪl] 動 名 微笑
4. **intimidating** [ɪn`tɪmə‚detɪŋ] 形 嚇人的
5. **eye contact** 片 眼神接觸
6. **glance** [glæns] 名 一瞥

226

實境對話

Jane: You look very uneasy. Is there anything wrong?
你看起來很不安，怎麼了嗎？

Kevin: No, but thank you for asking. I am just nervous.
沒事，謝謝你。我只是很緊張。

Jane: Why?
為什麼？

Kevin: My job interview is tomorrow. It's my dream job, and I really want to impress the interviewers.
我明天就要面試工作了。這是我夢寐以求的工作，我真想讓面試者有好印象。

Jane: Wow! First impressions are crucial to job interviews.
哇！第一印象對於工作面試非常重要哦。

Kevin: You're not helping. You're making me even more nervous!
你在幫倒忙，你讓我更緊張了！

Jane: Don't be. Just dress and talk appropriately, and you'll be fine.
別擔心。只要穿著、談吐都合宜，你沒問題的。

Kevin: What do you mean by "dress and talk appropriately"?
你說「穿著談吐都合宜」是什麼意思？

Jane: Wear a clean suit, which shows that you are not only disciplined but responsible.
「穿著合宜」，顯示你的自律和負責。

Kevin: Oh, I see. What about "talk appropriately"?
喔，我懂了。那「談吐合宜」呢？

Jane: It means you should answer the questions intelligently and with confidence, stressing that you are dependable and capable.
意思是聰明、有自信地回答問題，這可以展現你值得信任、也很適合這份工作。

Kevin: Now I know exactly what I should do. Thank you.
現在我知道該怎麼做了。謝謝你。

關鍵單字片語

7. **under the spotlight** 片 被注意到

8. **the pearly whites** 片 潔白的牙齒

9. **positive** [`pɑzətɪv] 形 有自信的

10. **adorable** [ə`dorəbl] 形 可愛的

11. **friendly** [`frɛndlɪ] 形 友善的

12. **appropriate** [ə`proprɪ.et] 形 恰當的

2. **天馬行空**
Talking about Anything
MP3 **107**

萬用好句

1. **What do you do for a living?**
   你做什麼工作？

2. **You have beautiful sparkling eyes.**
   你有美麗閃亮的雙眼。

3. **I like your hair. Where do you have your hair done?**
   我喜歡你的髮型，是在哪裡做的啊？

4. **I'd like to introduce myself. I'm Jason, Maria's cousin.**
   我來自我介紹：我是傑森，瑪利亞的表弟。

5. **How do you know Karen and John?**
   你是怎麼認識凱倫跟約翰的？

6. **I'd like you to meet my colleague, Linda. Linda, this is Ken.**
   我想介紹你認識我的同事琳達。琳達，這是肯。

7. **How many people are there in your family?**
   你家裡有幾個人？

8. **What kind of music do you like?**
   你喜歡哪一種音樂？

9. **Maybe we can have dinner some time next week.**
   也許下星期我們可以找個時間吃晚餐。

10. **Have you seen any interesting movies lately?**
    你最近看了什麼有趣的電影嗎？

11. **You have a very beautiful name. Does it have any special meaning?**
    你的名字很美，這有什麼特別的意思嗎？

12. **Have we met before?**
    我們以前遇過嗎？

關鍵單字片語

1. **introduce** [ˌɪntrəˈdjus] 動 介紹

2. **meet** [mit] 動 遇見

3. **hobby** [ˈhɑbɪ] 名 嗜好、喜好

4. **favorite** [ˈfevərɪt] 形 最喜愛的

5. **courteously** [ˈkɝtɪəslɪ] 副 有禮貌地

6. **encounter** [ɪnˈkaʊntɚ] 動 意外遇見

實境對話

Kevin: Hi, I'm Kevin, John's friend back in college. May I ask your name?
嗨，我是凱文，約翰以前的大學朋友。我有榮幸知道你的名字嗎？

Amanda: Sure. I'm Amanda, John's co-worker.
當然可以。我是亞曼達，約翰的同事。

Kevin: Oh, so you are Amanda.
喔，原來你就是亞曼達。

Amanda: What do you mean? Have you heard of me?
什麼意思？你聽過我的名字嗎？

Kevin: I heard a lot about you from John. He told me you're a big tennis fan.
我聽約翰說了很多你的事，他告訴我你很喜歡網球。

Amanda: Yes, I am. How about you? Are you into any sports?
沒錯。那你呢？你有特別喜歡的運動嗎？

Kevin: I like tennis a lot as well.
我也很喜歡網球。

Amanda: What a coincIdence! Did you hear about the 5-hour game between Djokovic and Nadal in the Australian Open final?
真巧！你知道那場澳洲公開賽喬科維奇和納道爾五個小時的比賽嗎？

Kevin: Yes, I did. It was really a great game between two fantastic tennis players. I really admire their sportsmanship.
我知道啊。那真是場兩位優秀選手間的精采比賽，我真的很佩服他們的運動家精神。

Amanda: So do I. To me, they both are winners.
我也是。在我心目中他們兩個都是贏家。

Kevin: I couldn't agree with you more. Well then, how about playing tennis together some time next week?
我非常同意你。下星期找個時間一起打場網球如何？

關鍵單字片語

7. **get to know** 片 開始瞭解

8. **shiny** [`ʃaɪnɪ] 形 閃耀的

9. **pleased** [plizd] 形 欣喜的

10. **break the ice** 片 打開話題

11. **potted history** 片 個人背景簡介

12. **small talk** 片 閒聊

3.相約出遊
Let's Go Out!
MP.3 108

萬用好句

1.	**How about going to the movies together this evening?** 今天晚上一起去看電影好不好？
2.	**What are your plans for the coming holiday?** 你這個假日的計畫是什麼？
3.	**Jill always hangs out with her cousins on weekends.** 吉兒週末總和她表姊妹一起閒晃。
4.	**When should I pick you up?** 我何時該去接你？
5.	**There is an exhibition of pottery from the Ching Dynasty on now at the museum. Would you like to come with me?** 博物館目前有場清朝陶器的展覽，你要和我一起去嗎？
6.	**Do you want to share a ride with me to the zoo?** 你想搭我的車去動物園嗎？
7.	**It is always a delight to tour with one's family in good weather.** 好天氣和家人一同出遊，總是令人心情愉快。
8.	**Do you want to join us for snowboarding next weekend?** 你下週末想和我們一起去溜滑雪板嗎？
9.	**I wish I could go to the movies with you, but I have to prepare for my mid-term.** 我想和你去看電影，但我得準備期中考。
10.	**How many people are coming on the company trip to Thailand?** 有多少人要參加公司的泰國旅遊？
11.	**Let's go to Hawaii for a vacation!** 一起去夏威夷度假吧！
12.	**Good companions can always add enjoyment to your trip.** 好的旅伴能讓你的旅程增色不少。

關鍵單字片語

1. **hang out with** 片 與某人消磨時間
2. **meet up** 片 碰面
3. **invite** [In`vaɪt] 動 邀請
4. **spend time with** 片 與某人度過時光
5. **spring break** 片 春假
6. **museum** [mju`zɪəm] 名 博物館

實境對話

Alan: Yeah! Spring break is just around the corner!
耶！春假馬上就要到了！

Jenny: You've already got a plan?
你已經有計劃了？

Alan: Sure. I made reservations two months ago.
當然有。我兩個月前就預定好了。

Jenny: Wow, you are really organized. Where are you going?
哇，你真有規劃。你要去哪裡？

Alan: I'm going to Switzerland.
我要去瑞士。

Jenny: Cool! Switzerland! It's No. 1 on my travel list, too.
酷！瑞士耶！那也是我旅遊名單的第一名。

Alan: Its natural treasure of mountains, lakes, glaciers, and the Alps are world famous.
瑞士以自然資源，像是山、湖、冰河和阿爾卑斯山聞名全球。

Jenny: How many days will you be there?
你要去幾天？

Alan: I'm staying in Switzerland for ten days.
我要在瑞士待十天。

Jenny: I've always dreamt about going to Switzerland one day. Why didn't you ask me to go with you?
我一直夢想著去瑞士。你為何沒邀我？

Alan: You know what? Here is your flight ticket. Surprise!
你知道嗎？來，這是你的機票。嚇到你了吧！

Jenny: Are you serious? Am I dreaming?
你是認真的嗎？我在作夢嗎？

Alan: Yes I am, and no you're not. We're going to Switzerland!
我是認真的，你不是在作夢。我們要去瑞士了！

關鍵單字片語

7. **schedule** [`skɛdʒul] 動 將…排入計劃

8. **family outing** 片 家庭出遊

9. **carpool** [`kɑr͵pul] 名 共乘制度

10. **glacier** [`gleʃɚ] 名 冰河

11. **fair** [fɛr] 形 天氣晴朗的

12. **stand sb. up** 片 放某人鴿子；失約

231

4.甜蜜約會
Dating

MP3 109

萬用好句

1.	**My mom wants to set my brother up with our neighbor, Jenny.** 我媽媽想幫我哥和鄰居珍妮安排約會。
2.	**Janice is totally my type of girl.** 珍妮絲完全是我喜歡的那種女生。
3.	**Kevin never takes a girl to a movie on a first date.** 凱文第一次約會從不帶女生去看電影。
4.	**Larry had a crush on Mary and decided to ask her out.** 賴瑞被瑪麗煞到，決定約她出去。
5.	**Where are you taking your girlfriend for dinner tonight?** 你今晚要帶你女朋友去哪裡吃飯？
6.	**When should I pick you up, seven or eight?** 我該幾點去接你，七點還是八點？
7.	**It's Jeff's first date with Lynn, so he couldn't be more nervous.** 這是傑夫第一次和琳恩約會，所以他非常緊張。
8.	**It never occurred to Tom that he would ever have the chance to date the girl of his dreams.** 湯姆從沒想過他會有和夢中情人約會的機會。
9.	**Do you know who Janice's date is tonight?** 你知道珍妮絲今晚要和誰約會嗎？
10.	**Kevin and Gina had a romantic candlelight dinner at a fancy French restaurant last night.** 凱文和吉娜昨晚在一間精緻的法式餐廳，享用了一頓浪漫的燭光晚餐。
11.	**Amanda was very touched when she saw Larry carrying a bunch of red roses, her favorite flower.** 當亞曼達看到賴瑞捧著一束她最愛的紅玫瑰時，她非常感動。
12.	**Frank is such a gentleman that he always opens the car door for his date.** 法蘭克很有紳士風度，他總幫約會對象開車門。

關鍵單字片語

1. **date** [det] 名 約會對象

2. **crush** [krʌʃ] 名 迷戀的對象

3. **fall in love** 片 墜入愛河

4. **pick up** 片 把上(男友或女友)

5. **double date** 片 兩對約會

6. **dress up** 片 盛裝打扮

實境對話

Frank: Which suit is better, the gray one or the white one?
哪一套西裝比較好，灰色還是白色的？

Joy: The gray one. Why? Are you going somewhere?
灰色的。怎麼了？你要去哪裡嗎？

Frank: I have a dinner date with Janice tonight.
我今晚要和珍妮絲吃晚餐。

Joy: Haven't you been seeing each other for six years? How come you look so nervous?
你們不是已經約會六年了嗎？你怎麼看起來這麼緊張？

Frank: That's because I am really nervous.
那是因為我真的很緊張。

Joy: Why is that? You've been on at least a hundred dates with her.
怎麼了？你們已經約會超過一百次了吧。

Frank: Tonight is different. Look.
今天晚上不一樣，你看。

Joy: Wow. A diamond ring! Are you going to propose to her?
哇，鑽戒耶！你要跟她求婚嗎？

Frank: Yes. I've contacted the restaurant, and they're going to hide the ring in a cake.
嗯。我和餐廳聯絡過了，他們會幫我把鑽戒藏在蛋糕裡。

Joy: It sounds very romantic. I'm sure Janice will be very touched.
聽起來很浪漫，我敢說珍妮絲一定很感動。

Frank: I hope so. I hope everything goes well and that she says "yes." to me.
我希望她會。我希望一切順利，她能答應我的求婚。

Joy: I believe she will. Good luck.
我相信她會的，祝你好運。

關鍵單字片語

7. **make-up** [`mek͵ʌp] 名 化妝；裝扮

8. **be seeing sb.** 片 與…約會

9. **escort** [`ɛskɔrt] 名 陪同赴宴者

10. **blind date** 片 相親

11. **flirt** [flɜt] 動 調情

12. **propose** [prə`poz] 動 求婚

5.糾團聚餐
Dinner Party
MP3
110

萬用好句

1. **How about having lunch at Lucy's together?**
一起去「露西小館」吃午餐好不好？

2. **Maria insisted on splitting the bill with Kenny.**
瑪利亞堅持要和肯尼分攤費用。

3. **Some of my high school friends are going to have dinner together next Wednesday.**
我有些高中朋友下週三要一起吃晚餐。

4. **Do you want to join us for dinner tonight?**
你今晚要和我們一起吃晚餐嗎？

5. **What do you want to eat for lunch, hot pot or teppanyaki?**
你午餐想吃什麼，火鍋還是鐵板燒？

6. **My colleagues just had a pizza party in celebration of the highest sales ever.**
我的同事們為了慶祝史上最高銷售數字，一起吃比薩。

7. **Excuse me. May I have two more plates?**
不好意思，我可以再要兩個盤子嗎？

8. **Do you want some dessert?**
你想要來些甜點嗎？

9. **I'd like to have some onion rings as my appetizer.**
開胃菜我想吃洋蔥圈。

10. **Frank tapped his glass with a spoon and then made a toast to Karen, the hostess of the dinner party tonight.**
法蘭克用湯匙敲敲玻璃杯，向晚宴的主人凱倫舉杯致詞。

11. **My family enjoys having Christmas dinner together and connecting with each other at the same time.**
我的家人喜歡一起吃耶誕大餐，並且和彼此交流。

12. **Let's meet over dinner at 7.**
我們七點晚餐見。

關鍵單字片語

1. **grab a bite** 片 隨便吃吃

2. **eat out** 片 外出吃飯

3. **diner** [`daɪnɚ] 名 小餐館

4. **restaurant** [`rɛstərənt] 名 餐廳

5. **hot pot** 片 火鍋

6. **make a toast** 片 舉杯致詞

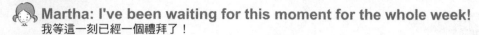

Martha: I've been waiting for this moment for the whole week!
我等這一刻已經一個禮拜了！

Stan: Haha. Are you going anywhere?
哈哈，你要去哪裡嗎？

Martha: I'm going to Sasha's new house for dinner.
我要去莎夏新家吃晚餐。

Stan: Her new house? Has she bought a new house?
她的新家？她買新房子啦？

Martha: Yes. She and her fiancé have bought a new house.
對呀，她跟她未婚夫已經買新房了。

Stan: Her fiancé? Is she going to get married soon?
未婚夫？她快要結婚了嗎？

Martha: Yes. Haven't you heard about this?
對啊，你沒聽說嗎？

Stan: No, I didn't know until you told me.
沒有，你告訴我之前，我都不知道。

Martha: Maybe she's going to tell you later. Do you want to come with me? I'm sure she would be very happy to see you.
也許她之後就會跟你說了。你想和我一起去嗎？她看到你一定會很高興的。

Stan: Of course. Can we drop by a department store before we go to the party?
當然好。我們去派對之前，可以先繞去百貨公司嗎？

Martha: Sure. Why?
當然可以，要做什麼啊？

Stan: I am going to get a housewarming gift and a wedding gift for her.
我要買新居落成和新婚的禮物給她。

關鍵單字片語

7. **tap** [tæp] 動 輕敲

8. **lazy Susan** 片 (餐桌中央的)圓轉盤

9. **takeout** [`tek.aut] 名 外賣

10. **take a rain check** 片 改天再約

11. **together** [tə`gɛðɚ] 副 一起

12. **be hungry for** 片 對…感到飢渴

235

6.電話漫談
Phone Chat

MP3 111

萬用好句

1.	**I'll phone back later.** 我晚點再打來。
2.	**I've got the wrong number.** 我打錯電話了。
3.	**Can I take a message for you?** 我可以替您留言嗎？
4.	**I'm sorry. Amanda is not at her desk now.** 很抱歉，亞曼達現在不在座位上。
5.	**Thank you for calling.** 謝謝你打來。
6.	**I can't get through. The line is busy.** 我打不通電話，佔線中。
7.	**There was no reply, so I left a message on the answering machine.** 沒人接電話，所以我在答錄機上留言。
8.	**The connection is bad. I can't hear you.** 收訊很差，我聽不清楚。
9.	**Can you speak louder?** 你可以大聲點嗎？
10.	**This is Jessie speaking.** 我是潔西。
11.	**Who is this, please?** 請問您是哪位？
12.	**I just want to spend some time alone, so I won't pick up the phone today.** 我只想獨處一下，所以我今天不會接電話。

關鍵單字片語

1. **hang up** 片 掛掉電話

2. **make phone calls** 片 撥電話

3. **answer** [`ænsə] 動 接電話

4. **ring off** 片 掛斷電話

5. **caller** [`kɔlə] 名 來電者

6. **dial** [`daɪəl] 動 撥號

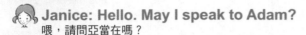

實境對話

Janice: Hello. May I speak to Adam?
喂，請問亞當在嗎？

Adam: This is Adam speaking. Who's this?
我就是，請問您哪位？

Janice: This is Janice. I haven't talked to you for ages.
我是珍妮絲，好久沒跟你講到話了。

Adam: Hi, Janice! How have you been?
嗨，珍妮絲。你最近好嗎？

Janice: Great. I haven't seen you since the end of the semester.
很好。自從學期結束我就沒見過你了。

Adam: You're right. I was away until last Saturday.
沒錯，我上週六才回來。

Janice: Where did you go?
你去哪裡啊？

Adam: I went to Paris with my parents. How about you? Where did you go?
我和我爸媽去巴黎。那你呢？去了哪裡嗎？

Janice: Nowhere. My parents have been too busy to travel.
哪裡也沒有。我爸媽一直很忙，他們沒時間旅行。

Adam: That's too bad. Why are you calling?
真是太糟了，你為什麼會打給我？

Janice: I'm wondering if you have finished your assignment. I really need some help.
我在想你作業寫完了嗎？我真的需要一點幫助。

Adam: Sure. Do you want to come over? I can help you.
好啊。你想要過來嗎？我可以教你。

Janice: There's no need. I just need to check the answers.
不用了，我只需要核對答案。

關鍵單字片語

7. **operator** [`ɑpə,retə] 名 接線生

8. **directory** [də`rɛktərɪ] 名 電話簿

9. **busy** [`bɪzɪ] 形 忙線中

10. **on the phone** 片 電話中

11. **leave a message** 片 留言

12. **speak to** 片 與…講電話

7. 臉書互動
Facebook
MP3 112

萬用好句

1.	Some people are able to get in touch with long-lost friends on Facebook. 有些人甚至在臉書上聯絡上失聯的朋友。
2.	I really hate being randomly sent game requests on Facebook. 我真的很討厭在臉書上收到任意寄發的遊戲邀請。
3.	Sometimes I find myself relying too much on Facebook. 有時，我發現自己太依賴臉書了。
4.	What is your favorite application or game on Facebook? 你最喜歡的臉書應用程式或遊戲是什麼？
5.	Many people get addicted to Facebook, and they are basically online the whole day. 許多人對臉書上癮，他們幾乎一整天都掛在線上。
6.	The News Feed is a list of updates about your friends on your own Facebook home page. 「動態更新」就是你臉書首頁上朋友的動態更新列表。
7.	You can always update your Facebook profile at the left side of your screen. 你總可以在螢幕左側更新你的臉書檔案。
8.	Jenny is a Facebook friend of mine; we have never met each other in person. 珍妮是我的臉書朋友，我們從來沒有見過面。
9.	Facebook me whenever you have anything interesting to share. 每當你有趣事要分享的時候，就用臉書通知我。
10.	If you forget your password, you have to answer the privacy questions for the sake of security. 如果你忘了密碼，為了安全起見，你必須回答私人問題。
11.	Maria posts a joke on her wall before going to bed every night. 瑪利亞每晚睡前，會在她的塗鴉牆上貼一則笑話。

關鍵單字片語

1. **delete** [dɪˋlit] 動 刪除

2. **poke** [pok] 動 戳

3. **post** [post] 動 張貼

4. **like** [laɪk] 動 喜歡(讚)

5. **tag** [tæg] 動 貼上標籤

6. **appear offline** 片 顯示為離線

Sally: Amy's posted the photos of our class reunion on her wall.
愛咪把我們同學會的照片貼在牆上了。

Kenny: On her wall? What do you mean?
肯尼：貼在牆上？什麼意思？

Sally: On her Facebook wall. God, are you still living in a cave?
貼在她的臉書塗鴉牆上啊，天啊，你是山頂洞人嗎？

Kenny: I know what Facebook is. But what's the wall about?
我知道臉書，但甚麼是塗鴉牆？

Sally: It's a Facebook page on which you can see your friends' status posts and photos once you log in. Also, your friends can see your wall.
那是個讓你一登入就可看到朋友動態、文章和照片的臉書頁面。朋友也可看到你的塗鴉牆。

Kenny: Cool. It sounds like a spider web of blogs.
酷耶！聽起來像是部落格組成的蜘蛛網。

Sally: Exactly. Now, let's check out our photos.
沒錯，現在我們來看照片吧。

Kenny: Are you telling me that these are Amy's pictures?
你不是跟我說這些是愛咪的照片嗎？

Sally: Yes. What's wrong?
對呀，怎麼了？

Kenny: Since they're Amy's, why is your name on the pictures?
既然這些是愛咪的照片，你的名字怎麼會在上面呢？

Sally: Oh, it's the tag. You can tag your friends who took the photos with you. Once you tag them, the system will send them a notice.
喔，這是標籤。你可標記與你一起拍照的朋友。一經過標記，系統就會寄發通知給他們。

Kenny: Wow, how convenient!
哇，真方便！

關鍵單字片語

7. **online** [ˋɑnˏlaɪn] 形 在線上的

8. **status** [ˋstetəs] 名 狀態

9. **chat room** 片 聊天室

10. **hook up with** 片 和⋯聯絡上

11. **obsessively** [əbˋsɛsɪvlɪ] 副 沉迷地

12. **album** [ˋælbəm] 名 相簿

8. 分享私事
Sharing Secrets
MP3 113

萬用好句

1.	What I'm going to tell you should stay just between you and me. 我要跟你說的事，勿出四耳。
2.	Can you keep a secret? 你可以保守秘密嗎？
3.	There is no problem in mentioning this to anyone else. 可以向任何人提起這件事。
4.	Maria and Karen are trying to cheer up Kim, who just broke up with her boyfriend. 瑪利亞和凱倫試著要讓金開心起來，她剛和男朋友分手了。
5.	You can trust me and open up to me. 你可以相信我，對我坦誠。
6.	True friends will listen to you when you are in trouble, and they will always keep your secrets. 真正的朋友當你有困難的時候會聽你訴說，他們也會保守秘密。
7.	Do you know who spread the confidential information about Mary? 你知道是誰把瑪麗的事說出去的？
8.	Secrets are best shared only among close friends. 秘密最好只有密友知道。
9.	Kenny confided in me that he was dating Jim's sister. 肯尼跟我坦白說他在和吉姆的妹妹約會。
10.	I've been a bit depressed lately. Could I talk to you for a while? 我最近有點沮喪，可以跟你說說話嗎？
11.	It had been a secret until Gina brought it into the open. 到吉娜說出去之前，這一直是秘密。
12.	Jenny is such a blabbermouth that you can't trust her with any secrets. 珍妮是個大嘴巴，你別相信她會守住任何秘密。

關鍵單字片語

1. **a shoulder to cry on** 片 可以哭訴的對象

2. **sleepover** [`slip,ovɚ] 名 在朋友家過夜

3. **cheer sb. up** 片 使某人開心起來

4. **chitchat** [`tʃɪt.tʃæt] 動 閒談

5. **gossip** [`ɡɑsəp] 動 閒聊、八卦

6. **keep a secret** 片 保守秘密

實境對話

Jason: Emily, are you alright? Why are you crying?
艾蜜麗，你沒事吧？你怎麼在哭？

Emily: It's no big deal.
沒什麼事。

Jason: Come on. Just tell me. Maybe there is some way I can help.
少來了。說出來吧，或許有什麼是我能幫忙的。

Emily: Thank you. You are really my best friend.
謝謝你，你真是我最好的朋友。

Jason: What's a friend for? Tell me what happened.
朋友是用來做什麼的？跟我說發生什麼事。

Emily: I don't know where to start, and it is supposed to be a secret.
我不知道該從哪裡開始說，而且這應該要是個祕密的。

Jason: You can trust me. I'm good at keeping secrets.
你可以相信我，我最會保守秘密了。

Emily: Really? Can you promise me that you won't tell anyone?
真的嗎？你可以答應我絕對不會跟任何人說嗎？

Jason: Of course. What is it?
當然，發生了什麼事？

Emily: It's that...I failed my math midterm.
是這樣的…我數學期中考被當了。

Jason: Again? Haven't you failed math three times already?
又被當？你不是已經被當三次了？

Emily: That's why I don't know what to do. My dad will kill me when he sees my test score.
所以我不知道該怎麼辦。我爸看到分數的時候，一定會殺了我。

關鍵單字片語

7. **open up to** 片 對…敞開心胸

8. **spill the beans** 片 洩密

9. **buddy** [`bʌdɪ] 名 好朋友

10. **listen to** 片 傾聽

11. **mention** [`mɛnʃən] 動 提及；說到

12. **advice** [əd`vaɪs] 名 建議；忠告

9. 有福同享
Sharing Happiness

MP3 **114**

萬用好句

1.	Jason bought everyone a drink in celebration of his promotion. 傑森為慶祝榮升，請每個人喝飲料。
2.	Maria wants to throw a surprise party for Helen on her birthday. 瑪利亞想要幫海倫在生日那天辦個驚喜派對。
3.	Do you know why Mr. Watson looks so overjoyed? 你知道華生先生為什麼看起來那麼開心嗎？
4.	Mike footed the bill for everyone at the table on his birthday. 麥克在他生日那天幫大家買單。
5.	Helen shouted for joy when she saw her favorite movie star, Jackie Chan, in front of her. 當她看見她最喜歡的電影明星成龍站在面前時，海倫開心地大叫。
6.	On the day his child was born, Jack was in a festive mood and called everyone in his family. 他小寶寶出生的那天，傑克開心地打電話給每個家人。
7.	Karen gleefully told her father that she had gotten her dream job. 凱倫開心地跟她父親說，她得到夢寐以求的工作了。
8.	Does anyone have any good news to share? 誰有什麼好消息要分享嗎？
9.	The class jumped for joy when the teacher said there would be no test for today. 當老師說今天沒有考試時，全班開心地跳了起來。
10.	I got a big raise. Let me buy you dinner. 我加薪了，讓我請你吃晚飯吧。
11.	Kenny is on top of the world because his girlfriend just said yes when he popped the question. 當他女友答應他的求婚時，肯尼非常開心。
12.	How should we celebrate Kenny's birthday? 我們要怎麼慶祝肯尼的生日？

關鍵單字片語

1. **celebrate** [`sɛlə͵bret] 動 慶祝

2. **festive mood** 片 歡欣的心情

3. **overjoyed** [͵ovə`dʒɔɪd] 形 狂喜的

4. **foot the bill for** 片 替⋯付賬

5. **share** [ʃɛr] 動 分享

6. **have fun** 片 玩得開心

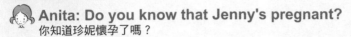
實境對話

Anita: Do you know that Jenny's pregnant?
你知道珍妮懷孕了嗎？

Manny: Really? I'm so happy for her. She has wanted a baby for a long time.
真的嗎？我真替她開心，她一直想要個小孩。

Anita: That's right. She was ecstatic when she told us the great news.
沒錯。她興奮地跟我們說這個好消息。

Manny: She surely was. When is the due date?
她一定是的。預產期是什麼時候？

Anita: It's in mid-June.
六月中。

Manny: Then it's just a month away. I haven't seen her for ages.
那不就是一個月後？我好久沒見到她了。

Anita: Gina and I are going to throw a baby shower for Jenny. Do you want to join us?
吉娜和我要幫珍妮辦個嬰兒祝福會，你要來嗎？

Manny: Absolutely! When is the party?
當然要！是什麼時候？

Anita: It's next Saturday afternoon at Gina's apartment.
下星期六下午，在吉娜的公寓。

Manny: I'll be there. How about the gift? What are you going to get her?
我會到。那禮物呢？你們要買什麼給她？

Anita: We've got a gift list. You can take a look and register for the one you want to get her.
我們有一份禮物清單，你可以看一下，然後登記你想買給她的東西。

Manny: Great! Where is the list?
太棒了，清單在哪裡？

關鍵單字片語

7. **party** [`pɑrtɪ] 名 派對

8. **live it up** 片 盡情享受

9. **be happy for** 片 為…感到開心

10. **baby shower** 片 新生兒派對

11. **buy sb. a drink** 片 請某人喝飲料

12. **glee** [gli] 名 喜悅；歡欣

10. 有難同當
In the Same Boat
MP3 115

萬用好句

1. Don't worry. I've got your back.
別擔心，我挺你。

2. I'll always stand by you.
我會永遠支持你。

3. Larry is really glad that he has so many friends to share the load.
賴瑞真的很高興有這麼多朋友分攤重擔。

4. Hang in there!
堅持下去！

5. Let me help you through your troubles since we are best friends.
既然我們是最好的朋友，讓我幫你度過難關。

6. A friend in need is a friend indeed.
患難見真情。

7. What would you do if your friend were in trouble?
如果你朋友有麻煩，你會怎麼辦？

8. Jessica was really worried about Maria, who just failed math for the second time.
潔西卡真的很擔心瑪利亞，她的數學又被當了。

9. Helen will never abandon her husband though he is heavilly indebted.
海倫絕對不會拋棄她丈夫，即使他負債累累。

10. Cheer up! Things will turn out to be fine.
開心點！都會沒事的。

11. Mrs. Watson always listens to her husband carefully whenever he talks about being depressed over his job.
每當她丈夫講到工作上沮喪的事時，華生太太總是仔細聆聽。

12. Maria will do whatever it takes to help out her little sister.
瑪利亞會做任何事來幫助她小妹度過難關。

關鍵單字片語

1. **take blame for** 片 承擔過失之責

2. **as a result** 片 結果

3. **in trouble** 片 在困境中

4. **bother** [`baðɚ] 動 麻煩、困擾

5. **on your mind** 片 在心上

6. **share the burden** 片 分擔負荷

實境對話

Jane: What's the matter? You look really upset.
怎麼了？你看起來很沮喪。

Tommy: Mr. Watson yelled at me. He was so furious.
我被罵了。華生先生很生氣。

Jane: Why was that? Were you late this morning?
怎麼了？你今天早上遲到了嗎？

Tommy: Yes, but just for two minutes. And that's only part of the reason he was so angry.
沒錯，不過只遲到兩分鐘，而那只是他那麼生氣的部分原因。

Jane: What else was the matter?
那還發生了什麼事？

Tommy: It's the sales report. He asked me to redo it by tomorrow.
是銷售報告，他要我在明天前重做一份。

Jane: By tomorrow? It's already four thirty now!
明天前？現在已經四點三十分咧！

Tommy: That's right, so I have to work overtime tonight.
沒錯，所以我今晚得要加班了。

Jane: How about I stay and help? Two heads are better than one.
不如我留下來幫你吧？三個臭皮匠勝過一個諸葛亮。

Tommy: Really? But it's Friday. It's too much to ask you to work overtime with me tonight.
真的嗎？可是今天是星期五，要你今晚陪我加班太過分了。

Jane: That's fine. Besides, we might be able to leave before eight if we work together.
沒關係，而且如果我們一起做，說不定八點前就可以走了。

Tommy: That would be great. Thank you. Let me buy you a drink later.
那就太棒了，謝謝你。晚點讓我請你喝一杯。

關鍵單字片語

7. **take full responsibility** 片 負全責

8. **weigh down** 片 使頹喪

9. **help out** 片 替…解圍

10. **speak out** 片 說出來

11. **upset** [ʌpˋsɛt] 形 沮喪的

12. **unsettle** [ʌnˋsɛtl] 動 使心神不寧

11. 漸行漸遠
Growing Apart
MP3 **116**

萬用好句

1. **Karen and Diana used to be very close friends.**
   凱倫和黛安娜以前是很好的朋友。

2. **Tim and Jerry drifted apart after graduating from university.**
   提姆和傑瑞在大學畢業後漸行漸遠。

3. **Time has changed Maria a lot, and I didn't even recognize her at first glance.**
   時間改變了瑪利亞很多，我第一眼竟認不出她來。

4. **Do you still enjoy a cup of tea after all these years?**
   這麼多年後你還喜歡喝茶嗎？

5. **My grandfather wants so much to get in touch with his high school buddies that he even hired a detective.**
   我的祖父太想聯絡上他的高中同學，甚至還聘了一位偵探。

6. **Jenna keeps everyone at a distance with her aloof attitude.**
   珍娜冷漠的態度把每個人拒於門外。

7. **We haven't seen each other for over twenty years.**
   我們已經超過二十年沒見到彼此了。

8. **When Maria found out everything was just a lie, she made up her mind and broke up with Tommy.**
   當瑪利亞發現一切都是謊言時，她下定決心要和湯米分手。

9. **Do your parents get along with each other well after their divorce?**
   你的父母離婚後，彼此處得還好嗎？

10. **I can feel that we have been growing apart recently.**
    我可以感覺到最近我們漸行漸遠了。

11. **I think this relationship is over.**
    我想這段關係已經結束了。

12. **Karen hasn't heard from Diana for a long time.**
    凱倫好久沒聽到黛安娜的消息了。

關鍵單字片語

1. **get over** 片 接受

2. **cheat on sb.** 片 欺騙某人

3. **separated** [`sɛpə,retɪd] 形 分離的

4. **keep a distance** 片 保持距離

5. **drift apart** 片 漸行漸遠

6. **aloof** [ə`luf] 形 冷漠的

實境對話

Karen: Dad, can I go to the movies this Saturday afternoon?
爸，我這週六下午可以去看電影嗎？

Dad: Sure. Who are you going with?
當然可以，你要和誰一起去？

Karen: Jessica and Anita.
潔西卡和艾妮塔。

Dad: How about Lauren? You haven't talked about her for a long time.
那羅倫呢？妳好久沒提到她了。

Karen: I don't want to talk about Lauren anymore.
我不想再談論羅倫。

Dad: Why is that? Didn't you say you were "BFF"?
怎麼了？你以前不是說你們是永遠的好朋友嗎？

Karen: That was the past. I have seen the truth.
那都過去了，我看清楚真相了。

Dad: What truth?
什麼真相？

Karen: The truth that she doesn't deserve my friendship.
就是她不值得我的友誼。

Dad: What actually happened?
到底發生什麼事了？

Karen: We've drifted apart ever since she stole Anita's boyfriend. I despise her for stealing my best friend's boyfriend.
自從她搶了艾妮塔的男友後，我們就不來往了，我藐視她搶了我好友的男友。

Dad: Hmm...that's really not something you do to your friends.
嗯…這還真不是你該對朋友做的事。

關鍵單字片語

7. **cold** [kold] 形 冷淡的

8. **silent treatment** 片 冷漠對待

9. **divorce** [dəˋvors] 名 離婚

10. **lose contact** 片 失去聯絡

11. **break up** 片 斷絕往來；絕交

12. **used to** 片 過去曾經…

12.老友相聚
Friends Reunited
117

萬用好句

1.	**How have you been all these years?** 你這些年過得如何？
2.	**I haven't seen you since the graduation ceremony.** 自從畢業典禮後我就沒見過你了。
3.	**The best things in life come in threes, like friendships, dreams, and memories.** 人生最棒的事有三件：友誼、夢想和回憶。
4.	**It was such a delight meeting all my best friends at my school reunion.** 能在校友會遇到我所有的好朋友，真是令人開心。
5.	**Have you ever attended a high school reunion?** 你有參加過高中校友聚會嗎？
6.	**Long time no see.** 好久不見。
7.	**I am sorry, but your name has escaped me.** 我很抱歉，但是你的名字我沒有印象。
8.	**Doesn't my name ring a bell?** 我的名字有讓你想起些什麼嗎？
9.	**What's new with you?** 你有什麼新消息嗎？
10.	**Ross made a PowerPoint presentation featuring his high school photos for the class reunion.** 羅斯為了同學會製作高中照片的投影片。
11.	**You've changed a lot.** 你變了好多。
12.	**I can hardly recognize you.** 我幾乎認不出你來。

關鍵單字片語

1. **catch up** 片 趕上

2. **fail** [fel] 動 忘記

3. **contact** [`kɑntækt] 動 聯繫；聯絡

4. **surprised** [sə`praɪzd] 形 感到驚喜的

5. **greeting** [`gritɪŋ] 名 問候、招呼

6. **cheerful** [`tʃɪrfəl] 形 感到開心的

實境對話

Ken: Hi. Do you remember me? I am Ken.
嗨。你記得我嗎？我是肯。

Ann: Oh, did you play basketball on the varsity team?
喔，你是不是在大學籃球代表隊裡的肯？

Ken: No, that's Ken Watson. I am Ken Jones.
不，那是肯・華生。我是肯・瓊斯。

Ann: I am terribly sorry. Time does make the memory fuzzy. I am Ann.
真的很抱歉，時間模糊了記憶。我是安。

Ken: I know. You used to be our class leader.
我知道，你以前是我們的班代。

Ann: That's right. It's really nice to meet all my classmates again after all these years.
沒錯。真的很高興在這麼多年後，可以再見到所有的同學。

Ken: I couldn't agree with you more. It has been more than ten years since we graduated, hasn't it?
我非常同意你。我們已經畢業超過十年了，對吧？

Ann: Twelve years, and we've all changed a lot.
十二年囉，我們都變了很多。

Ken: That's right, and do you know who the girl over there is?
沒錯。你知道那邊那個女生是誰嗎？

Ann: Do you mean the thin girl with long brown hair? I think that's Tina.
你是說那個棕髮的瘦女生嗎？我想那是提娜。

Ken: Are you serious? The once freckle-faced fat girl has turned out to be hot!
你認真的嗎？那個雀斑臉的胖女生變這麼辣！

Ann: Time really performs magic, doesn't it?
時間真的會變魔術，對吧？

關鍵單字片語

7. **gathering** [`gæðərɪŋ] 名 聚會

8. **BFF** 縮 永遠的好朋友

9. **hear from** 片 收到…的消息

10. **trust** [trʌst] 動 信任；相信

11. **memory** [`mɛmərɪ] 名 記憶

12. **recollect** [ˌrɛkə`lɛkt] 動 回憶

13. 互許終身
Getting Married
MP3
118

萬用好句

1.	John and Linda are going to get married this June. 約翰和琳達今年六月要結婚。
2.	Sara broke into tears when Josh proposed to her in the restaurant. 當喬許在餐廳向她求婚時，莎拉忍不住落淚。
3.	Karen was surprised to see there was a diamond ring in the cake. 凱倫很驚訝看到蛋糕裡有鑽戒。
4.	Will you marry me? 你願意嫁給我嗎？
5.	After dating for two months, Jessica and Tom decided to get married and start a family. 約會兩個月後，潔西卡和湯姆決定共組家庭。
6.	I still remember that romantic night twenty years ago when your father proposed to me. 我還記得二十年前你父親跟我求婚的那個浪漫夜晚。
7.	Can you tell me how your boyfriend proposed to you? 你可以告訴我你男友是怎麼求婚的嗎？
8.	Do you know when Maria and Kenny's wedding is? 你知道瑪利亞和肯尼的婚禮是什麼時候嗎？
9.	Julia is my best friend. She's perfect to be my bridesmaid. 茱莉亞是我最好的朋友，她是我伴娘的最佳人選。
10.	Mr. Watson had tears in his eyes when he walked his baby daughter down the isle of the church. 當他牽著寶貝女兒的手步上教堂走道時，華生先生眼眶泛淚。
11.	We're planning a bachelor party for Larry on the eve of his big day. 我們正在為賴瑞籌辦一場婚禮前夕的單身漢派對。
12.	We hope you will live happily ever after. 我們祝你們永遠幸福快樂。

關鍵單字片語

1. **fiancé** [ˌfiənˋse] 名 未婚夫

2. **get engaged** 片 訂婚

3. **lovesick** [ˋlʌvˌsɪk] 形 害相思病的

4. **spouse** [spauz] 名 配偶

5. **get married with** 片 與…結婚

6. **passionate** [ˋpæʃənɪt] 形 熱情的

實境對話

Father: Sweetheart, do you have a minute?
親愛的，你有空嗎？

Daughter: Yes. What is it?
有，什麼事？

Father: Your mother will have been gone ten years next month.
你媽媽下個月就逝世十年了。

Daughter: Yes. You've been grieving for her these years, and you've been really lonely.
嗯。這些年你一直都在哀悼她，你也一直很寂寞。

Father: My sweetie, it's been pretty tough for you, too.
我的小寶貝，你也一直不好過。

Daughter: What are you trying to tell me, Dad?
爸，你想跟我說什麼？

Father: I'm thinking of settling down again one of these days, to spend the rest of my life with someone special.
最近我想要定下來了，就是與一個特別的人共度一生。

Daughter: Hmm...
嗯…。

Father: And I'm wondering when that day comes, can you give me your blessings?
我在想，如果有那麼一天，我會不會得到你的祝福？

Daughter: Of course I can. Have you met that special someone yet?
當然會，你遇到那個特別的人了嗎？

Father: I think I have. It's Ms. Chen.
我想我遇到了。是陳小姐。

Daughter: Ms. Chen? You mean my history teacher?
陳小姐？她不是我的歷史老師嗎？

關鍵單字片語

7. **romantic** [rə`mæntɪk] 形 浪漫的

8. **atmosphere** [`ætməs͵fɪr] 名 氣氛

9. **couple** [`kʌpl] 名 夫婦；未婚夫妻

10. **ring** [rɪŋ] 名 戒指

11. **best man** 片 伴郎

12. **limousine** [`lɪmə͵zin] 名 加長禮車

萬用好句

1.	**How many brothers and sisters do you have?** 你有幾個兄弟姊妹？
2.	**Who are you named after?** 你是以誰命名的？
3.	**Do you live with your grandparents?** 你和祖父母一起住嗎？
4.	**In my opinion, family is much more important than friends.** 在我看來，家族比朋友重要多了。
5.	**Our family always gathers together on Chinese New Year's Eve.** 我們家族總會在中國新年的除夕夜團聚。
6.	**My father is going to take my mother to Toronto on vacation.** 我爸爸要帶我媽媽去多倫多度假。
7.	**Mr. and Mrs. Watson are my parents-in-law.** 華生夫婦是我的岳父母。
8.	**My father was very strict when I was little.** 我爸爸在我小時候非常嚴格。
9.	**Amanda doesn't know whether to tell her children that she is going to divorce their father.** 亞曼達不知道是否要告訴孩子們，她打算和他們的爸爸離婚。
10.	**Even though no family is perfect, family members should always be considerate to each other.** 縱然沒有家庭是完美的，家人間總該互相體諒。
11.	**Mr. Thompson is the breadwinner in the family.** 湯普森先生是家裡負擔生計的人。
12.	**What do you think is the best thing about your father?** 你認為令尊最棒的地方在哪裡？

關鍵單字片語

1. **family reunion** 片 家族聚會

2. **close** [klos] 形 親近的

3. **intimate** [ˋɪntəmɪt] 形 親密的

4. **family member** 片 家族成員

5. **lead to** 片 導致、造成

6. **pleasant** [ˋplɛzənt] 形 高興的

Hannah: Dad, you've got mail.
爸，你有一封信。

Father: Oh, thank you. It's from your grandmother.
哦，謝謝你。是你奶奶寄來的。

Hannah: Grandmother? What's it about?
奶奶？她寫些什麼？

Father: She said she's going to spend the Chinese New Year with us this year.
她說今年要來和我們一起過年。

Hannah: Cool! I haven't seen Grandma for two years, not since she moved in with Uncle John.
酷耶！自從她搬去跟約翰叔叔住以後，我已經兩年沒見過她了。

Father: That's right, and she said Timmy was coming with her, too.
沒錯，她說提米也要和她一起來。

Hannah: Who is Timmy?
誰是提米？

Father: Don't you remember Timmy? He is Uncle John's little son. You used to play blocks together at Grandma's place.
你不記得提米了嗎？他是你約翰叔叔的小兒子，你們以前都在奶奶家一起玩積木啊。

Hannah: Now I remember him. Wasn't he always wearing blue overalls with a weird dog on them?
現在我想起來了，他是不是總穿著一件有奇怪狗狗的藍色吊帶褲？

Father: Yes, that's Timmy. Can you give up your room to Timmy?
對，那就是提米。你可以把房間讓給提米睡嗎？

Hannah: No problem.
沒問題。

Father: Thank you, my dear.
謝謝你，親愛的。

關鍵單字片語

7. **relative** [`rɛlətɪv] 名 親戚

8. **vacate** [`veket] 動 空出來

9. **get along with** 片 與…和睦相處

10. **strict** [strɪkt] 形 嚴格的

11. **influence** [`ɪnfluəns] 名 影響

12. **be named after** 片 以…命名

15. 爭執鬥嘴
Arguing
MP3 120

萬用好句

1.	**I'm sick and tired of her excuses.** 我已經受夠她的藉口了。
2.	**What can I do to shut him up?** 我要怎麼做才能讓他閉嘴？
3.	**Jason and David's debate regarding the NBA ended in a heated argument.** 傑森和大衛的NBA籃球賽辯論以一陣大吵收場。
4.	**How do you avoid arguments with your siblings?** 你怎麼避免和兄弟姊妹爭吵？
5.	**Jason had a fight with a young man, who was very disrespectful to an old man on the MRT.** 傑森和一個年輕男人爭吵，那名男子在捷運上對一位老先生很不尊重。
6.	**Some hand gestures are very impolite and may lead to serious fights.** 有些手勢很不禮貌，可能會導致嚴重的爭吵。
7.	**I am sorry, but I can't agree with you.** 我很抱歉，但我不同意你。
8.	**Jessica and Amanda haven't talked to each other ever since their fight last week.** 潔西卡和亞曼達自從上星期吵架後，彼此就沒再說過話了。
9.	**You just really hurt my feelings.** 你真的傷了我的心。
10.	**I didn't mean to say that. Would you please forgive me?** 我不是故意說那些話的，可以請你原諒我嗎？
11.	**It's very mean of you to do things like that to your friend.** 你很過分，竟對你最好的朋友做出這些事。
12.	**It takes two fools to argue.** 爭吵是兩個傻蛋做的事。

關鍵單字片語

1. **irritate** [ˋɪrəˌtet] 動 使惱怒；使煩躁
2. **be angry with** 片 對⋯生氣
3. **tolerate** [ˋtɑləˌret] 動 容忍
4. **furious** [ˋfjʊrɪəs] 形 狂怒的
5. **mad** [mæd] 形 惱火的
6. **keep calm** 片 保持冷靜

實境對話

Emma: That's it! I'm breaking up with John.
真是夠了！我要和約翰分手。

James: Wait! Wait! Wait! What happened?
等一下！等一下！發生什麼事了？

Emma: I had a fight with him. I just can't take him anymore.
我受夠他了，所以我和他吵了一架。

James: Calm down. I've never seen you as furious as this before.
冷靜一下，我從來沒看你這麼生氣過。

Emma: That's because he is being ridiculous!
那是因為他太誇張了！

James: OK. Take a deep breath, and then tell me what happened. Did he forget your dinner date again?
好。深呼吸，然後告訴我發生什麼事。他又忘記你們的晚餐約會了嗎？

Emma: No, he picked me up at 7, carrying a bunch of roses. He had never been so punctual before.
沒有，他七點帶著一束玫瑰花來接我。他從沒那麼準時過。

James: Did he take you to a cheap restaurant?
他是帶你去廉價餐廳嗎？

Emma: No, we had a candlelight dinner at a fancy French restaurant.
沒有，我們在一間精緻的法式餐廳吃燭光晚餐。

James: Sounds like a perfect date! What did he do wrong?
聽來像是個完美的約會！他究竟做錯了什麼？

Emma: He held my hands while we were waiting for the dessert. I thought he would propose to me, but he just asked me if I could lend him some money!
我們在等甜點時，他握住我的手。我以為他要跟我求婚，結果他只是問我可不可以借他錢！

關鍵單字片語

7. **drive sb. bananas** 片 使某人發瘋

8. **had better** 片 最好

9. **take** [tek] 動 忍受

10. **settle the dispute** 片 平息糾紛

11. **mutual** [`mjutʃuəl] 形 共同的

12. **emotional** [ɪ`moʃən]] 形 情感的

1. 職涯探索
In Search of Career
MP3 121

萬用好句

1.	**The first step towards finding the right career path is to know yourself.** 尋找適當職涯的第一步，就是瞭解自己。
2.	**A personality assessment can help you find out who you are.** 性格評量可幫助你了解自己。
3.	**The right job can satisfy you both financially and psychologically.** 一份適合的工作可滿足你的經濟以及心理需求。
4.	**Where should I start looking to find the right job?** 我應該從何處著手找份適合的工作？
5.	**It takes time and effort to find the career that best suits you.** 找到最適合自己的職業，需要花費時間及力氣。
6.	**You can consult someone who is in the field of your interest.** 你可以請教那些在你感興趣領域工作的人。
7.	**What career suits your personality the best?** 什麼職業最適合你的個性？
8.	**The Student Affairs Office provides tips for finding the right job.** 學生事務處提供尋找合適工作的小訣竅。
9.	**The right job can make your life meaningful and satisfying.** 一份合適的工作可以讓你的生活有意義、又感到滿足。
10.	**Jeff can't decide which career path to take after graduation.** 傑夫無法決定畢業後究竟要從事什麼工作。
11.	**Although your family's expectations are important, it is your own desires that matter the most.** 雖然家人的期望很重要，但最要緊的還是你自己的想法。
12.	**The perfect situation is to make a living at what you are both good at and interested in.** 最好的狀態是，靠你既擅長又有興趣的工作謀生。

關鍵單字片語

1. **fulfill** [fuˋfɪl] 動 實現
2. **go after** 片 追求、追逐
3. **outlook** [ˋaut͵luk] 名 願景
4. **disposition** [͵dɪspəˋzɪʃən] 名 性格
5. **career explorer** 片 職業探索專家
6. **ideal** [aiˋdiəl] 形 理想的 名 理想

實境對話

Mother: Son, what do you want to do after you graduate?
孩子啊，你畢業後想做什麼工作？

Larry: I don't know. Isn't it a bit early to think about that now?
我不知道。現在想這些，不會太早嗎？

Mother: I don't think so. I saw on the news that some graduates start to look for jobs even in early April.
我不覺得。新聞上說，有些畢業生甚至四月初就開始找工作了。

Larry: Really? Why are they in such a rush?
真的嗎？為什麼他們要這麼急？

Mother: They're not rushing. I think they are being proactive.
他們不是急。我覺得他們是「先發制人」。

Larry: Really? Well, maybe you're right.
真的嗎？嗯，或許你說的沒錯。

Mother: So I think now is a good time for you to do something.
所以，我想現在對你來說是個做些準備的好時機。

Larry: Like what?
像是？

Mother: Well, you should try to know more about yourself.
嗯，你應該試著更了解你自己。

Larry: What does knowing more about myself have to do with finding a job?
更了解自己和找工作有什麼關係嗎？

Mother: Do you want to be stuck in a job you don't like?
你想從事你不喜歡的工作嗎？

Larry: No, I don't.
我不想。

Mother: Let's Google some aptitude tests for you to do first.
我們先上網搜尋性向測驗給你做吧！

關鍵單字片語

7. **career advice** 片 職涯建議

8. **possibility** [ˌpɑsəˋbɪlətɪ] 名 可能性

9. **proactive** [proˋæktɪv] 形 先採取行動的

10. **consult** [kənˋsʌlt] 動 請教

11. **focus on** 片 專注於…

12. **aptitude test** 片 性向測驗

2. 內勤工作
Office Jobs

MP3
122

萬用好句

1.	What's the job description of an office manager? 辦公室經理的工作內容是什麼？
2.	Mr. Watson has his secretary answer his phone calls. 華生先生讓秘書替他接聽電話。
3.	Who can copy these files for me? 誰可以幫我影印這些文件？
4.	Mandy is responsible for organizing Mr. Greggs's schedule. 蔓蒂負責安排桂格先生的行程。
5.	Staying in the office all day long sometimes bores me a lot. 整天待在辦公室，有時實在非常無聊。
6.	Peggy answers incoming calls and takes messages for us. 佩姬替我們接聽電話並記錄留言。
7.	It's enough for me if I can find a job where I don't have to sweat under the sun all day long. 無須整日出外揮汗如雨，對我而言已經夠好了。
8.	Karen is looking for a new secretary who can help her with organizing meetings with clients. 凱倫正在找位能幫她安排客戶會議的新秘書。
9.	The typical duties of an office manager vary according to the size of the organization and the management structure. 辦公室經理的常態工作，隨著組織大小以及管理架構而有所變化。
10.	Most office jobs nowadays involve computer skills. 現今大多數的辦公室工作都涉及電腦使用技巧。
11.	Without his secretary's help, Mr. Watson might even have trouble finding a note pad in his office. 若沒有秘書的協助，華生先生連在辦公室裡找本記事簿都有困難。
12.	What does a human resources manager do? 人資經理要做些什麼？

關鍵單字片語

1. **hustle** [`hʌsḷ] 動 催促、趕緊做某事

2. **run errand** 片 跑腿、作差事

3. **file documents** 片 分類、歸檔文件

4. **accurate** [`ækjərɪt] 形 準確的

5. **skill** [skɪl] 名 技巧

6. **incoming call** 片 來電

實境對話

Iris: Good morning. I am Iris.
早安，我是愛瑞絲。

Hank: Oh, you're the new girl, aren't you?
喔，你就是新來的秘書，對吧？

Iris: Yes. Mr. Lin told me you'll give me the orientation training.
沒錯，林先生跟我說你會給我到職訓練。

Hank: That's right. Shall we begin?
沒錯，可以開始了嗎？

Iris: Yes. Thank you so much.
好，非常謝謝你。

Hank: Your main duty is to organize Mr. Lin's daily schedule.
你的主要工作是安排林先生的每日行程。

Iris: OK. How do I do that?
好的。我要怎麼做？

Hank: First of all, you need to advice Mr. Lin at 8:30 every morning of his daily schedule. If two meetings overlap, you have to tell Mr. Lin about it two days in advance.
首先，早上八點半報告林先生的每日行程。若同時有兩個會議，你必須在兩天前告知林先生。

Iris: OK. What else?
好。還有呢？

Hank: You need to answer his calls and contact his clients.
你需要接聽他的電話並與客戶聯繫。

Iris: Answer calls...contact clients....What else?
接聽電話…聯繫客戶…還有嗎？

Hank: Never be late. Mr. Lin hates people being late, especially his secretary.
絕對不要遲到。林先生討厭有人遲到，尤其是他的秘書。

關鍵單字片語

7. **job description** 片 工作說明

8. **depend on** 片 信賴；依靠

9. **word processing** 片 文字處理

10. **data entry** 片 資料輸入

11. **secretary** [`sɛkrə,tɛrɪ] 名 秘書

12. **type** [taɪp] 動 打字

259

3. 外務工作
Non-office Jobs
MP3 123

萬用好句

1.	**An excellent salesperson should bond well with his clients.** 一名優秀的銷售員應和客戶建立良好關係。
2.	**The secret to Terry's success as a top salesperson is that he always remembers every client's birthday and sends him or her a card.** 泰瑞成為頂尖銷售員的祕訣是，他總記得每位客戶的生日並寄送卡片。
3.	**As a salesperson, what do you usually do first every day?** 身為銷售人員，你通常都做什麼來開啟你的一天？
4.	**Sales representatives are required to pay regular visits to clients.** 銷售經理人必須定期拜訪客戶。
5.	**The purchasing assistant has to hand in a report regarding customer orders by Friday.** 採購助理每週五前需繳交關於客戶訂單的報告。
6.	**What are the duties of a customer service representative?** 客服專員的工作是什麼？
7.	**Most real estate agents work every weekend.** 大多數不動產經理人週末不休息。
8.	**Customer needs always come first.** 顧客的需求永遠擺在第一位。
9.	**You need to have a truck driver's license for this position.** 這個職位要求你具備卡車駕照。
10.	**Hank always has lunch with his customers to bond with them.** 漢克總和客戶吃午餐以聯繫感情。
11.	**My mother is a sales agent who spends a lot of time associating with her clients.** 我媽媽是位銷售員，她花許多時間和客戶交際。
12.	**Sales representatives should keep in good contact with potential clients.** 銷售專員應和潛在客戶保持良好聯繫。

關鍵單字片語

1. **regularly** [ˋrɛgjələlɪ] 副 定期地

2. **brilliant** [ˋbrɪljənt] 形 傑出的

3. **constantly** [ˋkɑnstəntlɪ] 副 不斷地

4. **keep up with** 片 跟上⋯

5. **flexibility** [͵flɛksəˋbɪlətɪ] 名 彈性

6. **client** [ˋklaɪənt] 名 客戶

實境對話

Jason: Mom, I am so thirsty. Is there anything to drink?
媽，我口好渴。有沒有東西喝？

Mom: There's some Coke in the fridge. Why do you look so exhausted?
冰箱裡有些可樂。你看起來怎麼這麼累啊？

Jason: I've been working all day in the sun.
我今天在太陽下工作了一整天。

Mom: How come? I thought you were a real estate agent.
怎麼會？我以為你是不動產經紀人。

Jason: I am, and that's why I have to work all day in the sun.
我是啊，所以我得一整天在太陽下工作。

Mom: What actually do you do as a real estate agent?
房地產經紀人到底在做什麼呢？

Jason: We have to show the buyers the houses. Sometimes it's one house after another for the whole afternoon.
我們得要帶買家看房子。有時候一整個下午要一間看過一間。

Mom: I still don't understand the "working in the sun" part.
我還是不懂「在太陽下工作」這個部分。

Jason: In order to find more potential buyers, I drive around the neighborhood posting ads and even talk to passersby to see if they are interested in buying a house nearby.
為發掘更多潛在客戶，我開車到附近貼廣告，或和路人聊天，看他們是否想買附近的房子。

Mom: I'm so proud of you, my son. You're such a diligent worker.
兒子，我好以你為榮。你真是努力工作。

Jason: Indeed I am. Now, can I have a glass of Coke?
我真的是。現在我可以喝杯可樂了嗎？

Mom: Sure. Here you are, my dear.
當然可以。拿去吧，親愛的。

關鍵單字片語

7. **coordinate** [koˋɔrdn͵et] 動 協調

8. **real estate** 片 不動產

9. **public relations** 片 公共關係

10. **make sure** 片 確認、確保

11. **marketer** [ˋmɑrkɪtɚ] 名 行銷專員

12. **sales representative** 片 銷售員

4. 自己當老闆
Running a Business

MP3 124

萬用好句

1. You should start planning before you actually start a business.
實際創業前，你應先擬定計畫。

2. What should I do to start a business of my own?
我該如何創業？

3. Alan is thinking about starting a bakery in a building on the street corner.
亞倫考慮在街角那棟房子開間麵包店。

4. Running a business of your own takes a lot of effort.
經營自己的生意要耗費許多精力。

5. Mike's father agreed to give his son's company financial support.
邁克的爸爸同意提供他的公司經濟援助。

6. The bank won't give you a loan unless a financial plan is provided.
除非你提供財政計劃書，否則銀行不會核貸。

7. Running your own business is a rewarding but engaging choice.
經營自己的生意是個有回報、卻也很耗費心力的選擇。

8. Jack was a passionate young lad who decided to start his own computer business after graduating from university.
捷克是個有抱負的青年，他大學畢業後就決定創立自己的電腦公司。

9. There are thousands of people launching their own businesses, but only some thrive.
有數千人自行創業，然而僅其中一些人成功。

10. Where can I get some advice on starting up a business?
我要到哪裡獲得創業的建議？

11. Have you decided what type of business you are going to run?
你已經決定要經營哪種生意了嗎？

12. What are the risks of starting my own business?
自行創業有哪些風險？

關鍵單字片語

1. **tycoon** [taɪˋkun] 名 商業鉅子

2. **look to** 片 照顧、注意

3. **demanding** [dɪˋmændɪŋ] 形 苛求的

4. **oversee** [ˋovɚˋsi] 動 監督

5. **evaluate** [ɪˋvæljuˌet] 動 評估

6. **involvement** [ɪnˋvɑlvmənt] 名 牽連

實境對話

Jamie: What are you going to do after graduation?
你畢業以後要做什麼？

Flora: I haven't received any replies yet from the companies I have applied to. How about you?
我還沒有收到任何公司的回覆。你呢？

Jamie: I am going to start a business.
我要創業。

Flora: Are you sure? What are you going to do?
你確定嗎？你要做什麼？

Jamie: I'm thinking about starting a cleaning company on my own.
我想要開間清潔公司。

Flora: That will cost you a lot of money. Where willl you get the money?
那會花你很多錢。你要去哪裡籌錢啊？

Jamie: The government is encouraging youth to start their own businesses by providing low-interest loans.
政府為了鼓勵青年創業，有提供低利貸款。

Flora: How do you apply for those? Will that be hard?
你要怎麼申請？會很難嗎？

Jamie: Not at all. All I need to do is prepare a business plan. The government will make its decision based on that.
一點也不。只要準備好事業計劃書，政府會依計畫書做出貸款評估。

Flora: That's really useful information.
這真是個實用的訊息。

Jamie: Are you interested in starting a business as well?
你也對創業有興趣嗎？

Flora: I've always wanted to have a shop of my own selling models.
我一直想要開間自己的模型店。

關鍵單字片語

7. **budget control** 片 預算控制

8. **set up the goal** 片 設立目標

9. **assign** [ə`saɪn] 動 分派

10. **make decisions** 片 下決定

11. **run a business** 片 經營事業

12. **necessary** [`nɛsə‚sɛrɪ] 形 必要的

5.**尋覓工作**
Job Seeking
MP3
125

萬用好句

1. You can check out job bank websites for job openings.
你可以在人力銀行網站查詢工作職缺。

2. Each June, thousands of graduates search for jobs.
每年六月，數以千計的大學畢業生在找工作。

3. Jason has been looking for a job for two months.
傑森找工作已經超過兩個月了。

4. By joining GiveMeJobs.com, you will be updated with more than 5,000 jobs every week.
加入「給我工作網」，你每週可收到超過五千筆的新工作資訊。

5. Please enclose your C.V. with the application form.
請在申請書中附上履歷表。

6. There will be a job fair on campus in early June, and more than 500 jobs are available.
六月初學校會有就業博覽會，提供超過五百份工作。

7. You can ask Mr. Johnson to proofread your résumé.
你可以請強森先生校勘你的履歷表。

8. Is there anything I should know before having a phone interview?
進行電話面試需要注意些什麼嗎？

9. Can you give me some suggestions about job searching?
你可以給我一些找工作的建議嗎？

10. It is very important to develop your job searching skills, which can help you find your dream job.
培養找工作的技巧很重要，這可幫你找到理想的工作。

11. There will be more than 1,000 job seekers this month.
這個月會有超過一千名求職者。

12. Terry reads the classified ads in local newspapers to try to find a job.
泰瑞為了要找工作，閱讀地方報紙的分類廣告。

關鍵單字片語

1. **job fair** 片 就業博覽會

2. **work experience** 片 工作經驗

3. **cover letter** 片 附信

4. **employment history** 片 就職紀錄

5. **résumé** [ˌrɛzjuˋme] 名 履歷表

6. **testimonial** [ˌtɛstəˋmonɪəl] 名 證明書

實境對話

Dad: How is your day today?
你今天過得如何？

Jessica: Not good. I've been looking for job openings the whole afternoon, but it seems like there aren't any jobs available now.
不是很好。我找了一整個下午的工作，但現在好像都沒有職缺。

Dad: You must be doing something wrong. How are you looking for a job?
一定有什麼問題。你怎麼找工作的？

Jessica: I very carefully read through the job ads in newspapers.
我非常仔細地閱讀報紙的工作分類廣告。

Dad: Sweetheart, maybe you should try a different way.
親愛的，你或許該試試別的方法。

Jessica: What do you mean?
什麼意思？

Dad: There are plenty of job bank websites that you can sign up for. They have powerful search tools that save your time.
有很多找工作的網站可以註冊。它們有強大的搜尋引擎，可以節省你很多時間。

Jessica: But I still have to browse through them, right?
但我還是得花很多時間逐一瀏覽吧？

Dad: Don't worry. The websites will only mail you the jobs according to your needs, based on job titles, location, or even salary range.
別擔心。網站會根據你的需求，如工作職稱、地點甚至薪資範圍，寄職缺給你。

Jessica: Cool! Then I can stop reading those job ads in tiny font sizes.
酷！我不用再閱讀那些分類廣告的小字了。

Dad: You haven't told me what kind of job you want.
你還沒告訴我你想找什麼工作呢。

關鍵單字片語

7. **specialty** [`spɛʃəltɪ] 名 專長

8. **job search engine** 片 工作搜尋引擎

9. **instead** [ɪn`stɛd] 副 反而；替代

10. **region** [`ridʒən] 名 區域

11. **background check** 片 背景調查

12. **career field** 片 職業領域

6. **過關斬將**
The Job Interview

MP3
126

萬用好句

1.	**Mr. Johnson gave me some suggestions to improve my interview performance.** 強森先生給了我一些改善面試表現的建議。
2.	**Before the interview, try to learn more about the company.** 面試前，先行熟悉該公司狀況。
3.	**A behavioral-based interview is one based on discovering how the interviewee would act in specific employment-related situations.** 行為面試是要發現面試者在特定的職場情境下所做出的反應。
4.	**First impressions are of vital importance in a job interview.** 第一印象在工作面試中十分重要。
5.	**A neat appearance and a friendly smile might just win you the job.** 整齊的外表和友善的笑容或許就能幫你贏得工作。
6.	**Jack was so nervous that he kept stammering in the interview.** 傑克很緊張，所以在面試中一直口吃。
7.	**Many companies have their own unique job interview process.** 許多公司有特定的面試過程。
8.	**Most employers will be interested in your employment history because it tells them what kind of person you are.** 大多數僱主會對你的就職紀錄感興趣，因為這可以讓他們了解你是個怎麼樣的人。
9.	**There are many ways to impress the interviewer using gestures.** 有許多肢體上的動作可讓面試官印象深刻。
10.	**What is your greatest strength?** 你最大的優點是什麼？
11.	**A brief self-introduction is usually needed in job interviews.** 面試時，通常需要做簡短的自我介紹。
12.	**What experience do you have in this field?** 你在這個領域有哪些經驗？

關鍵單字片語

1. **scary** [`skɛrɪ] 形 令人害怕的

2. **think straight** 片 清晰思考

3. **interview** [`ɪntɚˌvju] 動 面試

4. **interviewer** [`ɪntɚˌvjuɚ] 名 面試官

5. **favor** [`fevɚ] 動 偏好

6. **aggressive** [ə`grɛsɪv] 形 有進取心的

實境對話

Interviewer: Good morning. Please take a seat. From your résumé, I can see that your job experience is quite diverse.
早安，請坐。從你的履歷裡，我看到你的工作經歷相當多樣化。

Jessica: Yes. I used to be a nurse, and my last job was as a driver.
是的。我曾經是護士，而我上一份工作是司機。

Interviewer: Would you like to elaborate on that?
你願意說明一下嗎？

Jessica: Sure. I graduated from a nursing school. After that, I worked as a nurse for some time. But I found that wasn't what I wanted.
可以的。我從護校畢業後，當了一段時間的護士，但我發現那不是我想要的。

Interviewer: Sounds like you're a young girl who knows what she wants.
聽起來你是個很有主見的年輕女孩。

Jessica: Thank you. I found that I need more freedom.
謝謝你。我發現，我需要更多自由。

Interviewer: That's why you gave truck driving a try?
所以你試著當一名卡車司機？

Jessica: Yes. That's very insightful.
是的，您真有見地。

Interviewer: So why did you quit your job as a truck driver?
那你為何離職、不當卡車司機了？

Jessica: That job indeed gave me the freedom that I wanted, but I found that I need more workplace security.
那份工作的確給了我自由，但我發現我需要更多的工作安全。

關鍵單字片語

7. **verbally** [`vɝblɪ] 副 口頭地

8. **blow it** 片 搞砸某事

9. **eligible** [`ɛlɪdʒəbl] 形 符合資格的

10. **neat appearance** 片 整潔的外表

11. **response** [rɪ`spɑns] 名 回覆

12. **HR** 縮 人力資源

7. **同事相處**
Workplace Relationships
MP3 127

萬用好句

1.	**Do you want to come to our potluck party this Saturday?** 這週六要帶菜來參加我們的聚餐分享派對嗎？
2.	**Jeff is always generous with his colleagues, and that's why he has such a good reputation.** 傑夫總對同事很慷慨，這也是他擁有好名聲的原因。
3.	**Do you want to grab something for lunch with us?** 你想和我們一起去吃午餐嗎？
4.	**Do you know why nobody wants to talk to Karen?** 你知道為何沒人願意和凱倫說話嗎？
5.	**Hank is so arrogant that no one wants to work with him.** 漢克太過高傲，沒人願意與他合作。
6.	**Some of our colleagues love to have a drink together every Friday night.** 我們有些同事喜歡在每週五晚上相聚喝一杯。
7.	**I really need some advice on getting along with coworkers.** 我真的需要一些與同事和睦相處的建議。
8.	**Try to keep a good workplace relationship with your coworkers.** 試著和你的同事保持良好的工作關係。
9.	**Do your best to avoid offending those who work with you.** 盡力避免冒犯與你共事的人。
10.	**Gina is such a chatterbox, and she nags people all the time.** 吉娜是個喋喋不休的人，總是在抱怨。
11.	**Many conflicts among colleagues arise from what starts out as harmless exchanges.** 許多同事間的衝突都起因於無心之言。
12.	**How do you ask a chatterbox to stop interfering with your work?** 該如何讓一個喋喋不休的人停止干擾你工作？

★ 關鍵單字片語

1. **bonding** [`bandɪŋ] 名 聯繫感情
2. **peer pressure** 片 同儕壓力
3. **newbie** [`njubi] 名 新人；新手
4. **communicate** [kə`mjunə‚ket] 動 溝通
5. **associate** [ə`soʃɪɪt] 名 同事
6. **colleague** [`kɑlig] 名 同事

實境對話

Mason: Do you want to have dinner together after work?
下班後想要共進晚餐嗎？

Anita: Sure. Do we have any company?
好啊，有誰會一起去嗎？

Mason: Yes. Maggie will take us to a great Indian restaurant.
有啊，瑪姬要帶我們去一家很棒的印度餐廳。

Anita: Really. Then I think I might need to skip tonight's dinner.
真的哦，那我可能不能跟你們一起吃晚餐了。

Mason: What's wrong? Don't you like Indian food?
怎麼啦？你不喜歡印度菜啊？

Anita: Actually, I prefer not to associate with Maggie after work.
其實，我寧可別和瑪姬在下班後有來往。

Mason: Why not? Do you two have something against each other or something?
為什麼不？你們之間有甚麼嫌隙嗎？

Anita: It's not like that. It's just that she likes to gossip about the colleagues in the office, which is very bothersome.
不是那樣。只是說她喜歡在辦公室講同事八卦，這非常令人困擾。

Mason: You're right. She did tell me that she had some little secrets to share with me tonight.
你說得沒錯。她確實有跟我說，今晚有些小秘密要與我分享。

Anita: Sounds like someone is going to be the topic of conversation very soon.
看來有人很快就要成為話題焦點了。

Mason: I think so. She also invited May from the Sales Department.
我也這麼覺得。她也邀了業務部的梅。

關鍵單字片語

7. **deal with** 片 應付；處理

8. **frank** [fræŋk] 形 坦白的

9. **tend to** 片 有…的傾向

10. **exchange** [ɪksˋtʃendʒ] 動 交換

11. **reserved** [rɪˋzɜvd] 形 有所保留的

12. **harmless** [ˋhɑrmlɪs] 形 無害的

269

8.辦公室文化
Office Culture
MP3 128

萬用好句

1.	**It's our tradition that the newbie has to buy drinks for everyone.** 我們的傳統是，新人要負責幫大家買飲料。
2.	**Every office has its unique office culture.** 每間辦公室都有其獨特的辦公室文化。
3.	**It's a tradition in our office that we leave cards and candies on the birthday boy or girl's desk.** 我們辦公室習慣在壽星的桌上留下卡片和糖果。
4.	**A positive office culture can both motivate workers and improve work efficiency.** 正向的辦公室文化可以激勵員工並改善工作效率。
5.	**I really hate the backstabbing culture in my office.** 我真的很討厭我們辦公室的背後捅刀文化。
6.	**Do you and your coworkers hang out after work?** 你下班後會和同事出去嗎？
7.	**Instead of dressing too casually or too formally, try to blend in.** 試著融入同事的穿著習慣，避免太過休閒或正式。
8.	**Allen always buys everyone dinner whenever a big deal is closed.** 艾倫總會在大案子結束後請大家吃晚餐。
9.	**Rumor has it that Amanda is seeing Kevin, the team manager.** 謠傳亞曼達正與團隊經理凱文約會。
10.	**Our leader tries to create a supportive office atmosphere.** 我們組長試圖創造支持性的辦公室氛圍。
11.	**What do you think of leaving a thank-you note on your colleagues' desk?** 你覺得在同事的桌上留一張感謝字條如何？
12.	**Most of my colleagues are tired of Maggie's gossiping.** 我大多數同事都厭倦了瑪姬的四處八卦。

關鍵單字片語

1. **group purchase** 片 團購

2. **in common** 片 共同的；共有的

3. **pep talk** 片 鼓勵性演說

4. **workplace** [`wɝk͵ples] 名 工作場所

5. **vital** [`vaɪtl] 形 極其重要的

6. **appreciative** [ə`priʃɪ͵etɪv] 形 感謝的

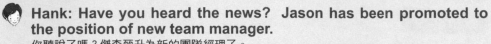

實境對話

Hank: Have you heard the news? Jason has been promoted to the position of new team manager.
你聽說了嗎？傑森晉升為新的團隊經理了。

Jenny: Really? That's such great news for him!
真的嗎？對他而言真是件好事！

Hank: And good news for us, too!
對我們而言也是！

Jenny: What do you mean?
你的意思是？

Hank: Don't you know that part of our office culture is that whomever is promoted will buy everyone afternoon tea for a week?
你難道不知道本公司的習慣，是升職的人要請大家吃一個禮拜的下午茶嗎？

Jenny: So that's what Anita meant when she said it was "something great."
所以這就是愛妮塔所謂的「好事」。

Hank: I think so.
我想是的。

Jenny: And it's such a nice gesture to have everyone in the office share in his achievement and happiness.
而且讓全辦公室的人分享他的成就與喜悅，是個不錯的舉動。

Hank: Indeed it is.
的確如此。

Jenny: It makes me feel more excited about this afternoon.
這樣我對今天下午感到更加興奮了。

Hank: Me, too. I hope someday I can be the one to buy you all afternoon tea.
我也是。希望哪天我可以成為請你們下午茶的那個人。

關鍵單字片語

7. **casual** [ˋkæʒʊəl] 形 非正式的

8. **leave a note** 片 留下訊息

9. **repay the kindness** 片 報答好意

10. **inviting** [ɪnˋvaɪtɪŋ] 形 吸引人的

11. **foster** [ˋfɔstɚ] 動 心懷(野心)

12. **friendliness** [ˋfrɛndlɪnɪs] 名 親切

9.部門會議
Departmental Meetings
MP3 129

萬用好句

1. The departmental meeting is a routine part of every Monday morning.
部門會議是每週一早上的例行公事。

2. Karen was sick and thus absent from the departmental meeting.
凱倫生病了，因此缺席部門會議。

3. Everyone should attend the departmental meeting on time.
每個人都應準時出席部門會議。

4. Who is responsible for the meeting minutes?
誰負責會議紀錄？

5. Sometimes it's kind of hard to stay awake during the departmental meeting.
有時要在部門會議中保持清醒狀態還真困難。

6. Our departmental meeting usually lasts for more than an hour and a half, which always drives me crazy.
我們的部門會議通常持續一個半小時，這總是讓我抓狂。

7. What are the questions under discussion for today's meeting?
今天會議中要討論的議題為何？

8. A cross-departmental meeting will be held in reaction to the latest company scandal.
為回應最新的公司醜聞，將召開跨部門會議。

9. Where is the departmental meeting this morning?
今天早上的部門會議在哪裡舉行？

10. A reminder should be sent two days before the meeting.
會議提醒應於開會前兩天寄出。

11. What should I do to organize a departmental meeting?
我該如何安排一場部門會議？

12. Who is the chairperson for today's meeting?
由誰擔任今天會議的主席？

關鍵單字片語

1. **conference call** 片 電話會議

2. **recurring** [rɪ`kɝɪŋ] 形 循環的

3. **minutes** [`mɪnɪts] 名 會議紀錄

4. **meeting request** 片 會議邀請

5. **attendance sheet** 片 簽到表

6. **closing remark** 片 結語

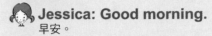

Jessica: Good morning.
早安。

Mr. Lee: Good morning. When is the departmental meeting today?
早安。今天的部門會議是何時？

Jessica: It's at 2:30 this afternoon, in Conference Room A.
下午兩點半在A會議室。

Mr. Lee: This afternoon? I thought it was in the morning.
下午？我以為是在早上。

Jessica: It was, but a notice was sent around that stated the time was changed to the afternoon.
本來是在早上，但有通知改到下午。

Mr. Lee: Fine. What's on the agenda for today?
好。那今天要討論哪些議題？

Jessica: The annual sales report and the sales targets for the coming year.
討論年度銷售報告與來年銷售目標。

Mr. Lee: OK. Will Lisa from the Ad Department be present?
好的。廣告部門的莉莎會出席嗎？

Jessica: I'm afraid not. She's on sick leave, so the vice director of the Ad Department, Ms. Chen, will be present on her behalf.
恐怕不會。她請病假，因此廣告部門的副主任陳小姐會代她出席。

Mr. Lee: One more thing, I need a favor from you.
還有件事，我需要你的協助。

Jessica: What is it, Sir?
先生，請問是什麼事呢？

Mr. Lee: Can you have these copied by 10? I will need them for the meeting.
可以幫我在十點前影印好這些嗎？我開會時需要使用。

關鍵單字片語

7. **take place** 片 舉行；發生

8. **annual** [`ænjuəl] 形 一年一度的

9. **absent** [`æbsn̩t] 形 缺席的

10. **agenda** [ə`dʒɛndə] 名 議程

11. **punctual** [`pʌŋkʃuəl] 形 準時的

12. **brainstorm** [`bren.stɔrm] 名 集思廣益

10. **協商談判**
Negotiations
130

萬用好句

1. I really need you to give me some negotiation tips.
我真的需要你給我一些談判小撇步。

2. You have to know your bottom line before the negotiations.
談判前,你必須清楚你的底線。

3. Can you give me any suggestions about negotiating with clients?
你能否給我關於與客戶協商的建議?

4. Being afraid of negotiations won't help you get the job done.
害怕協商的心態無法讓你完成工作。

5. First, know what your client wants and what you can provide.
首先,理解客戶的需求,以及你所能提供的。

6. Knowing the right time to negotiate is also very important.
知道適當的協商時機,也是非常重要的。

7. Is that compatible with what you would like to see?
這與你想看到的相符嗎?

8. Is there anything you would like to change?
有任何您想更改的地方嗎?

9. Your negotiation style is an expression of yourself.
協商的方式,是一種個人風格的展現。

10. Kenny just earned us two more days to complete the project.
肯尼剛剛幫我們的計劃多爭取了兩天的時間。

11. List the least desirable, but tolerable terms that you'd be willing to take, which will be your walk-away point.
列出最不想要、但能接受的條件,做為你的停損點。

12. Instead of focusing on what you want and trying to convince the client, consider what the client wants and aim to work toward a compromise.
與其著眼於你的需求以及如何說服客戶,不如考慮客戶的需求,並致力於彼此妥協。

關鍵單字片語

1. **negotiate** [nɪ`goʃɪˌet] 動 協商
2. **turn out** 片 結果是;證明是
3. **satisfy** [`sætɪsˌfaɪ] 動 使滿意
4. **bottom line** 片 底線
5. **accomplish** [ə`kɑmplɪʃ] 動 完成
6. **conniving** [kə`naɪvɪŋ] 形 默許的

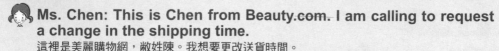

Ms. Chen: This is Chen from Beauty.com. I am calling to request a change in the shipping time.
這裡是美麗購物網，敝姓陳。我想要更改送貨時間。

Mr. Robins: Please give me your order number.
請給我您的訂單號碼。

Ms. Chen: It's 555-9895.
訂單號碼是555-9895。

Mr. Robins: A moment, please. Well, according to the shipping advice, you're expected to receive your items by next Tuesday.
請稍等。根據貨運資料，您將於下週二前收到您的訂貨。

Ms. Chen: I see. But the thing is, next Tuesday will be too late for our mid-seasonal sale. Can you make it a bit earlier?
我了解。但情況是，下週二將趕不上我們的季中慶。可以幫忙提前貨運時間嗎？

Mr. Robins: When would you like to receive your items?
您想於何時收到貨品？

Ms. Chen: It would be great if I could have them by this Friday.
如果可以在本週五前收到的話最好了。

Mr. Robins: This Friday will not be possible since we're now understaffed. How about this Sunday? I can make that happen.
由於我們目前人手不足，因此本週五不太可行。若本週日呢？我可以幫得上忙。

Ms. Chen: Sunday would be excellent. Do we have to pay an additional shipping fee?
週日非常好。我們需要另付運費嗎？

Mr. Robins: That won't be necessary. We have a contracted courier who can offer us free early delivery twice a month.
不需要，我們簽約的貨運廠商，每個月提供兩次免費提前送貨。

Ms. Chen: That's great. Thank you very much.
太好了，非常謝謝你。

關鍵單字片語

7. **false assumption** 片 錯誤假設

8. **proposal** [prə`pozl] 名 提案

9. **alternative** [ɔl`tɜnətɪv] 名 選擇

10. **settle down** 片 塵埃落定

11. **strategy** [`strætədʒɪ] 名 策略

12. **task** [tæsk] 名 任務；工作

MP3
131

萬用好句

1.	**A little bird told me that you are dating someone new.** 我聽說你最近有新戀情。
2.	**Is it true that Jason and Gina went out on a date last night?** 傑森跟吉娜昨晚去約會了，是真的嗎？
3.	**What's wrong with you? You look really upset.** 還好嗎？你看起來很沮喪。
4.	**I enjoy chatting with Hank in the coffee room from time to time.** 我很喜歡偶爾與漢克在茶水間閒聊。
5.	**Frank and his colleagues sometimes have lunch together to talk about their coworkers.** 法蘭克和同事們有時會一同吃午餐，談論他們的同事。
6.	**Gossip seems to be unavoidable in all workplaces.** 流言似乎在所有工作場域都無法避免。
7.	**Do you know who Mr. Watson went out with last night?** 你知道昨晚華生先生和誰出去嗎？
8.	**It's almost impossible to eliminate gossip from the office.** 要消滅辦公室流言幾乎是不可能的。
9.	**What do you think of Maria and Hank, who are both colleagues and a couple at the same time?** 瑪利亞與漢克身兼同事與伴侶，你有什麼想法嗎？
10.	**It's an open secret that Andy always slips out the door a little too quickly every day.** 安迪每天總是提早下班，這已經不是秘密了。
11.	**Laura told me that Tom and Jessica are dating on the sly.** 蘿拉告訴我，湯姆和潔西卡在暗中交往。
12.	**I want to keep my distance from a gossipmonger like Diana.** 我想和像黛安娜那樣愛說閒話的人保持距離。

關鍵單字片語

1. **tacky** [`tækɪ] 形 俗不可耐的
2. **instead of** 片 代替
3. **from time to time** 片 有時
4. **gossipmonger** [`gɑsɪp͵mʌŋgɚ] 名 饒舌人
5. **open secret** 片 公開的秘密
6. **bulletin board** 片 公佈欄

實境對話

Gary: Have you heard the news that Mandy is going to be the new director of the Sales Department?
曼蒂即將成為業務部主任，你聽說了嗎？

Sandy: What? Are you serious?
什麼？你是說真的嗎？

Gary: Yes. It's been on the bulletin board all this morning.
是啊，今天早上已經上公布欄了。

Sandy: I don't get it. How can a lazy worker like her get promoted?
我真的不解，像她一樣的懶惰鬼怎會升職？

Gary: I don't understand it, either. But she is really good at making herself loved by all her superiors.
我也不解。但她的確很討她的主管們歡心。

Sandy: She is indeed. Karen told me that she always runs errands for Mr. Gregg and Ms. Watson.
她的確是。凱倫告訴我，她總是幫葛雷格先生和華生女士跑腿。

Gary: I know, and she sometimes even leaves the office early.
我知道，而且她有時還會早退。

Sandy: I know that, too. It's an open secret in the office.
我也知道，這在辦公室已經不是秘密了。

Gary: Maybe it's essential to have an excellent relationship with our superiors to get promoted.
我們或許必須和主管保持良好關係才能升職。

Sandy: Maybe. Good workers like us are never appreciated.
或許吧。而且像我們一樣努力工作的人總是不被珍惜。

Gary: Maybe I should start to run some errands for Mandy.
我或許該開始幫曼蒂跑跑腿了。

Sandy: Come on. That will make you nothing but an apple polisher!
拜託，那你就成為一個只會拍馬屁的人了！

關鍵單字片語

7. **drift into** 片 逐漸陷入…

8. **tension** [ˋtɛnʃən] 名 緊張

9. **in general** 片 一般而言

10. **ruin** [ˋruɪn] 動 破壞

11. **reputation** [ˌrɛpjəˋteʃən] 名 名譽

12. **ignore** [ɪgˋnor] 動 忽視

12. 抱怨工時與薪資
Complaining about Jobs
MP3 132

萬用好句

1. The reduction in overtime pay forced many employees to resign.
刪減加班費迫使許多員工辭職。

2. Our manager never approves any of our overtime pay sheets.
我們的經理從不幫我們簽核加班費。

3. Salaries remain unchanged while the prices of commodities keep going up.
薪資靜如止水，而物價卻持續飛漲。

4. I've been working overtime every night for more than two weeks.
我已經加班超過兩週了。

5. I work such long hours that maybe I should just start living in my office cubicle.
我的工時那麼長，或許我該搬進辦公小隔間裡住。

6. Anyone who would like to file a complaint can reach the labor union representative at extension 885.
想申訴的人，可以撥打分機885聯絡工會代表。

7. Are you satisfied with your salary?
你對你的薪資感到滿意嗎？

8. I'm already so fed up with the long hours that I want to quit.
我已經受夠長時工作了，所以我想離職。

9. Considering the long hours I work, my salary isn't enough.
我的長時工作和我的低薪不成比例。

10. It is obvious that Mr. Watson is violating the labor laws by asking his workers to work over 12 hours per day.
華生先生要求員工一天工作超過十二個小時，這很明顯違反了勞基法。

11. A confidential complaint can be made upon request.
只要提出要求，就可以匿名申訴。

12. Mr. Gregg never pays his employees on time.
桂格先生從來不準時發放薪資。

關鍵單字片語

1. **underpay** [ˌʌndəˈpe] 動 少付工資

2. **salary** [ˈsælərɪ] 名 薪水

3. **work overtime** 片 加班

4. **double-shift** [ˈdʌblˈʃɪft] 名 連值兩班

5. **bonus** [ˈbonʌs] 名 紅利、津貼

6. **wage** [wedʒ] 名 薪資；報酬

實境對話

Sam: Did you check your e-mail today?
你今天收信了嗎？

Tina: Not yet. Is there any news?
還沒。有甚麼新鮮事嗎？

Sam: There will be a 20% cut in our overtime pay.
加班費將會減少兩成。

Tina: What? But we just had a cut in salary last month.
什麼？但是上個月我們已經減薪了。

Sam: You're right, and that's why some of our colleagues are planning to organize a strike next week.
沒錯，所以這就是為什麼我們有些同事下星期要罷工。

Tina: A strike?
罷工？

Sam: Yes, and more than 15 people have already indicated that they are in favor of a strike.
是的，已經有超過十五個人要參加了。

Tina: But is that permissible? The company will be very angry. Will those who signed up be punished?
但是沒問題嗎？公司一定會很生氣的。參加的人會不會被處罰？

Sam: They won't. The union will continue negotiating with the company. The strike is just to express our dissatisfaction.
不會的。工會將持續和公司協商，罷工只是用來表達我們的不滿。

Tina: Right. We can't just sit back and do nothing. How do I show I support the strike action?
沒錯，我們不能什麼都不做。我要怎麼參加罷工的行列呢？

Sam: You can register your support for the strike on the union's website.
你可以在工會的網站上報名。

關鍵單字片語

7. **fed up** 片 受夠了

8. **worth one's salt** 片 稱職的

9. **disgruntled** [dɪsˋgrʌntḷd] 形 不悅的

10. **permissible** [pəˋmɪsəbḷ] 形 允許的

11. **working hours** 片 工作時數

12. **file a complaint** 片 提出申訴

13. **抱怨同事與主管**
Complaining about Colleagues

MP3
133

萬用好句

1.	**I'm fed up with Maria: she complains a lot but can't do anything.** 我已經受夠瑪利亞，她只會埋怨，卻什麼事也不會做。
2.	**Hank is such an apple polisher that nobody wants to be friends with him.** 漢克是個馬屁精，沒有人想和他做朋友。
3.	**Is there any safe way to complain about your colleagues and your boss?** 有沒有安全的方法可以抱怨同事和老闆？
4.	**Sophie keeps nagging everyone, which is really annoying to us.** 蘇菲一直跟人嘮叨，我們都覺得很煩。
5.	**Constant complaining is so toxic in the workplace that it might erode your relationship with coworkers.** 持續抱怨是工作場所的毒藥，因為它會傷害你和同事間的關係。
6.	**Allen always tries to get others to do his work for him.** 亞倫總是把自己該負責的工作丟給其他人做。
7.	**I will simply not stand for any sexual harassment in the workplace.** 職場性騷擾是我最無法忍受的事。
8.	**Maria has been bugging everyone in the office to buy her kid's cookies to raise money.** 瑪利亞一直煩辦公室裡的人，要大家買她小孩的募款餅乾。
9.	**Kevin always has an excuse for being late, such as "My cat is sick."** 凱文總是有遲到的藉口，像是「我的貓生病了」。
10.	**Jason is a real backstabber who loves to speak ill of people behind their backs.** 傑森會在背後中傷人，他總愛在人們背後說壞話。
11.	**Debbie is a real downer. No one on her team likes to work with her.** 戴比是個掃興鬼，她組裡沒人想與她共事。

關鍵單字片語

1. **abusive boss** 片 虐待人的上司

2. **annoying** [əˋnɔɪɪŋ] 形 惱人的

3. **prank** [præŋk] 動 惡作劇

4. **brown nosing** 片 拍馬屁

5. **apple polisher** 片 拍馬屁的人

6. **let it go** 片 放手、不在意

實境對話

Vince: What are you doing, Peggy?
佩姬，你在做什麼？

Peggy: I am writing up the sales report.
我在做銷售報告。

Vince: Sales report? But it's already four thirty in the afternoon!
銷售報告？但是已經是下午四點半咧！

Peggy: Mr. Watson has asked me to have it done by six.
華生先生要我今天下午六點前做完。

Vince: That's unreasonable! He always hands out tasks at the last minute.
這不合理！他總在最後一秒才派工作。

Peggy: I know, but what can I do about it?
我知道，但我能怎麼辦？

Vince: Don't you get tired of working for him?
你替他工作都不會感到厭煩嗎？

Peggy: Sometimes I do, especially when he asks me to remake the coffee five times.
有時候會，尤其當他叫我重泡五次咖啡的時候。

Vince: Really? Did he really ask you to remake the coffee five times?
真的嗎？他真的叫你重泡五次咖啡？

Peggy: What can I say? He is very critical about coffee and people working for him as well.
我能說什麼？他對咖啡和替他工作的人都很要求。

Vince: It must be hard for you, working for such a neurotic boss.
替這種神經質的老闆工作，你一定很辛苦。

Peggy: Yes, indeed it is.
真的很辛苦。

關鍵單字片語

7. **attitude** [`ætətjud] 名 態度

8. **grumble** [`grʌmbḷ] 動 發牢騷

9. **stingy** [`stɪndʒɪ] 形 小氣的

10. **resentment** [rɪ`zɛntmənt] 名 怨恨

11. **backstab** [`bæk͵stæb] 動 陷害

12. **pushover** [`puʃ͵ovɚ] 名 易受影響者

萬用好句

1.	**Why is David the one who's getting promoted?** 大衛為何能被升職？
2.	**Congratulations on your big promotion and raise.** 恭喜你升職加薪。
3.	**How are you going to celebrate your promotion?** 你要怎麼慶祝升職？
4.	**Rumor has it that Jack is going to be promoted.** 據說傑克會升職。
5.	**Larry bought everyone in the bar a drink in celebration of his promotion to the position of new manager.** 賴瑞請酒吧裡的每個人喝酒，慶祝他成為新任經理。
6.	**Anyone who wins the contract will get a special bonus.** 贏得合約的人會拿到特別獎金。
7.	**Whether or not you can get a raise depends on your work performance.** 你能否獲得加薪，取決於工作表現。
8.	**Christmas bonuses are given to every employee as an incentive.** 發放耶誕獎金作為對員工的激勵。
9.	**Who do you think will get the promotion?** 你覺得誰會獲得這次升職？
10.	**Alan's outstanding sales figures earned him a big raise.** 亞倫傑出的銷售數字讓他獲得加薪。
11.	**Mr. Gregg will evaluate the performance of each of you to decide who will be the new team manager.** 桂格先生會評量你們每個人的表現，決定由誰來擔任新的小組經理。
12.	**Jessica was overjoyed to know she was promoted to the position of marketing manager.** 潔西卡很高興得知她被升為行銷經理。

關鍵單字片語

1. **raise** [rez] 名 加薪

2. **promotion** [prə`moʃən] 名 升職

3. **award** [ə`wɔrd] 名 獎

4. **deserve** [dɪ`zɜv] 動 值得…

5. **encourage** [ɪn`kɝɪdʒ] 動 鼓勵、鼓舞

6. **outstanding** [`aut`stændɪŋ] 形 傑出的

實境對話

Karen: Congratulations on your promotion!
恭喜你升職了！

Hank: Thank you so much.
非常謝謝你。

Karen: You've been working really hard. You really deserve it.
你一直都很努力工作，升職是應該的。

Hank: I was just doing my job.
我只是做我份內的工作。

Karen: But nobody works as hard as you. I've seen you working overtime alone in the office several times.
但沒人比你更認真工作了。我好幾次看你一個人在辦公室裡加班。

Hank: I indeed need more time to finish my work.
我的確需要更多時間以完成我的工作。

Karen: That's why you do a better job! And moreover, you have won several contracts for the company in the last six months.
所以你做得比較好啊！而且，你過去半年也替公司簽下不少合約。

Hank: I can't take the credit all by myself. It's due to good teamwork.
我不能獨自居功，這要歸功於團隊合作。

Karen: That's very modest of you to say that.
你那麼說真的很謙虛。

Hank: I really meant what I said. Everybody deserves credits.
我是說真的，這是大家的功勞。

Karen: Mr. Lee has high expectations for you. Please try your best in your new position.
李先生對你的期望很高，請在新的職位上繼續努力。

Hank: I will try my very best not to let him down.
我會盡力不讓他失望。

★ 關鍵單字片語

7. **modest** [`mɑdɪst] 形 謙虛的

8. **performance rating** 片 工作評比

9. **not only...but...** 片 不僅…還…

10. **be based on** 片 取決於、基於

11. **position** [pə`zɪʃən] 名 職務

12. **recognition** [ˏrɛkəg`nɪʃən] 名 認可

15. **轉換跑道**
Changing Jobs
MP3 135

萬用好句

1. **I am thinking about getting a new job.**
   我正考慮換新工作。

2. **Many people change jobs right after getting their annual bonus.**
   許多人在領到年終後就換工作。

3. **Getting a new job takes a lot of effort, but it's also a great opportunity to experience something new.**
   找份新工作要花很多努力，但也是個體驗新事物的好機會。

4. **Why do you want to find a new job?**
   你為什麼想找新工作？

5. **You are exactly the kind of person headhunters are looking for.**
   你就是人力仲介正在找的人。

6. **I know a headhunter who's looking for a market analyst like you.**
   我認識一位人力仲介，她正在找一位像你一樣的市場分析師。

7. **Jessie decided to try her hand at the real estate business.**
   潔西決定到不動產業界試試身手。

8. **There's no harm in trying out different kinds of jobs when you are young.**
   趁年輕時多試幾份不同的工作無妨。

9. **Laura is trying to build a better career by getting a new job.**
   蘿拉試著藉由換份新工作建構更好的職涯。

10. **Changing jobs in middle age can present challenges.**
    中年轉職較具挑戰性。

11. **The headhunter is offering a signing bonus of twenty thousand dollars, which is really enticing to me.**
    人力仲介提供兩萬元簽約金，這點很吸引我。

12. **Gina is trying to get a new, high-paying job that isn't stressful, which is almost mission impossible.**
    吉娜試著想找份高薪、低壓力的新工作，這幾乎是不可能的任務。

關鍵單字片語

1. **headhunter** [`hɛd,hʌntɚ] 名 人力仲介

2. **transfer** [træns`fɜ] 動 轉換

3. **opportunity** [,ɑpɚ`tjunətɪ] 名 機會

4. **intention** [ɪn`tɛnʃən] 名 目的

5. **career change** 片 轉職

6. **get on** 片 出人頭地

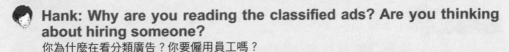

Hank: Why are you reading the classified ads? Are you thinking about hiring someone?
你為什麼在看分類廣告？你要僱用員工嗎？

Gina: No, just the opposite. I am looking for a job.
不，恰恰相反。我在找工作。

Hank: Why is that? I thought you already had a job as a manager for a big company.
為什麼？我以為你已經在大公司當經理了。

Gina: Actually, I am thinking about getting a new job.
事實上，我想要找份新工作。

Hank: Really? Why? Is your boss too demanding?
真的嗎？為什麼？你老闆要求太高嗎？

Gina: Not at all. Mr. Watson is very nice. He has taught me a lot.
一點也不。華生先生人很好，他教了我很多。

Hank: Then why?
那是為什麼？

Gina: I think it's time for me to challenge myself.
我想該是挑戰自己的時候了。

Hank: What do you mean?
這是什麼意思？

Gina: I love pets, and I have been taking pet grooming courses for three years. I hope that one day I can open up a pet beauty salon.
我很喜歡寵物，我學寵物美容已經三年了。希望有一天我可以開一家寵物美容店。

Hank: It takes great courage to make such a career change.
要這樣轉職，需要很大的勇氣。

Gina: Yet it is necessary for me to realize my dreams.
但卻是我實現夢想的必經之路。

★ 關鍵單字片語

7. **downsizing** [`daʊn͵saɪzɪŋ] 名 縮編

8. **switch departments** 片 轉換部門

9. **insecure** [͵ɪnsɪˋkjʊr] 形 不安全的

10. **transferable skills** 片 可轉換技能

11. **current** [`kɜnt] 形 目前的、現今的

12. **mentor** [`mɛntɚ] 名 良師益友

氣候異常
1. 氣候異常
Climate Anomalies
MP3 136

萬用好句

1.	**Global warming refers to the rising temperature of the Earth.** 全球暖化意指地球溫度的升高。
2.	**The increase in global temperatures causes the rise of the sea level.** 地球溫度的增加導致海平面上升。
3.	**The oddly high temperature in summer these past several years in Taiwan might be related to global warming.** 台灣近年來的異常高溫可能與全球暖化有關。
4.	**Extreme weather conditions, such as droughts and heavy rainfall, have happened a lot recently.** 極端的氣候狀況，如乾旱和狂雨，最近發生頻繁。
5.	**Global warming is a complicated and important issue.** 全球暖化是個棘手並且重要的議題。
6.	**Carbon dioxide emissions contribute to global warming.** 二氧化碳的排放造成全球暖化。
7.	**How can we slow down the global warming process?** 我們該如何減緩全球暖化的速度？
8.	**What are the side effects of global warming?** 全球暖化有哪些副作用？
9.	**Sadly, there is no single solution to global warming.** 令人難過的是，全球暖化並沒有單一解決方案。
10.	**Car pooling is a way to reduce our CO_2 emissions.** 汽車共乘是減少二氧化碳排放的一種方法。
11.	**What do you know about global warming?** 你對於全球暖化的了解是？
12.	**The impact of global warming is far greater than just increasing temperatures.** 全球暖化所造成的影響，並非僅止於溫度上的增加。

關鍵單字片語

1. **global warming** 片 地球暖化

2. **temperature** [ˋtɛmprətʃə] 名 氣溫

3. **iceberg** [ˋaɪsˌbɝg] 名 冰山

4. **degree** [dɪˋgri] 名 度數

5. **on the increase** 名 正在增加

6. **two times** 片 兩倍

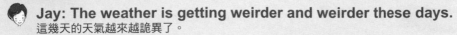

Jay: The weather is getting weirder and weirder these days.
這幾天的天氣越來越詭異了。

Gina: What do you mean?
你的意思是？

Jay: Can't you see? It was eleven degrees yesterday and twenty-five degrees today!
你不覺得嗎？昨天氣溫是十一度，今天卻是二十五度！

Gina: You're right. It's like winter transforming into spring in a single day.
你說的沒錯，這就像冬季在一天之內轉換成春天。

Jay: And the weather forecast said the temperature will drop to thirteen degrees this weekend.
而且氣象預報說這週末將會降溫至十三度。

Gina: Really? What's wrong with the Earth?
真的假的？地球瘋了嗎？

Jay: Maybe the end of the world is on its way.
或許世界末日就是明天。

Gina: Come on! Things can't be that bad.
拜託！沒那麼誇張吧。

Jay: Who knows? Maybe we just have to leave it to the scientists to save us.
誰知道？或許我們該把問題交給科學家解決。

Gina: Or maybe we can start protecting the Earth ourselves!
或者我們可以自己開始保護地球！

Jay: You're right. What do you think of walking home every day?
你說得沒錯。你覺得每天走路回家怎麼樣？

Gina: Great idea! Let's do that!
好主意！就這麼辦！

關鍵單字片語

7. **climate** [ˋklaɪmɪt] 名 氣候

8. **indicate** [ˋɪndə͵ket] 動 指出

9. **during** [ˋdjʊrɪŋ] 介 在…的整個期間

10. **retreat of glaciers** 片 冰川倒退

11. **adaption** [əˋdæpʃən] 名 適應

12. **shifting** [ˋʃɪftɪŋ] 名 變動

2. 族群融合
Ethnic Integration
MP3 137

萬用好句

1. **Racial integration aims to create equality for all people.**
   族群融合的目的是促進全人類的平等。

2. **Our government has been devoted to greater ethnic integration lately.**
   我們的政府近年來致力於族群融合。

3. **The Hakka culture has received more and more attention in Taiwan.**
   客家文化在台灣已越來越受注目。

4. **What do you think of racial integration?**
   你對於族群融合有什麼看法？

5. **The road to ethnic integration is never easy.**
   族群融合之路並不好走。

6. **Martin Luther King Jr. endeavored to advocate racial harmony.**
   馬丁路德金恩博士致力於提倡族群和諧。

7. **Why does racial discrimination exist?**
   為何有種族歧視？

8. **People should be treated equally and have equal opportunity.**
   人類應被平等對待，並享有均等的機會。

9. **Mutual respect and understanding are the best ways to achieve racial integration.**
   相互尊重與理解是通往族群融合的最佳途徑。

10. **To whom can I file a complaint of racial discrimination?**
    我應該向誰申訴種族歧視？

11. **The government of Taiwan has spent a lot of effort to protect the rights and quality of life of the aboriginal people.**
    台灣政府已付出許多努力以保護原住民的權利及生活品質。

12. **Racial discrimination is any act that treats people of other races in an unfair manner.**
    種族歧視是以不公平的方式對待其他種族者的任何行為。

關鍵單字片語

1. **ethnic integration** 片 種族融合
2. **reconcile** [`rɛkənsaɪl] 動 使和解
3. **unify** [`junə,faɪ] 動 統一
4. **language** [`læŋgwɪdʒ] 名 語言
5. **infusion** [ɪn`fjuʒən] 名 注入
6. **equality** [ɪ`kwɑlətɪ] 名 平等

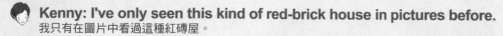
實境對話

Kenny: I've only seen this kind of red-brick house in pictures before.
我只有在圖片中看過這種紅磚屋。

A-Hui: Actually, no one is living in this house now. It's a museum.
事實上，這棟房子已經無人居住了，而是一家博物館。

Kenny: A museum? But it looks just like a house someone lived in a long time ago!
博物館？但它看來就像一棟久無人居的房屋。

A-Hui: It used to belong to the Lin Family, and they donated it to be used as a Hakka Cultural Park years ago.
它曾屬於林家舊厝，幾年前林家將房屋捐出，作為客家文化主題公園。

Kenny: Is that related to the Hakka Cultural Festival?
這跟客家文化祭有關嗎？

A-Hui: Yes. The government has both the cultural park and the Hakka Cultural Festivals to improve the understanding of Hakka culture.
有的。政府建立文化公園以及舉辦客家文化祭，以增進人們對於客家文化的了解。

Kenny: And thus to improve mutual tolerance among different groups?
因此可增進不同族群間的互相接納？

A-Hui: Right. Each group has its unique culture and history.
沒錯。每個族群都有其特殊的文化及歷史。

Kenny: Then what's special about the Hakka Cultural Festival?
那麼，客家文化祭有什麼特別的嗎？

A-Hui: Take the Hakka Tung Blossom Festival for example; you can enjoy traditional snacks and experience the unique Hakka lifestyle.
舉客家桐花祭為例，你可以享用傳統小吃和體驗客家人獨特的生活方式。

關鍵單字片語

7. **level the barrier** 片 弭平障礙

8. **diverse** [daɪˋvɝs] 形 多種多樣的

9. **on the other hand** 片 另一方面

10. **affirmative** [əˋfɝmətɪv] 形 肯定的

11. **unique** [juˋnik] 形 獨特的

12. **separate** [ˋsɛpəˏret] 動 分隔

3. 社會福利
Social Welfare
MP3
138

萬用好句

1.	People suffering from poverty should be taken care of. 經濟弱勢者應受到照顧。
2.	Incentives are sometimes offered as a way to increase the birthrate. 政府有時會以提供獎勵的方式提高生育率。
3.	Developed countries put more emphasis on social welfare. 已開發國家較重視社會福利。
4.	Social welfare refers to the provision of the minimal level of wellbeing and social support for all citizens. 社會福利意指提供人民的基本照顧和社會支持。
5.	There are many informal social groups and religious groups devoted to social welfare. 許多非正式社會團體及宗教團體投身社會福利。
6.	Families suffering from economic difficulties can apply for subsidies. 面臨經濟困境的家戶可申請津貼。
7.	Unemployment benefits are provided to people who lose their jobs. 失業給付提供給失去工作者。
8.	Do you know if there are any social programs that Jerry, who has just become a single dad, can apply for? 你是否知道任何適合剛成為單親爸爸的傑瑞申請的社會補助呢？
9.	In what ways does the government support people with disabilities? 政府如何幫助身心障礙者？
10.	What are the overall objectives of social security and welfare? 社會安全與社會福利的整體目標為何？
11.	Social workers are still undervalued in Taiwan. 社會工作者在台灣仍不受重視。

關鍵單字片語

1. **constitution** [ˌkɑnstəˋtjuʃən] 名 憲法
2. **implement** [ˋɪmpləmɛnt] 動 實施
3. **policy** [ˋpɑləsɪ] 名 政策
4. **social welfare** 片 社會福利
5. **well-being** [ˋwɛlˋbiɪŋ] 名 安康
6. **support** [səˋport] 動 名 支持

實境對話

Gavin: The new National Health Insurance policy was announced today.
新的全民健康保險政策已在今天公布。

Laura: What is that?
那是什麼？

Gavin: It's also called "Second Generation NHI," which is the revision of the current premium system.
它也叫做「二代健保」，調整了目前的保險費率制度。

Laura: Does that mean we have to pay higher insurance fees?
意思是我們必須支付更多保險費嗎？

Gavin: For some of us, yes, it does. But it is a necessary step to protect the whole NHI system.
對於某部分的人而言是的。但這對於整體健保系統有益。

Laura: But I really don't see the point! I'm not sick, so why should I pay so much money every month?
但我真的不太懂。我沒有生病，為何每個月需要付那麼多錢呢？

Gavin: Actually, the money you pay is used to promote social justice.
事實上，你所付出的費用被使用於促進社會正義。

Laura: What do you mean?
你的意思是？

Gavin: The money you pay is not only for your own sake, but is also used to help disadvantaged groups and low-income households, who would otherwise not be able to afford healthcare.
你的支出不僅用在你身上，也協助弱勢族群及低收入戶，支付無力自行負擔的醫療開銷。

Laura: It sounds like the realization of a supportive, egalitarian society.
聽起來像是互助社會的實現。

關鍵單字片語

7. **charity** [`tʃærətɪ] 名 慈善

8. **provide for oneself** 片 自謀生計

9. **monetary payment** 片 金錢給付

10. **subsidy** [`sʌbsədɪ] 名 津貼

11. **health service** 片 公衛服務

12. **NGO** 縮 非政府組織

4.教育制度
Education System
MP3 139

萬用好句

1. The K-12 system is designed to educate primary and secondary school students.
十二年國教系統為針對初等教育與中等教育學童所設計。

2. In many countries, including Canada and Australia, K-12 education is free.
許多國家,包含加拿大與澳洲,十二年國教免收費。

3. In this country, compulsory education is from elementary to high school grades.
在這個國家,自小學至高中為義務教育。

4. Educational reforms are based on the principle of social justice.
教育改革乃根據社會正義原則。

5. What are the pros and cons of the K-12 education policy?
十二年國教的優缺點為何?

6. The K-12 system is divided into two parts: nine years of compulsory education in the lower grades and the three years of high school education.
十二年國民教育系統分為兩大部分,分別為九年義務教育以及三年高中教育。

7. How do junior high school students apply to go to senior high schools?
中學生該如何申請就讀高中?

8. As of August 2014, senior high schools and vocational schools will be free for every student.
自二〇一四年八月起,高級中學及職業學校將免收費。

9. The new K-12 policy is designed to alleviate pressure on children.
新的十二年國教政策目的為減輕孩童的壓力。

10. What do you think is the core spirit of education?
你認為教育的核心精神為何?

關鍵單字片語

1. **education** [ˏɛdʒʊˋkeʃən] 名 教育

2. **aim** [em] 動 瞄準

3. **have an effect on** 片 對⋯產生影響

4. **transmit knowledge** 片 傳遞知識

5. **curriculum** [kəˋrɪkjələm] 名 課程

6. **intellectual** [ˏɪntlˋɛktʃʊəl] 形 智力的

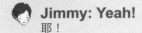

Jimmy: Yeah!
耶！

Mom: Why are you so happy?
你在開心什麼？

Jimmy: I read today's newspaper. The headline says the K-12 system is on the way, so there will be no more tests for me!
我讀了今天的報紙，頭條寫著十二年國教即將施行，所以我再也不用考試了！

Mom: So that's why you are giving away all your reference books.
所以你才把所有參考書送人哦。

Jimmy: Yes! From now on, I can play as many games as I want.
是啊！從今以後，我想玩多少遊戲就玩多少！

Mom: I am sorry, but that won't happen.
很抱歉，不可能。

Jimmy: Why not? There will be no more tests!
為何不？我不需要考試了啊。

Mom: The K-12 system frees you from taking entrance exams, but you still have to study hard to apply for the best high schools.
十二年國教取消了入學考試，但你仍必須認真念書，才得以進入頂尖高中。

Jimmy: I thought I would just go to a nearby school without having to do anything.
我以為我什麼都不用做，就可以就讀附近的學校。

Mom: That's only one of your choices. You can still apply for the school you like. Do you want to go to a school you don't like?
那只是其中一種選項。你仍然可以申請你想就讀的學校。你想就讀不喜歡的學校嗎？

Jimmy: No, I don't.
不，我不想。

Mom: Then you'd better go to your room and pick up your books.
那你最好回房間繼續念書。

★ 關鍵單字片語

7. **cultivate** [ˋkʌltəˌvet] 動 培養

8. **academic** [ˌækəˋdɛmɪk] 形 學術的

9. **K-12 grade** 片 十二年級

10. **primary school** 片 小學

11. **high school** 片 高中

12. **pursue** [pɚˋsu] 動 追求

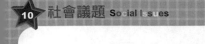

5. 景氣回暖
Economic Recovery
M.P.3 140

萬用好句

1. **The economy has rebounded after the previous downturn.**
經濟狀況於前次衰退後恢復。

2. **The gradually-dropping unemployment rate is a positive sign.**
逐步下降的失業率是一個正向的指標。

3. **Due to the European debt crisis and the weak US labor market, many countries have suffered from the economic downturn.**
歐債危機與美國勞工市場的疲軟，導致許多國家蒙受經濟衰退。

4. **It is said that the economic downturn will bottom out in 2012.**
據說景氣衰退將於二〇一二年探底。

5. **Do you think the new policy can boost the slumping economy?**
你認為新政策有助於提振衰退的經濟嗎？

6. **Taiwan's economic growth hinges on the global economic recovery.**
台灣的經濟成長與全球經濟復甦息息相關。

7. **The stock market is getting better along with the world economy.**
股市跟隨全球經濟狀況而逐步改善。

8. **The booming economy is definitely good news for our country.**
經濟繁榮對我國而言絕對是個好消息。

9. **Do you agree that the main cause of Taiwan's economic recovery is the boom in neighboring mainland China?**
您同意台灣經濟的恢復，是由於鄰近的中國景氣的帶動嗎？

10. **It seems that most European countries are beginning to recover from the worst downturn ever since World War II.**
大多數歐洲國家似乎正開始從二次大戰後最嚴重的經濟衰退中復甦。

11. **Did you suffer any losses during the economic downturn?**
經濟衰退時，你是否蒙受任何損失？

12. **The stock market is still in the red due to the previous slump.**
股市仍因前次的經濟蕭條而不振。

關鍵單字片語

1. **economic** [ˌikəˋnɑmɪk] 形 經濟上的

2. **boost the economy** 片 推動經濟

3. **investor** [ɪnˋvɛstɚ] 名 投資者

4. **bull market** 片 牛市(看漲)

5. **crisis** [ˋkraɪsɪs] 名 危機

6. **economic recovery** 片 經濟復甦

實境對話

Journalist: Mr. Johnson, can you say something about the third quarter sales report?
強森先生，可以請您談談第三季的財務報告嗎？

Spokesman: Absolutely. There was an obvious growth in the third quarter due to the global economic recovery.
當然可以。由於全球景氣回暖，第三季有明顯的成長。

Journalist: But rumor has it that your company lost more than 20 billion dollars in the previous economic slump. Is that true?
但有謠言指出，貴公司已於前次經濟衰退期間損失超過兩百億，此言當真？

Spokesman: The truth is that we did lose some money because of the reduction in European orders, which have continued to grow in the past few months and have made us optimistic about the fourth quarter.
我們的確由於歐洲訂單量的減少而稍有虧損，然而過去幾個月來歐洲訂單持續成長，讓我們對於第四季度充滿希望。

Journalist: Do you think this is the end of the economic slump?
你認為經濟衰退已至尾聲嗎？

Spokesman: To be honest, no one can be sure about that, but the growing numbers do make us very optimistic about the future.
很難說。但逐漸成長的數字的確讓我們對於未來抱持樂觀態度。

Journalist: Then do you have anything to say about the fourth quarter?
那麼，關於第四季您有什麼想法嗎？

Spokesman: We are expecting continuous growth in both orders and revenue with our latest model of cell phone, which will be available next week in Asia and next month in Europe.
隨著最新款手機即將於下週在亞洲、下個月在歐洲上市，我們預期訂單與收益將持續成長。

關鍵單字片語

7. **recession** [rɪˋsɛʃən] 名 衰退

8. **hinge** [hɪndʒ] 動 決定於

9. **abnormally** [æbˋnɔrməlɪ] 副 反常地

10. **growth** [groθ] 名 成長

11. **G.D.P.** 縮 國民生產毛額

12. **downturn** [ˋdaʊntɝn] 名 衰退

6. 勞資關係
Labor Relations
MP3
141

萬用好句

1. **Employers should provide labor insurance for every employee.**
雇主應提供每名雇員勞工保險。

2. **The failure of negotiations between owners and players in the NBA led to a lockout.**
全美籃球協會勞資雙方談判破裂，導致罷工。

3. **The NBA representatives expressed disappointment that they were unable to close the gap in salary expectations with the union.**
全美籃球協會的代表，因未能弭平與工會間對於薪資期望的鴻溝而表示失望。

4. **The union is designed to protect the rights of the employees.**
工會是維護勞工權益的組織。

5. **What are the benefits an employer should legally provide?**
雇主應依法提供給勞工的權益有哪些？

6. **Your employer must take measures to ensure job security.**
雇主應為你的工作安全採取措施。

7. **I'm in charge of labor relation disputes.**
我負責處理勞資間的糾紛。

8. **Do you want to file a complaint against your employer?**
你想要投訴你的雇主嗎？

9. **Any employer who fails to provide insurance for employees will be fined up to $20,000.**
未替勞工投保的雇主將被處以兩萬元罰鍰。

10. **In the event of labor disputes, the concerned parties can negotiate by themselves, or follow the jurisdiction channels.**
勞資糾紛中，相關人員可彼此協商、或訴諸法律。

11. **A good employer makes sure his workers earn enough to meet the cost of living.**
一個好雇主會確保員工的民生需求被滿足。

關鍵單字片語

1. **be conducted by** 片 由⋯處理

2. **union** [`junjən] 名 工會

3. **legally** [`liglɪ] 副 法律上；合法地

4. **in the trade** 片 業內；業界

5. **be aligned with** 片 與⋯結盟

6. **represent** [ˌrɛprɪˋzɛnt] 動 代表

實境對話

Journalist: I am now standing in front of the ABC Corporation Building. We have Ms. Chen, the union representative, with us. Good morning, Ms. Chen.
記者現在的位置是在ABC辦公大樓前方。我們邀請到工會代表陳小姐。陳小姐早。

Ms. Chen: Good morning.
早安。

Journalist: What's the purpose of this sit-in?
這次的靜坐抗議，您的目的是？

Ms. Chen: Today's sit-in is to express our dissatisfaction with the reductions in overtime pay and the extended work hours.
今天靜坐的目的，是表達我們對於加班費刪減以及延長工時的不滿。

Journalist: The company spokesman claimed the changes comply with all labor laws. What is your opinion on that?
公司發言人表示一切皆符合勞基法。您的看法是？

Ms. Chen: That's totally untrue! The company failed to negotiate with the union before implementing changes to overtime pay and work hours.
事實並非如此。公司在執行刪減加班費和延長工時前，並未和工會進行協商。

Journalist: So, what are you asking for?
那麼，您的訴求是？

Ms. Chen: We want the company to cancel the changes to overtime pay and work hours and reopen friendly negotiations with the union in the best interests of both sides.
我們希望公司取消上述政策，並重新開啟友善的溝通管道，以尋求雙方的最佳利益。

Journalist: Thank you for speaking with us, Ms. Chen. Back to you, Andy.
感謝陳小姐接受我們的訪問。鏡頭交還給安迪。

關鍵單字片語

7. **bargain over** 片 協議

8. **working condition** 片 工作條件

9. **dispute** [dɪ`spjut] 名 動 爭執

10. **employer** [ɪm`plɔɪə] 名 雇主

11. **advocate** [`ædvə.ket] 動 提倡

12. **fight against** 片 對抗

萬用好句

1.	**Keep your credit card number secret to avoid fraud.** 保密你的信用卡號碼以防詐騙。
2.	**Fraud can be committed via e-mail and phone calls.** 詐騙可經由電子信件與電話進行。
3.	**You can dial 165 to report fraud.** 你可撥打165通報詐騙。
4.	**The man used a fake identity to defraud the bank.** 男子利用偽造證件詐騙銀行。
5.	**Mrs. Cheng was almost defrauded; luckily, her son stopped her from making a big mistake.** 鄭女士差點遭詐騙，所幸她的兒子及時阻止大錯。
6.	**Some fraudsters pretend to be bank officers, asking you to provide your bank card information.** 某些詐騙分子假扮成銀行員，藉以要求你提供提款卡資訊。
7.	**Never operate an ATM under the instructions of other people.** 勿在他人的指示下操作自動提款機。
8.	**How do you know the call was a scam?** 你怎麼知道那是一通詐騙電話？
9.	**Phishing refers to e-mails, text messages and websites made and operated by criminals in an attempt to steal personal information.** 網路釣魚意指嫌犯藉由寄發電子郵件、簡訊及網頁，企圖竊取個資。
10.	**If you receive a suspicious e-mail, report it to the police.** 若你收到可疑電子郵件，請逕向警方舉報。
11.	**Keep an eye on your credit card, just in case it might be stolen or used to steal money from your account.** 謹慎保管你的信用卡，避免遭盜刷，或藉此竊取你的帳戶存款。
12.	**Some scammers may even pretend to be judges.** 某些詐騙分子甚至會假扮成法官。

關鍵單字片語

1. **fraud** [frɔd] 名 欺騙

2. **criminal** [`krɪmən!] 名 罪犯

3. **deception** [dɪ`sɛpʃən] 名 詐騙

4. **valuables** [`væljʊəb!z] 名 財產

5. **defraud** [dɪ`frɔd] 動 詐騙

6. **rather than** 片 而不是…

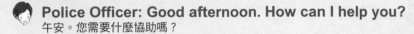

Police Officer: Good afternoon. How can I help you?
午安。您需要什麼協助嗎？

Mrs. Watson: I've just got a phone call telling me that the money in my account was stolen and that the police will seize all my money unless I wire all of it to a police account. What should I do?
我剛接到一通告知帳戶遭竊的電話，若我不將所有的錢電匯至警方帳戶，警方將會沒收我所有的錢。我該怎麼做？

Police Officer: Calm down. This is a typical scam, and you will lose all your money if you do what they ask.
請冷靜。這是典型詐騙，若你依照對方要求操作，將會失去你所有的錢。

Mrs. Watson: But they told me the police bank account will be under my name, so I don't have to worry about losing a dime.
但他們說警方帳戶將會列在我的名下，因此我不會損失任何錢。

Police Officer: It's a trick. They might have an account under your name, but you won't have any access to the account nor the money. Have you ever lost your purse?
這是他們的詐騙手法。帳戶或許會在你的名下，但你無法使用該帳戶。你曾遺失錢包嗎？

Mrs. Watson: Yes! I lost it last month on a train.
有！上個月掉在火車上。

Police Officer: They must have gotten your purse and ID to open a bank account on your behalf.
他們一定是拿了你的錢包和證件，用你的名字開了一個銀行帳戶。

Mrs. Watson: Wow! Luckily my grandson told me to come and confirm it before wiring the money.
哇！幸好我孫子要我在轉帳前，先到警局做確認。

Police Officer: You have a very smart grandson.
你的孫子真機靈。

關鍵單字片語

7. **hoax** [hoks] 動 欺騙 名 騙局

8. **reconfirm** [ˌrikən`fɜm] 動 再確認

9. **transfer** [`trænsfɜ] 名 轉帳

10. **Internet fraud** 片 網路詐騙

11. **PIN** 縮 個人識別號

12. **privacy** [`praɪvəsɪ] 名 隱私

8. 美股大跌
The Stock Market
MP₃
143

萬用好句

1. The largest stock market in the US is the NYSE.
美國最大的股票市場為紐約證券交易所。

2. Stock market investors include individual retail investors and institutional investors, such as insurance companies.
股市的參與者包括個別投資人以及法人投資者，如保險公司。

3. Why is the stock market going down?
股市為何會下跌？

4. The unemployment rate also contributes to the stagnation in the stock market.
失業率亦為造成股市成長緩慢的原因。

5. When do you think the best time is to invest in the stock market?
你認為投資股市的最佳時機為何？

6. Both the Dow Jones Industrial Average and Standard & Poors fell yesterday, which made my father very upset.
昨日，道瓊工業指數與標準普爾指數皆下跌，使家父非常沮喪。

7. U.S. stocks opened in the red for the first time in five months.
美國股市五個月以來首度開低。

8. The stock market tanked and investors lost tons of money.
大跌的股市使投資者損失慘重。

9. Does the interest rate fall as the stock market declines?
當股市下跌時，利率也會跟著下跌嗎？

10. What are the factors impacting the stock market?
影響股市的因素有哪些？

11. The stock market is currently on a slippery slope.
股市目前正逐步下滑。

12. You can see the U.S. stock market results on Channel 77 at 8 pm.
你可於晚間八點，收看七十七頻道的美股行情。

關鍵單字片語

1. **stock market** 片 股票市場

2. **DJIA** 縮 道瓊工業平均指數

3. **index** [ˋɪndɛks] 名 指數

4. **Wall Street** 片 華爾街

5. **interest rate** 片 利率

6. **business** [ˋbɪznɪs] 名 交易

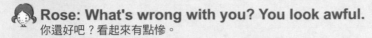

Rose: What's wrong with you? You look awful.
你還好吧？看起來有點慘。

Jay: It's because things are awful.
因為事情的確蠻慘的。

Rose: What do you mean?
怎麼說？

Jay: I've lost a lot of money in the stock market.
我在股票市場內大賠。

Rose: You did? I read about the crisis in the stock market in the newspaper. It is one of the most serious crises in decades.
是噢？我在報紙上讀到股市低迷的消息，是數十年來最慘的狀況。

Jay: It's been the most serious for me in five years.
對我而言是這五年來最糟的。

Rose: Cheer up. Mr. Wang told me yesterday that he had great faith in the stock market and that he was expecting a strong rebound.
開心點。王先生昨天跟我說，他對股市具極大信心，並預期股價會強力回彈。

Jay: Who is Mr. Wang?
王先生是誰啊？

Rose: The man upstairs who used to be a Wall Street broker.
住樓上的先生，他曾經在華爾街擔任股票經紀人。

Jay: Do you mean the old man who's always reading a newspaper and who walks with a cane?
你是指那位總在閱讀報紙和拄著拐杖的老人嗎？

Rose: That's right. Since analysts predict a rebound in the market, I think you will get your money back soon.
是啊。既然分析家預測股市即將回彈，我相信你在短期內就可收復失土。

關鍵單字片語

7. **trade** [tred] 名 貿易

8. **currently** [ˋkɝəntlɪ] 副 現在

9. **S&P 500** 片 標準普爾500指數

10. **targeted stock** 片 目標股票

11. **estimate** [ˋɛstə‚met] 動 估計

12. **nominal value** 片 面值

9. 東京地震
Tokyo Earthquake
MP3 144

萬用好句

1.	**An 8.9-magnitude earthquake hit off Japan on March 11, 2011.** 二〇一一年三月十一日，一個規模八點九的強震襲擊日本。
2.	**The earthquake in Japan caused a lot of damage and casualties.** 日本大地震造成嚴重傷亡。
3.	**The 311 Earthquake also triggered a 23-foot tsunami that killed thousands of local residents.** 三一一大地震也引發了二十三呎高的海嘯，造成當地數千名民眾喪生。
4.	**After the tsunami, there were vehicles among the debris.** 海嘯席捲過後，殘片瓦礫中可見汽車身影。
5.	**The nuclear power plants in Japan were shut down temporarily.** 日本的核能發電廠暫時關閉。
6.	**How do I make a donation to the refugees in Japan?** 我該如何捐款給日本的受災者？
7.	**Some volunteered to stay and monitor the nuclear power plant, running the risk of radiation exposure.** 一些志願留看核能發電廠者，冒著暴露於輻射線中的危險。
8.	**The 311 Earthquake was the most powerful one in Japan's history.** 三一一大地震是日本史上最強大的地震。
9.	**Japanese nuclear officials said a reactor in the nuclear power plant overheated after the cooling system failed.** 日本核能部門官員表示，核能發電廠內的一座反應爐在冷卻系統當機後過熱。
10.	**As a friendly neighbor, Taiwan raised at least three billion dollars for Japan, which suffered from the great 311 Earthquake.** 身為友善的鄰國，台灣為日本三一一大地震受災戶募集了超過三十億元。
11.	**What were the areas affected by the quake?** 受地震影響的區域為？
12.	**The damage was estimated to be at least $30 billion.** 損失估計超過三百億元。

關鍵單字片語

1. **earthquake** [ˋɝθ.kwek] 名 地震
2. **tsunami** [tsuˋnɑmɪ] 名 海嘯
3. **damage** [ˋdæmɪdʒ] 名 動 損害
4. **nuclear power plant** 片 核能發電廠
5. **missing** [ˋmɪsɪŋ] 形 行蹤不明的
6. **evacuate** [ɪˋvækjʊ.et] 動 使疏散

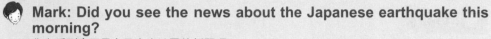

Mark: Did you see the news about the Japanese earthquake this morning?
你有看到今天早上日本大地震的新聞嗎？

Karen: Yes, I did. The magnitude of the earthquake was eventually determined to be 8.9.
有啊。地震規模上修至八點九。

Mark: And a reactor at the nuclear power plant overheated.
而且有個核能發電廠的反應爐過熱。

Karen: Really? What can they do?
真的嗎？那他們要怎麼辦？

Mark: Some power plant workers volunteered to stay, maintain and monitor the reactor.
有些電廠員工志願留守，以維護及監督反應爐。

Karen: Isn't that very dangerous? It's so brave of them to put their own lives at risk for the safety of the majority.
那不是非常危險嗎？他們真勇敢，冒著自身生命危險以維護大多數人的安全。

Mark: Yes, they are very courageous. In addition, Japan is in desperate need of international support.
是啊，他們真的非常有勇氣。另外，日本目前急需國際援助。

Karen: What can we do now?
我們現在能做些什麼？

Mark: The Red Cross Society of the Republic of China is raising funds for the refugees in Japan.
台灣紅十字會正為日本的受災者進行募款。

Karen: How do I make a donation?
我該如何捐款？

Mark: You can make your donation by credit card or go online.
你可使用信用卡或上網捐款。

關鍵單字片語

7. **warn** [wɔrn] 動 警告

8. **alert** [əˋlɜt] 名 警戒

9. **aftermath** [ˋæftɚ͵mæθ] 名 後果

10. **landslide** [ˋlænd͵slaɪd] 名 山崩

11. **massive** [ˋmæsɪv] 形 大規模的

12. **scale** [skel] 名 規模

10. 茉莉花革命
The Jasmine Revolution
MP3 145

萬用好句

1.	The Jasmine Revolution had a great impact on North Africa. 茉莉花革命對北非產生重大影響。
2.	The Jasmine Revolution is named after Tunisia's national flower. 茉莉花革命是以突尼西亞的國花命名。
3.	Right after the Jasmine Revolution in Tunisia, China had its own Jasmine Revolution as well. 就在突尼西亞的茉莉花革命之後，中國也發起了茉莉花革命。
4.	A lad aged 26 burned himself to death in protest of the regime. 一名二十六歲的男子自焚，以表對政權的抗議。
5.	The anti-government protest lasted for at least a month. 反政府抗議行動持續至少一個月。
6.	8,000 lawyers and teachers participated in the protest. 八千名律師及教師參與抗議。
7.	What do you know about the Jasmine Revolution in Tunisia? 你對於突尼西亞的茉莉花革命有何了解？
8.	The Jasmine Revolution resulted from people's dissatisfaction with the high unemployment rate and the slumping economy. 茉莉花革命是源於人民對於高失業率以及經濟蕭條的不滿。
9.	The former Tunisian president was accused of eighteen crimes. 突尼西亞前總統遭控十八條罪名。
10.	Many Chinese youths plotted their own Jasmine Revolution online. 許多中國年輕人在網路上策劃了他們的茉莉花革命。
11.	The Chinese authorities arrested the protestors immediately. 中國執政當局立即逮捕了抗議者。
12.	The Chinese authorities are still investigating who the conspirators of the Jasmine Revolution were. 中國執政當局仍在調查茉莉花革命的密謀策劃者。

關鍵單字片語

1. **Jasmine Revolution** 片 茉莉花革命

2. **democracy** [dɪ`mɑkrəsɪ] 名 民主

3. **slim chance** 片 渺茫的機會

4. **plot** [plɑt] 動 策劃；密謀

5. **arrest** [ə`rɛst] 動 逮捕

6. **corrupt** [kə`rʌpt] 形 腐敗的

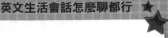

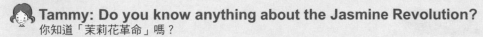

Tammy: Do you know anything about the Jasmine Revolution?
你知道「茉莉花革命」嗎？

Father: Yes, it was an anti-government protest in Tunisia. Why?
嗯，那是在突尼西亞的反政府示威行動，怎麼了嗎？

Tammy: I'm doing a report on it. Why was it so important?
我正針對這個議題做報告，這個事件為何那麼重要？

Father: Because this large-scale protest lasted for more than a month, and many people died in the confrontation as well.
因為這場大規模的抗議事件持續了一個多月，且有很多人在抗爭中喪命。

Tammy: Why did people protest against the government?
為何人民要抗議突尼西亞政府？

Father: The Tunisian government had been a corrupt regime for decades, and the demonstration was the largest-scale anti-government protest ever.
突國政府的貪污政權已行有年之，以至於會發生這起史上最大規模的反政府示威活動。

Tammy: At first, I thought the Jasmine Revolution originated in China.
一開始我以為「茉莉花革命」發生在中國呢。

Father: The one in China is a copy, and, unlike the one in Tunisia, it was suppressed by the government. There was even censorship of the related key words on the Internet.
中國那場是起而效尤。且和突尼西亞不同，它遭政府壓制，甚至還會審查網路關鍵字。

Tammy: Was that possible?
還可以這樣搞喔？

Father: Of course, they could do that.
行啊，中國政府的確辦得到。

Tammy: Wow! It looks like we do live in a free country.
哇，看來我國真民主啊。

關鍵單字片語

7. **protest** [`protɛst] 名 抗議

8. **sit in** 片 靜坐抗議

9. **suppress** [sə`prɛs] 動 壓制

10. **step down** 片 辭職；退休

11. **under pressure** 片 在壓力之下

12. **regime** [rɪ`ʒim] 名 統治；政權

11. **瑞典爆炸**
Sweden Bombing Incident
MP3 146

萬用好句

1.	**Sweden's Security Service is investigating two blasts which happened only a few hundred meters apart yesterday.** 瑞典安全部正針對昨天兩起距離僅數百公尺遠的爆炸案進行調查。
2.	**The explosion killed the suspected bomber on the spot.** 爆炸導致嫌疑炸彈客當場身亡。
3.	**The explosion in Sweden was investigated as an act of terrorism.** 瑞典爆炸案被視為一起恐怖攻擊，並展開調查。
4.	**How many people were hurt in the explosion?** 爆炸案中有多少人受傷？
5.	**The explosion could be an angry attack against the troops.** 爆炸案可能為一起針對軍隊的憤怒攻擊。
6.	**Did you read the news about the explosion in Sweden?** 你有看到關於瑞典爆炸案的報導嗎？
7.	**Two people were hospitalized because of the recent explosion.** 兩位民眾因最近這起爆炸案而送醫救治。
8.	**What did the police say about the explosions in Stockholm?** 警方對於斯德哥爾摩爆炸案有何說法？
9.	**Was there any connection between the two explosions in Sweden?** 瑞典的兩起爆炸案間是否有任何關聯？
10.	**One person was killed and two were hurt by two blasts in the center of Stockholm, the capital of Sweden.** 瑞典首都斯德哥爾摩發生的兩起爆炸案造成一人死亡、兩人受傷。
11.	**Do you believe that the blasts in Stockholm were not related?** 你相信在斯德哥爾摩發生的爆炸案之間毫無關連嗎？
12.	**The government will need to do more investigation and find more witnesses to provide information of what actually happened.** 政府需要進行更多調查，並需要更多目擊證人提供關於事實真相的資訊。

關鍵單字片語

1. **terrorist bomber** 片 恐怖炸彈客
2. **go off** 片 響起；進行
3. **the authorities** 片 當局
4. **bomb** [bɑm] 名 炸彈
5. **explosion** [ɪk`sploʒən] 名 爆炸
6. **injured** [`ɪndʒəd] 形 受傷的

實境對話

Frank: Take a look at this. It is terrifying.
快過來看，真可怕。

Karen: What is it?
怎麼了？

Frank: It's news of the bombing incident in Sweden, which might be another suicide bombing.
一則新聞有關瑞典發生爆炸案，有可能是另一起自殺炸彈攻擊。

Karen: Was anyone hurt or did anyone die in these bombings?
有人在爆炸中受傷、甚至喪生嗎？

Frank: One man, who was suspected of being the suicide bomber, died in the blast and two other people were injured as well.
一名疑似自殺炸彈客的男人死於爆炸、以及另有兩名傷者。

Karen: Oh, no. But luckily, there weren't too many people hurt or killed.
噢，不。不過，所幸沒有太多人傷亡。

Frank: But the explosion was downtown and the possibility of it being a suicide bombing made people panic.
但由於爆炸案發生在市區，且有可能為自殺式爆炸，引起人們的驚慌。

Karen: How did the government respond to the bombing?
該國政府對於爆炸案有何回應？

Frank: It was reported that the government has started to investigate the background of the dead man to see if he was associated with terrorists.
據報導，該國政府已針對死者展開調查，以釐清他是否有恐怖分子身分。

Karen: It sounds awful. I hope it was just an accident.
聽起來真糟糕。希望這只是一起意外事件。

關鍵單字片語

7. **suicide** [`suə,saɪd] 形 自殺的

8. **evidence** [`ɛvədəns] 名 證據

9. **victim** [`vɪktɪm] 名 受害者

10. **police** [pə`lis] 名 警方

11. **investigate** [ɪn`vɛstə,get] 動 調查

12. **occur** [ə`kɝ] 動 發生

萬用好句

1.	**There were copycat riots across London following the riots in Tottenham.** 托登罕騷亂後，數起模仿騷亂發生於倫敦各處。
2.	**Last year, London suffered widespread rioting, looting and arson.** 去年，倫敦經歷了大規模的騷亂、劫掠與縱火。
3.	**The London riot followed the shooting of a young man killed by the police, and came after a peaceful protest in Tottenham.** 一名年輕男子於托登罕的一場和平抗議中遭警方射殺身亡後，開啟了倫敦騷亂。
4.	**The shooting by police sparked the violence.** 動亂的導火線為警方殺民事件。
5.	**The London riots were characterized by looting and arson.** 倫敦騷亂的特徵為劫掠與縱火。
6.	**There is going to be a special report on the London riot and the economic crisis in Europe at eight tonight.** 今晚八點，將播出關於倫敦騷亂以及經濟危機的特別報導。
7.	**More than three thousand people have been arrested.** 已有超過三千人遭逮捕。
8.	**The riots in England reflect the effects of the sluggish economy and the high unemployment rate in Europe.** 英國騷亂事件為針對歐洲經濟遲緩以及高失業率的反映。
9.	**Stories and updates on the latest riots ran day and night.** 媒體版面完全被最新的騷亂事件所佔據。
10.	**Some youths in the mob threw rocks at the police.** 暴民中有許多年輕人朝警方丟擲石頭。
11.	**The Brixton tube station was closed due to the recent violence.** 布里克斯頓地鐵站由於近期發生的動亂而關閉。
12.	**What's the evidence that gangs were behind the riots?** 騷亂為幫派主導的證據為何？

★ 關鍵單字片語

1. **riot** [`raɪət] 名 暴亂；騷亂
2. **loot** [lut] 名 動 劫掠
3. **violence** [`vaɪələns] 名 暴力
4. **condemn** [kən`dɛm] 動 責難
5. **a wave of** 片 一股…浪潮
6. **disorder** [dɪs`ɔrdɚ] 名 混亂

實境對話

Danny: What are you doing, Amanda?
亞曼達，你在做什麼？

Amanda: I am writing to Karen, my pen pal in London.
我正在寫信給倫敦的筆友凱倫。

Danny: Then why do you look so worried?
那你為何看起來憂心忡忡？

Amanda: Didn't you see the news? There was a riot in London.
你沒看新聞嗎？倫敦發生騷亂。

Danny: A riot? In London? How come?
騷亂？在倫敦？怎麼了？

Amanda: Many young people protested the high unemployment rate and the economic recession. Some of them fought with the police.
有許多年輕人抗議高失業率及經濟蕭條，並發生了一些警民衝突的狀況。

Danny: That sounds like the usual protest. Why do you call it a "riot"?
聽似普通的抗議事件，為何你稱之為「騷亂」？

Amanda: It started as a protest, but some criminals used the opportunity to loot the nearby shops and occupy the subway stations.
一開始為抗議事件，但有些罪犯利用機會劫掠附近的商店、並佔領地鐵站。

Danny: It sounds terrifying.
聽起來真可怕。

Amanda: Cars were even set on fire all over town. The subway was forced to stop. Everything was in a mess.
各處有汽車遭燒毀，地鐵被迫停駛，一切陷入大亂。

Danny: You must be very worried about your pen pal.
你一定非常擔心你的筆友。

關鍵單字片語

7. **more than** 片 不只…

8. **smashed** [smæʃt] 形 破碎的

9. **gangster** [ˋɡæŋstɚ] 名 盜匪

10. **on behalf of** 片 代表

11. **copycat** [ˋkɑpɪ͵kæt] 名 模仿者

12. **set fire to** 片 縱火燒…

13. 兩岸互動
Cross-Strait Relations
MP3
148

萬用好句

1.	**Have you ever visited Beijing, whether for business or travel?** 你曾出於工作或旅行緣故造訪北京嗎？
2.	**What do you know about "The 1992 Consensus"?** 你對於九二共識有何了解？
3.	**The two sides across the Straits have seesawed back and forth over several important issues related to both politics and the economy.** 海峽兩岸針對重要的政治與經濟議題進行協商。
4.	**Sun Moon Lake is one of the popular tourist spots for Chinese tourists.** 日月潭是最受中國遊客歡迎的旅遊景點之一。
5.	**Nowadays, students from China are allowed to study in Taiwan.** 近來，中國學生可在台就讀。
6.	**Do you think a consensus will be reached in the meeting?** 你認為這次會議中將達成共識嗎？
7.	**Direct cross-strait flights cut down a lot on travel time.** 兩岸直航節省我們許多通勤時間。
8.	**The Three Mini Links is restricted to passengers who meet certain requirments.** 小三通僅限於符合特定資格者使用。
9.	**The Three Mini Links issue is still in the spotlight.** 小三通議題仍備受矚目。
10.	**Every party has its own opinion on cross-strait relations.** 每個政黨對於兩岸關係皆有其見解。
11.	**Economic ties across the Strait have thrived, with bilateral trade up to 10 billion dollars.** 兩岸經濟關係由於上達一百億元的雙邊貿易而繁榮。
12.	**We should tolerate different opinions when it comes to politics.** 談到政治，我們應該接納不同的觀點。

關鍵單字片語

1. **summarize** [ˋsʌməˌraɪz] 動 總結

2. **sensitive** [ˋsɛnsətɪv] 形 敏感的

3. **bilateral trade** 片 雙邊貿易

4. **Mainland China** 片 中國大陸

5. **remark** [rɪˋmɑrk] 動 評論

6. **delegation** [ˌdɛləˋgeʃən] 名 委任

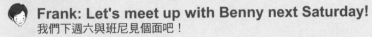

實境對話

Frank: Let's meet up with Benny next Saturday!
我們下週六與班尼見個面吧！

Denise: Benny? He won't be back for three months.
班尼？他三個月內不會回來。

Frank: Is that true? Why?
真的嗎？為什麼？

Denise: He got an offer from a company in China, and he decided to see what it was like in the biggest market in the world.
他得到一家中國公司的工作邀請，並決定到世界上最大的市場看看。

Frank: He is the third guy I know who has left to work in China.
他是我所認識第三個到中國工作的人。

Denise: I was on business in Shanghai last month, and it is such an international city with many skyscrapers and modern buildings.
我上個月到上海出差，發現上海是個國際化的城市，有著摩天大樓和現代化的建築。

Frank: And Shanghai is a popular tourist spot as well.
上海也是個知名的旅遊景點。

Denise: And Beijing, too. In addition, with the policy changes, people from China can also travel to Taiwan more easily.
北京也是。而且，隨著政策改變，中國民眾來台旅遊也更容易了。

Frank: This bring the two sides of the Strait even closer together.
這讓隔著台灣海峽的兩岸更加接近了。

Denise: I couldn't agree with you more. I saw a lot of visitors from China at the National Palace Museum last week.
非常同意。上禮拜，我在故宮博物院看到許多來自中國的遊客。

Frank: It must be really hard for the older generation to imagine.
老一輩的人一定非常難以想像這種情況。

Denise: That's a good observation.
非常入微的觀察。

關鍵單字片語

7. **The 1992 Consensus** 片 九二共識
8. **cross-strait** [`krɔs`stret] 形 海峽兩岸的
9. **negotiation** [nɪ͵goʃɪ`eʃən] 名 協商
10. **allow** [ə`lau] 動 允許
11. **deny** [dɪ`naɪ] 動 否認
12. **address** [ə`drɛs] 動 致詞

14. 總統大選
Presidential Election
149

萬用好句

1. **How many candidates are there in this presidential election?**
這次總統大選有幾位候選人呢？

2. **When is the televised presidential election debate?**
總統大選的電視辯論會幾點開始？

3. **President Ma is looking forward to a chance to continue his term.**
馬總統期待獲得連任的機會。

4. **The DPP has nominated Tsai Ying-wen as its presidential candidate.**
民進黨提名蔡英文為總統候選人。

5. **You can get updates on news of the campaign online.**
你可上網讀取最新選戰新聞。

6. **The 13th presidential Taiwanese election was scheduled for Jan 14th.**
第十三屆台灣總統大選訂於一月十四號。

7. **What month is the United States presidential election in 2012?**
二〇一二年的美國總統大選在幾月？

8. **The presidential election will be held together with the legislative election.**
本屆總統大選將與立委選舉合辦。

9. **When was the first direct election held to choose the President of the U.S.A.?**
美國第一次總統直選在何時？

10. **DPP challenger Tsai Ying-wen resigned her post as chairperson of the DPP after her electoral defeat.**
民進黨總統參選人蔡英文，在敗選後辭去她民進黨黨揆的職位。

11. **The 2012 presidential election, mainly between incumbent President Ma Ying-jiou and the challenger Tsai Ying-wen, was a tough race.**
在二〇一二年的總統大選中，現任馬英九總統與參選人蔡英文，有場激烈的競爭。

關鍵單字片語

1. **presidential election** 片 總統大選

2. **debate** [dɪˋbet] 名 動 辯論

3. **vice** [vaɪs] 形 副的

4. **campaign** [kæmˋpen] 名 選戰

5. **resign** [rɪˋzaɪn] 動 辭去

6. **party** [ˋpɑrtɪ] 名 政黨

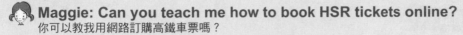

Maggie: Can you teach me how to book HSR tickets online?
你可以教我用網路訂購高鐵車票嗎？

Hank: Of course. When are you going to take the train?
當然可以，你要搭哪時候的車呢？

Maggie: January 14.
一月十四號的班次。

Hank: January 14? Isn't that the weekend right before the final?
一月十四號嗎？那不是期末考前的那個週末嗎？

Maggie: I know, but I don't think there will be many people on the campus that weekend.
我知道啊，但我想那個週末不會有太多人在學校喔。

Hank: Why not? The library is always crowded on "Super Weekend."
怎麼會？圖書館在「抱佛腳週末」總是人山人海呢。

Maggie: It's the date of the presidential election. Aren't you going back home to vote for the candidate you support?
因為「總統大選日」啊，難道你不回家投票給支持的候選人嗎？

Hank: You've given me a wake-up call. My mom warned me that if I didn't go back home to vote, she wouldn't give me any allowance for three months.
你提醒我了。我媽有警告過我，如果我沒回家投票，就要扣我三個月的零用錢。

Maggie: My dad said the same thing to me.
我爸也這樣說耶。

Hank: It looks like we have to cancel the study group in case both of our parents get mad at us.
看來我們要取消讀書會了，免得我們的爸媽抓狂。

Maggie: You're right. Let's book the tickets online.
有道理，我們上網訂車票吧。

關鍵單字片語

7. **nominate** [`nɑmə,net] 動 提名

8. **primary election** 片 初選

9. **political** [pə`lɪtɪkḷ] 形 政治的

10. **vote** [vot] 名 選舉 動 投票

11. **civil rights** 片 民權

12. **choose** [tʃuz] 動 選擇

15. 環境永續
Environmental Sustainability
MP3 150

萬用好句

1. Sustainability refers to how biological systems are able to remain diverse and productive over time.
永續性是指生物系統如何長期維持多元性並保有生產力。

2. Environmental sustainability is necessary for the well-being of human beings.
環境永續對人類的安康而言是有必要的。

3. Well established and healthy wetlands and forests are examples of sustainable biological systems.
健全的濕地與森林體系是永續生物系統的例證。

4. What actions should we take to protect the environment?
我們該為環境保護採取哪些措施呢？

5. We should only use what we need and retain enough for our future generations to utilize.
我們應僅取用所需，為後代子孫保留足以利用的資源。

6. We shouldn't treat non-renewable resources, such as fossil fuels, as if they were unlimited.
我們不該視石油等非再生資源為無限量的能源。

7. Driving less reduces the threat to environmental sustainability.
少開車可降低對環境永續性的威脅。

8. Cycling to work is very environmentally friendly.
騎單車上班很環保。

9. Environmental consciousness is now under the spotlight.
現在，環保意識已成為公眾的焦點。

10. It is everyone's responsibility to help sustain the environment.
維護環境是每個人的責任。

11. Making double-sided copies is very much encouraged in our office.
在我們辦公室裡非常鼓勵使用雙面列印。

關鍵單字片語

1. **ecology** [ɪ`kɑlədʒɪ] 名 生態學

2. **species** [`spiʃiz] 名 物種

3. **due to** 片 由於

4. **extinction** [ɪk`stɪŋkʃən] 名 滅絕

5. **wetland** [`wɛt͵lənd] 名 溼地

6. **utilize** [`jutl͵aɪz] 動 利用

實境對話

Gina: What are you doing? You've been in the garage for 2 hours.
你在幹嘛啊？你已經在車庫裡兩個小時咧。

David: I am recycling.
我在做回收啊。

Gina: That doesn't sound like a two-hour job. What've you been doing?
那也不需要花兩個鐘頭吧，你究竟在做啥啊？

David: I'm sorting things into the different types of recyclable material.
我在把垃圾分別歸到不同的回收類項去。

Gina: Why don't you just throw them into the garbage can?
你為什麼不把它們直接丟進垃圾桶裡呢？

David: It's much easier to simply throw them into the garbage can, but for the sake of our Earth, it is always worth spending time recycling.
直接丟進垃圾桶裡當然很省事，不過為了我們的地球，花時間做回收是很值得的。

Gina: What do you mean?
你是指？

David: The planet's natural resources are limited, and no one can be sure when the supply will be totally depleted. That's why we have to recycle everything as much as possible, for the sustainability of the planet.
地球資源有限，沒人能確定何時枯竭。為了地球的永續發展，我們要儘量做好資源回收。

Gina: You're right.
有道理。

David: And that's why I always ask you to turn off the lights after leaving a room.
那就是我總要你隨手關燈的原因了。

7. **greenhouse gas** 片 溫室氣體

8. **resource** [rɪˋsors] 名 資源

9. **co-exist** [͵koɪgˋzɪst] 動 共存

10. **recycle** [riˋsaɪkl̩] 動 回收

11. **garbage bin** 片 垃圾桶

12. **deplete** [dɪˋplit] 動 用盡

315

萬用好句

1. Happiness is not only an attitude but also a genetic disposition.
快樂不但是一種態度，也是一種天性。

2. Do you see the glass as half-full or half-empty?
你視杯內的水是半滿還是半空？

3. Always look on the bright side of life.
總要多看人生的光明面。

4. "Impossible is nothing" is Jason's motto.
「沒有不可能」是傑森的座右銘。

5. "When you think you can or think you can't, you are right."
「當你覺得你辦得到或者辦不到時，你永遠是對的。」

6. Pessimism may lead to failure, especially when you think things will turn out poorly and, as a result, take no action.
悲觀可能導致失敗，尤其當你覺得事情的結果會很糟，而因此不採取任何行動時。

7. What kind of person are you, a pessimist or an optimist?
你是悲觀者還是樂觀者？

8. Some people would rather expect the worst and be pleasantly surprised when things turn out fine.
有些人寧願把事情想到最糟，而當事情的結果還好時，感到喜出望外。

9. An optimist is more likely to think he or she is always right.
樂觀者較可能覺得自己總是對的。

10. Jerry is keen on pouring cold water on any exciting plans.
傑瑞喜歡對有趣的計劃澆冷水。

11. Which do you think is better, pessimism or optimism?
你覺得悲觀比較好，還是樂觀比較好？

12. Depending on the situation, both optimistic and pessimistic viewpoints can be motivating factors.
在提升動機上，悲觀和樂觀都能依情況派上用場。

關鍵單字片語

1. **pessimistic** [ˌpɛsəˋmɪstɪk] 形 悲觀的

2. **optimistic** [ˌɑptəˋmɪstɪk] 形 樂觀的

3. **attitude** [ˋætətjud] 名 態度

4. **to the extent** 片 到達…程度

5. **benefit** [ˋbɛnəfɪt] 名 益處、好處

6. **positive** [ˋpɑzətɪv] 形 正向的

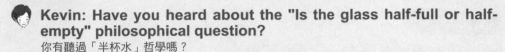

Kevin: Have you heard about the "Is the glass half-full or half-empty" philosophical question?
你有聽過「半杯水」哲學嗎？

Jessica: No. What is that?
沒有，那是什麼？

Kevin: It's a common expression to highlight that whether a person is optimisic or pessimistic is important.
那是普遍用來表達某人樂觀或悲觀的講法。

Jessica: Sounds interesting. Can you tell me more about that?
聽起來很有趣，你可以多說一點嗎？

Kevin: Sure. Upon seeing the half-full glass of water, optimistic people are happy because they have half a glass of water, but pessimistic people are depressed because they only have half a glass of water.
當然。看到半杯水時，樂觀者會因為還有半杯水而開心，而悲觀者會因為只剩半杯而沮喪。

Jessica: That makes sense. A particular situation may be seen in different ways depending on one's point of view.
有道理。有時候觀點不同，情況看起來就會不同。

Kevin: That's right. I couldn't agree with you more.
沒錯。我非常同意。

Jessica: Why did you mention this? Are you doing a report or something?
為何提到這個？你在做報告嗎？

Kevin: No. I just read about it in the newspaper, and I am kind of curious about it.
沒有。我剛好在報紙上看到，引起我的興趣。

關鍵單字片語

7. **inherently** [ɪn`hɪrəntlɪ] 副 天性地

8. **negative** [`nɛgətɪv] 形 負面的

9. **contribute to** 片 促成

10. **stressed out** 片 受到過多壓力的

11. **motto** [`mɑto] 名 座右銘

12. **curious** [`kjurɪəs] 形 好奇的

2.務實 vs.理想
Practicality vs. Idealism
MP3 152

萬用好句

1. **How do we find a balance between pragmatism and idealism?**
   我們要如何在務實主義與理想主義間取得平衡？

2. **In my opinion, in any realm of life, the only way to succeed is to take a practical, rather than idealistic, point of view.**
   我認為，在人生的各面向，成功的唯一途徑是採取實際、而非理想化的觀點。

3. **Which type of person are you, practical or idealistic?**
   你是實際、還是理想化的人？

4. **On the other hand, idealistism can offer us a vision to fight for.**
   另一方面，理想化的觀點可以給我們一個奮鬥的目標。

5. **An idealistic approach alone cannot bring prosperity. You have to take a practical stance as well.**
   空有理想無法帶來成功，必須同時抱持實際的態度。

6. **What are the practical concerns in this matter?**
   這件事實際的考量是什麼？

7. **Do you have any practical advice concerning the plan?**
   關於這項計畫，你有何實用建議？

8. **An idealist always dreams big.**
   理想主義者總是有遠大的目標。

9. **Jamie is always thinking too idealistically. She thinks everything will always run as smoothly as she planned it.**
   潔美總是太理想化。她覺得每件事都能如預期般順利進行。

10. **Jason is a practical person who has no interest in expensive cars.**
    傑森很實際，他對昂貴的車沒有興趣。

11. **Do you think Mandy's plan is practical or just an idealistic dream?**
    你覺得蔓蒂的計劃可行、或只是個理想的夢？

12. **Combined with dedication, idealism can lead to practical results.**
    藉由付出，理想化也可以帶來實際成果。

關鍵單字片語

1. **practical** [`præktɪk]] 形 實際的

2. **idealistic** [aɪˌdɪəl`ɪstɪk] 形 理想的

3. **realm** [rɛlm] 名 範圍

4. **devotion** [dɪ`voʃən] 名 奉獻

5. **dichotomy** [daɪ`kɑtəmɪ] 名 二分法

6. **standpoint** [`stænd,pɔɪnt] 名 立場

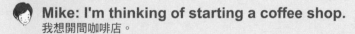

Mike: I'm thinking of starting a coffee shop.
我想開間咖啡店。

Peggy: A coffee shop? I didn't know you could make good coffee.
咖啡店？我不知道你會泡好咖啡。

Mike: I can't, but how hard can it be? It looks so easy on TV.
我不會啊，但會有多難？電視劇裡看起來都很簡單。

Peggy: Come on! Be realistic! You need more than zeal to start your own coffee shop.
拜託！實際點！開咖啡店要的不只是熱忱。

Mike: Then do you have any suggestions?
那你有什麼建議嗎？

Peggy: First, you have to know how to start a company, but most important of all, you need to know how to make great coffee.
首先你要知道如何開公司。最重要的是，你得知道怎麼泡出很棒的咖啡。

Mike: OK. But what should I do first?
好的。但我首先應該做什麼？

Peggy: The government has special classes for youths who want to start their own business, and it's free. Whoever passes the course can also apply for a loan.
政府替想創業的青年開辦免費課程，通過課程後還可申請貸款。

Mike: That sounds perfect. How do I register for the course?
聽起來很棒。我要怎麼報名？

Peggy: I can show you. You can just go to their website.
我開給你看，就在他們的網站上。

Mike: Thanks a lot!
感謝你！

關鍵單字片語

7. **correctly** [kə`rɛktlɪ] 副 正確地

8. **approach** [ə`protʃ] 名 方法

9. **in sum** 片 總括而論

10. **make coffee** 片 泡咖啡

11. **believe firmly** 片 強烈認為、深信

12. **apply for** 片 申請

3. 行動vs.觀察
Action vs. Observation

MP 3
153

萬用好句

1.	**Actions speak louder than words.** 坐而言不如起而行。
2.	**Henry always puts all of his ideas into practice.** 亨利總是將想法付諸實行。
3.	**Jessica is a self-described actionist who always focuses on inspiring people around her to take action to achieve their dreams.** 潔西卡形容自己為行動派，她總是鼓勵身邊的人努力實踐自己的夢想。
4.	**Do you take action first, or watch and wait for a while?** 你會先採取行動，還是先稍做觀察？
5.	**There are no flies on Janet.** 珍娜是個徹底的行動派。
6.	**It might take some time for an observer to figure out what to do.** 觀察者需要一些時間思考如何行動。
7.	**Active people like to walk around the city and explore.** 行動派會走遍城市加以探索。
8.	**Energetic people get their work done with enthusiasm and energy.** 有活力的人會投注熱情和能量將工作完成。
9.	**Look before you leap.** 三思而後行。
10.	**I evaluate what I can do and what I already have before taking any action.** 我總在行動前，謹慎評估我能做什麼、又擁有些什麼。
11.	**Because of their quiet and reserved nature, "owl personalities" tend to observe and even over-analyze before taking any action.** 因為安靜保守的天性，貓頭鷹性格者習慣在採取行動前先行觀察，甚至過度分析情況。
12.	**A good observer will observe both the inner and outer environments adequately so as not to rush into taking the next step.** 一個好的觀察者會充分觀察內外環境，才不至於讓自己倉促進行下一步。

關鍵單字片語

1. **actionist** [`ækʃənɪst] 名 行動派
2. **put into practice** 片 付諸實行
3. **inspiring** [ɪn`spaɪrɪŋ] 形 鼓舞人心的
4. **observe** [əb`zɜv] 動 觀察
5. **pay attention to** 片 注意到…
6. **take the initiative** 片 採取主動

實境對話

Hank: Where is Tina? I haven't seen her today.
緹娜在哪裡？我今天還沒看到她。

Peggy: She didn't come to work today.
她今天沒來上班。

Hank: Why is that? Is she sick?
怎麼了？她生病了嗎？

Peggy: No, she is going to Tibet on vacation.
不，她去西藏度假了。

Hank: Tibet? She mentioned Tibet last week, but I didn't know she would be leaving in such a short time.
西藏？她上星期才跟我提過，但我沒想到她這麼快就成行。

Peggy: She is an actionist, isn't she?
她真是個行動派，不是嗎？

Hank: She surely is. It would probably take me half a year to plan a trip like that.
她的確是。我可能得花半年來規劃。

Peggy: Me, too. There are so many things to plan, such as tickets and accommodations, especially when you are traveling all by yourself.
我也是。有很多事要規劃，像是車票和住宿，尤其是當你一個人旅行的時候。

Hank: Is she traveling alone? Isn't she joining a tour group?
她自己一個人去嗎？她沒有參加旅行團嗎？

Peggy: No, she said it would be a waste of time to have to go shopping with the rest of the tour group. She would rather spend more time sightseeing.
沒有，她說要和整團人一起購物，簡直是浪費時間，她寧願花時間觀光。

Hank: She is really courageous to travel that far away alone.
她真是勇敢，一個人跑那麼遠旅行。

關鍵單字片語

7. **active** [`æktɪv] 形 主動的

8. **passive** [`pæsɪv] 形 被動的

9. **explore** [ɪk`splor] 動 探索

10. **jump into conclusion** 片 妄下結論

11. **reserved** [rɪ`zɜvd] 形 保守的

12. **studious** [`stjudɪəs] 形 一心一意的

4. 愛情 vs. 麵包
Love vs. Life

MP3
154

萬用好句

1.	**Which would you choose, love or money?** 你會選擇愛情還是麵包？
2.	**Most young people tend to choose love rather than money.** 大多數年輕人會選愛情，而非麵包。
3.	**Janet thinks basing a decision on money is too materialistic, and what matters most is how your heart feels.** 珍娜覺得選麵包太拜金，最重要的是感覺。
4.	**It is true that money cannot buy happiness, but without money it's hard to survive in the real world.** 金錢的確不能買到快樂；但若沒有錢，也很難在現實世界中存活。
5.	**Even if you had all the money in the world, without love, you would not be able to enjoy it.** 沒有愛情，即使你擁有世界上的所有財富，你也無法享受。
6.	**Michelle believes that money, like bread, is the staff of life.** 蜜雪兒相信金錢好比麵包，對生活很重要。
7.	**As the old saying goes, "Poverty makes a couple pessimistic."** 諺語說得好，「貧賤夫妻百事哀」。
8.	**Money cannot do everything, but you can do nothing without it.** 錢不是萬能，但是沒有錢萬萬不能。
9.	**Is it true that no matter how strong a love is, it will finally be destroyed by reality?** 不論愛情多穩定，最後都會被現實打敗嗎？
10.	**Love what you choose and choose what you love.** 愛你所擇，擇你所愛。
11.	**Why can't you have both money and love?** 你為什麼不能同時擁有愛情與麵包？
12.	**Would your parents ask you to marry someone for his wealth?** 你的父母會要求你出於某人的財產而與他結婚嗎？

關鍵單字片語

1. **matter** [ˋmætɚ] 動 要緊

2. **pauper** [ˋpɔpɚ] 名 窮人

3. **bread-winner** [ˋbrɛdˏwɪnɚ] 名 養家者

4. **prefer** [prɪˋfɝ] 動 偏好⋯

5. **instead of** 片 代替

6. **material** [məˋtɪrɪəl] 形 物質的

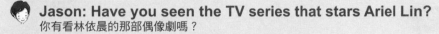

Jason: Have you seen the TV series that stars Ariel Lin?
你有看林依晨的那部偶像劇嗎？

Peggy: Do you mean "Love or Bread"?
你是說「我的億萬麵包」嗎？

Jason: Yes, that one. What would you have, love or bread?
沒錯，就是那部。你會選什麼，愛情還是麵包？

Peggy: That's a really tough question. Without love, I think it would be impossible for me to live with someone.
這真是個難題。沒有愛情，我無法和某個人一起生活。

Jason: So, are you saying that you would choose love?
所以，你是說你會選擇愛情？

Peggy: I think so. I just can't imagine being stuck with someone I don't love for the rest of my life. How about you?
我想是吧。我就是無法想像和一個我不愛的人共度一生。那你呢？

Jason: I think I would take the bread. After all, you need money to survive and raise your children.
我想我會選擇麵包。畢竟得要有錢才能生活和養小孩。

Peggy: Even if that means you had to forget about the one you truly love?
即使你得忘掉你的真愛嗎？

Jason: It's a dilemma, but I believe love can grow.
這很兩難，但我相信愛情可從生活中慢慢培養。

Peggy: Wow! You are very practical.
哇，你真的很實際。

Jason: Maybe I am, but I believe most people would make the same decision as me.
或許吧，但我相信大部分的人都會跟我做出一樣的選擇。

關鍵單字片語

7. **precious** [`prɛʃəs] 形 珍貴的

8. **star** [stɑr] 動 由…主演

9. **reality** [rɪˋælətɪ] 名 現實

10. **provide** [prəˋvaɪd] 動 提供

11. **in need for** 片 需要…

12. **dilemma** [dəˋlɛmə] 名 兩難

5. 單身vs.結婚
Single vs. Married
MP3 155

萬用好句

1.	**Remaining single means realizing that marriage is not necessarily better.** 維持單身就是知道結婚不一定比較好。
2.	**Married life is full of excitement and frustration.** 婚姻生活充滿了刺激和挫折。
3.	**Single life or married life, which one do you think is better?** 單身生活或婚姻生活，你覺得哪一種比較好？
4.	**Are you going to get married someday?** 你會結婚嗎？
5.	**Being single allows you to have more time to care for other people.** 單身代表你有更多時間關心其他人。
6.	**Do you think you are ready for marriage?** 你認為你已準備好進入婚姻了嗎？
7.	**Marriage is a magical thing that a single person may desire while a married person may regret.** 婚姻是如此神奇，令單身的人嚮往，已婚的人後悔。
8.	**What do you think the advantages of being married are?** 你覺得婚姻的好處有哪些？
9.	**Jason doesn't believe in love and hence he swears that he will never get married.** 傑森不相信愛情，因此他發誓永不結婚。
10.	**Who is happier, single or married women?** 單身女子還是已婚女子，誰比較快樂？
11.	**What do you think of marriage?** 你對於婚姻有什麼想法？
12.	**Maria wants to marry her Prince Charming as soon as she graduates from university.** 瑪利亞想和她的白馬王子在大學畢業後就結婚。

關鍵單字片語

1. **bachelor** [`bætʃələ] 名 單身漢

2. **widow** [`wɪdo] 名 寡婦

3. **married** [`mærɪd] 形 已婚的

4. **widower** [`wɪdoə] 名 鰥夫

5. **hence** [hɛns] 副 因此

6. **wife** [`waɪf] 名 妻子

實境對話

Larry: Are you going to Jason's wedding next Saturday?
你下週六要參加傑森的婚禮嗎？

Fran: What? Is Jason getting married?
什麼？傑森要結婚了？

Larry: Yes. He sent an email to everyone. Didn't you get it?
是啊。他有寄電子郵件給大家，你沒收到嗎？

Fran: I haven't checked my email yet. All I can say is a big wow.
我還沒收信。我只能說我太驚訝了。

Larry: Me, too. I almost choked on my soymilk when I found out.
我也是。我知道的時候還差點被豆漿嗆到。

Fran: Didn't he say he would never get married and that he didn't want to be suffocated by a marriage certificate?
他不是說他永不結婚、不被結婚證書束縛嗎？

Larry: That's right, and he also told me that only silly men get married because there are so many beautiful girls out there.
沒錯，他也跟我說只有蠢蛋會結婚，因為外頭有那麼多美女。

Fran: Do you remember what he gave David at his bachelor party? A tombstone. I still can't believe that he is really going to get married.
你記得他在大衛的單身派對上送大衛什麼嗎？一個墓碑。我還是不能相信他要結婚了。

Larry: Me, neither. I thought it was nothing but a prank, but Alice promised me it was true.
我也不相信。我一直以為這是惡作劇，但愛麗絲跟我保證是真的。

Fran: How can Alice be so sure?
愛麗絲怎能這麼確定？

Larry: That's because she is the one who is going to marry Jason.
因為就是她要和傑森結婚。

關鍵單字片語

7. **husband** [ˋhʌzbənd] 名 丈夫

8. **DINK** 縮 頂客族

9. **divorce** [dəˋvɔrs] 動 離婚

10. **single** [ˋsɪŋgl̩] 形 單身的

11. **be full of** 片 充滿

12. **remain** [rɪˋmen] 動 保持；仍是

6.機會vs.命運
Opportunity vs. Destiny
156

萬用好句

1. **What do you believe in, fate or opportunity?**
你相信機會還是命運？

2. **When the time comes, seize your chance and choose your destiny.**
當時機來臨，把握機會選擇你的命運。

3. **I don't believe in fate, only in my devotion and myself.**
我不相信命運，只相信付出和相信自己。

4. **Men propose, God disposes.**
謀事在人，成事在天。

5. **Be open to opportunity and embrace it while you can.**
接受機會，好好把握。

6. **Having the chance to work for such as well-known company is definitely the opportunity of a lifetime for Jason.**
在如此知名的公司工作，絕對是傑森一生一次的機會。

7. **William McFee used to say, "If fate means you to lose, give him a good fight anyhow."**
威廉‧麥克菲曾說：「如果命運要你認輸，總要好好抵抗。」

8. **Positive thinking can lead to more opportunities.**
正向思考可通往更多機會。

9. **Opportunity likely depends upon the effort you make.**
機會來自於你所付出的努力。

10. **You can't sit back like a turtle, waiting for your chance to come.**
你不能像隻烏龜整天坐著，等待你的機會降臨。

11. **What would you do if you got a lucky break?**
當你認為機會來臨時，你會怎麼做？

12. **My mom always tells me that success in life doesn't just happen. You have to fight for it.**
媽媽總是跟我說，成功不會自然發生，你得努力爭取。

關鍵單字片語

1. **seize the time** 片 把握時機

2. **luck** [lʌk] 名 運氣

3. **take your chance** 片 把握機會

4. **destiny** [ˋdɛstənɪ] 名 命運、宿命

5. **second chance** 片 第二次機會

6. **lifetime chance** 片 一生一次的機會

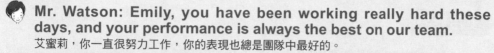

Mr. Watson: Emily, you have been working really hard these days, and your performance is always the best on our team.
艾蜜莉，你一直很努力工作，你的表現也總是團隊中最好的。

Emily: Thank you, Mr. Watson. I try to do the best job I can.
謝謝你，華生先生。我只是盡力而為。

Mr. Watson: I would like to send you to our New York branch.
我想派你到紐約分公司。

Emily: Wow! I am flattered. How long would I be working there?
哇！我受寵若驚。我得在那裡待多久？

Mr. Watson: At least three years. We are trying to expand our business in North America.
至少三年，我們正試著拓展北美業務。

Emily: Well, I am not sure if I can leave my family for that long.
嗯，我不太確定我是否能離開家人那麼久。

Mr. Watson: Running a branch of your own is a once-in-a-lifetime opportunity. You would certainly learn a lot from this experience.
這是你一生一次管理分公司的機會，你一定能從這次的經驗學到很多。

Emily: But I'm not sure if I'm capable. I don't want to let you down.
但我不確定能否勝任，我不想讓你失望。

Mr. Watson: I don't believe you would. In addition, you can work and study for a master's degree at the same time.
我相信你不會讓我失望的。而且，你可以一邊工作一邊讀碩士。

Emily: It sounds attractive. When should I leave for New York?
聽起來很吸引人。我應何時出發？

Mr. Watson: Next month.
下個月。

Emily: I will start packing immediately.
我會馬上開始打包。

關鍵單字片語

7. **fight for** 片 為…爭取、努力

8. **capture** [`kæptʃɚ] 動 捕捉、把握

9. **knock on** 片 敲門(形容機會來臨)

10. **likely** [`laɪklɪ] 形 有可能的

11. **in the future** 片 在未來

12. **doom** [dum] 動 註定、命定

7.創新vs.順應
Innovation vs. Accommodation
MP3 157

萬用好句

1.	**Innovation and tradition are both important for a company.** 對一家公司而言，創新和傳統都很重要。
2.	**Do you think innovation is vital to the prosperity of our industry?** 你覺得創新對我們企業的興盛很重要嗎？
3.	**Without traditions, we wouldn't know where we came from.** 沒有傳統，我們不會知道自己從何而來。
4.	**Usually, innovation is defined as the exploitation of new ideas, leading to the creation of new products, processes, or services.** 創新通常被定義為替產品、過程、或服務注入新想法。
5.	**Kevin was the first to adopt the symbolism of wind in architecture.** 凱文在建築界創先採納風的象徵含義。
6.	**Most of the time, innovation brings new ideas and products, however tradition is the keeper of our past.** 大多時候，創新帶來新想法和新素材，而傳統則守護著我們的過去。
7.	**Do you consider yourself to be innovative or traditional?** 你認為自己是創新的還是傳統的？
8.	**What do you think is more important, innovation or tradition?** 你覺得哪個比較重要，創新還是傳統？
9.	**Laura is a woman of innovation, and thus qualified for the position.** 蘿拉是位勇於創新的女性，因此很適合這個職務。
10.	**The local government is trying to preserve tradition in an innovative way in order to inspire the youth.** 當地政府為了鼓舞年輕人，正試著以創新的方式保存傳統。
11.	**Jason's sculpture successfully created innovation out of tradition by using clay and aluminum.** 藉由結合使用粘土和鋁，傑森的雕塑品成功地創新傳統。
12.	**Try thinking out of the box, and you'll find other possibilities.** 試著跳脫傳統，你會發現其他的可能性。

 關鍵單字片語

1. **innovative** [`ɪno͵vetɪv] 形 創新的

2. **comply with** 片 順應

3. **custom** [`kʌstəm] 名 習慣

4. **novel** [`nɑvl̩] 形 新穎的

5. **traditional** [trə`dɪʃən!] 形 傳統的

6. **aspect** [`æspɛkt] 名 方面

實境對話

Josh: Hi, have you seen the new manager?
嗨，你見到新任經理了嗎？

Jane: Do you mean Mr. Adams?
你是說亞當斯先生嗎？

Josh: Yes. He called a meeting of all the team members yesterday.
是的。他昨天召集所有團隊成員開會。

Jane: What did he say in the meeting?
他在會議裡說些什麼？

Josh: He told us that it's time for reforms and to make good changes.
他跟我們說，該是時候改革、做些好的改變了。

Jane: Good changes? What did he mean?
好的改變？什麼意思？

Josh: He said the team is not efficient enough, and each of us will have to be divided into groups and hand in sales reports to him every week.
他說團隊效率不足，我們每個人都得分成小組，每週繳銷售報告給他。

Jane: Is that true? It sounds like too much trouble.
真的嗎？聽起來太麻煩了。

Josh: Indeed it is, but he said it's to improve both the efficiency and our sales figures.
是真的很麻煩，但他說這是可以同時改善效率和銷售數字的方法。

Jane: Oh, crap! Why can't we just do things the same as usual?
噢，最好是！為什麼不能照以前那樣做事就好？

Josh: That appears to be an impossibility, and we have to hand in the first report by tomorrow.
看樣子是不太可能，我們明天就要繳交第一份報告了。

關鍵單字片語

7. **improve** [ɪmˋpruv] 動 改善

8. **as usual** 片 照例；如常

9. **exploit** [ˋɛksplɔɪt] 名 功績

10. **create** [krɪˋet] 動 創造

11. **break with tradition** 片 打破傳統

12. **reform** [͵rɪˋfɔrm] 動 改革

8. 成就與滿足
Accomplishment and Satisfaction 158

萬用好句

1. How much would you be willing to sacrifice for success?
你願意為成功犧牲多少？

2. The sense of achievement is the sweetest fruit in the world.
成就感是世上最甜美的果實。

3. Satisfaction and a sense of achievement drives happiness.
滿足和成就感能讓你快樂。

4. What is your goal in life?
你的人生目標是什麼？

5. Karen committed every inch of herself to trying to achieve the monthly sales target.
凱倫盡全力達成每月銷售目標。

6. Sometimes, the harder the task is, the greater the joy is.
有時候任務越困難，喜悅就越大。

7. Only when you face the challenge, can you know how sweet the fruit of success is.
只有當你面對挑戰時，才會知道成功的果實有多甜美。

8. What would make you happy?
什麼會讓你開心？

9. Are you satisfied with your life?
你對你的生活感到滿意嗎？

10. Miranda loves challenges, and she always seeks new opportunities to push herself to the limit.
米蘭達喜愛挑戰，她總是追求挑戰自我極限的機會。

11. Josh was overjoyed when he told everyone that he had sealed the deal.
喬許告訴大家簽到合約時，他欣喜若狂。

關鍵單字片語

1. **sacrifice** [`sækrə,faɪs] 動 犧牲

2. **challenge** [`tʃælɪndʒ] 名 挑戰

3. **goal** [gol] 名 目標

4. **push** [puʃ] 動 促使

5. **realize one's dream** 片 實現夢想

6. **achievement** [ə`tʃivmənt] 名 成就

實境對話

Ken: It's Friday night. Let's go party!
現在是星期五晚上，我們去狂歡吧！

Julia: Thank you, but I can't. I want to finish the sales report.
謝謝，但我無法。我想把銷售報告寫完。

Ken: Come on! Everyone deserves to have some fun tonight.
拜託！今晚每個人都該好好玩一玩。

Julia: Well, I just want to do my job well, which gives me a lot of satisfaction.
我只是想把工作做好，這能讓我感到滿足。

Ken: But, "all work and no play makes Jack a dull boy," or, in your case, "Jill a dull girl."
但是成天工作會讓你變得無趣。

Julia: I will get some rest right after I finish the report.
等我做完報告，我會休息的。

Ken: I know you are keen on earning brownie points from Mr. Watson, but there are always more important things than work.
我知道你很想讓華生先生幫你打出優良考績，但總有比工作更重要的事。

Julia: I know, but I love the excitement and sense of achievement that work brings. Is there anything wrong with that?
我懂，但我喜愛工作帶來的刺激和成就感。這樣有什麼不對嗎？

Ken: I believe that a sense of achievement and satisfaction can make you happy and feel competent, but that's not everything to life.
我相信成就和滿足感可以讓你快樂、感覺有能力，但那並不是生命的全部。

Julia: Well, I'll think about that.
嗯，我會想一想的。

關鍵單字片語

7. **commitment** [kə`mɪtmənt] 承諾

8. **overcome** [ˏovɚ`kʌm] 動 克服

9. **pick oneself up** 片 使⋯振作

10. **be satisfied with** 片 對⋯感到滿足

11. **think about** 片 考慮

12. **limit** [`lɪmɪt] 名 極限

9. 宗教信仰
Religious Belief
MP3 159

萬用好句

1.	**What does the term "religion" mean to you?** 「宗教」對你而言是什麼？
2.	**How do you define being a Christian?** 你如何定義基督教徒？
3.	**Can a person be both a Christian and a Muslim?** 一個人可以同時是基督教徒和回教徒嗎？
4.	**Everyone has his own interpretation of religious beliefs.** 每個人對於信仰都有自己的一套詮釋。
5.	**Do you have any religious beliefs?** 你有宗教信仰嗎？
6.	**Do you believe in God?** 你相信上帝嗎？
7.	**Conversation about religion may sometimes make people uncomfortable, and thus can be a conversation stopper.** 關於宗教的談話有時會讓人不舒服，因此是個談話殺手。
8.	**Do you consider yourself a religious man?** 你認為自己虔誠嗎？
9.	**My mom is very religious, and sometimes I think "superstitious" is an even better word for her.** 我媽媽很虔誠，有時我甚至認為「迷信」更適合她。
10.	**As a devout Christian, Jeremy goes to church every Sunday.** 身為虔誠的基督教徒，傑若米每週日做禮拜。
11.	**It's hard for me to decide whether Buddhism is a philosophy or a religion.** 我很難判定佛教是哲學理論，抑或是宗教。
12.	**Buddhism is a very popular religion in Asia, especially in Southeast Asian countries, such as Taiwan, Thailand, and Cambodia.** 佛教興盛於亞洲，尤其是在東南亞國家，如台灣、泰國和柬埔寨。

關鍵單字片語

1. **religious belief** 片 宗教信仰

2. **Christian** [`krɪstʃən] 名 基督徒

3. **go to church** 片 做禮拜

4. **compare** [kəm`pɛr] 動 比較

5. **religious affiliation** 片 宗教歸屬

6. **contrasting belief** 片 相異的信仰

實境對話

Andy: How about going to Tim's soccer game this Sunday?
這週日去看提姆的足球賽好不好？

Amanda: Sorry, but I already have plans.
抱歉，我已經有安排了。

Andy: That's too bad. What are you going to do?
太不巧了，你要做什麼？

Amanda: I always go to church on Sundays.
我週日都會上教堂。

Andy: Are you a Christian?
你是基督徒嗎？

Amanda: Yes. I was baptized when I was three years old.
是，我三歲時就受洗了。

Andy: I didn't know you were a Christian. I have never seen you pray.
我不知道你是基督徒。我沒看過你禱告。

Amanda: I always pray before dinner and before every contract negotiation.
我總在晚餐前和每次簽約談判前禱告。

Andy: Kind of in the same way Jeremy Lin does before every basketball game?
就像林書豪在每場籃球賽前做的一樣嗎？

Amanda: Exactly, but in a slightly different way. I don't have Tim Tebow making funny gestures in front of me. I just pray in my heart for the Lord to give me courage.
是，但有點不同。沒有提姆在我面前做滑稽手勢。我只在心中向上帝禱告，請祂給我勇氣。

Andy: You are very religious.
你非常虔誠。

Amanda: It's a comfort and a support in my life.
這是我生命中的安慰跟支柱。

關鍵單字片語

7. **shared** [ʃɛrd] 形 共有的

8. **ethic** [`ɛθɪk] 名 倫理

9. **Muslim** [`mʌzləm] 名 回教徒

10. **ritual** [`rɪtʃuəl] 名 儀式

11. **similar** [`sɪmələ] 形 相似的

12. **devout** [dɪ`vaut] 形 虔誠的

10. 家庭生活
Family Life
MP3
160

萬用好句

1.	**How often do you go traveling with your family?** 你多常和家人一同旅遊？
2.	**Family is undoubtedly the most important part of one's life.** 家庭無疑是人的一生中最重要的部分。
3.	**Strong and close ties among family members can help raise well-adjusted and self-confident children.** 家人間強而緊的聯繫可教養出適應力強且有自信的孩子。
4.	**The City Council offers free counseling sessions for couples who need advice on relationships and child-raising.** 市議會提供需要人際關係和教養小孩建議的夫妻免費諮商講座。
5.	**Do you have a good relationship with your grandparents?** 你和祖父母的關係好嗎？
6.	**What do you usually do with your kids on the weekends?** 週末時，你通常和孩子做些什麼？
7.	**My mom insists that the whole family has dinner together every day.** 我媽堅持全家人每天一起吃晚餐。
8.	**Every family has problems, which can be solved with love and respect.** 每個家庭都有他的問題，也都可用愛和尊重來解決。
9.	**My father used to spend some quality time with us before we went to bed.** 我父親過去在睡前會花時間與我們相處。
10.	**Our family is very close.** 我們的家族關係很緊密。
11.	**Despite all the conflicts, the love in our family remains strong.** 儘管有衝突，我們家人之間的愛緊密相繫。
12.	**My mom tries her best to provide care and safety for our family.** 我媽媽盡全力提供家人關懷和安全。

關鍵單字片語

1. **session** [`sɛʃən] 名 講習

2. **generation** [ˌdʒɛnəˈreʃən] 名 世代

3. **intimate** [`ɪntəmɪt] 形 親密的

4. **relationship** [rɪˈleʃənˌʃɪp] 名 關係

5. **together** [təˈgɛðɚ] 副 一起

6. **tackle the problem** 片 處理問題

Wife: Don't forget your son's soccer game this Saturday.
別忘了你兒子這週六的足球比賽。

Husband: I have a meeting this Saturday afternoon.
我這週六下午要開會。

Wife: But Jimmy has been looking forward to your coming to his game. He will be very disappointed.
但吉米一直很期待你能去看他比賽。他一定會很失望。

Husband: I am really sorry.
我真的很抱歉。

Wife: I told you about his game last month. Can't you reschedule?
我上個月就跟你說他有比賽了，你不能改時間嗎？

Husband: I'll see what I can do, but I am not sure I will be able to.
我會想辦法，但是我不能確定是否能改。

Wife: Please try. You also missed Janet's piano concert last week.
請盡力。你上星期也錯過了珍娜的鋼琴演奏會。

Husband: I'm really sorry. Mr. Watson asked us to work overtime.
我真的很抱歉。華生先生要我們加班。

Wife: You can't sacrifice your family time for work. The children are getting very upset.
你不能為了工作犧牲家庭。孩子們都感到非常沮喪。

Husband: Is that true? Did Janet say anything to you?
真的嗎？珍娜跟你說了什麼嗎？

Wife: Yes, she said she was very disappointed in you.
嗯，她說她對你很失望。

Husband: Oh, no! That's bad.
噢，不！真糟糕。

★ 關鍵單字片語

7. **close** [klos] 形 親密的

8. **relative** [`rɛlətɪv] 名 親戚

9. **despite** [dɪ`spaɪt] 介 儘管

10. **cooperate** [ko`ɑpə͵ret] 動 合作

11. **safe** [sef] 形 安全的

12. **care** [kɛr] 動 關心、關懷

11. 親職教養
Parenting

MP3
161

萬用好句

1.	**The first step in being a good parent is to express love.** 成為好父母的第一步，就是表達愛。
2.	**Even a gentle cuddle can fill your kid's life with sunshine and love.** 即使是一個小擁抱，也能讓你孩子的生命中充滿陽光和愛。
3.	**Mr. Huang tells his children "I love you" every single day.** 黃先生每天跟他的孩子們說「我愛你」。
4.	**Avoid comparing your children to others, especially siblings.** 不要拿你的孩子跟其他人做比較，尤其是手足間。
5.	**Keep in mind that your child is not an extension of yourself, but an individual who is dependent upon your care.** 牢記，孩子不是你的延伸，而是仰賴你的照顧而成長的一個個體。
6.	**Criticism not only hurts your children's feelings but also your relationship with them.** 批評不只傷了孩子的心，也傷了你們的關係。
7.	**Try to be assertive yet kind when pointing out what your children have done wrong.** 試著堅定但和善的指出孩子的錯誤。
8.	**Peggy expects her son to be a doctor in the future.** 佩姬期待她的兒子將來成為一位醫生。
9.	**How do you think a person should act to be a great parent?** 你覺得應該怎麼做才能成為好父母？
10.	**Don't be too quick to rescue your child from a problem, because life itself is the best teacher.** 不要太快幫你的孩子解決問題，因為生命本身就是最好的老師。
11.	**Take time to listen to your children and show your interest in them.** 花時間傾聽你的孩子，對他們表達興趣。
12.	**The best way to teach your child is to be a good role model yourself.** 教育孩子最好的方式就是以身作則。

關鍵單字片語

1. **raise** [rez] 動 扶養、養育

2. **develop** [dɪ`vɛləp] 動 發展

3. **character** [`kærɪktə] 名 人格、個性

4. **intimacy** [`ɪntəməsɪ] 名 親密感

5. **educate** [`ɛdʒə͵ket] 動 教育

6. **discipline** [`dɪsəplɪn] 動 訓導

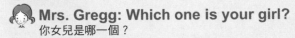

 實境對話 ●

👩 **Mrs. Gregg: Which one is your girl?**
你女兒是哪一個？

👨 **Mr. Watson: The one in a red skirt on the slide. Which is yours?**
在溜滑梯上穿紅裙子的那個。你的呢？

👩 **Mrs. Gregg: The twin boys playing on the seesaw over there.**
在那裡玩蹺蹺板的雙胞胎男孩。

👨 **Mr. Watson: Oh, I recognize them. Aren't they the twins in Ms. Dai's class? They are in the same class as my girl.**
喔，我認得他們。他們不是戴小姐班上的雙胞胎嗎？他們和我女兒同班。

👩 **Mrs. Gregg: What a coincidence.**
真巧。

👨 **Mr. Watson: My girl, Charlotte, told me that both of your boys do very well at school. What's your secret to educating them so well?**
我女兒夏綠蒂跟我說，你的兩個兒子在學校都很優秀。你有沒有教育他們的祕訣？

👩 **Mrs. Gregg: Thank you. I am flattered. In fact, there is no other secret but love and trust.**
謝謝你，我受寵若驚。事實上沒有什麼祕訣，不過就是愛和信任。

👨 **Mr. Watson: Love and trust? What do you mean?**
愛和信任？什麼意思？

👩 **Mrs. Gregg: Love and learn to appreciate your child as an individual.**
愛你的孩子，學著欣賞他為一個個體。

👨 **Mr. Watson: OK. What about trust?**
好的。那信任呢？

👩 **Mrs. Gregg: Trust your child, and believe that your child is capable of making decisions. Learn to let go.**
信任你的孩子，相信他能夠做決定，學習放開你的手。

👨 **Mr. Watson: Thank you for your advice.**
謝謝你的建議。

★ 關鍵單字片語

7. **cuddle** [`kʌdḷ] 動 擁抱

8. **praise** [prez] 動 稱讚

9. **sibling** [`sɪblɪŋ] 名 兄弟姐妹

10. **point out** 片 指出

11. **serious** [`sɪrɪəs] 形 嚴肅的

12. **rescue** [`rɛskju] 動 解救

12. 待人接物
Ways of Treating People
MP3 162

萬用好句

1. To summarize, the key to good human relations is having the skill or ability to work effectively with other people.
簡言之，良好人際關係的祕訣是擁有和其他人有效合作的技巧或能力。

2. Jason is socially awkward and lacks good human relations skills.
傑森對於人際關係很不拿手，缺乏良好的人際互動技巧。

3. Whenever Jason has a conflict with friends, he always turns to his older brother for advice.
每當傑森和朋友起衝突時，他總是尋求哥哥的建議。

4. How can I advance my understanding of social relationships?
我該如何增進對社交關係的理解？

5. Greeting people with a smile is the easiest way to win friends.
笑臉迎人是贏得友誼最容易的方式。

6. Jessica is not in my social circle, and we barely talk to each other.
潔西卡不在我的社交圈內，我們幾乎不和彼此說話。

7. The easiest way to meet new friends is to lead an interesting life.
遇見新朋友最簡單的方式，就是過著有趣的生活。

8. Inviting some friends to your place for a party is a great idea.
邀請一些朋友到你家開派對是個好主意。

9. With the popularity of the Internet, Facebook has become one of the most popular forms of social media.
隨著網路盛行，臉書已變成最受歡迎的社交媒介。

10. Spend more time around people, and you can make new friends.
多花時間與人相處，你就能交到新朋友。

11. It's impossible for you to sit at home playing computer games when new friends come knocking on your door.
你不可能坐在家裡打電動，而新朋友跑來敲你家的門。

關鍵單字片語

1. **human relation** 片 人際關係
2. **deal with** 片 處理
3. **socially** [`soʃəlɪ] 副 社交上地
4. **awkward** [`ɔkwəd] 形 笨拙的
5. **peer group** 片 同儕團體
6. **conflict** [`kɑnflɪkt] 名 衝突

實境對話

Mom: David, your teacher called today.
大衛，你的老師今天打電話來。

David: Really? What did she say?
真的嗎？她說什麼？

Mom: She asked me to come to school tomorrow afternoon. She would like to talk to me. Do you know what it's about?
她要我明天下午去學校一趟，想和我談一談。你知道是什麼事嗎？

David: Maybe I do. I guess it's concerning Frank.
我或許知道，我猜是法蘭克的事。

Mom: Frank? What's wrong between you and Frank?
法蘭克？你和法蘭克怎麼了嗎？

David: We had a fight today.
我們今天吵了一架。

Mom: Why? Aren't you best buddies?
為什麼？你們不是最好的朋友嗎？

David: We are, but I really don't like his way of doing things.
是，但我真的不喜歡他做事的方式。

Mom: Son, sometimes we meet someone we don't appreciate or even don't like. You can take that as an opportunity to know more about people and their ways of doing things. Who knows? You might even learn something from them.
兒啊，有時我們會遇到自己不欣賞或是不喜歡的人，你可以把這當成是識人和識其處事方式的機會。誰知道呢？或許你可以從他們身上學到東西。

David: I don't think so.
我不這樣認為。

Mom: Don't say that. We can always learn things from other people.
別這樣說，我們總是可以從他人身上學到東西的。

關鍵單字片語

7. **make friends** 片 交朋友

8. **social life** 片 社交生活

9. **come over** 片 過來

10. **friendly** [`frɛndlɪ] 形 友善的

11. **get along** 片 和睦相處

12. **lone wolf** 片 獨行俠

13. 身心健康
Physical and Mental Health 163

萬用好句

1.	**Is there any connection between mental and physical health?** 心理和生理健康之間有任何關聯嗎？
2.	**Keeping fit means keeping mentally fit as well.** 保持健康也意味著保持心理健康。
3.	**Getting enough quality sleep each and every night can help you relieve stress and live a healthier life.** 每晚擁有充足而良好的睡眠可幫助你減輕壓力，過著更健康的人生。
4.	**Good habits are the keys to a healthy life.** 良好的習慣是開啟健康人生的不二法門。
5.	**Negative emotions such as anger, aggression and fear are often harmful to your health.** 憤怒、挑釁和恐懼等負面情緒，對健康是有害的。
6.	**My grandfather gets up at five and does exercise every morning.** 我的祖父每天早上五點起床做運動。
7.	**What type of exercise do you usually do in your free time?** 你空閒時通常做什麼樣的運動？
8.	**Physical health and mental health are inextricably linked.** 生理和心理健康是相輔相成的。
9.	**Poor physical health also increases the risk of people developing mental health problems.** 生理不健康也會增加產生心理健康問題的風險。
10.	**Mr. Johnson has been suffering from headaches for many years.** 強生先生有頭痛的問題好幾年了。
11.	**Jessica is in the habit of going to the gym regularly.** 潔西卡有著定期上健身房運動的習慣。
12.	**Many chronically ill patients tend to have mental health problems, too.** 許多慢性病人通常也有心理上的狀況。

關鍵單字片語

1. **mental** [`mɛntl] 形 心理的

2. **physical** [`fɪzɪk]] 形 生理的

3. **health condition** 片 健康狀況

4. **emotional health** 片 情緒健康

5. **sound** [saʊnd] 形 健全的

6. **fit** [fɪt] 形 健壯的

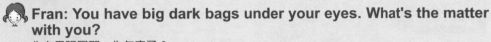

Fran: You have big dark bags under your eyes. What's the matter with you?
你有黑眼圈耶，你怎麼了？

Ken: I have been suffering from insomnia these days.
我這幾天失眠。

Fran: Most of the time, insomnia results from too much stress in your life. You can try to relax a bit more before going to bed.
大多時候，失眠是源於日常生活中的過度壓力。你可以試著在睡前放鬆一下。

Ken: I have tried to count sheep, but it didn't work.
我試著數羊，但是沒有用。

Fran: That's not what I mean. Counting sheep will make some people concentrate more and make it harder for them to fall a sleep.
我不是這個意思。數羊會讓某些人更專心、更無法入睡。

Ken: Then, what should I do?
那我該怎麼辦？

Fran: You can take a hot bath and drink a cup of hot milk before going to bed. Try some lavender essential oil as well.
你可在睡前洗個熱水澡，再喝杯熱牛奶。也可試試薰衣草精油。

Ken: Lavender essential oil? Isn't that a bit too feminine?
薰衣草精油？好像有點太女性化了。

Fran: Don't you know insomnia can be a silent killer? Being a little bit feminine is much better than being unhealthy. In addition, try not to watch TV 30 minutes before going to bed.
你不知道失眠是沈默的殺手嗎？有點女性化總比不健康好吧。且別在睡前三十分鐘看電視。

Ken: Now I know! I always watch the stock market news before going to bed!
現在我懂了！我總在睡前看股市新聞。

關鍵單字片語

7. **negative emotion** 片 負面情緒

8. **exercise** [`ɛksə͵saɪz] 動 運動

9. **disease** [dɪˋziz] 名 疾病

10. **suffer from** 片 遭受…疾病所苦

11. **blood pressure** 片 血壓

12. **cholesterol** [kəˋlɛstə͵rol] 名 膽固醇

14. 自我反省
Introspection

MP3
164

萬用好句

1. Self-reflection is the capacity to exercise introspection and the willingness to learn more about oneself.
自我省思是能夠自我檢視、並願意多瞭解自己的一種能力。

2. Do you think self-reflection can make you a better person?
你認為自我省思可以讓你成為更好的人嗎？

3. Introspection is self-observation, a process of learning more about one's inner thoughts, feelings, and desires.
自我檢視是一個更瞭解自己想法、感覺和欲望的自我觀察過程。

4. Self-reflection is one of the hardest things to do in life.
自我省思是生命中最難的事情之一。

5. Self-reflection requires us to stop and take a look at who we really are.
自我省思是要我們停下來、好看看我們是誰。

6. I always spend ten minutes before bed reviewing my whole day.
我總是在睡前花十分鐘的時間回顧一整天。

7. Self-reflection can help us gain a better understanding of ourselves and thus create a better future for ourselves.
自我省思可幫助我們更瞭解自己，帶領我們迎向更好的未來。

8. What is the best way to engage in self-reflection?
進行自我省思的最佳方式為何？

9. You can gain a better insight about yourself by asking yourself some important questions.
你可藉由問自己一些重要問題以深入了解自己。

10. Remember to be totally truthful to yourself.
記得要對自己完全誠實。

11. It might be unpleasant or even scary to deeply reflect on your personality and life.
深省自己的性格與生活，可能是很不愉快、甚至是嚇人的。

關鍵單字片語

1. **reflection** [rɪˋflɛkʃən] 名 省思

2. **retroflection** [ˌrɛtrəˋflɛkʃən] 名 內省

3. **be conscious of** 片 察覺到…

4. **desire** [dɪˋzaɪr] 名 欲望

5. **thought** [θɔt] 名 想法

6. **inner** [ˋɪnɚ] 形 內在的

Willy: Are you alright? You look terrible.
你還好吧？你看起來很糟。

Rose: Mr. Johnson asked me to see him in his office.
強森先生找我進他辦公室。

Willy: Really? What was it about? You didn't get fired, did you?
真的嗎？是什麼事？你不會被開除了吧？

Rose: Luckily, no, but I think I will be the next time he asks me to come to his office.
很幸運地，不是，但是我想下次他叫我進去時，就是了。

Willy: Why is that?
為什麼？

Rose: He was furious about my sales report, and he also said I don't know what self-reflection is. He is getting tired of me.
他對我的銷售報告感到很暴怒，他還說我不知道什麼叫自我反省。他對我感到厭倦了。

Willy: Don't be upset. He used to say similar things to me.
別難過。他以前也跟我說過類似的話。

Rose: Is that true? I wonder why he does that?
真的嗎？他究竟是什麼意思？

Willy: It's just because he has high expectations of you. He can't stand seeing you make the same mistakes over and over again. Maybe you can keep track of what you've learned from every sales report, so that you won't make the same mistakes again.
因為他對你期望很高，所以他無法忍受你一直犯相同的錯誤。也許你可以記下每次從銷售報告裡學到的東西，這樣就不會一再犯相同的錯了。

Rose: That's a good idea. Did you do that, too?
好主意。你也是這樣做的嗎？

Willy: Of course, and that's why you still see me here.
當然，所以你現在還能在公司裡看到我。

7. **reflect** [rɪˋflɛkt] 動 反省

8. **process** [ˋprɑsɛs] 名 過程

9. **fire** [faɪr] 動 解雇

10. **truthful** [ˋtruθfəl] 形 誠實的

11. **insight** [ˋɪn͵saɪt] 名 洞察力、眼光

12. **involve** [ɪnˋvɑlv] 動 牽涉到…

15. 空巢時期
Empty Nest
MP3
165

萬用好句

1.	**The Empty Nest Syndrome is a feeling of loneliness parents sometimes feel when their children leave home for university or work, or because they get married.** 空巢症狀是家長在孩子們因唸書、工作、或結婚而離家時所產生的感覺。
2.	**Parents with Empty Nest Syndrome may face challenges in re-establishing new relationships with their adult children.** 有空巢症狀的家長在重新與成年孩子建立新關係上面臨挑戰。
3.	**Most Empty Nest Parents need to re-adjust their daily routines.** 多數空巢期的家長需要重新調整生活步調。
4.	**Some parents with Empty Nest Syndrome may suffer from depression, as well as loss of purpose.** 某些有空巢症狀的家長會感到沮喪以及失去目標。
5.	**Have you ever heard of Empty Nest Syndrome?** 你有聽說過空巢症狀嗎？
6.	**Women are more likely to suffer from Empty Nest Syndrome.** 女人通常較容易有空巢症狀。
7.	**Many married couples divorce after their children leave home.** 許多夫妻在小孩離家後離婚。
8.	**Some Empty Nest mothers suffer from a loss of identity.** 某些空巢期的母親會失去身份認同感。
9.	**It might be a good idea for parents with Empty Nest Syndrome to find a new career or hobby.** 找份新工作或新興趣，對於有空巢症狀的父母或許是個好主意。
10.	**Karen weeps every time she thinks about her newly-married son.** 凱倫一想到她剛結婚的兒子就落淚。
11.	**How can one recover from Empty Nest Syndrome?** 如何從空巢症狀中恢復？

關鍵單字片語

1. **Empty Nest** 片 空巢期

2. **syndrome** [`sɪnˌdrom] 名 症狀

3. **re-adjust** [ˌriə`dʒʌst] 動 重新調適

4. **identity** [aɪ`dɛntətɪ] 名 身分

5. **result in** 片 造成…結果

6. **depression** [dɪ`prɛʃən] 名 沮喪

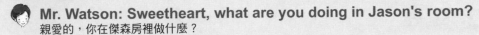

實境對話

Mr. Watson: Sweetheart, what are you doing in Jason's room?
親愛的，你在傑森房裡做什麼？

Mrs. Watson: Nothing. I am just thinking about him.
沒什麼。我只是在想他。

Mr. Watson: I know you must miss him a lot, but he will be home next Sunday.
我知道你一定很想他，但他下週日就會回來了。

Mrs. Watson: I know. I just feel a little bit empty, both in the house and in my heart.
我知道。我只是覺得有點空虛，不管是家裡還是心裡。

Mr. Watson: What do you mean?
你的意思是？

Mrs. Watson: It was just like yesterday when little Jason crawled all over this room, crying for milk and hugs. And now he has turned into a young lad, leaving for college.
小傑森在房裡到處爬，哭著要喝奶跟抱抱，好像昨天的事。而現在他已長大離家念大學了。

Mr. Watson: You're right. Time flies.
沒錯。時間過得真快。

Mrs. Watson: And I could always talk to him when he came home from school, and I used to get him snacks while he was studying for tests at night. Now I have nothing to do anymore.
我以前總是可以在他下課回來的時候跟他聊天，在他唸書準備考試的時候幫他準備點心。而現在我什麼都不能做了。

Mr. Watson: You have to be strong and get used to this. He is a grownup now, and he is going to have his own family soon. It's time for us to start our second life, too.
你要堅強並習慣這一切。他已長大成人，很快也會有自己的家庭。我們也該開始第二春了。

關鍵單字片語

7. **weepy** [ˋwipɪ] 形 淚汪汪的

8. **recover from** 片 從…中恢復

9. **better off** 片 好轉

10. **terrified** [ˋtɛrəˏfaɪd] 形 感到害怕的

11. **upcoming** [ˋʌpˏkʌmɪŋ] 形 即將到來的

12. **keep in touch** 片 保持聯繫

16. 退休養老
Retirement
MP3 166

萬用好句

1. Retirement is the point where a person stops being employed after years of work.
退休是一個人在數年的工作之後，停止工作。

2. How should we prepare for retirement?
我們該如何為退休做準備？

3. Nowadays, most developed countries have mechanisms in place to provide pensions on retirement.
現今，大多數已開發國家擁有健全的退休金制度。

4. When and how should I apply for retirement benefits?
我應何時、如何申請退休福利？

5. My grandfather has been saving up for retirement.
我祖父已經為退休存錢。

6. Jenny wants to travel around the world after retiring.
珍妮退休後想要環遊世界。

7. "The trouble with retirement is that you never get a day off."
「退休的麻煩就是你不能再休假了」。

8. What do you want to do after you retire?
你退休後想做什麼？

9. Sending retirement wishes to someone who is retiring is a good way to honor his or her hard work over the years.
給予即將退休的人士祝福，表達你對他過往辛勞工作的敬意。

10. Retirement is a new chapter in every person's life.
退休是你開啟人生新頁的機會。

11. Mr. Gregg started his own bakery after retiring from the bank.
桂格先生從銀行退休後，自己開了一間麵包店。

12. What do you think is the best age to retire?
你覺得最適合退休的年齡是幾歲？

關鍵單字片語

1. **annuity** [ə`njuətɪ] 名 年金
2. **retire** [rɪ`taɪr] 動 退休
3. **quality life** 片 有品質的生活
4. **pension** [`pɛnʃən] 名 退休金、養老金
5. **benefit** [`bɛnəfɪt] 名 福利
6. **tension-free** [`tɛnʃən`fri] 形 無壓力的

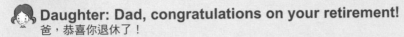
實境對話

Daughter: Dad, congratulations on your retirement!
爸，恭喜你退休了！

Father: It's next month, but thank you anyway.
是下個月，不過還是謝謝你。

Daughter: Aren't you excited about it?
你不興奮嗎？

Father: Actually, no. I am a bit worried.
事實上不。我有點擔心。

Daughter: Worried? How come?
擔心？為什麼？

Father: I really don't know what to do after I retire. I've been working for twenty-five years, and suddenly I'll have nothing to do.
我真的不知道退休後要做什麼。我工作了二十五年，突然間我無事可做。

Daughter: I think now is the best time to begin your second life.
我覺得現在是你開始第二春的時候。

Father: A second life? What should I do?
第二春？我應該做什麼？

Daughter: You can do anything you want, such as traveling.
你可以做任何想做的事，像是旅行。

Father: Hmm...sounds good.
嗯…聽起來不錯。

Daughter: You'll have plenty of time to do whatever you like. If I were you, I would travel around the world, or start a coffee shop.
你會有很多時間做喜歡做的事。如果我是你，我要環遊世界，或是開間咖啡店。

Father: Maybe I can start a bar of my own!
或許我可以開間酒吧！

關鍵單字片語

7. **farewell** [`fɛr`wɛl] 名 告別、告別辭

8. **retiree** [rɪ.taɪə`ri] 名 退休人員

9. **pastime** [`pæs.taɪm] 名 休閒喜好

10. **honorably** [`ɑnərəblɪ] 副 可敬地

11. **continue** [kən`tɪnju] 動 繼續

12. **finance** [faɪ`næns] 名 財務

17. 生離死別
Life and Death
MP3
167

萬用好句

1.	**Allen will have a memorial service for his father this Sunday.** 艾倫這週日將替他父親舉辦一場追悼會。
2.	**A memorial service is a ceremony in honor of the dead.** 追悼會是向死者致敬的儀式。
3.	**Do you know the difference between a funeral service and a memorial service?** 你知道葬禮跟追悼會的差別嗎？
4.	**Karen was devastated by the loss of her only son.** 凱倫失去她的獨生子，痛不欲生。
5.	**Ancient Egyptians believed in the afterlife, so they preserved corpses in preparation for the coming life.** 古埃及人相信來世，所以他們將軀體保存良好以供來世使用。
6.	**Mrs. Watson had tears in her eyes while reading out the prayers for her best friend during the memorial service.** 華生太太在悼念儀式上，含淚念出她對摯友的祈禱文。
7.	**Maria lost her husband in a car accident ten years ago.** 瑪麗亞十年前在一場車禍中失去她的丈夫。
8.	**The deceased would want you to take good care of yourself.** 為了亡者，要好好照顧自己。
9.	**The late Mr. Gregg left his estate to his beloved wife.** 桂格先生死後為他摯愛的妻子留下一筆遺產。
10.	**Mrs. Gregg died of heart attack last Sunday.** 桂格太太上週日死於心臟病。
11.	**I want to take two days off because of my husband's funeral.** 我要為先夫的葬禮請兩天喪假。
12.	**The mayor decided to build a monument for Mr. Darwin after his death for his great devotion to the city.** 市長決定在達爾文先生死後設立紀念碑，感念他對該市的付出。

關鍵單字片語

1. **remorse** [rɪˋmɔrs] 名 悔恨

2. **in honor of** 片 向…致敬

3. **funeral** [ˋfjunərəl] 名 葬禮

4. **memorial service** 片 悼念儀式

5. **ceremony** [ˋsɛrəˌmonɪ] 名 典禮

6. **abandoned** [əˋbændənd] 形 被遺棄的

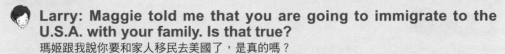

Larry: Maggie told me that you are going to immigrate to the U.S.A. with your family. Is that true?
瑪姬跟我說你要和家人移民去美國了，是真的嗎？

Diana: That's right.
沒錯。

Larry: When are you going to leave?
你什麼時候要離開？

Diana: Next month.
下個月。

Larry: Why so fast?
怎麼那麼快？

Diana: Because my dad's company wants him to start as soon as possible.
因為我爸的公司希望他儘早上班。

Larry: When will you come back to Taiwan?
你什麼時候會再回台灣？

Diana: I don't know. My mom told me that the next time we are back might be two or three years from now.
我不知道。我媽跟我說，我們下次回來也許是兩或三年後了。

Larry: So long? I am going to miss you very much.
這麼久哦？我會很想你的。

Diana: Me, too. Maybe you can come to visit me.
我也是。你可以來找我玩。

Larry: I will start saving money for the trip. Take good care of yourself and keep in touch.
我會開始存錢的。好好照顧自己，保持聯絡。

Diana: I will. Keep in touch!
我會的。保持聯絡！

關鍵單字片語

7. **immigrate** [`ɪməˌgret] 動 遷移

8. **pray** [pre] 動 祈禱

9. **bury** [`bɛrɪ] 動 埋葬

10. **prayer** [prɛr] 名 祈禱文

11. **monument** [`manjəmənt] 名 紀念碑

12. **tomb** [tum] 名 墳墓

18. 何謂幸福
The Happiness
MP3
168

萬用好句

1.	**No one but yourself can teach you what happiness is.** 除了你自己，沒有其他人能教你什麼是幸福。
2.	**The only way to know happiness is to experience it.** 理解幸福的唯一方法就是去體驗它。
3.	**Happiness is not simply fulfilling your desires and wishes, but gaining a sense of contentment.** 幸福不只是欲望和心願的滿足，而是一種知足。
4.	**For me, the happiest time is spending time with my children every Saturday afternoon.** 對我來說，最大的幸福就是每週六下午和我的孩子們相處。
5.	**What is happiness to you?** 對你而言，什麼是幸福？
6.	**Happiness can mean different things to different people.** 幸福對不同人而言，代表的意義不同。
7.	**What distinguishes happy people from unhappy ones is attitude.** 一個人幸福與否，取決於他的態度。
8.	**Positive thinking is the easiest way to help you obtain happiness.** 正向思考是幫助你獲得幸福最簡單的方式。
9.	**Understand what makes you happy and go for it.** 瞭解什麼能讓你快樂，並且努力爭取。
10.	**Don't let self-pity kill your happiness.** 不要讓自怨自艾毀了你的幸福。
11.	**Maintaining your health is also another way to achieve happiness.** 保持健康也是獲得幸福的一種方法。
12.	**Happiness may be the hardest thing to define.** 快樂或許是最難定義的事。

關鍵單字片語

1. **bliss** [blɪs] 名 福氣

2. **live in it** 片 把握當下

3. **as a matter of fact** 片 事實上

4. **self-pity** [`sɛlf pɪtɪ] 名 自憐

5. **distinguish** [dɪ`stɪŋgwɪʃ] 動 區分

6. **lottery** [`lɑtərɪ] 名 彩券

實境對話

Kenny: What do you think is the greatest happiness in life?
你覺得生命中最大的幸福是什麼？

Peggy: I haven't thought about it yet. What about you?
我還沒想過。你覺得呢？

Kenny: I'm not sure. It might be being healthy for your entire life.
我不確定。也許是一輩子都健康吧。

Peggy: Wow, don't you want to win the lottery or something?
哇，你沒想過要贏樂透之類的嗎？

Kenny: Having a lot of money is undoubtedly a dream for most people, and it can guarantee the best standard of living. However, I'm not sure if I would be happy and contented with nothing but money.
富有無疑是許多人的夢想，這也能保障良好的生活品質。然而，我不確定如果只有錢，我是否仍能感到快樂和滿足。

Peggy: You're right. As Abraham Lincoln said, "Most people are about as happy as they make up their minds to be."
你說的對。就像林肯總統曾說過的：「大多數的人就像他們所決定的那樣幸福。」

Kenny: I read an article about happiness and the price paid for it.
我讀了一篇關於幸福和其代價的文章。

Peggy: What was it about?
說了些什麼？

Kenny: It talked about most people spending most of their time chasing happiness, money in most cases, but losing the most valuable things in their life--their family and health.
是說大部分的人花了一生中的許多時間追求幸福，通常是錢，但卻失去了生命中最重要的東西——家人和健康。

Peggy: Sounds interesting. Do you still have the article? I want to read it, too.
聽起來很有趣。你還有這篇文章嗎？我也想讀一讀。

 **關鍵單字片語**

7. **attain** [ə`ten] 動 獲得

8. **sprout** [spraʊt] 動 使萌芽、茁壯

9. **define** [dɪ`faɪn] 動 為…下定義

10. **blessing** [`blɛsɪŋ] 名 賜福、祝福

11. **appreciate** [ə`priʃɪˌet] 動 欣賞

12. **price** [praɪs] 名 代價

國家圖書館出版品預行編目資料

不結巴！用英語會話交外國朋友 / 張翔、薛詩怡 著. --初版
.--新北市：知識工場出版 采舍國際有限公司發行,
2015.12 面；公分· --（Excellent；80）
ISBN 978-986-271-652-6（平裝）

1.英語　　　2.會話

805.188　　　　　　　　　　　　　104022037

 知識工場 · Excellent 80

不結巴！用英語會話交外國朋友

出 版 者／全球華文聯合出版平台 · 知識工場
作　　者／張翔、薛詩怡　　　　　印 行 者／知識工場
出版總監／王寶玲　　　　　　　　英文編輯／何牧蓉
總 編 輯／歐綾纖　　　　　　　　美術設計／蔡億盈

郵撥帳號／50017206 采舍國際有限公司（郵撥購買，請另付一成郵資）
台灣出版中心／新北市中和區中山路2段366巷10號10樓
電話／（02）2248-7896
傳真／（02）2248-7758
ISBN-13／978-986-271-652-6
出版日期／2015年12月初版

全球華文市場總代理／采舍國際
地址／新北市中和區中山路2段366巷10號3樓
電話／（02）8245-8786
傳真／（02）8245-8718

港澳地區總經銷／和平圖書
地址／香港柴灣嘉業街12號百樂門大廈17樓
電話／（852）2804-6687
傳真／（852）2804-6409

全系列書系特約展示
新絲路網路書店
地址／新北市中和區中山路2段366巷10號10樓
電話／（02）8245-9896
傳真／（02）8245-8819
網址／www.silkbook.com

本書全程採減碳印製流程並使用優質中性紙（Acid & Alkali Free）最符環保需求。

本書為張翔等名師及出版社編輯小組精心編著覆核，如仍有疏漏，請各位先進不吝指正。來函請寄
mujung@mail.book4u.com.tw，若經查證無誤，我們將有精美小禮物贈送！